Maverick

ALSO BY

LORA LEIGH

Secret Sins

Deadly Sins

Midnight Sins

Live Wire

Renegade

Black Jack

Heatseeker

Wild Card

Killer Secrets

Hidden Agendas

Dangerous Games

Dangerous Pleasure

Guilty Pleasure

Only Pleasure

Wicked Pleasure

Forbidden Pleasure

Maverick

Lora Leigh

St. Martin's Griffin
New York

This is a work of fiction. All of the characters, organizations, and events portrayed in this novel are either products of the author's imagination or are used fictitiously.

 For information, address St. Martin's Press, 175 Fifth Avenue, New York, N.Y. 10010.

www.stmartins.com

ISBN 978-1-250-03579-0 (trade paperback)
ISBN 978-1-4299-9187-2 (e-book)

First St. Martin's Griffin Edition: January 2013

10 9 8 7 6 5 4 3 2 1

Beauty is in the eye of the beholder…

Author's Note

IT'S NOT ALWAYS easy to write a hero such as Micah Sloane. He implants himself in your head, and he refuses to change. From the beginning, Micah was Jewish. He was Mossad. He was a man who saw death in far different ways than I did. A man who knew how to kill without guilt when killing was necessary. He made no excuses for who he was, for what he was. And he didn't need to make excuses.

I knew next to nothing about the Jewish faith or culture, so I had some studying to do. Many of the things I learned gave me a new respect for both the culture and the religion. But it also gave me new insights into my hero. I hope you see in him all the things I saw. A man as enduring, as strong, and as powerful as the land he came from. A man who knew love, honored love, and a man who understood love. Any mistakes I made in his character are mine alone.

But I want to give special thanks to a very brave friend who helped me with the character, the Hebrew, and a general understanding of the Jewish culture. Thanks, Kat. I couldn't have done it without your insights.

And thanks to the very dear character Micah. He helped me learn and to grow strong and that is truly the greatest gift of all.

Prologue

SHE WAS A MOTHER. She was a daughter. She was a sister and a wife. Delicate and so very beautiful. Dusky flesh stretched over aristocratic features that drew attention to the slope of her brow, the full delectable pout of her lips.

She was slender, well toned. She was a work of art for her age. A woman of forty-five shouldn't be in such peak physical condition.

Unless she was a killer.

Yes, she was a killer, the worst sort of killer actually. A woman of beauty, sparkling wit, and gentle hands. Those hands could fire a gun, wield a knife, or toss a grenade with the same merciless conviction as any male he had ever known. And yet, her soul was gentle. Gentle and strong.

"Pretty," he whispered as he touched the silken flesh of that hand, ran his finger over it, and finally found the subtle calluses of her trade.

She was a warrior. A warrior such as she should never have the light in her dark, pretty eyes extinguished.

"It's business, you understand." He kept his tone balanced, perfectly modulated.

He didn't want to frighten her. The blood pumped harder and faster through the body with fear. It would flow from her veins too quickly; there would be no chance to enjoy the beauty and rich satisfaction that came the moment one so strong gave up her last breath of life.

Did one such as she feel fear? he wondered.

He tilted his head to the side, an edge of curiosity pricking at him as she stared back at him with icy resolve. There was no fear in her eyes; there was no concern for her own life. She stared back at him with cold, flat eyes. Yet he knew those eyes. He had smiled into them many times. He had been charmed by her laughter and wit. But he had never known if she ever felt fear.

How very odd, he thought. He normally knew such simple things when he took an assignment. He made it his job to know all things about his victims.

"Do you fear?" He had to ask the question. He asked it in her own tongue; the beauty of her language had always fascinated him.

Many might not consider the Hebrew language one of grace and purity, but he did. He felt it each time he heard the words falling gracefully from an Israeli's lips. There was a certain cadence, a mystical, ancient fluidity, that fascinated him.

"Of you?" Her words slurred just the faintest bit from the sedative he had given her before carrying her to his lair. "I know no fear of you."

"Do you fear death?" He feared death. He faced it with each job he took, and sometimes he feared that when his own end came, it would come with pain and humiliation.

"I fear nothing on this earth." And he believed it.

"But you should," she continued. "You should fear, for a wrath such as none you have ever known will descend upon you."

"Your God?" he sneered.

"God will judge you, but Garren and David will destroy you."

Her husband. Her son. A CIA agent and a Mossad soldier. They were formidable adversaries.

"They will never know it was I who took you from this earth, Ariela," he promised her with a tinge of regret. "Angels may watch over them, but they won't speak my name."

She didn't give him the benefit of emotion. Instead, she turned her gaze from him, refusing to look at him.

His fingers trailed between her breasts once again, and he was glad he had cut her clothes from her. The chill air of the lair he had chosen peaked her nipples as though she were aroused. As though she waited for her lover, naked and spread out upon the metal table.

Her arms were manacled by the wrists, her hands hanging over the table, the chains attached to hooks in the floor. Her legs were lifted, spread, and held by the heavy chains he had attached to the ceiling.

His thumb brushed over a nipple, and still she didn't react.

"Does ice water or blood run through your veins?" he asked as he continued to touch her.

The feel of her flesh was exquisite. It was a shame that her husband would no longer feel the warmth of her beside him in his bed each night. Her arms would no longer embrace him. He would no longer know the slide of her silken flesh against his body.

"Does it matter which runs through it?" She didn't blink; she didn't cry; she didn't plead.

What satisfaction would he gain from this death? he wondered. Well, besides the nice fat payment that would be deposited in his account once her beautiful body was found. And the fact that his employer would continue to refrain from revealing his identity. That was becoming something of a problem for him. He would have never taken this job without that threat backing his required fee.

"Unfortunately, it doesn't matter," he sighed. "Are you not curious why you're here? Who ordered your death?"

"Would it matter?"

He smiled back at her. "You could take the name of the one who ordered your death into the afterlife with you. Does that matter?"

Her lips quirked. "Whether I know his name or not will make no difference in my afterlife. The One who matters knows his name; He knows the name of the one who hired you. He knows your soul. He knows who to punish."

He nearly flinched at the belief that resounded in her voice. She believed when he didn't, yet her belief had the power to send a jolt of concern through him.

Bah. He wouldn't allow this.

He grinned back at her mockingly. "Your God will punish me then?"

She said nothing more. Her gaze looked up, as though to the ceiling. Her lips moved, though he didn't know the words she whispered. She whispered them to herself. Perhaps to her God.

He fingered the one article he had left on her body. A symbol of her faith. The Star of David. He had always admired it. Her husband, Garren, had had it crafted for her. Each point of the six-sided silver star held a drop of gold inset in the point. It was simple, held to her neck by leather rather than gold or silver.

"Your son will find your body," he decided aloud, wondering if she would react to that decision.

There was no reaction. She stared ahead, her gaze fixed on something he couldn't see, wouldn't see. *Ah well. Whatever got her through death,* he decided as he moved from her and chose his blade.

"Perhaps I will give you my real name before the last breath eases from your body," he decided. "You might want to tell your God who I am. Just in case He gives a damn that you're dead."

No reaction, but had he really expected one?

This part was usually his favorite. He moved back from the table and didn't feel the familiar jolt of excitement, though.

He had always enjoyed playing with them. He enjoyed tracking them, kidnapping them. He liked the moment when their eyes opened and they realized they were standing on death's doorstep.

But this time, he felt only regret and a sense of anger. There was no reason for her death, not really. She wasn't close enough to identify his employer, but his employer was a bit psychotic at times.

He chose his weapon, a razor blade. Such a simple weapon, easy to purchase, so simple to use.

"You know, once, when I was a very young child," he mused, "I happened upon my mother."

He ran the edge of the blade against her arm, just enough for her to feel the cold metal and to know her fate.

"She lay in her bathtub, naked, blood dripped from her wrists onto the floor, and her eyes stared at me with such perfect peace."

He stared at her, and his mother's face flashed before his eyes. Blond hair, blue eyes, fragile features. His mother had been perfect.

"She wasn't dead," he continued. "I knelt by the tub. I knew she had chosen that path, and I asked her why. And she smiled." He smiled. "Because, she said, she loved the feel of the blade as it sliced into her vein. It was like a grape popping." He shook his head at the thought. "Unfortunately, Mother was more into cutting herself than truly dying. She didn't die that time, nor the next." He patted her arm. "She didn't die until I strapped her down to her own kitchen table and helped her along a bit."

He had told this story many times before. Always he had seen shock or horror on the face of his victim. On this one, he saw only that faraway look in her eyes and the soft ripple of her lips as she whispered to herself whatever words she formed with her tongue.

Her arm was turned up, her wrist vulnerable, the vein pulsing just below the flesh.

With his free hand he reached down and allowed his thumb to feather over the vein, his eyes to stare at it with sadness as he laid the blade to it.

There it was. He groaned at the feel of the vein popping beneath the blade. He let it slice deep, severing the vein before he moved to her other arm.

Anger was rocking through him now. Damn the egomaniacal bastard who held his identity as hostage. Were it not for him, this woman would be smiling. She would not be dying. She would be blessing the earth with her presence rather than bleeding into the dirt.

"Say something. You're dying," he snapped.

He wanted her to fight, to scream, to rage. And she did none of those things. Did she regret nothing? Were there no sins that she had yet to atone for?

She said nothing. She stared above him, whispered soundlessly, and only the smallest flinch betrayed her awareness of what he was doing when he let the blade slice into her other wrist.

The vein popped open, severed, and spilled its scarlet bounty over his fingers. His eyes closed as the silken hot, rich sensation feathered over his fingers, into his hand.

His breathing was harsh now, uneven as he reached down and touched himself and began to pump the aching flesh as pleasure tore through him.

He watched her face. He had to time this perfectly. Just right. It was bad enough he had to wear a condom when he played; he wanted to at least achieve this ecstasy at the same moment as his lovely victim achieved hers. He might regret her death, but her beauty had always inspired him. Amazed him.

Her blood flowed sweet and dark from her veins; it fell to the floor and ran in scarlet ribbons along the cement as he watched her face, watched her eyes. Yes, she was close, so close. He pumped harder, and heard his own strangled groan as it left his throat.

"Die," he moaned. "Die, sweet beauty. Die."

The light slowly left her eyes, her last gasp of life fell from her lips, and the scent of her body giving up its final pulse of life threw him over the edge until a shudder of completion finally tore through his muscles.

Breathing hard, he gripped himself and stared at the bounty laid out before him. Beautiful, so very beautiful in death.

But when had she closed her eyes?

He watched her closely, his head tilting as he blinked

back at her in curiosity. Her eyes were closed. There was no horror on her face, no blank fear or agony.

He stepped back from the body, careful not to step in the blood, and watched her in fascination.

Amazing, he thought. *Such strength of will. Such beauty.*

Mossad taught their agents well, he thought with a sigh. In all the years he had been taking lives, never before had he taken one who died with such grace.

"A perfect death," he whispered as he breathed in deeply and smiled back at her in admiration. "Absolutely perfect."

He moved to the head of the table, touched her cheek, then gently worked the knot of the leather that held her pendant free. He never kept mementos, but he couldn't resist this one small part of her that he could keep always.

There was nothing left to do now but to shower, clean all traces of his presence from the small underground cellar he had used, and take his leave. Her husband and son would receive a call later with the location of her body. Once it was found, the money would hit his account. There was a particularly lovely villa he had his eye on in France.

After wiping the last traces of himself from the area, he dressed carefully, picked up his briefcase, and slid open the narrow door.

Outside, the nightlife was in full steam. Israelis did so enjoy their entertainment. The nightclubs were, as usual, packed.

Smiling at one particularly lovely girl who passed by, he drew his cell phone from the pocket of his jacket and made a call to his handler. At least he could trust the mousey little man who dealt with arranging his assignments around his other job. It was often difficult to be both a CIA agent as well as the world's most secretive assassin. His handler managed it all very smoothly and, in all the years he'd had the job, had never breathed so much as a whisper of betrayal.

"I'm heading to the airport." He never spoke directly. "My flight to New York leaves in less than two hours; please make the necessary calls."

He closed the phone, pocketed it, and lifted his hand to stop one of the many taxis making their way through the streets. In less than two hours he would be heading to another job, another challenge. He did so love the challenge. But there was a heaviness in his chest as well. This job didn't set well on him at all.

As he boarded the plane two hours later and took his seat, he unfolded the American newspaper he had bought in the airport. The front page caused his brows to lift.

POPULAR INDUSTRIALIST KILLED
DURING SENATOR'S DAUGHTER'S RESCUE

He rubbed his finger against his lower lip as he read, a frown pulling between his brows. One of his favored employers, it seemed, had been killed during the rescue. Jansen Clay. He almost smiled when he read that Clay had died during the rescue of Senator Stanton's daughter, Emily. Evidently the American government didn't like the truth. Jansen Clay was no hero. He'd proven that when he'd arranged the first kidnapping of Emily Stanton along with two other girls, one of whom was Clay's own daughter. No doubt he had wished his plain little daughter had been killed during the kidnapping nearly two years before.

Emily Stanton and Risa Clay had survived, though. The third had died. And now, Clay was dead after trying to arrange the kidnapping of the Stanton girl again. The fool.

He stared at the picture before frowning. Another of his employers was involved in this affair. He knew Diego Fuentes had acquired the scientist's services just months before, because the man had actually approached Orion's handler to price the hit on Fuentes. Unfortunately, Orion hadn't finished this assignment as of yet.

Interesting.

He stared at the picture of Risa Clay and Emily Stanton again and grimaced. So plain. A man would have to put a bag over Risa's head or hide her face in the blankets to fuck her, as his employer had done nearly two years before. Were Orion to kill her, he'd definitely have to turn her facedown.

He nearly shuddered in distaste at the thought of it.

Ah well. Clay was dead; his daughter, it was rumored, was in some asylum, her brain destroyed from the drug she had been given during the kidnapping. Risa would remember little of that singular event in her life, and should be no risk to Orion's future profits. The man who had played a role in her destruction had little to worry about.

Chapter 1

Six Years Later

TONIGHT RISA CLAY was going to take a lover.

Behind her, in the bathroom garbage were the overly large cotton pants and t-shirt she normally wore. None of that tonight. With her heart beating an erratic tattoo in her chest, she forced herself to turn and stare into the full-length mirror, at her naked body. She had to force herself to look, to be objective, to push back the panic rising inside her at the thought of what she was about to do.

She was pale. Pale skin, pale breasts, and pale pink nipples. Her gaze went lower to the bare pale lips of her sex and she had to swallow quickly to hold back the nausea that rose in her stomach. She was pale there as well. Perhaps she should have tried the tanning bed, she thought. If her body didn't look like her own, perhaps this would be easier to do.

She could cancel until she tanned. But she immediately vetoed that idea. *No excuses,* she told herself. *No more backing out, no more cowardly nights hiding.*

She could do this. She had gone to the spa yesterday, hadn't she? She had sat in the chair and spread her thighs while the technician had waxed her most private parts. Parts that she had hated for so long. The part of herself that she blamed for the worst episode in her life.

She forced her eyes to close and inhaled quickly. She wasn't thinking about that tonight. She wasn't going to let the past ruin the plan she had come up with. She had promised herself she wouldn't. This was the right decision. She could do this. If she was ever going to regain her life and her independence, then she had to grab it with both hands and hold on, no matter how frightened she became.

Staring back at the mirror, she checked her hair. The thick, heavy dark blond strands that had once fallen halfway down her back were now shoulder length and fell neatly around her face. They weren't pale, at least not any longer. Highlights had been added by the beautician. Dark and golden brown strands were mixed with the sandy color now. At least it no longer faded into Risa's face.

There wasn't much she could do with her face, with the exception of the makeup she had learned how to use. The smoky shadow highlighted her pale blue eyes and rather nondescript features and gave her an interesting appearance instead. Her lashes were longer, darkened with mascara and eyeliner. Her lips were more lush than she had thought they were. Bronze lipstick had brought out their shape, and a light coating of blush highlighted her rather high cheekbones.

The makeup specialist Risa had gone to had complimented her on her cheekbones and the arch of her eyes and taught her how to bring out the best in them. If only that addition of makeup could instill the confidence she had lost so long ago.

Risa forced in another deep breath before reaching for the soft bronze silk panties she had bought. The low-rise thong was daring and terrifying. It was an invitation. A silken bit of nothing that would take no time to pull from her body.

But that was what she wanted, she reminded herself. Something that would be easy to remove, that wouldn't give her time to think or to consider what she was doing once she started doing it.

Next came the stockings. In ways, the stockings were even harder to put on. The thigh-high shimmering color made her legs appear longer, sexier. Another invitation. She was painting a "fuck me" sign on her body and she was doing it deliberately.

God help her to go through with this, because if she didn't, she might never have the nerve to try again.

Smoothing the stockings over her legs, she turned to the dress that hung on the hook by the bathroom door. The dress was her own challenge, the challenge being in actually putting it on and walking out of her apartment.

She didn't give herself time to think. The brown silk beaded baby doll dress ended well above her knees in a fall of sheer shadowy color. The bronze underslip showed through clearly and ended a few inches higher along her leg. The empire waist was banded by darker brown silk while the thin slip straps were the pale bronze of the underslip.

She smoothed the material over her hips before forcing herself away from the mirror and slipping on the chocolate brown stiletto heels that matched the dress.

She couldn't look at herself in the mirror again. If she did, she might chicken out of this and hide beneath the blankets as she did night after night.

Her hands shook as she opened the bathroom door and stepped into the bedroom. Picking up the little bronze beaded evening bag, she dropped her house keys inside along with some cash, a credit card, ID, and lipstick. The brown wrap she threw over her shoulders would protect her from the chill of the air against her shoulders but little else. It was thin enough that it was no more than dark smoke against her naked shoulders and arms.

She was ready. But for what?

To be a woman for a change, rather than a thing? A memory? To be something more than the automaton she had become over the years? Stilted, doing nothing but getting through the day and facing the night alone. She was so very tired of always being alone, of never knowing what she could have been or what she was missing out on as a woman. But would tonight do anything to free her, or would it only give strength to the demons that chased her through the night?

The feel of her hair brushing her shoulders as she shook her head at her own question spurred her to move to the door. A cab was waiting for her downstairs, her friends were waiting for her at the club, and if she was lucky, tonight she would find out what pleasure was, rather than pain.

If she was lucky. If she wasn't lucky, it wasn't as though she hadn't known the pain before. At least tonight, it would be her choice.

Still, her hands shook and her stomach rioted as she stepped off the elevator and walked into the main lobby of her apartment building.

The open, airy atmosphere of the lobby was given an almost intimate, welcoming touch by the low padded couches and chairs in various conversational arrangements. Huge potted plants provided an air of privacy for the groupings and aimed to set an air of intimacy and ease for those who used the lobby.

The security guard's eyes widened as he saw her, and the doorman stepped forward with a wide smile.

"Miss Clay, your cab is waiting on you," the doorman, Clive Stamper, announced as he opened the wide glass door for her. "And may I say you look especially lovely tonight."

Her smile trembled. "Thank you, Clive." Her voice was firm, low, as she moved past him and waited for him to open the passenger door of the cab.

Risa slid onto the leather seat, her fingers clenched around her purse as she gave the driver the name of the club.

Clive closed the door and stepped back and the cab moved forward.

It wasn't too late to turn back, she told herself. She could have the driver stop now. She could run back to her room as she had done last month, the last time she had tried this. She could put her baggy clothes back on and she would be safe.

Safe and so very miserable.

She was tired of being miserable. And there was always the chance that for the first time in six years, she could find a place inside her that wasn't tormented by the past. She just had to make that place, she told herself. That was all. She could do this. After all, she had survived hell, hadn't she? If she had survived hell, then she could survive one night in a lover's arms.

* * *

"WILD CARD AND Maverick pulling out." Noah Blake spoke into the mouthpiece as he pulled out behind the cab in the dove gray Lexus that had been provided to follow Risa Clay on her way to the nightclub where some of the former members of SEAL team Durango were waiting with their wives for the arrival of Miss Clay and Noah's passenger, Micah Sloane.

"Heat Seeker and Hell Raiser coming up behind you." John Vincent, the Aussie of the Elite Ops teams, and Nik Steele, the former Russian special forces soldier, were in the blue gas-guzzling Dodge that pulled up in Noah's rearview mirror.

"Live Wire has the club; Black Jack is inside." Jordan Malone, the team commander, spoke through the receiver.

"Black Jack has the table in view. Everything looks good to go."

Noah glanced over at his passenger, Micah Sloane, and almost grimaced at the emotionless, cold façade the former Israeli Mossad agent carried.

Micah was an enigma, even now, more than four years after the formation of the Elite Ops unit. He was a man who kept to himself, didn't share secrets, and never gave shit away.

He could get pissed, but it was a cold, icy fury. He could slice through flesh with words alone and leave others quivering in fear. He was the type of man that Noah would hesitate to make an enemy of, and there weren't many men in the world that Noah would really give a damn if they were friend or enemy. But Micah wasn't the type of man that Noah felt comfortable leaving the broken little Risa Clay with. He was too hard, too cold. Risa needed a man who knew how to be gentle, who knew how to be warm.

"You know, that cold, blank look could put a woman off," Noah told him quietly as he maneuvered through Atlanta's early evening traffic.

"I'll worry about my look; you worry about the traffic." There was no accent to Micah's voice, no Middle Eastern hint or so much as a tonal shift that would reveal he wasn't fully American.

His American father with his pale Nordic looks and height had added to the lightening of Micah's skin, as well as contributing to his tall, lean frame. Micah was over six feet, his black hair cut close and lying over his head to his neck in an almost haphazard manner. Black eyes in a face that appeared to be just darkly tanned and topped with thick slashing brows gleamed with menace. His lips were just a little too full, just a little too sensual. "Wide, mobile lips," Noah's wife, Sabella, had stated once. Noah hadn't been happy that she had noticed.

"I worry about this op," Noah stated. "I'd like to get home before the baby is born, if you don't care."

Noah's wife was carrying their first child. The wife he had nearly lost because of his own stupidity, his own pride. Being away from her didn't sit well with him. But it was his hand that had signed on to the Elite Ops; it was his decision that had placed him with the teams when he could have easily walked away from it all to be with Sabella.

That pride thing. He'd learned his lesson, he had his Sabella back, but he was still a member of the team and would be until the day he died.

"You signed on, you take the heat." Micah shrugged as he laid his arm along the armrest of the door and watched the traffic closely.

"One of these days," Noah muttered, almost to himself.

Micah was a hard bastard, there was no doubt. What the hell made him think he was the best man to charm a woman who knew nothing but fear where men were concerned, Noah hadn't figured out yet.

"One of these days your wife will do us all a favor and shoot you with your own gun," Micah grunted as his gaze continued to watch the traffic closely. "I hear she threw you to the couch last month."

Noah frowned. How the hell had Micah found out about that?

"Hell," Noah growled. "She told Kira, didn't she?" Kira being the wife to one of the ex–Navy SEAL commanders Micah would be having dinner with that night.

The members of the Durango team had all officially resigned their commissions with the SEALs over the past three years, though none of them were actually free of their covert status. They were the Elite Ops backup team, though Elite Ops was using backup less and less for the smaller operations.

"Maybe she didn't tell anyone," Micah stated. "Maybe I was testing your home security and saw you sleeping on the couch. I could have sliced your throat in your sleep."

"Dream on, asshole." Noah grinned. "Admit it. Sabella told Kira and she blabbed like the little minx she is. You didn't pass my security and we both know it." Wasn't possible, he had made certain of it.

Micah didn't so much as smile.

"Look, I'm serious," Noah sighed. "You go into that club looking like you're ready to kill and that kid is going to go running for the hills."

"She isn't a child."

Noah paused at Micah's statement and flashed the other man a curious look.

"She's not exactly an experienced, worldly woman, either," Noah assured him. "She's twenty-six years old, Micah, and all but a virgin."

"She is a virgin still." Micah's tone never changed.

"She was raped." Noah felt as though he were talking to a brick wall. "She's wounded, man. You can't show her the killer face and expect her to trust you."

Micah turned to look at him now. "The killer face?" he asked evenly.

"Yeah, that icy Mossad façade you're wearing right now," he growled. "Ease up, man. Practice smiling or something."

He flashed Micah a glare as the other man turned his head once again.

"I'll worry about her reaction to me; you worry about getting us to the club in one piece."

Noah almost gritted his teeth in frustration. Hell, he still remembered the night he had helped rescue Risa Clay from

Diego Fuentes's cell. She had been like a broken little doll. Vacant-eyed, shuddering from the drugs pumped into her, and fighting the reaction from them with every breath in her body.

She had been such a damned tiny thing. Naked and bruised, blood had marred her thighs, and pain had filled her eyes. *Traumatized* was a kind word for the state that kid had been in.

"Micah," he began.

"Noah, you want to stop now." Micah's voice hardened, and Noah hadn't thought that possible. "I know how to deal with Miss Clay. This is a meet and greet, nothing more. A chance to gauge her reaction to me, and therefore her reaction to the plan we intend to put before her tomorrow afternoon. Rest assured, I know how to treat a woman."

He might know how to treat one, Noah thought, *but he sure as hell might not know how to present an unthreatening demeanor.*

"Hell, what was Jordan thinking giving this op to you?" Noah questioned his uncle's decision roughly. "You'll terrify her."

"I demanded this op."

Noah glanced back at him in surprise. "Why?"

Micah's expression hadn't changed. His face was still closed, set. His eyes were like black ice and his voice like frozen air. It was enough to give a person frostbite.

"Why is for me to know." Micah shrugged. "It's your place to accept. Now if you wouldn't mind, your chattering is getting on my nerves. Perhaps Jordan could find a muzzle that would fit you."

Noah grimaced and tightened his hands on the wheel of the car as he made a turn behind the cab and gauged the distance to the hotel where Risa was heading.

Hell, she deserved better than the operation that was going to be thrown at her tomorrow. She deserved more than to be used as he knew this operation would use her. She wasn't mentally or emotionally capable of handling the stress it would lay on her fragile shoulders.

He'd mentioned his fears to his wife, Sabella. Worried that this operation would tax the girl's ability to heal and to get on with her life. But they had no choice. This wasn't just their best chance at capturing an assassin whom no one could seem to pin, but it was also their only chance to save her from a horrifying death. Risa was beginning to remember what everyone had believed she would never remember: the night of her kidnapping and rape and the man who had been in league with the father who had masterminded it.

Those memories could be the death of her.

"Risa Clay isn't a broken woman." Micah's comment surprised Noah into glancing back at him.

"What makes you think that?" Noah asked.

"You know the same things I do," Micah stated. "The trips to the spa, the shopping trip, and the clothes she's bought. The intimate toys found in her bedside drawer. No, Noah, she is not a broken woman. She is a woman trying to heal."

"And you think handing her over to you will complete that healing?" Noah snorted. "Hell, from what I've seen you can't keep a woman past the time it takes to fuck one, Micah. You're like a robot, man. That's fine with a woman that's not looking for anything more."

"Noah, you are becoming a mother hen," Micah sighed. "You remind me much of one here of late. I need to discuss this with Sabella. She's becoming a bad influence on you."

Noah grinned. Damn, his Sabella was his lifesaver.

"She'll just laugh at you," he promised the other man.

"I have no doubt she will laugh, simply because she knows you're a lost cause."

Noah let the argument go. There was obviously no convincing Micah that charming a woman took more than an invitation to his bed. Especially a woman like Risa, one who had known the horror she barely remembered. She may think she had forgotten details and faces due to that fucking Whore's Dust, but Noah knew her mind remembered, her body remembered.

He knew because he had been there. For nineteen hellish months he had been pumped full of that shit. He knew what it did to a body, to a mind. What it would do to the child she had been, and to experience the humiliation and pain of a rape on top of it wouldn't be that damned easy to get over.

Risa hadn't been as lucky as the other victims pumped full of the date rape drug. She hadn't completely forgotten that night, nor had she forgotten the endless months she had been held in the asylum. She sure as hell hadn't forgotten that it was her father who had consigned her to both hells.

The bastard Jansen Clay. Noah prayed he was burning in hell now.

"Live Wire, be advised, mark is bearing on your location," he spoke into the mic attached to his wrist as Risa's cab patted into the predetermined checkpoint. "Maverick is four doors down and coming in cold."

Four cars back and cold as ice. The man had to be made of computer chips.

"Ease in," Jordan ordered softly. "Let's see we have interest."

"Orion wouldn't be that sloppy," Micah stated as the cab turned into the club's receiving area and drew to a stop.

Seconds later Noah pulled in behind the cab, and he and Micah watched as Risa stepped from the vehicle.

Micah saw her face, each exquisite detail, and felt his body tense in familiar, but unwanted arousal and interest. It had been happening ever since they had started this op and he had been ordered to tail her. She's a mark, he reminded himself. A very vulnerable, very innocent mark, he had to remember that.

But the mark looked like an earth angel. Dressed in the bronze and brown, her sun-lightened hair swaying about her shoulders, her expression equal parts fear and valor.

He fought his body's reaction to her, fought his interest in her. He was here for one purpose: to capture that bastard Orion, and Risa Clay was a means to that end. As he had told Noah, tonight was a meet and greet, nothing more. A little chitchat, a dance or two, and tomorrow she would be forced to realize her world was changing. She had become the hunted, and Micah was her only chance at survival.

As she entered the club he stepped from the car, adjusted the black evening jacket he wore, and followed behind her at a sedate pace.

She was simply beautiful. Micah had seen her before, several times, though she was unaware of it. She was friends with the wives of the Durango team, all of whom were based in Atlanta.

Each time he had seen her, he'd been interested, attracted, but in a very objective manner. Her innocence and vulnerability touched something in him that hadn't been touched in years. She made him ache to take the pain from her eyes, and that was very dangerous for a man like him.

"Maverick, mark is in place," Jordan announced. "Go in naked. Black Jack in place to take your cover."

Micah slipped the receiver from his ear unobtrusively and unclipped the mic from beneath his jacket sleeve. Palming them, he slid in close to Travis Caine, the former MI6 agent, dropped them into the pocket of his jacket, and continued across the room.

Micah paused before heading to the table. Standing at one of the support columns several feet from the table when Risa was now taking her seat, he let himself draw in perhaps the final moments where he would see her expression unguarded.

There was fear in her eyes. Her body was stiff with it, and her gaze shadowed with it.

She looked around the room, glanced over him, and Micah waited.

Her gaze passed by him again, then again. On the third pass she lingered as he continued to watch her, allowing his gaze to memorize those features just before her eyes met his.

A jolt of power flashed through him. Her light blue eyes flickered with interest, fear, then interest again, as though she wasn't certain which she should feel.

He let his gaze continue to hold hers, let his mind reach out to her, soothe her, ease her. He used his eyes rather than his expression to calm the fear that he knew would be rising within her.

Micah knew the power of a look. When two people touched

from across a distance, that touch could be frightening, wary, or a stroke of gentleness. He stroked her gently. He never let his eyes dip below her chin; rather, he let himself take in every nuance of expression, every shift of each facial motion, the flicker of her lashes, the shadows in her eyes, the tension in her small body.

She was like a bird ready to fly. Poised at the edge of her seat, her body stiff and prepared to run.

Easy, little bird, he thought, letting his thoughts touch his gaze. *There's no pain here; there's no fear.*

He stroked the delicate line of her jaw with his gaze, then came back to her eyes. He let her inside him, let her see into the soul and the parts of him that were just a man, just a lover willing to touch her in gentleness. He let her see there was nothing to fear if she let him close to her.

Eyes were more than the windows to the soul. They could lie as well. And Micah was a consummate liar. But as he stared into her wary gaze, he found himself wishing he could be more. That he could be the man she needed in truth, rather than in deception.

She blinked, and he saw the minute softening in her gaze. It wasn't surrender and it wasn't desire, exactly. It was a hint of interest mixed with caution and resolution. She had made a decision. Now he wondered what that decision was.

He moved forward slowly, holding her gaze, too aware of the eyes that were watching. There were four members of the Durango team here along with their wives. Clint and Morganna, Reno and Raven, Kell and Emily, and Ian and Kira, who spent part of the year in Atlanta or wherever they were needed with the team. The other part they spent at their home in Texas. Macey was currently doing something somewhere with his fiancée, Emerson.

The couples pretended to be unaware of the tension that sizzled across the distance between him and the very delectable Risa Clay. He saw concern in their gazes, though, protectiveness in the shifts of their bodies.

This woman was their friend, and one they worried about. They were as uncertain about this mission as Noah was, and

Micah understood that concern. What they didn't know was that the wary little creature watching him so closely had nothing to fear from him.

He realized in that moment that Risa Clay had become more than the means to an end for him. She was a tool created for his hand. A weapon he would mold to respond to his every move. She was the very path he must walk in order to exorcise the ghosts that haunted him. And for that reason alone he would see that she came to no harm.

She was bait. He knew it. Tomorrow she would know it. And tonight would be his only chance to ensure that he was there when his enemy attempted to strike.

Micah had sworn years before that he would be the one to wield the weapon that would bring Orion to his death. Six years Micah had been haunted by that vow. Haunted by the death of his mother and, six weeks later, the death of his father.

Risa was his chance to cut the heart from the assassin who had destroyed his family and ruined the life Micah had dreamed of for himself.

It was time for payback, and Risa was his only connection to the bastard.

Orion had been hired to hunt her. Maverick would protect her. And when the time came, he would be there to kill the hunter.

Chapter 2

"THAT'S MICAH."

Risa heard Morganna's statement at her ear, but she couldn't turn away from the black eyes that held her. Eyes as deep, as dark as the night, yet there was something that sparked with warmth, that kept those eyes from being cold.

His expression was still. There was a hint of hardness, a suggestion of danger carefully leashed. But she couldn't expect anything less from a friend of four former Navy SEALs.

Still, the very stillness of expression was comforting. As though he knew himself, his strengths and weaknesses, and had learned to live with his own demons. He wouldn't wear his heart on his sleeve, or on his face. He was reserved. She understood reserved.

His entire body reflected his expression. He didn't move as though he were in a hurry. There was no anticipation, no sense of urgency. His body was coordinated, lean, tough. Fit.

Black slacks conformed to his muscular legs and hips. The white shirt beneath the black jacket was a hint of color in an otherwise dark ocean of still emotions and graceful male confidence. His hair was cut close to the scalp, but still the thick black strands would be long enough for a woman to thread her fingers through.

And what made her think of that? she wondered. Why did her fingers suddenly clench on her purse as she wondered what his hair would feel like beneath them.

It was his eyes that held her, though, that called to her. They stroked over her face, always came back to her eyes, and some softening within them, a hint of male interest, of determination, had her heart racing through her body with a force that left her trembling.

She had expected him to be strong, powerful. He was, yet it was a subtle strength and power. His body wasn't bulky with muscle and straining against his clothes. He was lean, corded. Male power shimmered around him, but it wasn't heavy and wide such as Kell's was. Kell Krieger was tall, his shoulders like a football player's, padded with muscle. Even Reno and Clint were like towers of muscle and strength. Micah Sloane was just as tall as they were, but the bulk was absent. Some might suspect the strength was absent. She had a feeling whoever made that mistake would come to regret it.

"It's about time you arrived," Clint drawled from the other side of Morganna as Micah Sloane moved to the vacant chair across from her.

He shook Clint's hand as the other man rose, repeated the move with Reno, Kell, and Ian. His eyes didn't leave Risa's.

"Micah, would you like to meet our friend Risa?" There was a hint of amusement in Morganna's voice now.

"I believe I just have." His words didn't rise above the music. It was as though the music paused for him alone, certain it would regret foiling his wishes if it didn't.

"Mr. Sloane." Risa nodded, barely able to swallow past the nervousness that rose in her throat.

His hand moved across the table. She had no choice but to loosen her fingers from her purse and allow him to take them. She expected a handshake, firm and determined. She didn't expect his hand to encase hers, his fingers to stroke against her wrist for one brief second, as though to ease the pulse pounding out of control there.

Then the warmth of his hand was gone, leaving her to regret the brevity of the contact as he loosened the button on his jacket and took his seat.

He leaned back in the chair and answered some question

Kell had asked. His gaze came back to her, though it was never gone for long.

He didn't demand that she stare into his eyes. The caress of his gaze was subtle, slow. It wasn't enough to draw others' interest, it was shielded by thick black lashes, but nothing could dim the effect it had on her.

"Risa Clay, meet Micah Sloane, a SEAL assigned to Durango team," Clint introduced them.

Micah never once looked below her chin, but she swore she could feel the warmth of that look flowing over her body. His attention wasn't crude; it wasn't obtrusive. It was simply there. A stroke along her brow, along her chin. It touched her hair, her ear when she tucked the strands nervously behind it.

"Risa, Micah likes to play with cameras as well." Kell leaned forward to speak to her, his green eyes bright in his somber expression. "The man carries a camera with him everywhere he goes."

Risa's heart was pounding; she felt flushed, frightened. She needed to get away from the careful stroke of his eyes on her.

She couldn't answer Kell. She couldn't form a reasonable reply. Pushing to her feet, she tried to form an excuse to escape to the ladies' room, but Micah's eyes were on her, probing, questioning. She couldn't form a single reasonable sentence. She turned and rushed from the table, weaving her way through the crowd and escaping to the dimly lit corridor and the tastefully appointed ladies' room beyond.

She pushed through the door, let it swing closed behind her, and felt like crying out in relief that the room was empty. The velvet and tasteful walnut chairs sat in several groupings outside the main stall area. A long counter of sinks could be glimpsed on the other side of the wall, the bright lights picking up the forest green and amber gold color in the walls and floors.

It was cool, soothing, and she felt like a complete fool. Her heart was racing, perspiration dotted her forehead, and fear was like a maniacal pulse of searing heat burning inside her veins.

Pressing her hand to her stomach, she breathed in deeply and straightened from the wall. She was going to get a handle on this, she promised herself. She wouldn't run again.

Turning on the cold water in one of the faucets, she held her wrists under the stream of soothing water and berated herself for her reaction. What the hell was wrong with her? She was going to do this. Micah Sloane was a damned good-looking man. He was safe. He wouldn't hurt her. And he was interested.

She might be a plain Jane, but he was a man, and she wasn't stupid. There had been interest in his eyes. Sexual interest.

One night, she wailed silently. *Just one night. God, please give me the strength to make a memory instead of a nightmare*. Her breathing hitched at the need burning inside her, the electrical pulse of feminine need, a woman's need just to be held.

Pulling her wrists back from the water, she shut the stream off, then dried her hands. Straightening her shoulders, she stared into her reflection. She wasn't ugly, not as she had been as a teenager, when her face had been all angles and sharp lines. It had filled out, softened. He wouldn't have to push her face into the blankets—

She broke off the thought as sickness roiled in her stomach and nightmares threatened to replace determination.

He had been interested. She could do this. God, just one night.

Licking her lips nervously, she blew out another hard breath, then turned and moved to the door. Pulling it open, she stepped out, then came to a hard, shocked stop.

Micah stood propped against the wall across from her, his hands shoved negligently into the pockets of his slacks, his jacket falling open, his shirt lying against what appeared to be lean, hard abs.

"Morganna wanted to race after you." His voice was black velvet, dark, whispering with magic and sexuality as she finally stared into his dark eyes and felt that pulse of need throbbing between her thighs.

"I needed . . ." She waved her hand to the door and swallowed tightly. "A moment."

"The crowd out there can get overwhelming." He spoke and his lips were firm and full. Wide, tempting lips. What would it be like, she wondered, to kiss a man? She hadn't been touched since she was eighteen years old. The kisses she had known before then had been sloppy, inexperienced. What would it be like to kiss a man? A man who knew a woman's body.

And this man would know. Sexual experience oozed from his pores in a subtle aura that had drawn the glance of every female who could see him as he walked toward the table earlier.

She licked her lips again. She should speak; she knew she should. She should say something.

"I'm sorry." Her smile was nervous; she was shaking on the inside, equal parts fear and the flush of need racing through her. "I must seem like a lunatic."

His head tilted to the side, his black eyes watched her with a hint of fire. "On the contrary," he stated as he pushed away from the wall and drew his hands from his pockets. "You seem like a lovely young woman uncertain with the animal your friends have introduced you to." For the first time a smile touched his lips. It was wry, a bit mocking. "They're used to dealing with testosterone overload, I believe. Those men of theirs are like teenage boys pushing and shoving at each other for dominance. They don't consider the effect it would have on someone unused to the phenomenon."

She almost laughed. The sound stuck in her throat as her gaze slipped to his lips again. Her breathing was rough, heavy. She didn't understand the sensations suddenly rioting through her, and they were frightening. Terrifying.

He moved closer, a subtle shift of his body, and only inches separated them as she stared up at him, aware of too many things at once. The feel of his body, the heat surrounding her. The strength of him. The clash of need and fear inside her.

"I'm sorry." She brushed at her hair nervously, then watched in shock as his hand lifted.

Like a frightened doe she stared up at him as though expecting the bullet at any second, Micah thought as he reached out and tucked her hair behind her ear for her.

The strands were as soft as silk, warm beneath his fingertips.

Risa froze at the light caress, and he was aware of the conflicting emotions, the fears that were tearing through her. Beneath her makeup her face was pale; he could see the hint of panic in her darkening eyes, as well as the arousal.

Yes, arousal. Her body, awakening and demanding touch, comfort, ease. But there were also the lingering effects of that fucking drug they had pumped her full of. Whore's Dust didn't just flush from the system. The synthetic drug attached to the brain, forced the body to feel arousal at the most inopportune times.

Her medical records told the tale. There were still minute quantities of the drug in her system, even eight years later. It didn't have the same hold on her that it had had on Noah, who had suffered continued injections for nearly two years. But it was there, and it affected the female body in different ways than it did the male body.

"They'll get worried if we don't return soon," Micah told her, forcing his voice to remain even, allowing his gaze to stroke her face as his fingers wished to. "We should join our friends, don't you think?"

She stared back at him, her lips parted, her eyes dilated as a flush of need mantled her cheekbones.

"If we don't," he allowed his voice to lower, "then I'm going to kiss you, Miss Clay. And I'm certain you'd find offense should I take such liberties so soon."

He almost winced. *Fuck.* His accent was slipping free with her. A hint of the desert colored his words, and the effect of it darkened her eyes.

Where the hell was the ice he kept firmly in place inside his soul? Where was the careful control that was so much a part of him?

"I'm sure I would," she whispered, but her tongue licked over her lips, a quick little foray, dampening them for him.

Was she growing slick? he wondered. Was her body preparing for him? Micah urged himself to caution, but he was also a man who had lived and died by knowing how to read a body.

This night was to establish interest. To see if she could tolerate the thought of what must be done in the coming days. If her body language was anything to go by, then tolerating it would be no problem.

"I'm going to kiss you, Risa," he warned her one last time. "Move away from me and we'll return to the others. Otherwise, those pretty pouting lips are going to belong to me."

Belong to him? Risa blinked back at him, her lips parting. But . . . *It was safe here, right? One kiss.*

"I—" She tried to speak, tried to think. She didn't want to appear whorish, but what else was she going to appear to be before the night was over? It was her night, damn it! He was a stranger. He would remain a stranger after the night was over. That was all that was important.

One night.

"One kiss," she whispered, shocked, amazed at her own daring.

His jaw clenched, a muscle ticcing at the side as his hand came up, cupped her neck, and his thumb whispered over her lips.

His head lowered until she felt his breath against her lips, the warmth of him sinking into her.

"I want to watch your eyes as I kiss you," his voice whispered through her. "I want to feel your lips, Risa, soft and sweet, and taste the nectar of your tongue. I want to taste you, and know the essence of you." He looked around, a teasing smile quirking his lips. "Impossible here, wouldn't you agree?"

She trembled. One hand gripped her purse; the other was flat against the wall behind her as she stared back at him.

"Why?"

His head tilted again. "Why do I want to kiss you like that?"

She nodded jerkily.

"Is there another way to kiss a beautiful, desirable woman?" he asked her then. "If there is, then I am unaware of it."

There was a hint of conviction in his tone, a hint of hunger. She was woman enough to see it, to feel it.

"You want to kiss me?" she whispered. Had anyone ever wanted to kiss her?

"My sweet, *want* is a mild word for the need to kiss you." There was a hint of self-mockery in his smile then, in the gleam of his eyes. "I should be ashamed of my lack of control." His hand lifted again, his fingers tucking her hair behind her ear once more. It was always falling free; the thick strands refused to anchor in any way.

"Such pretty hair," he said then. "Silken and warm."

His head lowered, his lips whispered over hers. A kiss. Firm, heated. Risa felt a surge of excitement. She felt pleasure. His lips warmed hers, his tongue tasted her until she was panting and nearly begging for more. A soft cry left her lips as his head lifted and he moved back marginally.

He held his hand out to her. "Shall we return? If we're lucky, the band could play something soft and slow. I'd like to dance with you, Risa."

Her hand lifted from the wall, her fingers trembled as she laid them in his hand.

"I—" Her lips trembled then. She laughed self-consciously. "I'm not used . . ."

"No explanations needed." His voice was darker, warmer. "None, Risa. Tonight, there's no need for anything but to be yourself. However you wish to be. Whoever you wish to be."

Morganna had sworn that no one had mentioned Risa's past to him. That they hadn't told him about the nightmares that haunted her. He didn't know her. He only knew that she was their friend. That she had been sheltered. Morganna had been fierce about that. That Micah would know Risa wasn't a woman to be played with. She had silently objected to that. Maybe, she had thought then, she wanted to be played with. Now she knew she did.

She could be whoever she wished to be.

She let his hand curl around hers and draw her forward.

When he released her, she didn't object when his arm went behind her, that same hand pressing possessively against her lower back.

She felt damned strange. She was damp between her thighs as she had never been before. Her clit was swollen; she could feel the sensitivity of the little bud between the folds of her sex. Her nipples rasped against the material of her dress; they felt swollen, heavy. They didn't feel too small now; they felt too large. She didn't feel plain; she didn't feel beautiful. She felt wanted. Had she ever felt wanted?

Micah could feel the violence threatening to explode through his system as he felt the tension gathering in her back. God, she was ready to explode. He could feel the heat of her flesh, see the blaze of need in her piercing blue eyes.

Did she know what that did to a man? he wondered. Even a man as controlled, as experienced, as he was. It was like a shaft of fire cutting through his balls. The need to sink inside her was a hunger unlike anything he had known previously, with any other woman.

Micah was a man who understood his own sexuality, his own hungers. He was a man who understood a woman's body. Each nuance of it. Each spark of hunger, each measure of arousal. And he wanted to kill Fuentes. He wanted to kill Risa's father. That son of a bitch had ordered his daughter injected with the evil of that drug and had watched. The fucker had watched as another man had raped his child.

A baby. She had been a fucking baby, and Jansen Clay had allowed another to touch her, to abuse her in the most monstrous fashion.

Micah led her back to the table, lifted his hand imperiously, and gained the attention of a waitress. Leaning close, he whispered to Risa, "I need to speak to Reno and Clint for a moment. I'll be back soon."

Her hair brushed against his cheek as she nodded, and she saw the trembling of her fingers in her lap. He didn't touch her further. Her body was already sensitized, her mind was thrown into confusion, and for the first time in his life Micah was on the verge of unadulterated fury.

His gaze lifted and connected with Kell Krieger's. The message in Micah's gaze was clear, and he knew the other man received it perfectly as his green eyes narrowed. *Protect her*. No other man was to approach her.

Micah knew himself; he was a man who knew his own central core as he knew nothing else in this world. And he knew, for the space of time that it was needed, this woman would belong to him. She would be his, completely. There was no other option.

Straightening, he turned and followed the other two men through the club and out the back entrance. The night wrapped around them, but that didn't mean there were no eyes to see them, that no else was watching them, no ears listening to them.

"What the fuck are you doing?" Clint's voice was furious as he jerked open the door of the soundproof van he and his wife had brought to the club.

Entering the interior, Micah eased himself into the seat along the back and watched as Clint slammed the door after Reno entered.

Both men glared back at him.

"She's fucking terrified." Clint was enraged. "That wasn't the deal, Micah. Meet and greet. What the hell are you doing, backing her into a wall and all but molesting her?"

Micah's hand jerked out, his fingers wrapping around the other man's throat before he could say anything further. The move surprised Micah. It clearly shocked both Clint and Reno.

"Let him go, Maverick," Reno warned him softly as Micah's eyes refused to leave Clint's.

"Accuse me of hurting her again and we'll have words, McIntyre," he told Clint harshly. "You don't know that woman as you believe you do. You don't know the effects of that demon dust they shot into her veins, and you don't know the hell she lives through each night. I know." His fingers almost tightened. "I've heard her nightmares, and I've heard her screams. Don't dare to interfere here."

He released Clint slowly, aware that the other man had

shown no fear; he had shown only a silent watchfulness, as had Reno after his initial protest.

Micah leaned back in the seat, forced his body to relax, his mind to center.

"Did you bring me here for any reason other than to berate me over Risa?" he finally asked. "Let's hope you did."

Reno snorted at the comment. "Live Wire tracked a tail on you," he told him. "Or rather one on Risa. She was followed from the apartment to the club. The car circled the club twice, then disappeared into traffic, and they lost it. Do you know how hard it is to lose one of you bastards in traffic?"

Micah's jaw clenched. "She's already being watched. Were they able to identify the driver?"

"All we have is dark hair and glasses. He was careful to keep his face hidden. We have some pictures, but it's going to take a few hours to get a clear idea of who we're looking for."

"It's not Orion." Micah rubbed his hands over his face, wishing he had the lack of control that would allow him to punch something. Or someone. "He wouldn't make that mistake. You'll not know when he's watching and when he's not."

He looked up in time to catch Clint and Reno exchanging glances and carefully stilled all expression on his face; even his eyes would be blank. He knew how to do it. These men were good, but Micah had learned, even at a young age, that any hint of emotion could get a man killed.

He did breathe in heavily. "Have a crew go into her apartment before she returns home, check for bugs. Orion will lay in listening devices sometimes, to track his mark. Several were found in his last victim's hotel room. That's how he knows where to strike and when. Make certain her apartment is clean."

"That could give us away," Clint pointed out. "He'll know we're on to him and he could run."

Micah shook his head. "He's been tracked before and escaped. He's a master at his craft and the execution of it. He'll know I'm her protection, there's no hiding that. Orion will see it as a challenge, but he won't back off. Nothing will stop him from attempting to kill her."

He and his father had found the devices in Micah's parents' home when his mother had turned up missing. How long they had been there, Micah wasn't certain. Definitely long enough for Orion to have tracked her schedule and to know where and when to take her.

"I'll get Live Wire on that." Reno nodded. "What are your plans tonight with Risa?" There was a vein of protectiveness in the other man's voice.

Micah stared back at him coldly. "What I do tonight is none of your concern. From this moment on, she's under my protection; that's all you need to concern yourself with. Watch my back; watch for Orion; follow Live Wire's commands. Do not involve yourself in whatever I do with Miss Clay."

They stared back at him, their gazes hard, defiant. Micah almost grinned at their expressions. He would hate to have to fight them, because damn if they wouldn't be hard to beat together. He might have a chance one-on-one, but these two men weren't that insane. They'd strike together.

"Don't fuck up, Maverick," Reno warned him then, his voice hard. "She's not just a mark; she's a friend. Hurt her and you won't have just me and Clint gunning for you; you'll have the entire team on your ass. You don't want that."

No, he didn't want that because he would need these men in the future during other missions. They watched his ass, protected it when the need arose. He'd have to move carefully.

He nodded at the warning. He could expect nothing less.

Chapter 3

THINGS WERE HAPPENING too fast.

Risa sat, poised on her chair, after Micah, Reno, Ian, and Clint moved away from the table.

She tried to join in the conversation and the teasing of the one remaining male at the table, but her efforts were stilted at best.

The club was too warm. There were too many people and she was too used to cowering in her apartment, alone.

She wasn't accustomed to the sensitivity in her own body or the confusion tearing through her. Or to being racked by shudders of . . . something that didn't make sense. Sensations she could not put her finger on.

She'd been around other men in the six years since she had been rescued from the asylum her father had had her placed in. After she had been rescued from Diego Fuentes's cell, her father had rushed her straight to a private hospital. It wouldn't do, of course, for her to start screaming in hysteria when she became conscious. Which was exactly what she had done.

She had been sedated and kept quiet for nineteen months. She remembered a few times that a doctor had come to her room, one she hadn't been familiar with. Her father had laughed and joked, petted her arm, and she had been injected with that hated drug again.

Why? She still questioned that. They hadn't raped her.

After that first time, no one had touched her. Jansen Clay had told her she was so ugly he couldn't pay anyone to fuck her, even in the interests of the test they needed to run on the drug.

They had let her suffer. Suffer while they petted her arm or stroked her hair.

She flinched at the distant memory. It was like that, except in her nightmares. The memories and the knowledge of her pain at that time were so distant, almost as though it had happened to someone else. Unless she dared to allow a man to touch her. Then the fear and the bleak sickness rolled inside her like a tidal wave ready to consume her.

Until tonight. Tonight, she would have given all she possessed for all the promises behind that one kiss. What made Micah different? What made her body react in this new way? Was it the man or the instinctive knowledge of the man's control?

They were questions she couldn't answer. Instead, she turned her attention to the dance floor and watched the gyrating bodies in fascination.

She had loved to dance when she was younger. As a teenager she had gone to every ball, every party, every dance that her father allowed her to attend. She would beg for weeks to go until he finally relented.

She had danced with friends then. Other girls who weren't paired with a date, who were left out of the male/female dynamic. But it had been fun. She had laughed then, she had felt free during those hours.

Oh, let her go, Jansen. It's not as though you have to worry about her virtue.

Her stepmother Elaine's frustrated anger at Risa's begging struck through her mind. Risa shook her head, fighting against the self-consciousness, the familiar pain that assailed her.

She promised herself she wouldn't do this tonight.

Tonight, she was going to have a lover. It was a promise she had made to herself.

She could do this. Micah thought she was merely sheltered, that she had been overprotected throughout her life.

He had been given that warning, Morganna had told her. Risa had been embarrassed by it, but now she felt a mild thrill at the thought of it. Micah would think of that, and he'd understand her hesitation, maybe.

"What do you think, Risa?" Morganna leaned forward, a bright smile on her lips as she asked the question.

"About what?" Risa shook her head; she'd obviously not been following the conversation.

"About you, me, and Raven showing those men the hazards of deserting us?" the other woman laughed. "Would you go out on the floor and dance with us?"

Dance with other girls like she had as a child? God, she didn't need anything else to dim her confidence at the moment than standing out there knowing she was there because a man didn't want to dance with her.

Suddenly panic assailed her. It lodged in her check, tightened in her throat.

Her head jerked back until she was staring at the dance floor, and anger pushed through her, tearing at her mind as she fought against the knowledge that not once had a man asked her to dance.

Not that she could have forced herself out on the floor with a man she didn't know. But she hadn't even been asked. Not once.

The other women had been approached; she had been distantly aware of that. The advances had been laughed off, but there had been advances.

"Come on, Risa. We'll have a blast," Morganna laughed.

Her lips parted, Risa lifted a shaking hand to her throat and fought the feeling of suffocation. She could not, was not getting on that dance floor.

"I'm sorry, but Risa promised me her first dance."

Her head jerked around and Micah was there. He stared down at her with a hint of a smile on his lips, his dark gaze warming, wrapping around her like a sultry summer night as he held his hand out to her.

"Reno and Clint chatter like old gossips," he told her teasingly as she placed her hand in his, rising to her feet as though in a dream, and allowing him to lead her through the press of bodies to the dance floor.

As they reached the edge of the gyrating mass of bodies, the music changed, slowed, eased.

"Ah, they must have read my mind," he commented as he turned her to him. "Still interested?"

She had never slow-danced.

The world around her seemed to fade as he placed one hand at her hip, held her hand with the other, and eased her against his body.

A harsh gasp tore from her at the contact of her nipples through her dress, against his hard male chest. Even through the layers of clothing the stroke of sensation was violent, electric.

"I don't dance often," she tried to cover her reaction to him even as she fought to make sense of it.

"Neither do I."

The hand at her lower back urged her closer without demanding it. Risa flowed into him, her fingers curling against his shoulder at the feel of his erection pressing against her belly, the feel of the warmth of his body surrounding her.

Her eyes closed and her head settled against his chest. Slowly, she forced herself to relax, let herself feel what it was like to be a woman, rather than a frightened child.

The fear was still there, waiting to attack. But oh God, this was . . . pleasant. More than pleasant, actually. It was comforting even as it made her feel more sensitive, more alive, than ever before.

One broad male hand stroked her back; the other held her hand against his chest, so close to the side of her breast. If she moved just right, she could feel his fingers stroking against the needy mound.

She didn't want the song to end. She didn't want the night to end. She wanted to become trapped in this moment, to relish the feel of his body against hers.

"You move like a fantasy," he whispered at her ear. "As graceful and fluid as a doe."

She wanted to believe him, and she couldn't, but the words stroked the pain and fear inside her.

Neither of them spoke then. Risa let herself be caught in the moment, let herself relax and flow against him, let her body move with his, closer, warmer, until her arms were around his neck, his wrapped around her back, holding her closer. His head was bent, his cheek against the top of her head. She could feel him wrapped around her, holding her, and there was no fear.

She could do this.

She lifted her head and stared up at him. "We don't have to stay here," she whispered. He might not be able to hear her, but she watched his eyes, saw the flare of heat in the darkened color, and knew he understood.

"Are you sure?" His lips moved; his expression shifted for just a second, a hint of male hunger showing through the normally still set of his face.

"I'm sure." She was already shaking inside.

His hand ran up her back, a whisper of sensation against the silk material covering her, then across her bare arm until he had her hand in his and drew back.

"We'll need to let our friends know we're leaving," he warned her gently.

Risa nodded. Yes, she would have to face her friends and their concern.

"Very well." With his free hand he tucked her hair behind her ear again and allowed his thumb to caress her jaw. "We'll leave now."

ORION WATCHED the couple as they moved from the dance floor, carefully controlling the frown that would have creased his forehead. It wouldn't do to show interest in them. At the moment he was allowing a particularly slutty little brunette to run her fingers up his thigh and pretending interest. But he kept his peripheral vision on the man and woman.

He knew that man; he knew he did. He never ever forgot

a face or the name that went to it, but in this case he couldn't put the face and the name together. How odd?

Plastic surgery? he wondered. That had to be it. Otherwise, he'd have instantly recognized the man who led Risa Clay from the dance floor.

He wanted to grimace at the thought that her companion had that look of a man who intended to fuck the woman he was with.

Even with makeup and the very appealing little slip dress, the girl wasn't particularly pretty. She wasn't as ugly as she had been as a teenager, but she wasn't exactly attractive, either. There was just a quality to her that offended his refined senses.

What was it about that girl that just bothered him? he wondered. Her cheekbones were high, her eyes slightly tilted. The odd pale blue color of her eyes showed up more with the artificial highlights in her hair.

She cleaned up okay, but he still couldn't find it in him to forget how very ugly she had once been.

He had hoped he wouldn't receive the job to kill her. He remembered, eight years before when she had first been kidnapped, her face had been in the papers. He'd grimaced then. Two years later when Jansen Clay's death had been announced, he'd had that vague premonition of what was coming.

It was a shame. His employer should have been more picky in his friends and the women he fucked. If he hadn't been with Jansen that night to take his pick of the girls, then he wouldn't have been stuck with only one choice, the Clay girl.

He'd done her, though. He'd pushed her face to the floor of the cargo plane and in front of her father, he'd pushed her skirts to her hips and rammed into her.

He'd been furious, he'd told Orion. The girl had been so pumped on Whore's Dust, his employer had been certain she wouldn't remember the event. But it appeared she had remembered parts of it, and he had learned she could be remembering more. It wouldn't do for her to remember who had raped her.

Orion was going to have to kill her. Damn, it would be so much easier to just put a bullet in her brain, but he just couldn't bring himself to kill her in such a manner. He was proud of each job he took and if he didn't bleed her, then no one would believe he had been the one to do her.

Pity. But it couldn't be helped.

She lived alone. That was a pleasant plus. He could slip into her apartment, gag her, and kill her in her own home. He didn't get to do that very often. He'd definitely have to put her facedown, though. There was just something about that face that he couldn't tolerate. Those eyes. She would be a particularly interesting test for him. He'd never had to kill a woman who made him as uneasy as this one did.

CHAPTER 4

HER GRANDMOTHER had always said she was stubborn, but Risa had never believed her. As she stepped into Micah's hotel room, she wondered if perhaps her grandmother Abigail wasn't right. Maybe she was too stubborn.

She had made herself go this far, and now that she had, her body was rioting with nerves. She didn't know this man. She knew nothing about him.

Well, next to nothing. Morganna, Raven, and Emily had imparted some information. He was thirty-two, born to Israeli immigrants, six two, tough. Their husbands respected him. He was clean as of his latest Navy-regulated blood tests. Morganna had stated that Clint believed he was kind. He was good with animals and children.

Hell, it was more than Risa knew about the men her friends were married to.

"Would you like a drink?" She jerked, startled as his hands touched her shoulders, but only to draw her wrap from the death grip she had on it as it lay over her shoulders.

She let the material slide over her arms as she shook her head.

"No, thank you," she finally breathed out. She didn't drink often. It had a curiously heated effect on her. It made her want things, things she didn't understand, touches she had only read about or seen in movies.

"Are you certain this is what you want, Risa?" he asked

then, his warm breath caressing the side of her neck as he bent his head to hers. "It's not too late to turn back. We can go to the bar and talk. I could drive you home."

She stiffened in sudden self-consciousness. "If you'd prefer not to." She moved to turn, to take her wrap, to let him off easy. God, had the lights of the club somehow hidden how plain she truly was?

"Prefer not to? I don't think so." His hand moved hers to his leg, pressed her palm against the tight muscle of his thigh.

Risa stared down at her hand, noticing how much larger his was as he held her palm against his muscular leg.

Curiosity overtook her. Curiosity and the electric slide of arousal that seemed to build inside her until she wondered that sparks weren't reflecting between them.

"I don't know how."

A finger pressed against her lips as he halted her words. "There's nothing either of us needs to know," he said softly as she continued to stare down at their hands. "Whatever you wish is yours. If you don't wish, then you have only to say so and I'll stop. Agreed?"

She licked her lips nervously and lifted her head. Her attention was caught and held by his lips. His lower lip was a touch fuller, more sensual, than the upper lip. On him, it looked good, sexy.

Her lips parted. "Would you kiss me?"

She felt as though she was begging, but she was helpless against the temptation, against the needs rioting through her body.

"I dream of kissing you," he whispered, his hand curving around her neck, his fingers heated against her flesh as she let herself accept the lie for now.

He couldn't have dreamed of kissing her, but she liked the sound of it. It soothed something inside her, and heated another part of her.

She watched as his lips lowered, watched as she felt his breath against her, then the heated rough velvet touch of lips against her own.

Risa inhaled roughly at the static surge of sensation that raced across her lips. She jerked back involuntarily, her hands flying to his chest, palms flat as she blinked back at him in surprise.

His lips tilted into a gentle grin.

"Should we try it again?" he asked softly. "Perhaps next time neither of us will be caught off-guard by the pleasure."

That was pleasure?

His hand tightened on her neck.

"Watch me, just like that," his dark voice crooned. "Your eyes wide, your gaze dark because I please you. I want very much to please you, Risa."

He did? Oh God, was this really pleasure? Could she bear much more of it if it was?

"Easy," he whispered. "Soft and easy."

Soft and easy. His lips settled against hers as they parted, a whimper of surging hunger escaping her throat as his head tilted, his hand tightening at her neck as her lashes fluttered closed and she let the waves of pleasure wash through her.

His tongue licked at her lips, then slid past them, just a little as he teased the tip of hers. Her lips parted further for him, her tongue reaching out as she trembled in his grasp.

Oh God, what was he doing to her? Her heart was thundering in her chest, but his was racing just as hard beneath her hands. A hard pounding rhythm that sank into her palms and filled her with wonder.

It was incredible. This kiss. His lips were heated and dominant, determined. They mastered hers, led her through a sexy, sultry dance that had her lifting to her tiptoes to get closer, to sink into him, to sate herself against the hunger surging inside her now.

Her hands slid up his chest, around his neck. Her head fell against his arm and she let the sensations inside her surge over her.

Lips and tongues met and meshed. Liquid fire raced through her veins, pounded into her sex. Her clit was throbbing with such aching need that she found herself pressing into him desperately, rubbing herself against the hard ridge of his cock as his hands tightened on her hips, pulling her closer.

Mewling cries of need were barely forced back. Many slipped free. She was a pleading mess of sensations that she had no idea how to handle.

She fought to breathe and couldn't, and didn't care. She tried to lift closer, to press her nipples tighter into the warmth of his chest, to grind her clit harder against his erection. She didn't know if she could stand the rapidly whirling sensations tearing through her now. They were unlike anything she had ever known; even that distant memory of flames burning her from the inside out didn't compare to this.

"Micah." She tore her lips from his, only to have his hand move to the side of her neck once more to hold her still. His lips were back on hers, his kiss as hungry and desperate as the sensual needs pouring through her body.

"Easy," he groaned, finally tearing his lips from hers, his big body tense and suddenly harder than ever before. "Hell, Risa, you make a man lose his head."

She did?

Her eyes opened, and for a second she almost believed him. His face was flushed from lust, his eyes gleaming back at her in hunger.

He wanted her. He couldn't fake this. This wasn't anger or depravity. It was simple hunger, for her.

Her hands fumbled at his shoulders before pushing beneath the edge of his jacket and pushing.

Surprise sparked in his eyes, but he let her push the material from his shoulders.

She licked her lips slowly, wanting his kiss again, but wanting something more as well.

Her hands slid back to his chest and moved to the buttons of his shirt. The first one fell free before she lifted her gaze to his.

"Whatever you want." His voice was thick, rough.

She wanted his shirt off. She pushed the second button free as his head lowered, his lips moving along her shoulder to the sensitive line of her neck.

Risa trembled at the pleasure. The scrape of his teeth sent tremors tearing down her spine and sensation to attack her womb, convulsing it violently as she gasped in surprise.

It must be natural. He didn't pause. His hands caressed her hips now, stroking the silk of her dress against her flesh and making her long for the touch of his hands.

She worked on the buttons, fingers fumbling, trembling, her neck arched, and she strained closer to the touch of his mouth against her shoulders.

"Take the shirt off and I get to take your dress off," he warned her, and he meant it. She could hear the determination, the hunger, in his voice.

She wanted her dress off. She wanted to rub against him, feel his skin against hers. She wanted to know what it was like. How much more pleasure could she bear? How much of his touch could she stand without melting to the floor with the heat rising inside her.

Her fingers reached the band of his slacks and her fingers formed fists in the material to drag his shirt out of his pants. It was open now, falling away from his surprisingly broad chest. Soft, silky chest hairs were scattered over it and arrowed down his taut stomach.

Her fingers touched the silky stuff, curled, and ran down that dark line until they met his pants once again.

She could do as she wished, he'd said.

His head lifted from her shoulder as hers straightened, and she stared back at him as her fingers touched the buckle of his belt.

"Whatever you wish," he whispered again. "Tonight, I'm all yours, Risa."

Tonight, just for tonight. She could have this, no explanations, no knowledge of each other. This was what she needed. She didn't have to face him in the morning; she could leave when it was over. She would never see him again. He would never know her shameful secrets.

Her fingers pulled at the buckle, loosened the leather, and left it free as they moved to the clasp and zipper.

This wasn't so hard. She could do this.

His slacks came loose easily. Beneath were soft cotton briefs and straining thick, hard flesh. The backs of her fingers felt the heat of that flesh; her hand ached to touch it.

"Your turn." His voice was a heavy growl.

She felt the hidden zipper at the back of her dress loosen and stilled. She watched him carefully as he eased the straps over her arms and pushed the material from her body.

It caught at her breasts, and she swore he swallowed tightly before pulling it over her straining nipples. The sensation of silk brushing against the tight nubs had her moaning. A sound she tried to cut off and couldn't.

"Risa." His hands smoothed down her arms as she felt a latent hunger burning inside him.

Her womb clenched, she felt her vagina tightening, the slick essence of need coating the bare lips as he stared down at her breasts.

"I want to touch you." His groan was rougher now, filled with a primal power that sent a shiver down her back. "Sweet mercy. You make me shake with the need to touch you."

She stared at him in wonder, wondering if he was lying, if they were just pretty words. Her mind and her heart doubted, but her body overruled it. The clash and clamor of demand shuddered through her as his hands cupped the swollen mounds.

Her knees weakened. How was she supposed to stand? The room felt as though it were spinning around her as weakness assailed her. She gripped his shoulders and watched, eyes wide as he palmed the flesh. His thumbs raked over her distended nipples and a surge of heat caught her unaware, causing her to stumble.

"You're making me weak!" she cried out as he caught her against him.

His lips stole anything else she would say. Slanting across hers he kissed her with a power and a demand she was helpless to fight against. Her arms wrapped around his neck as he lifted her. A moan slipped past their kiss as she felt him lowering her to the bed, easing over her, his heavy, heated body encasing her in warmth.

"Risa, you make a man lose control," he charged as he pulled back, his hand going to her breast once again, cupping it, shaping it with his palm. "I want to taste you here. I want to draw every ounce of sweet hunger from your body."

She couldn't protest. She wanted to protest. Violent pulses of sensation were charging through her body, drawing her tight, trembling through her as his head lowered.

She didn't know what she expected. She'd read about this. She'd seen it in movies; she hadn't expected this. Both hands encased her breast, plumped her nipple high; then his mouth covered it, sucked it in, and caused her to cry out with the turbulent surge of pleasure that seemed to tear through her womb.

"Micah. I can't stand . . ." She arched; her head shook. She wanted him to stop. She didn't want him to stop. His lips were drawing on her, electricity was tearing through her, and between her thighs fingers of electrical explosions tore through her clit, her vagina.

She was torn, terrified of herself now more than she was of the man.

"Easy, love." He was breathing hard, his features flushed as his head lifted. His hand smoothed down her side as the other plumped her other breast now, preparing it for his mouth.

His hand stroked over her hip, his head lowered. His fingers moved to her thigh, his mouth sucked in her other nipple, and his fingers crazed the super-slick swollen folds of her sex.

"Oh God, no."

What was happening to her? Something, something dark, primal, something unbidden, rose inside her, thrust her hips against his hand as her thighs closed on it.

"No." Her arms wrapped around his neck, her hands splaying against the back of his head as he tried to move. "Micah. Help me."

She couldn't breathe. She couldn't make sense of what she was feeling, where she was flying, and the frightening roller coaster of sensations was tearing her apart.

"Easy, love. I have you." He spread small kisses over her breasts as her hips writhed, the hand trapped between her thighs doing her bidding now, almost. Oh God, almost.

Then two fingers curled, parted her flesh, and notched against the entrance to her pussy.

Risa closed her eyes and fought the tears, fought the fear. She stilled beneath him, panting, waiting for the pain.

"Look at me, Risa," he crooned, his lips caressing her jaw now, brushing against her lips. "Open your pretty eyes. You promised to watch me, yes?"

Her lashes fluttered open. She saw him, but she was aware of little else than the slightest impalement between her thighs.

"Part your legs for me. Loosen for me, Risa. How can I please you if you're stiff against me?"

His wrist flexed between her thighs, raked against her sensitive clit, and sent a gasp of a breath falling from her lips.

"There." He gentled her with his voice, his eyes. "Part your legs, sweet. Let me show you how beautiful your passion is. Come now; open for me."

She forced her thighs to part. Whimpering cries lodged in her throat as she spread her legs.

"A little more, darling." She parted them farther, watching his eyes, his face. "Look, sweetheart," he urged her then, his gaze moving from hers and following to the point where his hand cupped her mound.

Risa's eyes widened, her hips arched, knees bending as she lifted to him, desperate to feel what she knew would be nothing more than pain.

"Slow and easy," he whispered at her ear. "Watch, love. Slow and easy."

His fingers curved, tilted, and entered.

Risa felt herself shaking, felt the slow slide of her juices meeting his fingers as her inner muscles tightened around the penetration, clenching and spasming as her back arched and pleasure tore through her. Pleasure or pain. A mix of burning relief and agonizing tension.

"Fuck me, yes," he suddenly groaned, his teeth nipping at her ear. "Take my fingers, Risa. Just my fingers."

They surged deeper as she lifted to them, her nails digging into his shoulders now, her flesh rioting with a surge of insane hunger. It was tearing through her, tightening her, making her crazed for more.

"Micah, I'm scared!" She hated it. There was nothing so humiliating as admitting it, as feeling the tears that slid from the corners of her eyes and met his lips.

"No fear, Risa." His fingers stilled inside her. "See, no pain, no fear."

No pain, no fear. That made sense. She drew in a shaking breath and clenched around his fingers again.

There was no pain, no fear.

"Now." She turned her head to meet his gaze. "Take me now."

She couldn't wait. The fears were building in her along with the pulse and power of the pleasure. Her mind fought her body; distant memories clashed in her head.

She kept her eyes on his. She fought to push back the past. His eyes anchored her, steadied her.

"You're not ready yet," he whispered. "Soon."

"Now." She shook her head as he moved, spreading kisses over her breasts, between her breasts. "I can't wait, Micah."

She was frightened to wait. Too many sensations were tearing through her. She felt locked between the past and the present, her mind battling the raging lust that rose like a tide of molten sensation inside her.

"Just a few more minutes, Risa," he groaned. "Soon."

His lips moved between her breasts, down her stomach as she fought to breathe. His shoulders pressed her thighs wider; his gaze stayed locked with hers as his fingers moved inside her, pressed deeper, and tore a throttled scream from her as the pleasure shocked the tense muscles, the tender nerve endings.

"I'm dying to taste you," he whispered, his lips poised over her clit. "Just a sweet kiss, Risa."

His head lowered. His eyes held hers. His lips pursed, covered her clit and his fingers moved, pulled back, then pushed inside her, parting her flesh with a surge of sensation that terrified her.

She fought for release, she fought to get closer. Her body turned and he flowed with her. On her side, one leg straight, the other bent to accommodate his head, and still his lips suckled at the tender bud between her thighs.

He followed as she twisted back, her heels dug into the bed, her hips arched, and her mind lost the battle with her body. Risa twisted beneath him, thrust into his fingers, his mouth. She was shaking, shuddering with sensation as she fought to breathe.

She needed, needed something. The tension was tearing through her, marking her with the perspiration that dotted her flesh, with her muscles straining for relief. There had to be relief.

"Fuck me, damn you." The words tore from her lips as her hands moved to his head. She felt like an animal, a creature that hungered for this, only for this.

His fingers moved, thrust, fucked inside her with deep, strong movements as his lips suckled at her clit. His tongue stroked over it, rasping it until she froze at the wave of sensation that suddenly rose inside her. Her eyes flared wide, her muscles locked against it. When it crashed over her, it wasn't so bad. It was a shudder of pleasure rather than a blinding, horrifying loss of consciousness.

"Ah, Riss." His head pressed against her abdomen as she shuddered through the little shocks of pleasure, his voice filled with somber regret as his lashes lifted from his eyes and he watched her with a tenderness that brought tears to her eyes.

"What's wrong with me?" she whispered, her hips still moving, the need still tearing through her vagina, her womb. "Micah, do something; please do something."

He rose to his knees, his fingers sliding from her body even as she tried to hold him inside.

Only then did she notice the condom he had somehow managed to work over his heavy, thick erection. His hand stroked over it, spreading her juices over the latex before he gripped the base tight and tensed before her.

"Are you sure, Risa?" His hand gripped her thigh, lifted her leg until her knees were bent, her legs spread wide. "Be sure, love."

She watched the wide, throbbing head as he came over her. Watched as he drew her hips up along his thighs as he knelt before her. The wide crest of his erection parted the glistening folds of her sex as she licked her lips and pressed closer.

"Slow and easy," he said again.

The heavy head pressed against her opening, parted it, and began to work inside her. His thighs widened as he came over her, propping his body up with one arm, allowing her to watch. His hips moved, shifted, working his cock inside her, stretching her until she thought she was going to burn alive from the slow, steady impalement.

It was too much. It wasn't enough. The clawing, vicious talons of lust were tearing through her until she was begging him, arching, her hips working against his, thrusting and pressing him deeper as she fought back the tears.

It was terrifying, but she couldn't stop. She wanted, she needed, but the dark void that seemed to rush around her was too frightening, too filled with the unknown, with sensations she couldn't accept.

Above her, Micah groaned her name. His lips lowered to her nipples. He sucked them until she fought the gathering void again. He kissed her, his lips slanting over hers as she ate at his, until the void threatened to rush through her.

"Risa, let go, baby." His voice was dark, shattered with his own pleasure. "I'll hold you; I swear it."

Her head shook. She didn't understand what he wanted, couldn't make sense of her own body, let alone his words.

"Risa, let it go!" His voice strengthened as his hips churned, his cock thrusting harder, deeper, stroking her into a storm of never-ending sensations. Darkness gathered behind her eyes as the wave rose again, stronger, harder.

Her nails dug into his shoulders; her head dug into the mattress as she fought it, struggled against it. She screamed against it, and once again, when it took her, it wasn't so bad. She fought it back until it was no more than a small surge, racing through her, shivering over her body as he gave a hard, harsh groan and shuddered above her before stilling.

His breathing was harsh, heavy. His cock inside her pulsed violently, so hard it felt like iron inside her. But he wasn't coming. She could feel the difference, knew it. He wanted to come, he needed to, but he hadn't.

The storm eased inside her, leaving her strangely bereft now, as his forehead touched her shoulder and he shuddered against her.

"I'm sorry, love," he whispered, his voice heavy. "I'm so sorry."

She blinked up at him as he moved from her, pulling free of her as a hard surge of renewed need shook her body. He was moving from the bed before she could get a handle on the pulse of hunger. His hands ran over his hair as he glanced back at her, his expression heavy, his cock still fully erect.

He hadn't come.

The thought slashed through her like a dull knife. Somehow, she had failed. He hadn't released. He hadn't known pleasure.

She swallowed tightly, staring back at him, and he paced to the bathroom.

"Don't you move!" He turned, pointed his finger back at her, his expression bleak and commanding. "I'll be right back."

She nodded, but as the door closed, she jumped from the bed as silently as possible. It took only a moment to jerk her dress over her head, her wrap around her shoulders. She carried her purse and her shoes and she escaped.

Humiliation burned inside her, tightened in her chest, and left her shaking as she took the stairs rather than waiting for the elevator. She raced down them, holding back her sobs, fighting the ultra-sensitivity in her body and screaming inside her mind.

She had failed. *A pity fuck,* she thought. The big, tough SEAL had felt sorry for her. He had seen her fears and had tried to make it better. But he couldn't get off. He couldn't come with her. That was a pity fuck. She was certain it was, and she couldn't bear it.

After she waved down a cab and gave the driver the address for her apartment, she huddled in the cab and thanked God that she never had to face Micah again.

He should have done as her father's friend had done. He should have taken her from behind.

A tear fell. The memory attacked her, sharp, brutal, the voice at her ear. *Ugly little bitch. I'd never get off if I had to look at your face.*

She flinched, covered her mouth, and held back her sobs as she stared into the brightly lit streets of the city. She had hoped she could survive just one night of pleasure. She had been wrong.

CHAPTER 5

MICAH WAS IN a lousy mood the next morning when he showed up at the Federal Building and made his way to the rooms that had been set aside for this morning's meeting.

He strode through the narrow underground corridor to the appropriate door, knocked, and waited for it to open. Stepping into the darkened room, he glanced through the hidden window in the next room and felt his fists clenching at the sight of Risa, her grandmother Abigail Clay, and their attorney as they sat silently in the other room.

The lawyer looked up, scowled into the mirror that hid the viewers from sight, and glanced at his watch.

Micah's Elite Ops team was there, as well as Clint, Reno, Kell, Ian, and Kira. The others cast Micah several odd looks before turning back to the window that looked into the consultation room.

"We have the rest of her doctor's reports." Jordan, a.k.a. Live Wire, commander of the group, slapped a file in his hand. "Can you believe that old biddie in there browbeat the doctor that's been overseeing Risa's care? She had no idea of the long-term effects of the Whore's Dust."

Micah snapped the file open, read it quickly, and felt a boiling rage building inside him.

"Does she know yet?" he asked as he read the reports on the tests that Risa was required to take monthly. The presence of the Whore's Dust in her system hadn't abated, and put last night into clear perspective for Micah.

It didn't help the rage building inside him but made it understandable. The Whore's Dust created an almost violent reaction during intercourse, especially for a woman. The explosive clash of sensations was often terrifying; the sexual release, if it was even attained, was stronger, and only built the need higher.

This was how Risa had handled it. She didn't let it happen. The toys in her drawer didn't help. And the night before, in his arms, she had fought her release with such strength that if she'd orgasmed, it had been no more than a weak facsimile of what it could have been.

Damn her.

Damn Fuentes and that fucking drug.

"According to her doctor, and we had to send Nik in to talk to him, Abigail Clay threatened his reputation, both public and private, if he informed her granddaughter of the effects. She stated Risa was terrified enough of her own body; she didn't want to make matters worse."

In ways, Micah almost agreed with her.

"Who's going in to talk to them first?" he asked.

He knew what had to be done. There was a contract on Risa's life, and the enemy Micah had been searching for for six years was rumored to have been given the job. The same man who had killed his mother, and ultimately his father, was now waiting for the opportunity to slice into Risa as well.

It was tied directly to her kidnapping. The U.S. government had known there were other men involved, especially an as yet unnamed scientist who had been trying to reproduce the date rape drug after the death of Fuentes's scientist.

Diego Fuentes hadn't known the scientist. All he had known was that his contact, Jansen Clay, was working with the other man to re-create the drug. Diego had blocked them several times, simply out of greed. He wanted to control the creation he had bankrolled. He hadn't wanted others' greedy fingers involved in it.

But why strike at Risa now? The only answer was her

medical records. Someone, outside of the government, was finding a way to keep watch on both her medical and psychological files, because in the past months she had begun having flashes of memory. Voices, shadowy faces. She was remembering more than just a hazy, distant dreamlike version of what had happened to her that night and during her stay at the asylum. She was actually beginning to remember details.

"I'll go in first with the attorney from the Department of Justice," Jordan finally answered Micah. "We'll need Risa to sign off on this, otherwise, the DOJ will walk away from her. If he walks out, then we're pulled off the assignment. Let's pray she listens to reason."

Oh, she would listen to reason, one way or the other, Micah promised silently.

He laid the file aside and focused on her now. She wasn't wearing makeup. Her hair had been pulled back from her face and tied at the back of her neck. Her eyes were shadowed with dark circles, her lips were compressed, and there was a flush mantling her cheeks—remnants of lust. He well understood that, though he knew the strength of it was more from the Whore's Dust than her inability to climax the night before.

Hell, if he'd had that doctor's report he would have known what the hell was wrong with her. Instead, the team had relied on the abbreviated report that Abigail Clay had overseen.

That old biddie was so damned protective of Risa now that she was worse than a junkyard dog. The old woman had nearly collapsed when she had learned the truth of what her son had done to her granddaughter. Micah had heard Kell and Clint's report of the night they had rescued her from the asylum and contacted the grandmother. When she had arrived at the hospital and learned the truth of what had happened, the grandmother had attacked Clint. Not because her son was dead but because she hadn't been able to kill him herself.

She had overseen her granddaughter ever since, despite Risa's refusal to allow it.

"The attorney is here, Jordan." Nik opened the door and stuck his head inside, his long Nordic blond hair falling over his face, his icy blue eyes piercing the darkness. "He says rock and roll."

Jordan nodded, collected his files, and left the room.

Micah turned his attention to the room.

Risa sat in full view of the mirror, giving Micah a clear view of her from the other side. Those damned baggy clothes she was wearing pissed him off. The long white blouse was pulled out over loose slacks. She wore flat shoes. She was hiding. If she thought dressing like a bag lady was going to still his desire, then she'd better think again.

He inhaled slowly, deeply, and watched as the federal attorney stepped inside with Jordan.

"Mr. Landowne. Ladies." The attorney nodded to them as he took his seat at the end of the table. Jordan sat at the other end, remaining silent.

"What's the meaning of this, Carl?" Attorney Landowne flashed the federal attorney a glare. "Since when do you call me Mister?"

"Sorry, Marion." The federal attorney grimaced. "This is official. We have some news that affects your client, and an official proposition for her. I wasn't certain you'd want to keep this on a first-name basis under those circumstances."

Carl Stephens stared back at the private attorney coolly. Stephens's graying brown hair was brushed back from his face, his hazel eyes were somber.

"What is the meaning of this?" Abigail Clay leaned forward in her chair, her renowned fiery temper sparkling in her light blue eyes. "Carl, I've known you since you were in diapers. You were a friend of the family for years, before Jansen's evil infected that relationship. Don't start pulling bull on me, because I know you too well to tolerate it."

"Grandmother." Risa's voice was warning. "You promised to behave yourself."

Risa appeared calm. She sat, her arms crossed on the table, her expression composed, but Micah saw the fear in her eyes.

Abigail Clay grimaced, her lined face tightening as a flash of agony pierced her gaze as she looked at her granddaughter. The old woman's hands trembled and her lips tightened as she sat back with a furious look at the attorney.

"Thank you, Miss Clay." The federal attorney glanced at Risa. "We informed your doctor of the penalties of withholding information from the government, Miss Clay, and from his patient." He nodded at her before turning back to Abigail. "I should inform you before we begin that I need to take a moment to explain to Miss Clay the truth of the tests her doctor has done each month."

Abigail paled as Risa stared back at the attorney, her expression becoming still, frozen.

Micah tensed, forcing himself to remain in his chair as the attorney explained the tests she had taken each month and what they were for. When the attorney explained that the Whore's Dust was still present in her system, and the ramifications of it, heat blazed in her face and fear filled her eyes.

The explanation was shaming her. Micah could see it. The knowledge that any arousal she had would be increased at least tenfold. That orgasms would be explosive. That the sexual needs would be more painful at times than others and sometimes torturous, according to how the drug worked on her system. If she had been pale before the explanation, then she was paper white when the attorney finished.

"What was the reason for this?" Abigail rasped furiously as she shoved her chair back and rose to her feet. "Look at her, and you wonder why I wouldn't allow that morbid doctor to tell her about it? She's been fine without knowing."

Dressed in silk tan slacks and a creamy blouse, the older woman paced a few steps, came to a stop, then ran her fingers through her short, stylish hair.

"Enough, Grandmother," Risa said softly. "You shouldn't have lied to me."

"It was for—"

"If you say it was for my own good one more time, then I will leave Atlanta." Risa looked up at her, and Micah saw the determination on her face, as well as the pain. "I'm not a child that you need to shelter. If you have to lie to me, then you aren't helping me."

Abigail covered her lips with her hand as she propped her other hand on her hip and turned away from her granddaughter.

"This is all very interesting, Mr. Stephens," Risa said then, her voice hoarse, rough, Micah knew, from her tears. "But I'm sure you have more to do than to oversee doctors' reports. Why are we here?"

Carl Stephens leaned forward, his gaze somber. "Your psychologist's reports are quite factual and they've been sent to us monthly. In the past months you've reported that the memories are becoming clearer, you actually remember phrases, and you remember that the other man with Jansen Clay the night of your kidnapping mentioned stability tests and an amount of money to be paid if he managed to reproduce a drug."

Micah watched as she followed tightly. "I was unaware you were overseeing that as well," she said faintly.

"Miss Clay, anything you remember of that night, or your time in the hospital, is important to us. As you know, that drug is damned dangerous. Keeping it off the streets is imperative."

She nodded jerkily. "You have the records; they're accurate. I haven't remembered anything more. What does this have to do with why we're here now?"

She was lying. Micah saw it flash in her eyes. She had remembered something more, perhaps last night; was that why she had run?

Carl looked down for a long second before lifting his gaze and meeting hers.

"Someone else has managed to get hold of those records as well," he said gently. "There's a contract out on your life, Miss Clay. Two million dollars." Abigail Clay cried out in protest as Risa sat frozen. "The assassin rumored to have picked it up is called Orion. His methods aren't pleasant. Actually they're particularly painful. He's an international concern to the United States. This is the first time we've had advance notice of his intent to strike and we mean to capture him. We need your help."

Risa swayed.

Micah was out of his chair and bursting out of the room the second he saw her eyes glaze, saw the imminent shock racing through her system. *Damn Stephens. Damn them all to hell.*

He didn't knock on the door where the meeting was being held; he threw it open and stepped inside, moving quickly to Risa's side, his arms going around her as she stumbled from her chair.

He caught her against his chest, glaring at Stephens as her nails clawed at his jacket and an animalistic sound of pain left her throat.

"Bastard," he snarled furiously. "You could have done this easier."

"Who the hell are you?" Abigail stood behind Risa like a protective tigress. "Release her this minute. I'll care for her. I cared for her when you bastards left her on my doorstep like she didn't matter." Tears ran down her face as she yelled up at him, her hands reaching for her granddaughter, trying to pull her from Micah's arms. "Damn you!"

Risa was dying inside.

She couldn't cry. It felt locked inside her. She wanted to hide. She wanted to find a hole and sink inside it; she wanted to scream in agony; she wanted to plead for answers.

Why? Why her?

Her father had sat and watched as another man raped her. Helped hold her down while they injected that vicious drug inside her that made her respond, made her beg. He saw her as unworthy to even sell to the highest bidder. How sick was that? And now, just when she thought she could live, it was to find out this.

She laughed. She couldn't believe she was laughing. Evidently others couldn't, either, because all sound ceased in the room.

She lifted her head from Micah's shoulder and pushed away from him. God, she didn't want to be touched; she didn't want his pity.

She turned to the federal attorney and laughed in his face.

"Two million dollars?" She wanted to scream in agony.

"My father didn't think I was worth fucking, my own government didn't even get a clue when I was institutionalized for nearly two years, but someone out there thinks my life is now worth two million dollars?"

Pain lashed at her chest, stealing her breath at the compassion in both attorneys' eyes now. Pity. They felt sorry for her.

"Risa. That's enough." Micah's hands settled on her shoulders, his grip firm, warm.

She wanted to turn into him and soak in that warmth. She wanted to beg him to make it all better, to make the demons go away, to take the pain away, to find her one moment of peace. She wanted to plead for it, and she couldn't.

"Miss Clay, I understand your anger," the federal attorney began.

"Do you, Mr. Stephens?" she questioned him roughly. "Do you understand any damned thing at this moment?" She stared around the room. Her grandmother and her attorney. Her grandmother had kept the doctor's reports from her, had denied allowing her the knowledge of what was going on with her own body.

"Why did you lie to me?" she whispered. "Why didn't you tell me the truth?"

"Risa, you were finally finding some peace," Abigail cried softly. "I couldn't tell you. The doctor has to be wrong; it's been years."

"I had a right to know." Her fists clenched at her side. "God, do you think I'm stupid? Do you think I hadn't realized something was wrong with me? Do you have any idea how I felt, Grandmother?"

Of course she didn't. No one asked, no wanted to hear, so Risa hadn't spoken of it. And she couldn't very well tell her grandmother she was dying to be fucked.

"And what the hell are you doing here?" She turned to Micah, avoiding his gaze, avoiding the demand in it, the pity she was terrified of seeing.

"Miss Clay, Mr. Sloane is private agent on loan to the Department of Justice. He and his team will be your protection."

She was going to throw up. She turned to the mirror, the

two-way glass, wondering who watched now. Then she turned to Micah.

"They knew," she whispered, her lips numb now. "Last night, all of them, they knew who you were."

"They knew," he said, his tone firm, quiet.

They had lied to her. Morganna and Clint, Ian and Kira, Kell and Emily, Reno and Raven. They had all lied to her.

"Did they even know you?" she asked then, wondering at the extent of the lies.

"I've worked with Reno and the others several times," he stated. "I've known them for years. When the Department of Justice contacted my team for your protection, we contacted Reno's because they're here in Atlanta."

"They're no longer with the Navy." She remembered that. Morganna and Raven had thrown a party when their husbands had finally left the Navy.

"No, they aren't with the Navy. They're private now, Risa, the same as I and my team."

They were private. That was why they were gone so often, because they were private. Like Micah. Because they were liars. Because Clint had stood in her face and chided her for hiding in her apartment, convincing her to come to the club with them and to meet his very good friend Micah.

"Perfect." She laughed again, a hollow, mocking sound that tore at her chest as it escaped. "How fucking perfect. Is Clint back there?" She waved her hand toward the mirror. "Is Morganna with him? Do you think they both know just how pleased I am to be used this way?" She screamed the question at him.

She was coming apart inside. She could feel it. She was unraveling like a ball of twine and she couldn't seem to stop the destruction.

Turning away from Micah, she faced the attorney instead. She didn't know him. He didn't matter. The fool she had made of herself the night before didn't affect his little world one way or the other.

"So tell me, Mr. Stephens." Breathing was almost impossible. She felt as though she were going to go to her knees at any moment. “Exactly what does the all-powerful United States of America need from me? Should I paint a target on my chest? How about taking out an ad in the newspaper? You can watch me then? See who bites?”

She hated the pity in that bastard’s eyes. How dare he stare at her with such somber compassion?

“No, Miss Clay,” he said gently, his hands braced on the table as her own attorney wiped his hands helplessly over his face. “We want you to work with us, and with Mr. Sloane. We want you to allow our agent into your home, pretend he’s your lover. While you do this, his team will watch you; they’ll cover you completely. When Orion tries to strike, we’ll be there. If you remember anything at any time, then we’ll know and we can assist you.”

She licked her dry lips and fought the dry heaves that twisted in her stomach. Maybe she should have eaten that morning after all; at least then she would have had something to throw up.

“How do they protect me against a bullet?” She shook her head mockingly. “I’m not stupid, Mr. Stephens. He’d be impossible to track.”

His expression flickered with regret before he looked over her shoulder.

“Risa, sit down for this.” Micah’s hands touched her shoulders again.

This time when she tried to jerk away, they tightened. A second later he turned her around, stared down at her, his black eyes flickering with fury as she slapped at his chest.

“Stop fighting me,” he demanded roughly. “You don’t want to stand up for this. If you want the truth, then sit your ass down and listen.”

His harsh tone broke through the ice forming in her belly. She had to swallow tightly, had to grip her control with the last of her strength as she pushed back from him and slowly took her seat again.

She glared at him when he sat down beside her. She wasn’t happy with the glare she received in return.

Turning back to the attorney, she forced a tight smile to her face. "So he doesn't use bullets?"

Attorney Stephens took his seat and shook his head. "He doesn't use bullets."

"Go ahead and spit it out," she demanded. "Let's not pretend to care about my feelings at this late date if you don't mind."

His nostrils flared, but the compassion in his eyes never dimmed.

"He finds a way to sedate his victims and kidnap them. As I said, this is the first advance notice we've had of one of his marks. This is our chance, Miss Clay, to make certain he never kills again. And, with any luck, our chance to find out who hired him, and what they're afraid you know."

"How does he kill them?"

Stephens looked down at the table for a long moment before lifting his gaze back to hers. "He has two manners of killing. If it's a male, he's rather merciful. He simply cuts their throats. His female victims, he's not so gentle with. He ties them down, legs raised, wrists down. He slices their wrists and watches them bleed out."

She blinked back at him. She could sense the edges of her vision growing dim and forced her head to the table, forced herself to close her eyes and fight back the need to faint. Hell, she was going to swoon for damned sure. Wasn't that so Southern?

"Risa." She felt Micah's hand at her back, a warm, comforting weight that sent talons of aching need slicing through her. "We can protect you. As Carl said, this is the first time we've had warning. We can protect you."

She shook her head, lifted it, and stared across the table at her grandmother. Abigail was deathly pale, her face streaked with tears, her expression tormented.

Her hand reached out to Risa. Shaking, fighting the terror rising inside her, she took her grandmother's fragile hand in her own.

"I'm so sorry, baby," Abigail sobbed, her tears running

freely now, her voice hoarse with anger and pain. "I'm so sorry I gave birth to that monster. God forgive me, Risa, I'm so sorry."

Risa's grandmother laid her head on the table and sobbed as their attorney rose from the table and moved to her. Risa could only watch her helplessly. *Poor Grandmother. How much pain was she supposed to endure? She had faced her son's atrocities, and now she was facing her granddaughter's imminent death.*

Risa turned to the attorney, feeling a strange, dark calm settle over her.

"I will require another agent," she stated. "I can't work with the one you've chosen."

She couldn't face him, couldn't pretend with him. Not after the night before. Humiliation crawled inside her, blistering, threatening the ice she needed to remain calm, to remain sane.

"Unacceptable."

Her head jerked around to Micah as he bit out the word with harsh emphasis. His black eyes were furious now. He stared down at her, a muscle ticcing at his jaw as she fought to hold on to her own control.

"Why?" she whispered. "Don't do this to me, Micah. You'll kill me. How much more do I have to endure? Do I have to face you every day, pretend to be your lover when we both know the truth?"

"You don't want to get into this here." His head lowered, his lips pulling back in a snarl. "You don't even want to get this started, Risa. There will be no other agent taking my place. No other man will take my place. If you want to live, then damn you, you'll accept the man that can keep your ass alive."

"Why?" Agony was a burden she didn't know if she could bear much longer. Humiliation ran as hot and as deep as the arousal she couldn't get rid of. She had failed with him, and now he wanted to do what? Rub her nose in it? Make her accept it?

"Accept the deal," he commanded furiously. "You will accept it, and you will accept me. If I have to force your hand, I will. Am I understood?"

A frown snapped between her brows as fury flooded in her eyes.

"Don't order me," she snapped back. "I'm not your lapdog, Mr. Sloane. And you will not make me do anything."

"Don't bet on it." Fury snapped between them, nose to nose, glaring, as she felt her clit swell further, her nipples tighten harder.

"I hate you!" She wanted to hit him. She wanted to wipe the command and dominance off his face with her fist.

"Hate me all you like." His smile was tight, confident. "But you will live, Risa. You will live, or I'll paddle your ass until you can't sit for a week."

Her eyes widened as outrage flooded her. "You wouldn't dare!"

"Oh, my little sweet, trust me. I'd dare that and much more."

Chapter 6

THE DOOR DIDN'T slam behind them when Risa closed it later that afternoon. It closed quietly, the dead bolt clicked into position, and when she turned, she froze. Two men stood in her living room, dressed in light overalls with the name of a cleaning company emblazoned on them.

Micah didn't seem overly concerned by the fact that two strange men were in her apartment.

One was tall, six and a half feet at least, white blond hair hanging to his shoulders, ice blue eyes regarding her with a hint of somber interest rather than pity. The other was shorter, with dark blond hair and gray eyes. The second man watched her with more than somber interest. There was hint of mischief to his expression, a decided curl of amusement about his lips. She decided to dislike him on the spot, simply because he was the only one who appeared as if he might protest it.

"Hey, Micah, are you introducing us?" The darker blond, amused male lifted his brows in query as he lifted a vacuum. "Here we've been sweeping up your bugs and being good little boys. There were some bad boys in here, too."

"I have bugs in my apartment?" She frowned. "You're not pest control. Call them."

"They're both pests and pest control," Micah grunted as he glanced at the vacuum. "Did you deactivate them?"

Risa paused and stared at the vacuum as the meaning began to sink in. Not real bugs, listening devices. Someone had placed listening devices in her home?

"All of them. We, umm, found something interesting, too." The darker-haired one glanced at her again. "We cleaned the overhead light fixtures, changed the bulbs and all that good stuff. She had an interesting little camera above her bed. Wireless. Snazzy as hell."

Risa drew in a hard breath as Micah cursed under his breath.

Surprise, surprise, she thought with a rather distant feeling of extreme humiliation. Not only was someone listening to her, but they also were watching her. Had she done anything embarrassing lately? Had she masturbated or attempted to since that camera had been installed?

"You're a bastard, John," Micah growled. "Take your toys back to base and let the others go over them, see if they can track the wireless link."

Risa turned from them all and moved to her bedroom. She couldn't deal with them. She couldn't deal with herself at the moment.

As the bedroom door closed behind her, Micah grimaced and turned to Nik and John. The Russian and Australian rarely worked well together, but today it seemed as though they had come to blows.

"Thanks for letting her know about the damned bug in the bedroom," Micah snapped at the shorter agent.

John's brows rose. "Mate, you're getting a little intense, aren't you?" he drawled, a frown working on his tanned brow as his accent grated across Micah's nerves. John only let that accent slip free when he wanted to piss someone off.

"I'll worry about my intensity," Micah told him. "You worry about getting those bugs to Jordan. See if he can get anything off them."

"On our way then." John nodded, though he continued to watch Micah carefully.

John moved for the door as Nik held back. When the door closed behind John, Micah turned to the Russian and lifted a brow questioningly.

"We have base set up across the hall," Nik told him. "As well as surveillance. Tehya and Kira are on-site and want to discuss Risa's medical records with you as well as the psychological report. They asked that you come over as soon as possible."

Micah nodded. He had some questions he needed answered and he knew the two women had consulted with one of the government scientists working to understand the drug and exactly how it worked on the human body.

"I'll be over there in a few hours." He nodded as he glanced toward the closed bedroom door where Risa had disappeared.

She was too calm. From the moment she'd backed down from him and agreed to the operation, she had been too damned calm.

"I'll let them know." Nik nodded. "We have surveillance on her apartment from across the hall, and we'll have someone on you whenever you leave. We have Black Jack and Wild Card with the grandmother providing protection there and the Durango team is providing backup here. We should have all our bases covered."

Should have. If. Maybe. Son of a bitch, Micah didn't like this. He hadn't liked it from the beginning, simply because he'd known that even if she survived, Risa would be damaged again by the whole op.

And he'd been right. Last night had been a fucking fiasco. He should have never walked away from her and left her alone in that bedroom, no matter how shaky his control had been.

Two minutes, he'd told himself. All he'd needed was two minutes to get a handle on the need to fuck into her, regardless of the tension that had begun building in her. That tension hadn't been sexual. It had been fear. Each time she had come close to release, she had locked up, fought it back, and managed to escape the explosive release he had felt building inside her.

Two minutes had given her just enough time to run from him. Just enough time to escape before he could return and ease her into her climax.

He'd been too damned hard, too horny. The need for her had risen inside him like nothing he had ever known before. No woman had ever made him as hungry, as fast, as Risa had.

Micah locked the dead bolts after Nik checked the hall and left the apartment. Turning, Micah stared around the room, wondering how the hell he was supposed to handle this one.

He'd managed to fuck up last night. The combination of the minute quantity of Whore's Dust that he hadn't known was in her system and her fears mixed with his own needs had made for a fiasco that had obviously ended up frightening her away. Thank God Nik and John had been outside, seen her leaving, and followed her. With the presence of the bugs in the apartment, it was obvious Orion was already on the job.

And it was obvious Micah and Risa were going to have to talk, very soon. He'd deliberately provoked her earlier, pissed her off, and pushed her into anger rather than shock.

That look of blank horror on her face had stripped his control. For the first time in years, Micah had felt something other than the need for vengeance. The need to protect, the fury at her pain, the control-stripping need to shelter her, had taken hold of him with a stranglehold he had been unable to break. It was no wonder the other members of the unit were watching him warily now.

Pushing his hands wearily over his hair, he stalked into the kitchen, checked the refrigerator and pantry for groceries, and spent time making a grocery list. Next, he moved around the apartment, except for her bedroom, and checked the windows and shades.

Then, he broached the bedroom.

Risa was on the bed staring up at the light fixture curiously. Where would someone have planted a camera? The decorative glass light cover was frosted with a series of designs cascading over it. It took her a while, but as she stared at it, she noticed that within the pattern of raised rosebuds, one was missing. Right in the center.

A glass rosebud for a camera? She imagined it could be done; technology was clearly able to produce one. Too bad that the men who used that technology couldn't be sane.

Maybe sanity, like beauty, though, was in the eye of the beholder.

God, she was a mess. She could feel herself shaking from the inside out. It had been all she could do to sign her name to the papers the attorney had given her at the Federal Building.

Running and hiding wasn't an option, he had assured her, as though he had known that was exactly what she wanted to do. Unfortunately, there didn't appear to be a hole deep enough or dark enough to protect her from the man they called Orion.

A killer. A man who strapped his victims down and drained them of their blood. Watched them die and probably found immeasurable pleasure from it.

She had to press her hand to her stomach. Again. She fought back the need to gag, because there was nothing in her stomach to throw up.

She hadn't even eaten today. She almost laughed as she remembered that. Hunger hadn't been high on her list of priorities this morning. When her attorney had called requesting that she and her grandmother accompany him to the Federal Building to sign some papers, Risa had never imagined that the thought of food would only make her sicker later.

Now she understood why he had been so vague about explaining why they had to sign those papers immediately. He'd implied the papers had to do with the vast holdings the government had seized from Jansen Clay.

Risa had been fighting for years for items that had belonged to her mother, who had died years before Risa's kidnapping. Jewelry, a few antiques Jansen's second wife had taken possession of, and some pictures. Risa had prayed that was being resolved, only to learn that her life was only going to hell faster than it had been.

She still couldn't make sense of it. Jansen hadn't thought she was worth trying to sell, but someone else thought it was worth 2 million to kill her. It was enough to be laughable. She would laugh again if she weren't afraid she would end up screaming.

Sitting up on the bed, knees bent, she laid her head against her arms, closed her eyes, and breathed out as she fought the panic rising inside her.

She had agreed to play bait. Here she sat, in her apartment, for all intents and purposes with her new lover. That was enough to make her cry. Her body was still sizzling, despite the truth of her situation, and the need to touch him again was like a fever burning inside her. Because of that fucking drug. Because it was messing with her normal arousal and making it worse. It was destroying her from the inside out.

At the sound of the bedroom door opening, she tensed, biting her lip as she swore she felt Micah enter the room.

"I ordered dinner." His voice washed over her and sent ripples of awareness coursing over her.

She nodded in reply.

"I've also sent out an order for groceries." His voice hardened, Risa nodded again.

"We need to talk about this, Risa. Now, while it's safe to talk here. Ignoring the situation isn't going to make it better."

"I'm really good at ignoring things," she muttered. "Trust me, it's not that hard to do, and it really does make life easier."

"Until you're dead?" he asked coldly.

Her head lifted at that. "Fate's a bitch, isn't she?"

His lips tightened. "Get out of bed and get in here and talk to me, before I join you."

She laughed at that. She was amazed that she could laugh without breaking into hysteria.

"Well, wouldn't we just hate to make you do that?" she stated mockingly as she pulled herself from the bed and moved for the door. "I'd hate to put you out to that extent again."

Electricity seemed to race over her body as she passed him at the doorway. It was all she could do to control the gasp that built in her throat, or the need to touch him.

"You ran out on me last night," he stated as she moved to the couch and curled into the corner. "Why?"

She stared back at him in surprise. "That's rather self-explanatory, wouldn't you think?"

Why did he care? It wasn't as though she had done anything for him.

"If you had waited, Risa, we could have fixed the problem."

Looking away from him, she wondered rather mockingly exactly how they could have fixed that problem for him.

"There's nothing to fix," she pushed out between stiff lips. "We're stuck together; I understand that. I'll try to stay out of your way as much as possible."

"Yeah, you do that," he snarled back at her.

She looked away from him, concentrating instead on the small office area she had created in the corner of the room. The corner desk, file cabinet, and computer. She had work to do there, but she couldn't seem to get a handle on actually doing the work. The accounting she did from home kept the bills paid; it kept her from having to dip into the small trust fund her mother had left her, and kept her grandmother from having to support her.

"Did we need to discuss anything else?" she asked. "I'm tired. I thought a shower and a nap—"

"I said I ordered dinner." He sat down in the chair across from her. "And I said we needed to talk."

"Just because you said it doesn't mean I agree with your decision." There was a chance she didn't have much longer to live anyway; she wasn't going to spend her last days on earth kowtowing to his arrogance. It was bad enough that now that he was here, she couldn't seem to get a handle on her own arousal. She needed to change panties, she was so damned wet.

He ran his hand over his face, and for a second Risa saw the weariness that marked his expression. He must not have slept last night, she thought, then felt perversely glad. Because she hadn't slept last night, either.

"Risa, we need to come to an understanding to make this work," he warned her, his dark eyes flashing with frustration.

"We have an understanding," she assured him. "I understand you have to stay here to catch a killer. There's a spare bedroom and bathroom; make yourself at home. I'll try to stay out of your way as much as possible."

Something dark and dangerous flashed in his eyes. His expression became emotionless, cold. For a moment fear skated down her spine; then her shoulders straightened. It wasn't as though he could kill her for talking back to him. And God, she was tired of putting her head down and simply trying not to antagonize fate.

Fate had slapped her so damned hard already that she was still reeling.

"Look." She lifted her hand as he started to speak. "Last night was a mistake, and I apologize for dragging you into my problems. I . . ." She swallowed tightly. "Sometimes, you just need to be touched, you know? I shouldn't have chosen you. I should have walked away and just picked up a damned drunk stranger or something."

She wondered if Micah could have fucked her drunk. She hated that he hadn't found any pleasure with her. It sliced into her with a sharper pain than her own inability to find the satisfaction she had needed. It wasn't his fault. He'd been dragged into this. He had probably felt that he had to go through with taking her because of this operation he was on. He appeared willing to do anything to catch Orion. Even fuck her.

"You amaze me." His voice was cold; his eyes were like pits of black ice.

"Yeah, I amaze myself sometimes." She held back the tears, the need to cry. She held back the need to curl into his arms and find some hint of comfort. She was tired, shaky, and terrified. And in her entire life she had never known a place as secure as she had felt when he had held her the night before.

"What else do we need to talk about?"

"Your inability to climax."

She flinched at the statement. Humiliation curled in the pit of her stomach.

She shrugged. "That wasn't your fault."

"I should have waited on your doctor's report," he said. "If I had known the Whore's Dust was still in your system, then I would have known what to do."

She crossed her arms over her breasts and stared away

from him. Heat seared her face, her neck. She didn't want to talk about this. She couldn't bear to talk about this.

"Risa, the effect of the Whore's Dust is frightening. We've been gathering reports for years on the men and women who survived the initial wave of that drug. You were given enough that it attached to the pleasure receptors in your brain. It leaves the body slowly, very slowly. To understand what's going on when it kicks in, you need to understand the effects of it."

No. She didn't want to know. She swallowed convulsively, remembering last night all too well as the need for touch built inside her again.

"After the initial injection, it doesn't make you want sex so much as it makes the need for sex stronger. It makes the sensations stronger."

"I can't talk about this." She came to her feet as hysteria threatened to break through the fragile control holding it back.

"We have to discuss this, Risa." He rose as well, facing her now, staring down at her with the inky ice of his gaze. "We have to deal with it. Because I won't be sleeping in your spare bedroom, or using your spare bath. I'll be sleeping in the bed with you. This isn't just a cover, because no doubt Orion knows I'm your bodyguard. This is about us. Period."

She shook her head. She couldn't do it. She couldn't let Micah in her bed; she couldn't share that much of herself with him. God, she didn't want to share that much with herself. The nights she awoke, her fingers beneath her pajamas, stroking her flesh because she couldn't protect herself in her sleep. The nightmares. Waking herself with her screams, her pleas. Begging Jansen Clay not to hurt her. *Please don't, Daddy, don't let him hurt me.*

"No." The word was a hoarse, desperate sound. "That's not possible."

She couldn't bear it. She couldn't stand knowing she couldn't satisfy Micah, that she would awaken them both trying desperately to achieve her own satisfaction, or that she would awaken them with her screams.

"That's very possible," he assured her. "I'm to be your lover, Risa. You are aware of what a lover is for, aren't you?"

She shook her head. "No. That wasn't the deal. The papers didn't say I had to sleep with you. No one said it had to go that far."

"But you want it to go that far," he stated then. "Deny it. You're aroused."

She was going to lose the battle with her tears. She was going to collapse to the floor in agony. The ache in her mind, her body, was too strong. The pain was physical, it bit into her so deeply.

She wanted him. Oh God, she wanted to touch him, wanted to be touched. She wanted to feel him inside her again, pressing into her, stretching her, burning her. She wanted him to fuck her so wild and so hard that she felt nothing but the burn, that pleasure and pain combined, and she couldn't fight either. She needed it until her nails bit into her palms. Until she could taste the need surging into her mouth, reminding her of his kiss.

He had said she wanted it to go that far. That she was aroused. Not that he did. Not that he was. And she was too frightened to even look to see how unaroused he was. If she looked and saw nothing, saw no sign of his erection, she was afraid it would finally break that last thread she had on the control that kept her trying to live day by day.

How sterile had her life become? In the six years since she had been taken from the asylum, she had fought just to live, day by day. To get up in the morning, to make friends, to learn how to defend herself, to find a balance in her life when sometimes she feared there would never be balance.

Now here she stood in front of the only man in those six years whom she had been able to touch, who had touched her. She had gone out several times in the past year determined to find a lover and had always chickened out. Until last night. Last night she had gone to his bed, and she still hadn't repaired the wound she had suffered from it.

"You can't deny it, Risa." His voice was lower, warmer. It throbbed with knowledge, with a false arousal she knew he couldn't actually feel. He couldn't want her now. Not after last night.

"Don't do this to me," she whispered, feeling the tears building in her throat, nearly strangling her with their strength. "Please, Micah. Don't hurt me like this."

Too much was building inside her, too much information she couldn't handle, that she couldn't deal with. The Whore's Dust making her hurt for sex, making her willing to beg to be touched. A contract on her life. And now Micah, a man stronger, more arrogant and dominant, than any she had ever known, and a fascination she couldn't seem to break away from.

All this for the ugly little girl who couldn't get a boyfriend when she was a teenager and couldn't get a lover now unless he had an agenda that required he force an interest in her. A man who hadn't been able to achieve his satisfaction with the ugly woman she had become.

She covered her mouth with her hand and turned away from him, all but running from him. She was running away. She was hiding because she was weak, because she couldn't face the truth of what she or her life had become.

"Risa, dammit," he cursed as the door slammed closed behind her.

She pressed her back to it as her legs gave out and she slid to the floor. As she hugged her knees to her chest, the tears began to fall. She couldn't hold them back; the pain was too intense. It dug inside her soul and sent a wash of ugly black emotion tearing through her.

For the first time in her life, she hated. Hated with a vicious, horrible strength that frightened her. And the awful truth of it was, there was no one she hated more than herself. She hated her weakness, she hated the helplessness she felt against the events transpiring against her, and she hated the face that Jansen Clay had always assured her was so ugly. So ugly he couldn't pay a man to fuck her. And God forbid, he had once said, that she would have children and pass that ugliness on.

God forbid that Risa should ever believe that she deserved the things other women did.

FRUSTRATION ATE at Micah as he paced the living room in the apartment across from Risa's. Morganna was in the apartment with her, giving him a chance to gather his control after she had run back to her bedroom. She was running away from him and running away from the danger. She had to face both. She would face him, and she would do it soon, he assured himself.

He was willing to let her bury her head in the sand for the moment, because he understood that the implications of the danger she was in were overwhelming. But tonight she would face him, and she would face the fact that there would be no turning away any longer.

"I have her psychologist's report here." Kira Richards was sitting on the floor in front of a long coffee table scattered with files. "This is a mess, Micah," she sighed. "Her father did a job on her before he ever allowed her to be raped." Micah flinched at the word but turned back to Kira and retook his seat on the couch.

He hadn't had the reports before meeting with Risa last night. There hadn't been time. They knew Orion had accepted the job. Moving quickly had been imperative. It was still imperative, but for different reasons.

Micah had read the files when he stepped in the room. He'd spent over an hour reading them as he waited for the delivery time that the restaurant had quoted for the food. Blanchard's, one of his favorite restaurants, didn't deliver fast; they delivered good food instead.

That extra time had given him the chance to go over the files, pages and pages of childhood events that Risa had told the psychologist about, as well as the psychologist's diagnosis.

"How did she survive this?" Kira whispered as she read one of the papers. "He told her she was so ugly he couldn't imagine her passing it on to her children?" Horror crossed her face as she lifted her gaze to Micah. "She remembers when he helped drug her, that he laughed that he'd never be able to sell her. He was lucky to pay someone to fuck her? She had no boyfriends when she was younger, and only a few friends." She shook her head. "Her psychologist is amazed she doesn't have to put her on drugs. According to her report—"

"According to her report, 'Risa is sound mentally, physically, and psychologically, with only a few issues that need to be worked out. Most important is that of her worth to herself as well as to others,' " he quoted. "I read the report." He may not totally have agreed with it. Risa was wounded, but she was strong. Healing her would require more than dealing with a few issues.

He forced himself to calm as he checked his watch again. He wanted to be there when dinner was delivered. He was going to make certain she ate. She had lost too much weight in the past year. She was still healthy, but he knew it wouldn't take much longer before that changed. She hadn't eaten before the meeting this morning, and she definitely hadn't eaten afterward.

"Risa is our best chance to catch Orion." Jordan spoke up from where he sat at a bank of security monitors. "If she cracks emotionally or mentally, then there's a chance he'll take her and we'll lose her."

"She won't crack." Micah was going to make sure of it.

"Micah, you might not be able to stop it," Morganna said softly. "She's twenty-six; she's had a lifetime to believe the crap her father filled her head with. With the addition of the Whore's Dust and now Orion, she may not come out of this without scars none of us can fix."

"There will always be scars." He flashed her a harsh look. "Her soul is scarred from the inside out, Kira. No one can change that. That doesn't mean she can't be happy. It doesn't mean she's not a beautiful, vibrant woman."

Kira knew that Risa wasn't ugly in any way—she had pretty eyes, a beautiful smile when she bothered to smile—but she wasn't exactly pretty, either. The girl leaned a bit to the plain side. Her features weren't distinguishing. She was a woman who would easily be overlooked unless you knew her. But the more Kira got to know her, the more she saw that there was a uniqueness to Risa that made her very pretty.

Kira watched as Micah picked one of the eight-by-ten black-and-white pictures that had been snapped of Risa during their surveillance of her in the past week. Black-and-white did nothing to compliment her, but Micah's expression was . . . entranced?

"Her eyes sparkle when she finds a reason to be happy," he murmured. "And even saddened, there's a light in them that assures me she will fight to live." He touched the face in the photo. "Why do you think she doesn't see herself as pretty?" He lifted his gaze back to Kira as he frowned. "Her smile is filled with warmth, and even in these pictures you can see the need for laughter, for passion, lighting her features." He tossed the picture back to the table. "How could a father be so vile, Kira? So evil?"

Kira almost smiled. When she looked at that picture, she saw it, too. She saw the life on Risa's face that Micah had picked up on. She saw the curiosity in Risa's eyes; she saw the latent passion. She had missed it all before, and seeing it gave the girl a prettiness that couldn't be denied.

Hell. Beauty was in the eye of the beholder; she had always heard that. In this case, perhaps it was more true than she had ever known.

Chapter 7

NIGHTFALL CAME too soon. Risa had never realized how much she'd hated the earlier winter nights until that night. When she was faced with the prospect of getting ready to go to bed with Micah.

She couldn't do it. Every time she thought of it, she remembered being in his bed the night before, and that farce it had turned into.

But it was dark. She always went to bed early. She got up early. If she managed to sleep at all. Last night, she hadn't slept, and her body was demanding rest.

Her mind was another matter entirely.

"You're worrying too much," he stated as she found herself staring at her computer screen, the numbers in the accounting program blending in front of her eyes. "You're tired, Risa. Get ready and go on to bed. I'll come in later."

She hated that tone. That compassionate let's-pamper-the-baby tone. She didn't need him to pamper or patronize her.

She turned slowly in her chair and glared at him. He was sitting back on her couch as though he owned it, the television blaring some news program as those black eyes flicked over her body before coming back to her face.

As though he was remembering the night before. How did he remember it? she wondered. As the total failure it had been on her part?

"Why would I want to do that?" she asked carefully. "It's barely ten."

His lips seemed to thin. God, those lips were so gorgeous, and they could kiss like a dream. Like a particularly hot, wicked, sensual dream. She knew. His lips had been on hers, licking at her lips, nipping at them. He had kissed her as though he had meant to devour her.

"You're so exhausted, you're close to falling asleep at the computer." He frowned back at her. "You should be well aware by now that I'm not going to hurt you. Sleeping in the bed with me won't be nearly so traumatic as fucking me in one, surely."

Her face flushed. Risa felt the rise of red-hot color washing over her features as she stared back at him in furious amazement.

"That was completely uncalled for." She jumped from her seat, outraged. "If you can't keep a civil tongue in your mouth, then don't speak."

She fell back on her grandmother's antiquated superiority. God, was she so lacking that she couldn't even bear hearing the word from his lips? *Fucking*. They had *fucked*. He had *fucked* her. She wanted to cover her ears in the hopes of blotting out the thoughts. Because she didn't find it nearly as distasteful as she wanted to. The implications of the word brought to mind the sweaty, slick movements of their bodies together. Her cries. His groans. The touch of his hands, the thrust of his cock inside her.

She nearly had to clench her thighs together to hold back the overpowering lust.

Whore's Dust, was it? She couldn't imagine it. Nothing had felt so natural as wanting Micah.

"You go to bed if you're so tired," she finally snapped. "I'll be in later."

He grinned. That sensually full, mobile mouth curved into a grin of sheer male confidence and superiority. The kind of grin she had seen her friends' husbands give their wives when they were determined to get their way.

"I'm very tired," he informed her. "A little minx kept me up well past my bedtime last night, then skipped out on me and forced me to follow after her. I stared into her window like a lovesick Romeo pining for her attention."

"Or a covert agent hoping she hadn't managed to get herself kidnapped before you could capture her murderer," she snarled back in reply. "Orion matters so much to you that you were willing to fuck someone you didn't even know to get to him?"

His brow arched. "Such language, Risa." Amusement glittered in his black eyes. "Be careful. You're liable to give me a hard-on talking that way. I'd be extremely uncomfortable sleeping if you did."

She almost lost her breath at the thought. Micah, aroused, in her bed. A shiver worked up her spine before she managed to turn away from him and stomp to the window on the opposite side of the room.

She stared into the park across from the apartment building, fighting to make sense of her response to him rather than any other man.

Not that there had been men to choose from, unfortunately. But Micah was like the epitome of men. Look in the dictionary for "male" and there most certainly would be a picture of him staring back.

He was tall, dark-skinned. Jeans hugged his ass. A white cotton shirt emphasized his leanly muscled shoulders. And he wore boots. He was wearing boots. Cowboy boots that were well worn, faded, and scarred. The perfect kind of badboy boots.

"Risa."

She jumped as his face joined hers in the glass of the window; then his hands fell on her shoulders as he pulled her back, allowing the curtain to fall into place once again.

Risa shuddered at the warmth of his hands even as she pulled herself away from him and turned to glare at him.

"What?"

He watched her, his eyes no longer amused, but somber instead.

"You should stay away from the curtains," he said. "A direct line of sight will allow certain devices to hear anything you're saying. The heavy curtains over the windows and the interference of the television would otherwise block it."

Oh.

She stared at the television, then back to the window as dismay washed over her. She'd spent so much time in a perpetual shadow during the months she had been in the clinic. She loved the sunlight. She loved having it shine through clean windows and brighten the rooms that she lived within. Just as she loved staring into the black velvet night as well.

"I see." She hugged her arms over her breasts before turning away from him once again. "I'll go shower. Or something."

She wanted to sit in the middle of the floor and start wailing in fury. Where was it fair? She had endured enough; she didn't need a killer adding to the nightmares she already knew.

"Risa." His hands gripped her shoulders again, this time refusing to allow her to jerk away. "We're going to keep you safe. I promise."

"Of course you will," she said faintly. Did she have any other choice but to believe it? "Tell me, Micah, has he ever failed?"

She knew he hadn't. The man the federal attorney had told her about was nothing short of a perfect assassin. He had never been caught. He had never been identified. He had never failed to kill the person he had been hired to kill.

"His past has nothing to do with our present. We know who he's after; wherever he gets his information whenever he's investigating a victim won't know about us. We're not a part of any government, nor are we part of a traceable agency. He'll see us as a nominal threat. When he makes his move, we'll be here, and we'll capture him."

His hands kneaded her shoulders, his head lowered until his lips were so close. Until she could almost taste them.

"And then what?" She shook her head against the rising need. "Someone else takes his place?"

"Then he'll talk."

Risa almost flinched at the icy tone of his voice. Pure menace glittered in his eyes.

Her lips parted, and she almost believed he would.

"You'll kill him before he can talk," she whispered, suddenly knowing that whoever or whatever Orion was, Micah hated him with a passion that most would reserve for love.

But he shook his head. "No." His thumb touched her lips. "I won't kill him until I know who threatens you. Then yes," the word hissed between clenched teeth. "Oh yes, Risa. Then, I promise you, I'll kill Orion, then I'll kill the bastard who dared to think he could continue to torment you."

She didn't have to tear herself away from him this time. He stepped away. The shadows on his face gave him an almost cruel, faintly savage look. A foreign look, for just a space of a moment.

Risa swallowed tightly.

"Go shower," he told her, his back to her as he headed for the kitchen. "It's nearly bedtime." He stopped at the doorway and turned back to her. "And you will learn to sleep with me, starting tonight. If by chance he manages to get into this apartment to lay another listening device, then there will be no doubt in his mind that you're not sharing a bed with me. There will be no doubt in any man's mind, Risa, whose woman you are."

MICAH WATCHED the widening of her eyes before he turned and moved into the kitchen. He paced to the sink, ran a glass of water, and drank it down as though the fire that raged inside him could be quenched so damned easily.

It couldn't be. Lust for Risa. Hatred so overwhelming it was barely contained for Orion.

His jaw clenched as an image flashed before his eyes. His mother, so delicate, so white. She'd been bled dry, her wrists slashed. And she would have suffered. Orion had stripped her of her clothes and of her life, but he hadn't stripped her of her dignity. Of all his victims, only Micah's mother had been found with her eyes closed, a serene expression on her face.

Knowing she had died as she had lived gave Micah no comfort, though. Ariela Abijah had been the epitome of female strength. It had been in her eyes, in the way she held her head, in her love for her husband, her son, and her country.

His fingers dug into the counter as he gripped the edge with lethal force. He imagined Orion's neck there, feeling the life slowly ease from his body. Watching his eyes. The hatred that filled Micah couldn't be contained. It burned like a black flame inside his soul, corrupting it. Staining it with the dark emotion.

Then, the image of that faceless enemy was erased. Instead, Micah saw Risa's image. He saw her as they danced, her expression filled with wonder as she experienced her first taste of passion. Her face flushed with lust, her blue eyes darkening with it as she fought to reach her orgasm, then pulled herself back from the brink.

He saw her, so filled with a quiet beauty that asked for nothing. He saw the strength in her beautiful eyes, the struggle to survive, the determination to fill her life with more than nightmares.

His head lowered as he grimaced at the hunger that rose inside him, as fast, as hard, perhaps more so than the hatred he had for Orion.

He had believed nothing could be as all-consuming as his need to kill that bastard. But he had learned in the past twenty-four hours that something could rise inside him with the same force and knock him on his ass.

Lust. A hunger for one woman, not just any woman, a need for Risa that bit into his balls like sharp teeth and left him almost shaking in his need to touch her.

And tonight, he would be sleeping with her.

He reached up to wipe the sweat from his brow at the thought of that.

He was going to have to slide into that bed beside her, sleep beside her, and hold back his lust. Because if he didn't, he could very well ruin the delicate plan he was laying in place for her. Something far different from using her to catch his.

No, Micah wanted Risa for much more than the fact that she was the only lead they had to Orion. He wanted her because her warmth reached into him. For the first time in his life, someone had touched a part of his soul that he didn't know existed. A part reserved solely for her.

His father had once told him that every man knew when he found his mate. That one woman who could change a man simply because he loved her. Whether he could actually have her wouldn't matter, Garren Abijah had warned Micah. What would matter was that loving her, knowing her, would make him a better man.

He feared Risa would be the one woman whom walking away from would destroy the man he was now. He sensed it, like a wolf sensed his mate. Like the flower sensed the sunlight. Like a dead man sensed his ultimate destruction, he thought darkly.

Because he couldn't have her, not forever. She would never carry the false name he had taken, she would never know what they could have had, because he could never let her know of the feelings that rose inside him whenever he saw her.

He hadn't just seen her last night.

No, he had seen her before. Many times. Leaving her friends' homes as he was arriving in the past year or so. The few times he had gone out of his way to find her during the times he had worried that he hadn't seen her in a while.

Yeah, he'd done that a time or two. Watched for her. Waiting for her. Always knowing, like a damned buck in rut, whenever she was near.

He pushed his fingers through his hair and blew out a hard, weary breath. He was damned tired himself, and sleeping next to her tempting heat was going to be hard.

"Hard" didn't come close to describing it. And even worse? Damned if he wasn't looking forward to it.

He took a moment to adjust his stiff cock in his jeans before moving around the apartment. He checked the door and the dead bolts, then the windows. The security system the apartment used was state of the art, but John and Nik had added a bit before Micah arrived at the apartment with Risa.

The advanced electronics now installed would detect a fly if it managed to slip past the seal.

Pursing his lips, he blew out another silent breath before he headed for the bedroom door. She'd finished her shower long minutes before. She was either in the bed or hiding in the bathroom attempting to come up with an argument that would keep him out of her bed.

There was no argument sane enough, he thought. Because the hunger to sleep next to her wasn't in any way logical.

He opened the door, his eyes quickly adjusting to the dim room and finding her shape in the bed.

Closing the door behind him, he moved to the bed and sat gingerly on the mattress to pull off his boots.

"You didn't get your pajamas," she informed him, her voice trembling a bit.

Micah closed his eyes. Did she have any clue how much he hated doing this to her? Could she sense in any way his reluctance to frighten her, or to force her to face her demons?

"I don't sleep in pajamas, sweet," he said quietly as the last boot dropped to the floor and he picked it up to set it next to the other before pulling off his socks.

Rising to his feet, he shucked his jeans and underwear first, then his shirt.

"I don't think I can do this." She sounded breathless but not frightened. She sounded aroused, and fighting it oh, so hard.

"Do you have a choice?" He didn't give her time to think.

Flipping back the sheet and comforter, he moved into the bed beside her, almost grinning at the small amount of space the bed afforded both of them.

He pulled the sheet over his hips, adjusted the pillow, and closed his eyes. He didn't have to see her to sense her. He didn't have to look at her to feel the warmth of her body next to him.

She was stiff, silent. Micah could feel the tension moving around her, and that tension would keep her from sleeping.

"Are you so frightened of me, Risa?" he asked quietly.

"After last night, isn't there some semblance of trust that will allow you to share this bed with me? Something that tells you I would lay down my own life before I'd harm yours?"

There was nothing, no one, that could convince him to harm her. That could make him further wound the spirit that fought so desperately to survive within her.

"It's not a matter of trust," she finally whispered into the darkness.

"Then what's it a matter of?" He turned to her then, letting his hand uncurl, allowing his fingers to curve over her hip despite the flinch that jerked through her body. "Tell me, Risa. Why deny yourself when you don't have to?"

She was still and silent, her breathing jerky.

"Because," she finally whispered. "The night will come that you won't be here any longer. And then I'll have to face reality rather than the illusion. And I don't think I want to face either."

Strangely enough, he understood that comment. The reality that he would leave, the illusion that he could stay. Yes, facing either would hurt them both. But Micah was a man who never allowed himself illusion. He knew only the reality, and the reality involved one simple fact.

"Memories can warm you in the cold of the night," he told her softly. "I know this well, sweet. If you want to make those memories, you have only to let me know."

SHE HAD ONLY to let him know.

Risa stared into the darkness for several more long moments before she turned slowly to her side, feeling his hand lift, only to return to the opposite hip as she faced him.

There was a sliver of light falling from the bathroom, just enough to make out his shadowed features. He was just as roughly handsome in the dark as he was in the light. His strong jaw was clearly defined, the fullness of his lower lip prominent despite the thinner, brooding upper curve.

And he had the rasp of a beard covering his face.

She wanted to touch it, yet she was too frightened. She wanted to run her fingers over it, feel it against her palm.

Who was she kidding? She wanted to feel it all over her body. She wanted it stroking against her breasts, her belly, her thighs.

"Making memories is a lousy excuse," she finally whispered, her breathing short and choppy from the mere thought of having his body cover hers again.

He was warm and hard, muscular and so intensely male that he made her mouth water.

"Is it?" His fingers moved against her hip. It took her several seconds to realize he had pushed his hands beneath the loose hem of her long T-shirt. It rested on her bare waist, the calloused flesh of his palm warm and decidedly inviting against her sensitive skin.

"You should think about it," he whispered, his head moving closer, his lips holding her attention, his need driving spikes of hunger through her system. "Remember how hot it was, baby? How the sweat built on our flesh? How we strained together?"

How he didn't come?

Risa closed her eyes, her head shaking as her hand pressed against his chest while she fought to hold her hunger at bay.

It was the Whore's Dust; that was what they said. But was it? If it was related to that damned drug, wouldn't it happen at a time other than when Micah was near? Why burn her now with such depth when it hadn't before? Not like this. Not until she wanted to throw caution to the wind and beg him to bury himself inside her.

"Don't." She finally managed to push the words past her lips: "Please, Micah."

His lips brushed her forehead instead and she wanted to cry out with the need to feel that caress against her lips.

"I won't hurt you, Risa." His voice caressed her senses, stoked her desires. "I promise you this."

A whimper of need passed her lips. "No, Micah, you'll destroy me, and we both know it."

But he was a man a woman couldn't help but fall in love with. The type of man a woman could never hope to hold.

She forced herself to turn her back on him once again, to lie alone, except for the touch of his hand against her hip. And it wasn't the fear of his touch that drove her. It was the fear of learning his touch, craving it, and never having it again.

Chapter 8

TWO DAYS OF HELL.

Risa stepped from her bedroom two days later, feeling the lack of sleep that had haunted her, the exhaustion edging at her mind.

She couldn't sleep with Micah in the bed with her. He slept naked. He crowded her in the bed. His arm always ended up against her, over her, something. At one point, his fingers had curled around her breast, his palm searing her nipple.

It had taken everything she had to remove his hand, the bastard. It didn't matter what she slept in, he ended up finding bare skin to touch. She was terrified to go to sleep. She knew if she did, she would awaken to find herself draped over him, probably begging him to fuck her.

That was all she needed to round out the most humiliating week of her life.

"Breakfast and coffee, sunshine," he called out from the kitchen as she paused in the living room and glared at him in irritation.

"I told you"—and she had, just the morning before—"I don't do breakfast."

"And I told you"—no, he had badgered her—"breakfast is the most important part of the day."

She wanted him, bare-chested, wearing nothing but low-slung jeans, his feet bare, his hair damp, for breakfast. Rather than fighting another useless battle, she moved to the kitchen table and gratefully accepted the coffee. She stared at the eggs, bacon, and toast he set before her. Hell, she might as well eat. She was too damned tired to fight with him.

"You didn't sleep well last night," he commented as he carried his own plate, minus the bacon, and cup to the table. Swinging his leg over the chair, he sat down and sipped at his coffee. "I hope I'm not distracting you."

He was so damned cheerful she wanted to snarl at him in violent irritation.

"I'm used to sleeping alone," she reminded him for what had to be the hundredth time. "I don't sleep well with you in the bed with me."

"You'll get used to me." He nodded as though it were a foregone conclusion.

In his dreams she would get used to him.

"We have to go out today," he informed her as she bit into her toast. "We need to take you clothes shopping."

"I have clothes." She sipped at her coffee to wash down the toast.

"New lovers always go clothes shopping," he told her. "Morganna circled it at the top of the list of things we should do immediately. If Orion's going to strike soon, then we need to control each time he has that chance. So we're going shopping."

She shrugged. Fine, they'd go shopping. That didn't mean she had to actually buy anything.

"You can throw out those baggy-assed clothes before we go and make room for the new stuff I'm buying you," he told her, causing her to pause, her fork inches from her mouth, to stare back at him in surprised anger.

"I don't need new clothes." The fork clattered to her plate. "Don't get out of hand in this, Micah. I can't afford a new wardrobe, and what's more, I like my clothes fine."

"But I'm your new lover and I don't like them," he informed her as he swallowed his eggs. "You hide in those clothes, and as your lover, I'd never allow you to hide that gorgeous body of yours."

Her lips thinned. "Look, let's not play games here." Her

fingers gripped the edge of the table. "My body doesn't concern you one way or the other. Neither do my clothes. We'll go through the motions and leave it at that."

His expression was composed, cool. It was always composed and cool. He hadn't gotten angry in the past two days; he hadn't argued with her. He had been like a steamroller just pushing her where he wanted her to go.

She pushed her plate back and opened her mouth to argue when his gaze lifted.

"Do you really want to turn this into a battle?" he asked her carefully.

Did she? There was something in his eyes the past two days that had made her wary of pushing him.

"Fine," she snapped. "I didn't have anything else planned. If you want to waste your hard-earned cash, that's your business. As long as we don't use my money for a bunch of clothes I neither need nor want."

He nodded. "Agreed. Finish your breakfast so you don't collapse on me, then. You look sleepy, sweets. Drowsy and sensual. It looks good on you. If Orion's watching, maybe he'll at least suspect I'm fucking you."

A flush washed up her cheeks at the thought of the dreams she had had during the few hours she had actually slept.

Dreams that were vivid, sexual. Dreams where he demanded she fuck him, ride him, where he spoke to her in explicit, naughty words that only made her wilder.

"Let's hope he tries to kill me soon then," she said in irritation. "Or I might kill you while we are waiting."

"Didn't your grandmother say you were even-tempered?" he asked her suspiciously. "I could have sworn she mentioned that when she was here yesterday."

Risa really wanted to forget that visit. Her grandmother had watched them both suspiciously, as though trying to decide if they were actually having sex. It had been embarrassing. Before her grandmother finally left, she had glared at Micah and fretted over Risa as though she were an invalid. Risa didn't want to remember it, and she didn't want to discuss any portion of it.

"My grandmother doesn't live with me," she informed him. "She wouldn't know if I was even-tempered or not."

"Did she know you very well before the kidnapping?" he asked as he lifted his cup to his lips again. God, she wanted to be the cup.

"No. Jansen didn't visit much and he didn't like for her to visit. I've only gotten to know her in the past six years."

Abigail had been a very infrequent visitor when Risa had lived in Virginia with Jansen and Elaine.

He nodded at that. "Jansen would have wanted to keep you from anyone who would have influenced you in any way counter to his wishes. I can see Abigail definitely protesting his treatment of you."

She thought about that, then shrugged. "Until the kidnapping, he wasn't cruel. Just rather strict." He had been verbally abusive. He had made certain she understood that her lack of beauty placed her at a disadvantage. He had been mean. He had been hurtful.

"He convinced you that you had no worth, according to your psychologist's reports," he stated. "That's untrue, Risa. You have much worth."

Risa took another drink of her coffee before forcing more of her eggs down along with part of the bacon. She knew cruelty now. Nothing she had experienced before her kidnapping had prepared her for the true monster her father had been.

"I heard you talking to Reno last night when he came over," she commented, refusing to acknowledge his topic of conversation. "You said you'd take Orion down with your last breath if you had to. Why?"

He leaned back in his chair, his bare shoulders flexing beneath the dark skin as he inhaled deeply.

"He killed someone close to me six years ago," he finally stated. "A Mossad agent. She had been missing for more than twelve hours before her husband and . . ." He hesitated. "Before her husband and son were contacted and told her location." His black eyes flashed for a moment with rage. "Six weeks later her husband was involved in a confrontation with a suicide bomber in Tel Aviv. He attacked the bomber, threw himself on top of the young man. I consider Orion responsible for both their deaths and Reno knows this."

"Why their son?" she asked faintly. "What happened to him?"

He was silent for long moments. "He continued the investigation. He thought he was getting close when he was betrayed by a friend. He drowned."

"I'm sorry," she whispered. "They must have been very close to you. Did you ever know why your friend's mother was targeted?"

He shook his head. "She was involved in an investigation into the rumored sale of a biological weapon by an American scientist. She thought she was getting close to his identity; then she disappeared. I suspect it was tied to that."

"So you went back to Israel to investigate?" She frowned.

He shook his head. "I'm American. There was little investigating that I could do."

But that hadn't stopped him, she guessed.

"I can hear the accent in your voice sometimes," she told him. "Your parents were immigrants?"

He nodded sharply before picking up his cup and finishing his coffee. "There, I've answered your questions. Now we discuss what I want to discuss. Jansen Clay."

"Jansen has nothing to do with this." She couldn't discuss the man who had donated the sperm to her birth. He had destroyed parts of her. There were still areas of her soul that were blackened with what he had done to her and the hatred she felt for him.

"Jansen has everything to do with this, Risa." Bare arms folded on the table as he pushed his plate away and stared back at her. "The FBI has been tracking your progress with the psychologist, going over the recordings made of your sessions, as well as the doctor's notes. You gave them permission to do that, remember?"

"I'm not a moron," she snapped back at him. "Nor am I so simpleminded that you need to patronize me. Yes, I remember giving them permission to follow my progress. But I haven't remembered anything."

"You haven't remembered faces or names, yet, but you have remembered things," he said gently. "You remember the rape now."

She cringed, her arms going over her breasts as she fought to hold back the horror of what little she did remember.

"Don't," she whispered. "I can't talk about this to you."

"Why? What better person to discuss it with, Risa? Whatever they did to you doesn't affect what's between us. There is nothing you could remember that would change my perception of you."

She shook her head, a mocking laugh passing her lips. "Well, isn't that incentive enough to discuss it," she stated bitterly. "Let it go, Micah. I talk to my psychologist and you are not my psychologist."

"What you've remembered in the past months is the reason this assassin has been called out to kill you. If we could identify whoever it is hiding in your subconscious at the moment, then we could put a stop to this now. Orion never completes a project if his pay is jeopardized. His reputation is exacting; he never deviates from it. If we knew who hired him, we could stop this now."

"But it's Orion you're after." She forced the words past her lips. "How would that serve you, Micah? You wouldn't have the hold card you need to trap him."

He wouldn't be here with her any longer. She was pathetic. She wanted him away from her, and yet she didn't want him gone. The appearance of a lover was a salve at least to her public ego.

"I'll have my chance at Orion. It's fated," he said coldly. "If I could take the risk from you, I would do so. What makes you think I would do otherwise?"

She shook her head. Because he was sleeping with a woman he didn't truly desire, she thought. Because to catch a killer, he was forced into her bed.

"I haven't remembered much more." She heard the sound of her voice, strained, rough. "I remember being held down." Bile rose in her stomach. "He said . . ." She inhaled roughly, feeling a cold sweat pop out on her skin. "He said he couldn't look at me, because I was too ugly." Her head lowered as she shook her head. "If he had to look at me, he wouldn't be able to get off. He was angry with Jansen because he wanted the younger girl. Jansen told him I was the only choice, and he laughed. Said he had to pay someone to fuck me after all."

She pushed back from the table, stumbling from her chair as his expression remained composed, icy. She was shuddering now, thinking about it. It wasn't a memory; it was like a dream. Like a horrible nightmare she couldn't escape from whenever she let herself think about it.

"I don't know who it was," she cried out, keeping her back to him as she moved into the living room. "I don't want to know who it was."

"Because you're afraid you know him. Your mind knows who it is, and it's protecting you." God, his voice. With her back turned, she could hear something in it, something so dark and dangerous in the hard, emotionless tone that she instinctively shied away from it.

"My psychologist, Dr. Brinegar, she tried hypnosis. I asked her to." She shook her head. "I wanted it over. I wanted whatever was in my head to just go away. But she didn't get any more answers than I'd already given her." She turned to him. "Maybe I didn't see who it was. Maybe this is something else. Retaliation because Jansen is dead. Something else."

He shook his head as he gazed at her, his eyes deep, deep pools of black savagery.

"Our intel says otherwise, Risa."

"Maybe your fucking intel is wrong," she cried out, her arms falling away from her breasts as her fists clenched at her sides.

He rose slowly from his chair. "My intel isn't wrong, Risa. It's taken me six years to develop this contact. My intel is very, very accurate. This hit went out because you remembered something in the last three months that you shouldn't have remembered. Something that makes someone believe you will remember more."

She shook her head. "I don't know what it is. What could it be?"

"The identity of your rapist," he stated. "Everything you've remembered in the past three months, the little details, what was said, the fact that you could see Jansen as you were raped. The hands that held yours down to the floor of the plane. Emily screaming out at Jansen. It all has to do with the rape. You're trying to remember your rapist, and he's been afraid you would remember. He's watched you, just as the FBI has been watching, hoping you would remember while he's been terrified you would. He's covering his ass now."

For a moment, just for a moment, she was back in that plane. The drone of the engines, the terror that smothered her as she stared at Jansen. The way he laughed, the amusement in his eyes as her body began to burn and she began to cry.

She shook the image away, fought it with everything inside her. She'd been fighting the memories for years and she knew it. She wanted to live in the present; she didn't want to live in the past. She didn't want to remember, because she was afraid if she remembered, remembered what it felt like, she would remember how she had begged.

"I don't want to talk about this," she choked out desperately. "I won't talk about this. You can stay here until you find the bastard. Find him and kill him."

But she knew what he wasn't saying. Unless they found the identity of his employer, and he always learned who was employing him, then it wouldn't matter. There were always more killers out there. And the majority of them didn't mind using a bullet.

She was dead.

Risa turned and stared at the heavy drapes covering her windows. She hated drapes on the windows. The living room was dim, despite the bright winter sunlight outside. The apartment had a shadowy, sinister feel to it, one that seeped inside her and left her shaking with fear.

She was standing there locked in her own thoughts, her own certainties. She was unaware of Micah moving behind her until she felt his palms against her shoulders.

She couldn't jerk away from him. The feel of him behind

her, heated and so strong, his hands against her, his entire maleness just there, feeding whatever the hell that drug did to her.

It had to be the drug, didn't it? It made her knees weak, made her womb flex and convulse while her vagina ached with emptiness.

Memories of hell were replaced with memories of one night. His kiss. The touch of his lips along her body, on her nipples, between her thighs. The feel of him pressing into her, stretching her, burning her until she'd wondered if she could accommodate the erection impaling her.

"I won't allow you to be hurt," he whispered behind her, his breath feathering the top of her hair. "I will give my own life to protect you, Risa. And should that happen, then there are others who will come after me, to ensure you live."

She shook her head, a tear falling. "Don't do this, Micah. Don't say this."

Because it didn't mean anything. When it came right down to it, it wasn't because he loved her, or because his life would suffer without her. It was because Orion had killed Micah's friends. It was because he was a man who would do whatever it took to protect those he considered his responsibility.

She was his responsibility now.

"Risa, look at me." His hands eased her around slowly.

Her palms pressed against his bare chest, her fingers curling as she breathed in roughly at the feel of the heat of his flesh, the pleasure against her hands.

The silky mat of chest hair drew her attention as she felt it under her palms. It rasped the sensitive flesh, tickled against it. Made her wonder what it would feel like to have her nipples pressing into his chest.

She couldn't stop herself; she had to stroke him. Just a little touch.

Her eyes closed as her hands stroked over him. She felt the tight, hard press of male nipples, felt the thunder of his heart racing beneath her hands.

"Yes, Risa." His voice seemed to come from a distance. "Touch me, sweet. Ah damn, your hands are like silk, love."

His voice was like rough, black velvet. His hands were on her back, stroking it beneath her shirt. She couldn't protest. She didn't want to protest. She just wanted to sink into the heated sensations, the pleasure whipping through her, over her.

She wanted to feel him against her, skin on skin as they had been once before. Her hands slid to his shoulders; her fingers tested the hard muscle there. He was broader than she had thought at the club, more muscular. Harder than she had imagined then.

She remembered the hardness of him.

"Risa." His head lowered, his lips feathered over her brow. "You're pushing a damned hungry man here, love."

He was hungry? She was starving. She felt as though she had never been touched, as though those touches nights ago had been another lifetime. She needed more, ached for more.

"Give me your lips." His hand cupped her neck. She loved that, the feel of his fingers wrapping around her neck, his thumb pressing beneath her chin. It was powerful and dominant and made her feel feminine, desired.

For this moment, just for a moment, she let herself believe she was desired.

"Micah," she whispered his name as she felt his lips against her brow, her cheek, her jaw.

A shiver went through her, then a rush of heat as his lips sent swells of pleasure cresting over her nerve endings. Her lips parted, ached. His kiss, she needed his kiss, just one more time.

"Tell me," he whispered. "I won't take this time, love. Tell me what you want."

If only it was love. If only she could make sense of the emotions that rose inside her, the needs she couldn't control.

"Kiss me." She told him; she didn't beg. She didn't hear a plea in her voice; she was certain of it. God, if he didn't kiss her soon . . .

A groan sounded at the side of her lips; then he was there. His lips slanted over hers and that dark magic sucked her in again.

Was it the drug already in her system that did this? Or was it the man? He was dark magic all on his own. His kiss was addictive. That was the drug, not the Whore's Dust. She could bear the arousal until he touched her. Until his lips were on hers, and then she was lost.

She was lost now. Her lips parted for his tongue. She tasted coffee and male heat; it might as well have been an aphrodisiac, because now all she wanted was more. She wanted it badly enough that she arched against him, stretching into his body, her arms twining around his neck as she tried to follow his kiss, tried to find a way to satisfy the need for more when she had no idea how to still the need to begin with.

"Sweet." His lips drew back; he pressed a kiss to the corner of her lips, held her head still, and pressed another to her jaw as she heard a sudden ringing blaring around her.

Her eyes opened as she stared back at him, dazed, uncertain where the sound was coming from.

"Morganna and Clint." His thumb ran over her sensitive lips. "It's a couples' day out. They're going with us."

"They are? Why?"

"Couples' day out," he stated again. "Morganna and Raven put that on the list. All serious couples hang together, you know. When a man is thinking forever and marriage and all that good stuff, then he develops married friends. We're lovers, remember? Serious lovers."

"He does?" Raven hadn't told her that. Of course, she hadn't discussed couples, marriage, and forevers with Raven, either. "Are you sure?"

"Positive." He released her slowly. "Go dress. I'll entertain them while you do; then you can entertain them while I finish dressing." He pulled a T-shirt from the chair behind him, and she couldn't help but watch as he pushed his arms into it and tugged it over his head.

"Go." He turned her toward her bedroom, then delivered a light, surprising tap to her rear as he pushed her toward the door. "Hurry, or they'll believe we were otherwise occupied."

She flushed. They *were* otherwise occupied. But she went to her bedroom, closed the door behind her, and leaned against it weakly. She really wanted to be otherwise occupied.

Even more, she wanted to be otherwise occupied with Micah in ways that she knew would only destroy her world further.

Chapter 9

THE SHOPPING trip was a disaster of major proportions. No wonder he insisted they needed another couple with them; he was counting on the fact that Risa wouldn't stomp out of the mall if there were witnesses. And damn him, he was right.

Instead, she fumed. She refused to try on outfits, not that it did her any good, because he bought them anyway as Clint and Morganna looked on in amusement.

Then, at the lingerie shop. Risa had never been so publicly humiliated as she was when Micah dragged her into that shop. Even worse, when he picked out the scraps of lace and silk, satins and stretchy cottons. He bought enough lingerie to clothe twenty women. In her size. Bits of material that there wasn't a chance in hell of her wearing.

He was insane. The amount of money he spent would have bought her groceries for a year. Groceries for her and a small family, she later decided.

He carried the bags. He encouraged her to buy snug jeans; when she didn't, he bought them himself. He bought tops. He even bought her a snug leather jacket that looked as soft as butter.

He bought dresses. Dresses she swore she would never have the nerve to wear. Evidently private investigation or whatever the hell he did paid a hell of a lot more than accounting.

"You are spending too much money," she protested.

"Enjoy it." He'd shrugged as though cost didn't matter. "I hope you took my advice and emptied your closets."

"Do I ever take your advice?" she snarled under her breath.

"Well, I do remember one night that you came close." He bent and whispered the words in her ear, and she wanted to melt into the floor.

As they walked through the mall, he held her hand or kept his at the small of her back. And he watched everyone. His black gaze was never in one place long unless he was contemplating some article of clothing, looking between the clothing and her.

By time they left, she had five pairs of jeans, innumerable tops, enough lingerie to start her own shop, a pair of leather running shoes, a pair of black heels that were decadent, and three club dresses. Evidently, Micah liked to go to clubs.

Leading her back to the car they had driven in, she noticed the tension in his and Clint's bodies. Their watchfulness. She wasn't certain what they were watching for until Clint said, "Car's clear. Nik and John had surveillance. No one's been around it."

"The apartment?" Micah asked softly.

"Not so much as a blink on the surveillance. Travis moved into the apartment after we left. He says all quiet."

Micah nodded, deactivated the locks while they were several vehicles away, and hit the auto-ignition on the keypad he carried.

It wasn't cold; winter in Atlanta didn't often get cold. There was a chill to the air, but that was about it. He opened the trunk and the bags went inside; then she and Morganna were put safely in the backseat while the big bad tough guys sat in the front.

Risa was starting to dislike men.

"I know that look," Morganna murmured in amusement as she leaned closer, a smile tilting her lips. "You're imagining how he would look with his head displayed on your mantel, minus his body."

She shot the other woman a look. Risa still hadn't decided

just how involved Morganna was in the deception the night she had met Micah.

"Come on, Risa." Morganna watched her somberly now. "You're life was in danger and I knew it. I have clearance because of my work with the DEA to aid when Clint works certain assignments. You're my friend. I'd rather tell a little lie to save you than see you dead."

Risa stared into the rearview mirror as Micah glanced back at her.

"Don't worry about it," she finally said, turning to stare out the window of the door. "No harm done."

And why had she said that? There had been harm done. She was still burning; she was still terrified of her own body since that night.

"You're hurt," Morganna pushed. "I don't like that."

Risa shrugged. "It was slight, Morganna. Please, just let it go."

Risa watched the scenery fly by as Micah navigated through the traffic. She was aware of the two men talking quietly to each other, discussing surveillance and precautions.

She had never been out with a man and another couple before. She wondered if this was how it was. The guys sitting in the front and discussing whatever. The women in the back, perhaps discussing fashion. She'd always imagined the couples would sit together instead. She would have preferred it that way if she were part of a true couple. She'd prefer to have Micah beside her, perhaps with her leaning against him as they all discussed topics they could share.

She'd imagined that was a real couple outing. And it very well may have been; she had to remind herself that she wasn't really part of a couple.

"We're moving into the parking garage," Micah announced quietly into whatever was attached beneath his jacket sleeve. A mic of some sort. There was also a receiver tucked into his ear, the little wire to it tucked behind his ear and hidden by his hair until it disappeared beneath his collar.

"All's clear," Clint stated as Micah pulled into the closest slot to the elevator.

"We'll come back for the bags," Micah decided. "I want to get Risa upstairs first."

Clint nodded. They exited the front of the car and each opened a door to the back. Micah reached in, took her hand, and helped her out, then placed her carefully in front of him, keeping her there as they moved to the elevator.

They stayed together every step of the way until they arrived at the apartment. As they neared the door, it opened. Another man stepped out, nodded to them, and entered the apartment across the hall.

Another stranger had been in her home?

"It's okay; he's part of the team," Micah leaned close and whispered in her ear. "We don't have any more of those nasty bugs in your apartment."

The bugs. She hadn't wanted to think of what that camera might have caught her doing at any given time. She touched her brow as she bit back the sniping reply she wanted to make. It wasn't his fault, she reminded herself; he was trying to help. He was trying to save her life; the camera wasn't his fault.

They stepped into the apartment. Clint and Micah went through it carefully, then left her alone with Morganna while they went for the shopping bags.

"This must be hard on you; you're used to being here alone," Morganna commented as she curled into the easy chair in the corner of the room, leaving Risa the couch.

Risa shrugged as she sat down, feeling helpless and very much alone as she stared around the apartment.

"It's different," she finally said, mostly because the other woman obviously expected an answer.

"Risa, if you need to talk, I'm willing to listen," Morganna offered. "It must be difficult, being thrown in this situation."

"I don't need to talk, Morganna." She forced herself to stay on the couch rather than pace the room. "I'm fine. Really."

"You have a monster trying to kill you, you're thrown into a situation with a man you don't even know, one you're forced to sleep with, but you're okay?" Morganna stared back at her, disbelieving. "Somehow, I doubt that."

"What do you want me to tell you?" she asked the other woman with no more than a hint of the anger that she felt at the situation. "He's bossy, domineering, and that fucking drug Jansen Clay shot me full of, too many times, ensures that I'm ready to fuck on a moment's notice. Having him in my bed is hell. I'm not sleeping. And I'm not fucking happy with the situation. Is there anything else you need to know?"

Morganna breathed out deeply, her gaze compassionate.

"The Whore's Dust to begin the arousal," Morganna finally said. "It only makes it worse. You don't want him because of the drug. You want him because you're a woman and he's a very sexy, very desirable man. There's nothing wrong with that, Risa."

"Isn't there?" She snorted mockingly. "You know, Morganna, if my friends had been so kind to just tell me what the hell was going on the night I met him, perhaps I would have understood that. I wouldn't have made the mistake of going to bed with him, and I wouldn't have to lie in that bed night after night, aware that it would take a bag over my head for him to get off. Thank you for that, by the way. It was a very enlightening experience."

She came off the couch as Morganna stared back at her in blank shock.

"You . . . he . . ." Morganna breathed out roughly. "Damn. I didn't know about that. He didn't add that in his report of that night."

"No kidding," she muttered.

"What the hell happened to make you think he'd have to put a bag over your face to get off?" Morganna came out of her chair then. "That is simply not true, Risa. You have got to get over what Jansen Clay did to you in that regard. You are not an ugly woman."

"Yeah, boy. I'd just win the next Miss America, wouldn't I?" she sniped back angrily.

"Well, I wouldn't go that far," Morganna admitted, which did little to soothe Risa's anger as she turned to her. "Risa, you're a very pretty young woman," Morganna said then.

"No, you're not the next Miss America, but you're a far cry from coyote ugly, I promise you that. And if there were issues that night, then you need to discuss them with Micah."

"Why don't I just do that?" She laughed mockingly. "I could just say, 'Oh, by the way, Micah, remember when you couldn't fucking get off? Well, why not just tell me—' "

She broke off as a flash of movement caught her attention. Heat filled her face at the sight of Micah and Clint standing in the open doorway, their hands full of bags, their expressions making it clear that they had heard every word of that last tirade.

Damn, damn, and double damn.

"Just tell you what?" Micah's lips were a straight, furious line as he moved into the apartment and tossed the bags carelessly to the couch as Morganna moved quickly to the door.

Risa was aware of the couple leaving, the door closing and locking behind them.

"Why not just tell me what it would have taken to get you off?" she sneered. "What would I have had to do, give you my back so you didn't have to look at my face?"

Micah tried. In all the years of his life he had never tried to push back the overwhelming anger as much as he tried to push it back now.

He reminded himself that she could be forgiven for her anger, for her snipishness at the mall. She could be forgiven for every damned thing she had said and done in the past two days. She was frightened. She was being put through another kind of hell and it couldn't be easy for her. But this one. This one he wasn't quite as willing to let go.

He had to admit, she was stronger than he had expected her to be. She wasn't cowering; she hadn't cowered a single time. She was trying to fight; unfortunately, she was fighting the wrong damned things and pissing him off in the process.

"You want to rethink that accusation you just made," he told her carefully, attempting to push back the anger and draw forward the ice he used to protect himself and others. "You want to rethink it carefully and rephrase it quickly, Risa."

She glared back at him. "Why should I?"

As she stood there dressed in a baggy silk blouse and loose black pants, her arms crossed over her breasts, her expression flushed and furious, Micah felt his erection flex and throb painfully. What was it about this woman that kept him hard? That kept him ready to fuck her at a moment's notice? If only he had the excuse of the Whore's Dust, he thought mockingly.

"Because I'm about five seconds from dragging you into that bedroom and spending the rest of the night showing you just how wrong you are," he informed her. "I can't believe you'd spout such idiocy from your mouth. Do you think if I didn't find you attractive, didn't ache for you, I would have been hard enough to pound nails?"

"You didn't come," she accused him roughly. "I know you didn't. You couldn't."

He pushed his hands over his head, clenched his teeth, and tried to keep his hands off her. If he touched her, he'd never be able to stop.

"Because you didn't get off," he pushed between gritted teeth. "Did you think I would take my pleasure of you when you hadn't taken yours of me? What the fucking hell is in your mind, woman? Have you lost your damned senses? I had to leave the bed to keep from pounding into you when you had obviously grown too tense to climax. I wanted to give us both a second to calm down. Just a moment to find my control. And when I returned, what did I find?"

He stepped closer when he hadn't meant to. His hands gripped her shoulders and he jerked her closer, staring furiously down at her surprised little face.

"You were gone!" he snarled. "You ran from me, Risa, rather than giving me a chance to help you find the pleasure you were seeking."

She shook her head, a jerky movement, as she swallowed tightly, her hands pressing against his chest.

"But I did," she whispered. "I did."

"You call what you gave me your release?" he bit out furiously. "You fought it. I understood why you fought it, and I understand even more now. The strength of it would have been frightening. You were with a man you did not know. Running was not the answer."

She pulled away from him and it was all he could do to keep from jerking her back to him. Instead, he let her go. He had to take this slowly. She had already been hurt by one man; he wouldn't add his name to her pain. He'd plotted out his seduction of her, and he would seduce her. She would come apart in his arms the next time he managed to get his dick inside that hot little pussy, and she would come apart with everything inside her. He'd accept nothing else. But he knew she wasn't ready for that yet. Fear still held her back. Her own demons held her back.

He watched as she pushed her fingers through her hair, feathering it around her shoulders and face like multi-hued strands of silk. Turning back to her, he watched as her light blue eyes seemed darker, the shadows under her eyes more pronounced. She hadn't slept in two nights. She had lain on her side of the bed and done no more than doze. She was killing them both and seemed unaware of it.

How did she affect him this way? There was something about the pain in her eyes that made him want to kill. The unsmiling curve of her lips made him hungry to kiss her, to make her smile. The mischievous tilt of her nose made him wonder at the many ways she could make a man insane, if she were to just be herself.

"Running was the only option," she finally stated proudly.

Pride kept her shoulders straight, her head high, no matter what was thrown at her.

"How can you consider that an option?" he growled back at her. "Running is a coward's way out, Risa. If there is one thing you have never displayed in the six years you've tried to rebuild your life, then it's cowardice."

Her smile was mocking, bitter. The pain that filled her eyes, her expression, tore at the heart he thought had already been ripped from him years ago.

"No, Micah," she whispered, her voice laden with the haunting pain that filled her eyes. "You're wrong. It took me six years to try to take a lover. Six years to get up the nerve, for that damned Whore's Dust to make me desperate enough to try. I failed. Evidently I failed more than I thought I had. You see, I thought I had orgasmed." Bitterness shaped her lips. "I guess I didn't. And we both know you didn't. So evidently, I'm a bigger coward than you believed, because I'll be damned if I can face allowing it to happen again."

She swung away from him again. She ran from him again. She closed herself in that bedroom, and it took every ounce of his control not to follow her, not to rip that damned door from its hinges and show her exactly what happened when she ran from her man.

Her man. He was losing his damned mind. Micah Sloane was no more than a man. The man who faced her daily was a dead man. Dead men didn't claim a woman. Dead men didn't dream of holding one forever. Dead men didn't talk, and dead men didn't dream. Because hell exacted an incredible price for allowing a dead man to walk. And that price might very well be the life of the woman he knew a part of him was already beginning to claim.

He breathed out roughly and reminded himself of his seduction schedule. He wouldn't think about claiming or loving. He couldn't. He would think of healing and protecting. That he could do. He could heal her, he could protect her, and he could destroy that last demon intent on taking her life.

He was two days into his campaign to seduce his lovely little lover. Getting her used to his body at night, lying against her, touching her, letting her feel his heat. The couple thing today was inspiration. He remembered his mother mentioning that when a man was seeking a bond with a woman, then he should develop friends who already had that bond, and have outings.

She hadn't been pleased with the shopping.

He moved to the fallen bags and picked them up. He straightened them on the couch and noticed a scrap of violet lace that still lay on the floor. She had looked at this particular piece and he had seen the need for it in her eyes, despite her protest. With each piece he had bought, he had seen her curiosity build.

His Risa wanted pretty clothes and pretty underthings. He had seen that the night he had taken her to his bed. She had worn silk and lace beneath her dress. Silken stockings and a lacy thong. Pretty, feminine, and delicate. As she was.

And just as damned fiery.

She was killing him. He'd once heard his father say that Micah's mother had caused him to grow gray hairs when he was trying to get her to commit to him. Micah wasn't after the commitment, but he could definitely feel the gray hairs coming on.

ORION SMOOTHED his hand over the metal table, his eyes narrowed as he tested the strength of it. Risa Clay was a little thing, but his employer had assured him she had some strength when attempting to escape. Fear could provide an amazing amount of power, even to a fragile, delicate little woman such Risa Clay.

Patting the metal table in satisfaction, he then turned his attention to the metal bars attached by chains to the roof. He pulled himself up, but he couldn't quite touch his chin to it. He chuckled a bit; he was obviously losing a bit of strength himself.

Ah well, it happened once a man passed that forty mark. But it didn't take strength to do his job. It took cunning, calculation, and patience. He was still at the top of his game there. Perhaps even more than he had been in his youth. With age and experience came wisdom, he decided as he dropped from the bar and moved to test the tilt of the table he had found. He would have preferred to do this deed in Risa Clay's home, but her new bodyguard had changed Orion's original strategy.

He never bought the articles he needed in a way that could be traced. He stole them for the most part. This table had come from a junk dealer's yard. Orion and managed to slip in and take it with no one the wiser. The bar was taken from the apartment he had leased. It was the clothes rod. A simple metal bar, clean of prints and ready for use. Everything in his little lair was clean of prints. He made certain it was spotless and prepared. He didn't want the poor little thing to die in filth. She wasn't pretty, she was really rather ugly, but from all he'd gathered, she was a kind girl. One who tried to do nothing but live her simple life.

Hell, she didn't even cheat on her taxes.

That was frightening. Perhaps she deserved to die. Anyone that conscientious needed to be taken out before she could breed and make more moralistic little bastards for the world to deal with.

He had enough to deal with himself. The bounty on his head by several government agencies was causing him a bit of concern. His last hit, an American scientist who had nearly cracked a cure for a particularly nasty man-made virus, had caused several governments a bit of worry.

That job had netted Orion several million when it was finished. He had enough to retire in peace now, buy him a nice little island somewhere, and import several luscious little girls to take care of his needs. He wouldn't have to work. Wouldn't have to balance his play any longer. He could retire.

This would be his last job, he decided. The excitement had fizzled; it didn't pique his interest as it had before. Now, it was simply a job.

When had this begun?

Ah yes, six years ago. Ariela Abijah.

He shook his head. Mossad hadn't taken kindly to her death, and neither had her son. The boy had nearly caught up with him. If it hadn't been for a bit of luck, then David Abijah would have managed to capture him on the merchant vessel Orion had used for his escape from Russia several years after he'd killed Abijah's mother.

Thankfully, luck had been with him. David Abijah had fed the fishes that night. He was no longer a problem that Orion had to deal with.

But yes, this was the reason the excitement had faded. Abijah had tracked him tirelessly, especially after his father had thrown himself on a suicide bomber.

Orion shook his head. He hadn't enjoyed killing the boy. There had been something in those black eyes that touched

Orion. A strength, a flame of determination. A look very similar to the look that had been in Ariela's eyes.

The memory of that look rather reminded him of the man Risa Clay had moved into her apartment. He hadn't seen his eyes, but Orion had seen his face clearly. There was a stamp of determination and arrogance on it that had sent a chill up his spine.

What a bit of timing there, he thought angrily as he tapped his latex-covered fingers on the metal table.

The little wretch hadn't even looked at a man in the six years she had been out of the asylum; now, she had a lover—a very experienced, intuitive lover. One who had disposed of the bugs Orion had placed in her apartment. After a single night at some club, a friend of a friend had managed to pick her up, and to move in with her.

He'd learned that much. And she had Navy SEALs for friends. That had caused him a moment's hesitation when he had identified them. Retired SEALs, but SEALs were SEALs until the day they died. Perhaps even beyond. They were like a plague that refused to go away when they were riled.

He'd nearly backed out of this deal, but he'd never backed out of a deal with this particular employer. It wasn't possible.

Shaking his head, he moved to his opened laptop and once again clicked through the digital pictures he had taken of them.

The man wore glasses; Orion had yet to see his eyes or snap a picture of them. The identification program Orion used didn't work very well with glasses. So far, it had pulled up only five pictures and two were of dead men, Abijah being one of them.

He was going to have to talk to the programmer he had bought it from. Or perhaps not. It was his last job; he was going to make certain of it.

He stared at the couple again, tilted his head, and stared at the woman. Was that a flash of prettiness in her face as she stared up at the man who walked with her? She looked furious, yet there was a hint of prettiness there that Orion hadn't seen before.

It had to be a trick of the light, he thought. He'd seen many pictures of her, and never had he seen this, this something that made him wonder if she wasn't so very ugly after all.

Not that she was dog ugly. She was very, very plain, he decided, looking at her closely. And when had he decided she was simply plain rather than ugly?

He must definitely be getting on in age. He shuddered at the thought that he could be so old that his eyes were giving out on him. The eye doctor he saw once a year had assured him that his eyes were fine. Twenty-twenty vision, the doctor had promised him. Orion had never had trouble with his vision.

He clicked through a few more pictures, tilted his head again, and frowned deeply. Yes, there it was. One he had snapped as they moved through the mall. The man had his hand at her neck, as though he were rubbing it. There was a hint of sensuality in her face. A certain tilt of her eyes. Her too-large mouth seemed sensual rather than out of place here. Even with her baggy clothes she looked almost pretty.

He shook his head. What new phenomenon was this? And what did it matter? He'd make his move soon. A rather public one, simply because it wouldn't be expected. No one could anticipate his next move. He'd made certain of it.

Chapter 10

"I HAVE THINGS I need to do," Risa announced the next morning after breakfast dishes had been cleared away and an uncomfortable silence had descended between them.

"Things?" A dark brow arched as Micah watched her from the easy chair.

He was entirely too confident, too arrogant, she decided as she eyed him. And too damned sexy. The blue cotton shirt he wore did nothing to hide the power beneath it, and the jeans and boots made him look much too male, too virile.

"Yes, things," she told him. "I need to go to Grandmother's and discuss some last-minute details for the party she's having in a few weeks. I'm handling the arrangements this year for her, and I want to make certain everything runs smoothly."

"Your grandmother could come here," he suggested, his gaze running over Risa's body.

He was always doing that. Looking her over, his black eyes gleaming with an intent she didn't understand. But her body responded to it. She almost sighed at the rush of desire that washed over her and pulsed between her thighs.

"I need to go to the house, Micah. I shouldn't have to argue over that. It's a simple enough trip and one you should be able to arrange." Besides, her grandmother was worrying and Risa needed to reassure her.

"Come here, and we'll discuss it." His hard hand patted his lap as he stared back at Risa with an edge of amusement.

"You can convince me you need to go to her, rather than her coming here."

She blinked back in surprise. Was he teasing her?

"There's nothing to discuss," she stated stiffly, forcing her hands not to form fists as she fought he need to do as he asked.

"There's actually a measure of risk involved in the trip," he mused. "Sit down here and we'll talk about it."

He patted his hard leg again.

"Stop playing with me, Micah," she demanded, frustration clawing at her now. "The situation is difficult enough; there's no sense in adding to the complications."

His eyes gleamed with laughter, and with lust. She wanted to sink into that link, holding it inside her. But the memories of the single night they had shared sliced through her mind and filled her with shame.

She couldn't handle a man like Micah, she had decided. He was obviously more exacting in his sexuality than she had heard of men being. What happened to the wham-bam-thank-you-ma'am sexuality that men were supposed to possess? When had the rules changed?

"I like adding complications, Risa, they make life interesting," he told her. "Now, you can sit down here and let me pet you a little bit while you explain this need you have to escape the safety of your apartment, or we can stay here."

"Or I can walk out and go anyway," she pointed out with a tight smile. "You'll still follow, your friends will follow, and I'll still be protected without having to humiliate myself to do it."

"You would of course have to get past me to get out that door," he pointed out. "How do you intend to do that?"

With a baseball bat, probably. That was most likely what it would take, and she didn't own one.

"Micah, please don't be difficult," she protested, trying to restrain her anger. "Nothing will be solved or gained by sitting on your lap and playing this asinine game you're intent on playing."

He stared back at her archly. "Much will be gained, Risa.

Just to begin with, our pleasure. Orion will be thrown off balance, and we'll be much more relaxed."

She felt her hands fisting into the loose material of the T-shirt she wore as she glanced at his lap and swallowed tightly.

He had an erection. It wasn't hard to detect. His explanation the day before for his reasons for not releasing the night they were together made sense, but still her mind wanted to reject it. Nerves and fear gathered in the pit of her belly each time she thought about that night, each time she remembered the waves of sensation that she had fought.

They had been frightening. The thought of experiencing them again was both terrifying and exciting. Unfortunately, the thought of disappointing him again held her back. She couldn't control that pleasure, and the thought of not controlling her body, of once again being helpless beneath the tide of sensation, had the power to send her into a panic.

"We discuss it here." He patted his lap again. "Or we stay inside today. Your choice."

Her choice. Was anything about this entire situation her choice?

"This is insane." Her voice was hoarse; her gaze flicked again to his erection.

Risa felt the flesh between her thighs pulsing, her juices gathering on the bare lips beneath the new panties she had slipped into and worn.

His brow arched again.

"What—" She swallowed tightly. "What are you going to do?"

A smile tugged at his lips. "What would you let me do?"

A shudder raced down her back.

Micah saw the widening of Risa's eyes, the hunger that darkened the light blue irises, and had to stifle a groan as his cock throbbed with the need to be buried inside her again.

He could make it better for her this time. He swore he would. Not today; it was too soon. She wasn't used to his touch yet, wasn't used to his hand upon her body, or the needs that burned between them.

A woman's body was the finest work of art. It was created for pleasure. From the top of her head to the soles of her feet, a woman was a man's greatest temptation. He would fight wars to protect her; he would give his life to see to her security. She was man's greatest strength, and his greatest weakness. She was created as his other half, and Micah had never understood that completely, until Risa.

"What I would let you do isn't the point." His body tensed further at the throb of hunger in her voice. "We both know this doesn't work for me."

"Nothing has to work, love," he promised her, his body tightened as she seemed to try to take that last step to him. "This isn't about having sex. It's about touch, nothing more. It's about learning your lover's body, your lover's touch. Wouldn't you like to learn my touch, Risa?"

Her eyes dilated; the most incredible flush washed over the creamy flesh of her face and neck. A hint of color, a mere suggestion of the fire that blazed in her body.

And he knew that fire. He knew the heat of her tight pussy, the stiff points of her hard little nipples, the taste of her. She was an aphrodisiac to his senses, and his hunger for her refused to abate.

"Come, Risa," he whispered as he gauged the weakening need that filled her eyes.

He held his hand out to her. "Come to me; feel your lover's touch."

Her hand trembled as she laid it in his. That slight tremor touched his heart in ways it shouldn't. She was innocent of a lover's touch, except his own. Still, she had no idea of the power of her own sexuality, or its effect on him. Would she be surprised, he wondered, to know she could make him feel weak with his need for her?

"Ah, love." He drew her to him, catching her hips and pulling her legs into place on each side of his legs until she was kneeling in front of him, watching him in confusion. "There." His hand stroked up her back. "I like looking at your pretty face when I'm touching you. I can watch your eyes darken, see the heat that builds beneath your flesh. I make you hot, Risa; admit it." His teasing grin was met with another flash of confusion in her expression.

"You frighten me," she whispered as he brushed her hair back from the gentle lines of her face. "I can't control what you do to me, Micah."

Ah yes, control. There was no control when lusts raged out of control, and the addition of the drug that still affected her small body would make the pleasure terrifying for her. She hadn't been able to control her body's response to touch when she was first injected with the Whore's Dust. It had made her beg for touch, despite the degradation she felt at the act. Control now would be uppermost in her mind.

Controlling her response, her pleasure. She needed to learn her own body, learn the depth of the pleasure, before she learned that control wasn't needed when it was a touch she desired with not just her body but her heart and her mind as well.

"Kiss me." He whispered the demand. "Take what *you* want, Risa."

He watched her eyes, watched the throb of her pulse at her neck. The thought of touching him sent a response tearing through her. He could see it, felt it in the tensing of her slender thighs alongside his.

She was dying for this touch. He was so hungry for it, he wondered if he would survive the wait.

RISA LICKED HER lips nervously as she stared back at Micah.

"What do I want?" The words fell from her lips before her head had a chance to censor them.

Her hands moved over his chest to his neck. She felt the heat of his flesh, the throb of his pulse, the thunder of his heart.

"You want to kiss me." His lips formed the words, drawing her gaze to their tempting lines.

"What more do I want?" she asked, knowing she wanted so much more. "Will you touch me as I kiss you, Micah?"

She needed to be touched. Her flesh felt tight, achy. The need to be touched was overwhelming. She ached. The ache was like a sickness, like a fever she couldn't get rid of.

"I'll touch you whenever you like, Risa; you have only to ask."

Weakness flooded her; need exploded inside her. Her hands moved to his shoulders, gripped the hard muscle there, and her lips lowered to his.

She had never kissed anyone, by her own instigation, her own initiation.

Micah sat beneath her, his body tense, humming with power and promise as her lips touched his and she felt a cry welling in her throat.

For the first time she had the chance to learn the shape of his lips against hers, the feel of them. Her lips parted, her tongue stroked over the fuller line of the lower curve, and she tasted coffee and heat. She tasted the man slowly, rather than simply the hunger that poured through her.

Her head tilted, lips parted over his, her tongue touched the seam of his lips and she felt lost in the wonder of the sensuality that began to build slowly between them.

Not just lust. It was so much more.

"Touch me," she breathed against his lips. "Please, Micah, touch me."

A groan rasped from his throat and his hands moved from the hard grip they had on her hips as his lips parted beneath hers, and then she didn't know who was kissing who, who controlled and who led.

One hand lifted to her face, his palm cupping her neck. She loved that touch. It made her feel cherished, made her feel surrounded by him. The other hand pushed beneath the loose hem of her shirt. It stroked up her back; his fingertips touched her flesh on the way back down. Electric pleasure seemed to surround her as she allowed herself to sink beneath the waves of sensation that built inside her.

The uncharted waters of slow, building heat were exhilarating. The touch of his lips against hers as she learned the shape, the hunger, of a kiss gave her a heady confidence. The feel of his neck and shoulders beneath her touch, the feel of his heartbeat thundering in his chest, gave her courage.

He had to enjoy her, she thought desperately. Would he kiss her with such hunger if he didn't? Would his heart race with excitement?

She jerked, her thoughts flying from her head as his palm cupped a breast, his thumb finding her nipple as a ragged cry tore from her throat.

Her head jerked back, eyes opening. She should have kept them closed, because the sight of his kiss-swollen, damp lips sent a punch of reaction to her womb.

"Micah. Tell me what to do," she gasped, her hands clenching his biceps now. "Tell me what to do."

"What you're doing," he groaned. "Let me touch you, Risa. Just feel good for me, love. Just let it feel good. This is all, just touch. Just touch, baby. Nothing more."

Just touch. She could handle just touch, maybe.

"Here. Let's take this off for you." The hem of her shirt rose.

Risa lifted her arms, eager to be rid of the confining material as he stripped it from her.

"Damn. Look how pretty."

Both hands cupped her breasts, framing the violet lace of the half bra that framed her flesh and lifted the swollen mounds to him.

Risa ran her hands over his shoulders, pushed them beneath the edges of his shirt, and rasped over his flesh with her nails.

It wasn't enough. As his lips moved over her neck, angling too slowly to the rise of her breasts, she tugged at his shirt. Her fingers fumbled with the buttons; she was certain one might have popped off.

She wasn't watching for the building arcs of dark intensity inside her now. It was just touch, he had promised her. She didn't have to worry about being thrown into a maelstrom that might tear her soul from her body.

Just touch was safe.

Her breathing was harsh, heavy. The thunder of her heartbeat echoed in her ears as hunger settled heavily between her thighs.

Her clit was tormented. Inside, her pussy throbbed and ached; her juices slid from her, preparing her, begging for touch as she pulled at the open edges of his shirt.

He released her long enough to tear it off and throw it aside. Once the material dropped from his hands, he was touching her again.

His lips were on her breasts; his tongue stroked over her distended nipples as they rose beneath the lace cups of her bra. His groan echoed around her, but his flesh was there for her touch.

Touch. He promised her touch.

She felt her hair across her shoulder, stroking her, feathering against her flesh as his fingers lowered the lace covering her breasts and his mouth captured a tight nipple in the wet, heated confines.

She jerked, arched. Flares of explosive pleasure tore along the nerve endings from her nipple to her pussy. Her juices were hotter, coating her pussy now, electrifying her clit.

It was just touch. Touch alone would swamp her in the dark abyss that threatened at the reaches of her mind.

"Yes, love." His whisper was a dark croon to her senses. "Let me touch you. Taste you. You're sweet, Risa. As sweet as sunshine."

A moan gathered in her throat, a trailing little cry as she felt the closure of her pants release, the zipper rasping down.

Then he was touching her there. Touch, just touch. His fingers circled her clit, rubbed against it. His teeth rasped over her nipple, sending a surge of painful pleasure to attack her system.

She moved against his fingers, lost in the building sensations. She wasn't frightened. There were no waves of darkness. The darkness was already there. It eased around her, slowly, washed her in warmth. It wasn't dizzying. It wasn't frightening.

She was barely aware of the cries falling from her lips. Her hips writhed against his fingers as he continued to rub around her clit, against it. He didn't go lower. He didn't invade the spasming, desperate clench of her pussy. He didn't penetrate it, didn't touch it.

His lips suckled at her breasts; his fingers rubbed at her clit. He stroked and she swore she might have screamed out his name.

One arm wrapped around her hips, but he didn't restrain her; he didn't hold her in place. He let her move. His fingers followed. Bright pinpoints of light began to flare behind her closed eyes. Flames began to race over her body, and before she could control the darkness, it rose in a sudden wash of light and color and exploded through her system with an ecstasy she couldn't imagine.

She screamed his name. She arched, bucked in his grip, and then flowed with the next eruption of pleasure as his fingers finally eased. But he didn't move. His palm cupped her mound, the pad pressing into her flexing clit as she rubbed against him, taking the last remaining pulses of sensation as she rubbed against him with jerky abandon.

She finally collapsed against his chest, her breathing ragged as shudders continued to race through her body. Her nails eased their grip on his bare shoulders; her thighs melted; then each muscle in her body followed suit. She was limp against him, torn by the knowledge that such pleasure could exist from touch alone.

"Precious Risa." He kissed her forehead, pulled her hair back from her cheek, and kissed there as well.

He touched her with gentleness, though she could feel the tension in his body and sensed his lust raging through him.

"You didn't," she whispered, knowing he hadn't found his release. "Again."

"Shh. My time will come," he told her, his voice raspy as he kissed the lobe of her ear. "This was for you, love. And trust me, feeling your pleasure race through you more than makes up for any discomfort I may feel."

His hand still cupped her, but his palm rasped against the ultrasensitive bud of her clit, but only when she wanted it to rasp.

Risa kept her face buried in his neck as the final shudders eased through her.

She had never known that touch alone could be so destructive. She couldn't have imagined that such pleasure could exist. This was what she had fought the night he had taken her? How insane could she have been?

"Do you know," he whispered at her ear then, "a man who understands true pleasure understands that his woman's pleasure is tied directly to his own? It's a very hollow release, Risa, for a man who understands that, when his lover has not found her pleasure as well. But it is a pleasure untold simply to see and to feel his lover's release, whether he gains his or not."

She burrowed closer to him, feeling a blush heating her skin. "Your accent is slipping again," she said weakly.

He chuckled at her ear. "So it is. You'll have to forgive me. I'm still immersed in my lover's pleasure."

She almost laughed. A smile did curve her lips, because she could still sense his own unrelieved need.

"Does it hurt?" she asked then.

"Does what hurt?" His hand eased from her, only to pull her closer, to allow her to feel the hard ridge of his cock rising beneath his jeans. "This? After several days in your presence, I'm becoming quite familiar with the situation."

Risa lifted her head and stared back at him. There was amusement in his black eyes, in the shape of his lips. He wasn't angry, but he was still very much aroused.

"I could try." She swallowed tightly. "That wasn't fair to you. We could go to the bedroom."

She didn't quite know how to handle this situation. She had just come on his fingers, had known an explosive release that left her weak and almost sated in his arms. There was an awareness, though, that something was missing. That she had managed once again to cheat not just herself but him also. She just wondered if she would survive knowing what she was cheating herself out of.

"Risa, love, the time that we come together again will arrive soon enough." He fixed the little latch to her slacks and drew the zipper up before easing the cups of her bra back over her breasts. "Come now." He lifted her from his lap and set her back on her feet. "Let's see about getting you into those butt-snugging jeans I bought you, and one of your pretty tops to go over your new lacy panties. I must admit, I'd find great pleasure in that today."

After the climax he had just given her, balking at that seemed a little childish. Besides, she'd wondered how the jeans and snug tops would look. She'd never worn clothes designed to cover and yet show off her body. She had always been self-conscious, too afraid to want to draw attention to herself, as a teenager. And after the kidnapping and her confinement in the private institution Jansen had placed her in, Risa had been terrified of wearing clothes that would reveal any part of her body.

Until the night she met Micah.

What had made her so determined to draw his attention? she wondered as she pulled her shirt on. She'd bought clothes designed to draw attention, to tempt a man. And, she knew now, not just any man, but the man her friends had spoken so highly of.

"I'll wear the clothes." She lifted her shoulders almost defensively at the thought of wearing them. "But I'm not used to wearing clothes like that."

"You should get used to it," he told her. "You should learn what you like, and make certain you have it. A few days at the mall, trying on whatever catches your eye, looking for what pleases you as a woman, you would have no trouble, Risa, filling your closet with clothing that would please you. A beautiful woman should always have clothing that makes her feel confident and in charge."

She almost laughed bitterly at that. "Yeah, I'm just real confident and in charge, with a hit man watching for me and a damned date rape drug messing with my arousal."

The pleasure of moments before was fading now and the familiar anger taking its place. She was tired of the anger. She was tired of the building frustration and the lack of control in her own life. Every step, every breath, seemed measured to guard against this new threat.

Wasn't it enough, she wondered, that she had had to survive what Jansen Clay, a man who should have wanted to protect her, had done to her? No, he'd compounded it by locking her in an asylum and keeping her in a drug-shadowed existence for nearly two years. If it hadn't been for the kindnesses of the staff there, God knew she would have given up in the first months.

She had learned later that two of the orderlies, a husband and wife, had made it their personal mission to see that she was looked after and wasn't abused. But they hadn't been able to keep Jansen Clay from visiting, and they had never seen the other man who she was aware had arrived with her father several times.

Those times were remembered because of the pain, rage, and horrifying arousal that had sped through her system after she was injected with something during those visits.

She had later learned she had been injected with a drug similar to the Whore's Dust.

She paused and turned to Micah.

"He was at the clinic," she said, frowning, aware that the memory was hovering just out of reach.

It was the hands. She had always noticed his hands. Large, blunt, as soft as silk.

"Who was at the clinic?" Micah's voice was soft now, distant, as though he didn't want to intrude on whatever she was remembering.

She lifted her gaze to his. "The man that raped me in the cargo plane. He was at the clinic. He came with Jansen several times. The doctors would almost let me slip out of the sedated haze they kept me in. They did it because the man that came with Jansen always injected me with that drug. It wasn't Jansen that did it. It was him."

As she stared at Micah, a hazy memory whispered through her.

"His hands hurt," she said. "I thought he'd break my arm when he held it down. Then he would shove the needle in and force the drug inside me, as though he had to do it quickly. It hurt."

"The attempts they made to duplicate the Whore's Dust," Micah said. "They used it on you several times."

She nodded slowly. "It wasn't like Whore's Dust, though." She lifted her head and stared back at him miserably. "It was worse, Micah. What he had was worse than the Whore's Dust. It didn't go away as easy. The pain of it seemed to last forever. Long after they left. It seemed like it was never-ending." She shook her head and shut her eyes quickly as she swung away from him.

"Don't fight the memories, Risa." His hands caught her shoulders when she would have run from him. "You were not at fault for what they did to you. You have no shame in this. It is entirely theirs. You can't fight the memories, because they're your only defense."

Her defense against a killer.

Her breathing hitched as the memory receded faster than it had flowed into her. The knowledge remained, though. The knowledge that whoever had raped her hadn't been content to destroy her that way. For some reason, he had wanted to torture her further. He'd wanted to watch her pain.

He had hated her.

CHAPTER 11

RISA WORE THE jeans with a long-sleeved dark blue silk blouse and the leather jacket Micah had forced on her at the mall. On her feet she wore thick cotton socks and the white leather sneakers.

She had to admit that below the neck she didn't look too bad. She'd tried to do something about above the neck. She'd styled her expertly highlighted hair around her face and used makeup sparingly, hoping she wouldn't feel like an over-made-up clown.

"Beautiful," Micah announced as she re-entered the living room, his black eyes frankly admiring as they went over her. "Risa, my love, I'm doomed to walk around in a haze of arousal whenever you're near."

She flushed, told herself he certainly didn't mean it, but she glanced this time. And yes, he was still aroused. His expression was wry as he shrugged on his own leather jacket, covering the proof of arousal that strained at his jeans.

"We could have gone to bed," she whispered, still a bit embarrassed at the fact that he hadn't released.

"You're not ready for bed yet," he told her. "When you're ready, sweet, your body will let me know."

He led her to the door as she shot him a frown over her shoulder. "That's a very arrogant statement, Micah," she told him, irritation seeping into her voice.

He had to be the most arrogant, irritating, frustrating man in the world.

"I'm a very arrogant man," he informed her as they stepped from the apartment. Before the door closed, the apartment door across from them opened and Risa watched as the agent Micah called John sprinted across the hall into her apartment.

"What does he do in there while we're gone?" she muttered as she heard the locks click behind them.

"Trust me, with John, you really don't want to know," Micah growled, his voice low. "Now be a good girl. We don't discuss the pests in your apartment while outside it."

She almost laughed at the comment before he nipped at her ear gently and led her to the elevator. The smile lingered on her face. Micah had a way about him that made her want to smile, made her want to join in whatever amusement twinkled in his black eyes.

"Those jeans are killing me," he sighed as they rode down the elevator.

"I could have worn the slacks," she tried for a sober look as she glanced over her shoulder at him.

"I could spank you," he muttered. "Such vile words should never come from such pretty lips."

She had to turn her back and bite her lip to keep from laughing. But she felt him behind her, and she swore she felt him looking at her butt. The jacket did nothing to cover it.

As she stepped out of the elevator, it felt natural to have his hand riding at the small of her back, leading her through the lobby.

"Mr. Sloane, your vehicle is waiting outside." The doorman handed him the key. "Have a nice outing, sir."

"Thank you, Clive." Micah accepted his key before moving to the car.

Micah opened the door for her, helped her in, then moved quickly around the vehicle to the driver's side. Sliding in and shutting the door, he started the engine and pulled out into the traffic.

She stared around the car, wondering how safe it was here. Were there "pests" in the car as well?

His chuckle drew her gaze back to him.

"I can almost read your expression." His smile was quick, warm. "The car is safe, sweet."

"How do you know?" she asked. "It's been parked in a public garage."

"Locked, secured, and under the eagle eye of Nik's camera," he told her. "We rigged enough security to ensure we didn't have any surprises."

"That's good then." The plush interior was comfortable and warm, the car smooth as Micah flicked on the turn signal and headed for the interstate.

"What kind of party has your grandmother arranged?" he asked her then.

"Just a small one," she told him. "She nearly canceled it once she learned I was in danger. She was afraid the same thing would happen to me that happened to Emily."

Her friend Emily. She wanted to cringe when she thought of the older girl. Emily had been with her the night of the kidnapping. Jansen had arranged for Emily's second kidnapping six years before. He'd been determined to acquire her as his own personal pet. It had been during her rescue from that kidnapping that they had learned Jansen was involved. He had died in the cell where Emily had been held.

Such a tangled web of evil, she thought as she watched Micah take the ramp onto the interstate. There had been so many lives that Jansen had affected, so much pain that he had dealt.

He had been the cause of the disappearance and death of Nathan Malone, a friend to the SEALs whose wives had befriended Risa. He had nearly killed Emily and Kell, and only God knew how many other lives he had destroyed. He had been a monster, and the world should have been told what he was, rather than allowing the fictional reputation he had built for himself to stand.

"We're not going to let anything happen to you," Micah promised. "You definitely won't be visiting the ladies' room without plenty of company though."

Emily had been taken through a concealed door in the

ladies' room when she had accompanied Jansen's second wife, who had pretended to be upset and ill.

That woman had been diseased, Risa knew. Risa had spent years seeing the manipulating evil that had filled Jansen's second wife as well as Jansen.

"I think I'll just stay out of the downstairs ladies' room to be certain," Risa told Micah. "I only need to be at the party a few hours; then I can leave. It's just a hundred people, her best friends and their guests, so there shouldn't be any surprises there."

"And unless Orion is intimately acquainted with your grandmother, then we should have no problems," Micah told her as he handled the vehicle through the early evening traffic crush.

"I rather doubt it," she said as she watched the traffic nervously. It was running fast and aggressive as it usually did at this time of the day. If it had been up to Risa, she would have left earlier or later. She hadn't considered the traffic, though, when they left. Her mind had been on other things.

Things such as the erection beneath Micah's jeans, and the flash of a fantasy that had run through her mind. The same fantasy that had followed her into her dreams last night. Her on her knees, his rough, aroused voice telling her to take him into her mouth. How to pleasure him.

She almost shivered, only barely managed to restrain the urge. She wanted that. She wanted to experience everything she could experience with him while he was in her life. And yet there was still the fear. She'd already been with him once, she'd felt his possession, knew he wouldn't hurt her, but the fear was still there, and it wasn't that easy to push out of her head. Because with the fantasies, there was also a mix of the nightmares. They intruded at the worst possible times, reminded her that pain could very well await her.

And she still wasn't certain whether Micah wanted her because he found her desirable or because he felt sorry for her. She knew a man could become hard and could even climax whether he truly desired a woman or not, according to the Internet research she had done the day before while Micah was talking to several members of his team in the kitchen.

One site on military personnel had even stated that adrenaline alone could cause a man to get an erection and after the erection was attained, finding release wasn't that difficult.

"You're thinking too hard?" Micah stated, a question in his voice.

Glancing over at him, she felt a flush mounting in her face before she turned quickly away from him.

"Just quiet," she said, trying to cover her embarrassment.

She was sitting here thinking about his erections while he was driving her to her grandmother's home. Obviously she had little or no self-control, despite the promise to herself that she would force herself to stop focusing on the needs that she couldn't seem to halt.

It hadn't been this bad before Micah, except in her sleep.

"Well now, if that isn't a pretty blush," he crooned, and the sound of his voice was like black velvet. Or black magic. Completely tempting and forbidden. "Maybe you'll tell me what you were thinking about when I get you home this evening."

Home. She cleared her throat and risked another glance at him. There was a hint of a smile at his lips. It made them look even more kissable than before.

"Maybe," she said breathlessly, remembering how he had convinced her to sit in his lap earlier, and the results of it. "You may have a chance at convincing me."

He chuckled. No sooner had the sound left his chest than he tensed. Risa saw his hands clenching on the steering wheel as the car jerked, nearly throwing them into the lane of traffic next to them.

His eyes jerked to the dash, then the road. His hands had a white-knuckled grip on the car as he cursed viciously.

"Hold on," he growled, his voice still calm, the vehicle his attempts to steer it.

Risa felt her heart rise to her throat. It was obvious there was a problem. The car was shuddering, the steering wheel jerking in his grip as he attempted to steer onto the center median.

The car wasn't wanting to be steered. The steering wheel kept jerking to the left as he attempted to pull it to the right. He jerked the gearshift down, tore the parking brake up. There was a scream of tires against the blacktop as the car seemed to jump partially into the opposite lane.

Micah was fighting the wheel as horns blared around him. A black SUV plowed into the side of the car, throwing it back into the lane, then onto the median.

Risa fought the screams rising in her throat as she heard the sound of glass shattering. Her hands were braced against the seat, her fingers digging into the cushioned side as they bumped over a dip a second before the car tilted.

Something hit the back, throwing her into the door as she wondered frantically where the air bags were. Their seat belts were latched securely but weren't protecting Micah from the glass that flew around them as the front end hit a cement barrier and the windshield shattered.

"Micah!" she screamed out his name as the car rocked to a stop, smoke drifting from the engine as he slumped against the seat.

She reached for him, her hands almost touching him when her door was jerked open and hard hands reached for her.

She turned, expecting Nik or Travis, one of the men she had seen from Micah's team. It was a stranger reaching for her. Dark glasses, dark hair. A vehicle was parked too close to the car, doors open as strong hands gripped her arm and pulled at her.

"Micah!" she screamed his name as hysteria began to take over.

She clutched at his arm, her nails digging into the leather of his jacket as she clawed for purchase and fought the hands trying to tear her from the vehicle.

"Micah, wake up!" she screamed as she lost her battle. Those brutal hands grabbed hers, squeezing until she released Micah with a scream of pain.

She was torn from the car with enough force that she slammed to her knees. Scrambling against the grass beneath her, she fought to find her footing, to throw herself back into the car as she screamed out for Micah.

Why wasn't anyone helping? She could hear the horns, the cars passing. She glimpsed the shocked faces as she was lifted by her hair and thrown toward the SUV.

"Micah!" She couldn't let this happen. No one would do this unless it was the man sent to kill her.

She tried to see his face, tried to slap the glasses from it, to identify him. She had to get details. Micah would save her. He would need to know what this man looked like. Micah needed to know who Orion was.

"Bitch!" Her claws raked his face as she fought him, twisting and jerking against his hold, her hands flying out, slapping at him, trying to claw him again.

He was pushing her closer to the SUV. Dragging her by her hair and her arm, trying to throw her inside it. She felt a pinch at her arm and a feral insanity surged through her.

An injection; the bastard had shot something into her arm. Her scream was enraged as she tore as his arm, clawed at his hand, and felt the darkness edging at her vision.

No. No. She couldn't let this happen. She couldn't let him take her. Micah would never forgive himself. She wouldn't have a chance to live if this man got her in that SUV.

"Micah!" She felt herself weakening.

Tears streamed from her eyes as her knees collapsed and the darkness began to swell through her. She felt herself falling, felt her face scrape the grass, and before she lost consciousness, she could have sworn she heard a gunshot.

MICAH CAME BACK to consciousness with Risa's screams ringing in his head. He could hear her terror, the sharp, imperative sound of rage and pain, and he knew in that instant what had happened.

The steering had been sabotaged as well as the brakes. He'd felt the explosion beneath the car a second before everything had gone to hell. He'd almost had a handle on it, almost had them safely out of traffic, when that damned SUV plowed into them.

The air bags hadn't deployed. Somehow they, too, had been deactivated. A gunshot through the back windshield had also taken out the front one, shattering the already-broken window and throwing glass through the car.

Blood filled his vision as he struggled against his seat belt. It took precious seconds to tear his weapon from the pocket of his jacket and too damned long to struggle to lie across the seats where he could glimpse her struggling with the hulking form of a male trying to push her into the black SUV that had pushed them off the interstate.

He couldn't see. He swiped at the blood that smeared over his eyes, but the figures were wavering. His vision was fucked the hell up. He was seeing double for too long. He couldn't tell where she was, and the bastard had her too close. There was no way to fire at the man attempting to take her without possibly hitting her instead.

He had to do something. He pushed himself from the car as he aimed to the side of the assailant and fired. Risa was to his right—well, two Risas. There were two versions of her assailant on the left. Micah fired to the left.

The bastard was still trying to shove her into the SUV.

Micah aimed at the ground and fired again, close to the other man's foot. Had the bastard jerked?

Risa fell from his grip as he jumped into the SUV. The assailant's foot was on the gas before his door was closed and Micah was struggling away from the car.

Where the hell was his backup?

He rolled from the car, catching his weight on his shoulder as he struggled to get to her still form where she had been left, crumpled on the ground.

"Risa!" he choked out her name.

God, had he hit her with that bullet? Had his vision been worse than he thought it was?

He could hear sirens, the sound of brakes, and voices rising as he stumbled to her.

"Risa. Baby." He touched her hair. There was blood on her face, her arm. Her eyes were closed, her body limp.

"Risa. Please. Baby, please." He hunched over her, rabid fury coursing through him as he fought to run his hands over her body, to check for injuries.

She couldn't be hurt, he prayed. He couldn't have shot her. Not Risa. How could he live with himself if he had hurt her, even in his effort to protect her?

Shaking his head, he lifted it, his weapon coming up as a shadow fell over them. Shadows.

"Micah, it's Jordan. Dammit, stand down."

Jordan came to a hard crouch as the other shadows, Nik and Noah, were suddenly there as well.

Micah wiped his arm over his face again, feeling the blood that seeped from his forehead and altered his vision as it dripped into his eyes.

"Is she shot?" he screamed. "I fired. I fired, Jordan. Did I hit her?" His hands ran down her arms, her waist. He couldn't find a wound, but he was terrified to turn her over, too scared he would hurt her worse before help could arrive.

"Ambulance is on its way!" Noah yelled over the sound of sirens approaching. "Son of a bitch, Noah. We could see him jerking at her and couldn't get past those damned cars deadlocked back there. I haven't run that far that fast in my life."

Micah shook his head. Dammit, he couldn't see her clear enough. He couldn't keep the blood out of his eyes.

"Risa," he choked out her name as Jordan began moving her. "Did I hit her? I fired. The bastard almost had her, Jordan. He almost took her."

Control. He was losing control, losing focus. He'd just held her in his lap no more than a few hours ago and given her her first taste of pleasure. There had been a smile on her lips before the world had gone to hell. She had been thinking about him. He'd eased her, gentled her. He couldn't have hurt her.

"I said stand down, Micah!" Jordan's tone was a lash of command. "She's been injected. He broke the skin. Looks like a sedative. She's out cold. No wounds other than surface cuts. Ambulance is here."

Dizzying weakness tore through Micah.

"Noah, ride with her. Make sure." He felt something on his forehead. "Don't leave her alone."

"Dammit, we're not leaving her alone," Jordan cursed. "Hold that on your stubborn-assed head until we get the paramedics over here. Son of a bitch, you're as bad as Noah."

As bad as Noah? Hell no. No one was as bad as Noah when he was wounded. The man was like a kamikaze when he saw his own blood. Unless his wife was around. No, if Bella was there, then he was like a big-assed baby crying for attention. Micah was doing neither.

He lifted Risa against his chest, lowered his head over hers, and whispered a prayer against her forehead. She was okay. He could feel her even breaths. She wasn't struggling to breathe. He let his fingers find her pulse; it was slow but steady.

She had been injected. A sedative. She'd been given a sedative. But she had fought the bastard. Micah had heard her screams; he'd seen her lash out at her assailant's face.

"Fingernails." He lifted his head to find Jordan. "Her fingernails. DNA. She raked his face."

"Good girl!" Jordan exclaimed. "The paramedics are here. I'll have them preserve anything they find. Get ready now, dammit; we have to move her."

Micah's hold tightened on her. He couldn't let her go. He wouldn't be certain she was safe. He had almost failed her once, he couldn't fail her again.

"Dammit, Micah—"

"Jordan, get them in together and fucking let it the hell go," Noah suddenly cursed. "He's not going to let her go."

He wasn't letting her go. He gripped his gun in one hand, his arms wrapped around her as he held her to his chest.

"Get them in the ambulance together. Micah's injuries are worse; she's sedated. You have the power to do it, now do it, and let's get them the hell out of here."

Micah let the argument drift away. He struggled as they lifted Risa onto a stretcher. The paramedic tried to push him back until he found the business end of Micah's weapon in his throat. Micah was pushed into the ambulance with her moments later as he fought to blink the damned blood out of his eyes. Weak but conscious, he let the paramedic check the head wound, Micah's gun held carefully at the side of his leg as he heard Jordan in the front of the ambulance barking out orders to the driver.

Hell, this was going to screw with the op, Micah knew. Hopefully Orion had run far and fast when he realized that Micah was shooting at him and others were running for the wreck.

He might not know that the people running for them were members of an operational team. Jordan could cover this, and he would, to the best of his ability. He was already directing the ambulance to a private clinic rather than the public hospital.

That would work. The paramedics would be briefed before they could leave with whatever story Jordan was cooking up in his head. Jordan was damned good at lies. It was what made him a helluva team leader. He got things done. He fixed things.

"How is she?" Micah turned to the paramedic as he finished radioing their stats to the clinic.

"She's out like a light."

Micah had his first look at the medical tech. He was older, possibly in his forties. His gray eyes were concerned, his expression confident. He was a man who had pretty much seen it all. He didn't seem fazed.

"How's your vision?" He held up two fingers.

"You have two fingers up, three down. One head and two eyes," Micah growled. "When we arrive at the clinic, stay the hell out of my way. Where she goes, I go."

"I got that part when you pushed that gun into my face," the paramedic grunted. "Don't worry, man; we're not standing in your way."

"Two minutes," Jordan called back to him. "Doctors are waiting at the entrance. Stay the hell out of their way, Micah, while they get her prepped and examined. Don't make me knock you the hell out."

Micah grunted. "Where she goes, I go. Period."

Jordan was cursing.

"She must be damned important to you," the paramedic murmured. "That's one dude I wouldn't want to mess with."

"She's important." She was more important than Micah had let himself believe until he'd seen her struggling with the man he knew had to be Orion.

He could have lost her. Not just his opportunity to take Orion down, but he could have lost Risa. Her smile. Hell, he hadn't heard her laugh yet. He could have lost her wonder at each touch they shared. He could have lost the fragile sense of warmth he was beginning to feel with her when he had never felt it with another woman.

WHERE HAD HE messed up? Orion was almost screaming in pain from the bullet that had torn into his foot as he'd tried to shove that little bitch into the SUV.

Who knew that the man riding with her was carrying a gun? Orion knew he should have found a way to get into their apartment and check out the unknown lover before making this attempt. He had argued with his employer that it was too soon to make the attempt. He needed to be certain; he needed to check out the new lover before he made his move.

His employer had refused to listen. It had to be done quickly, before she remembered anything more.

Orion groaned in pain as he turned the SUV off the interstate and looked for a quick place to stash it, and for another to steal for long enough to get him to a safe area where he could treat the gunshot wound and get a cab back to the apartment he had taken.

He'd tried several times to slip into Risa Clay's apartment since the bugs had been swept up by the housecleaning crew.

It happened sometimes. To get what he needed, he had to use electronics that were sometimes easy to sweep away. He'd thought he was safe with the lightbulb camera, but the cleaning crew had changed the bulbs as well.

It should have been simple, should have been easy to sneak back in and replace the bugs. Except they never fucking left the apartment. In three days, not once had they ventured out, and his employer had called daily.

Orion knew better than to let that son of a bitch rush him. This was the same reason Jansen Clay had fucked up and ended up dead, because he had allowed this man to rush him, to force him into readjusting his schedule. Jansen had paid the ultimate price for allowing himself to be bullied.

Orion had almost paid it.

Hell, he was too old for this shit. He should have retired six years ago instead of waiting. No, what he should have done was killed the son-of-a-bitch partner Jansen Clay had for being so stupid. He wouldn't have had to make that hit six years ago, and he wouldn't have had to take this job, either.

Because the only man who knew his identity would have been dead.

CHAPTER 12

FOUR HOURS LATER, Risa was still unconscious. Micah sat beside her bed, watching her closely, gauging the time as the monitors tracked her vitals.

Jordan was at the foot of the bed. Outside her private room the rest of the team was placed in strategic positions to watch the door as well as anyone who entered the clinic.

Noah, Jordan, and Nik had been several cars behind them. With the confusion that had ensued when Micah and Risa's vehicle had been run off the road, they had been back too far for immediate help.

They had been close enough to see Orion, though. Dark glasses that covered most of the upper face, dark hair, broad build, older. It wasn't a lot to go on.

Beneath Risa's nails had been torn flesh, though, enough that Micah was confident they could collect the DNA from it.

He ran his hand wearily over his lower jaw before rubbing at the back of his neck and continued to watch Risa closely.

This was the first time a victim had escaped from Orion. How long she stayed under and how she awoke would answer some important questions for them.

Micah had lied to her when he told her that he wanted Orion because a friend's mother had died. It hadn't been a friend's mother; it had been his own. It wasn't a friend's father who had thrown himself at a suicide bomber. It had been Micah's. And it hadn't been a friend who had managed to track Orion to that freighter. It had been Micah. And there he had learned Orion had friends. Somehow information had leaked from the Mossad to Orion, and the bastard had been waiting for Micah.

Orion's bullet had grazed his head as he threw himself from the freighter into the waters off Israel's shores. He would have drowned if a SEAL team hadn't been practicing in those waters and heard the gunshot.

If the team commander hadn't notified Jordan of the nearly dead Mossad agent they had rescued, Micah wondered which way would his life have gone. Would he have done the same as his father? Realized that whoever Orion was working for had enough ties to his government that eventually he would have been killed either way?

Micah had realized as the waters closed over his head that night that the investigation his mother had been involved in hadn't been sanctioned. She had been told to let it go, that the rumors were just that, rumors. Ariela Abijah had ignored that directive, and she had died for her efforts.

Orion had destroyed Micah's life as he had known it, and Micah was determined to destroy Orion. When this mission had first begun, nothing had mattered to Micah but catching Orion. He'd never imagined that in a few short days, saving the girl would become more important.

"I need skin tags," he told Jordan, speaking of the small skin-colored discs that housed a one-time-use electronic tracker. "Match them to her skin tone. I also want a bracelet, something simple that she can wear daily, with a GPS chip set in it that activates remotely. I don't want anything that could trip an electronic detector if he has one."

"Orion strips jewelry from the body," Jordan pointed out. "He also washes them down before they awaken. A skin tag won't work if it's wet."

"Jewelry and clothes are always found close to where he's taken them, normally in the same room where they're killed. Only once did he take a personal effect. That being the Star of David that Ariela Abijah wore," Micah argued. "Cell phones and electronics are disposed of on the way." He turned and stared back at Jordan fiercely. "He almost took her, Jordan. She would have been defenseless if he had gotten her into that SUV. I can't risk it happening again."

He had been so certain he could keep her safe. That with him, as well as the team for backup, there was no way Orion could get to her. And he'd been wrong.

"Has Nik figured out how he got to the car?"

Jordan shook his head. "He's back at the apartment going over the camera feed now. He hasn't found anything yet."

"We have to assume he's guessed that there's the possibility that this is now an operation." He breathed out roughly. That was going to make protecting her harder. "We need to contact the informant, see if he has any information."

"Travis is working on that." Jordan nodded. "We should have something within the next twelve hours."

"They're always awake when he slices their wrists," Micah said quietly. "Tox reports on the victims suggest he kills them within an hour of consciousness. His drug of choice has always been GHB. He wouldn't want to waste too much time. Get them where he's going to kill them, time to strip and wash the body, another hour, then perhaps thirty minutes to an hour before they awaken. He'd give himself enough time that they wouldn't awaken before he has them chained."

"He has medical knowledge then," Jordan stated.

Micah nodded at that. "At least enough medical knowledge to know how to adjust the drug; otherwise he'd kill them. That shit is too dangerous to mess with blind."

His fingers curled over the metal bar at the side of the mattress as rage threatened to burn through him. He'd promised that he would protect her. He'd given her his word, built her trust. And she had nearly been taken.

He reached out and touched her hair, just her hair, tucking it gently behind her ear. The weight of her hair behind her ear seemed to comfort her when she was nervous. It was a habit he found completely charming.

This woman had fascinated him over the past four years. Even though he had only known who she was, had only glimpsed her coming or going from Emily's, Raven's, or Morganna's homes, still she had drawn him. The knowledge of her courage, her strength, had always astounded him. He'd seen it in her face, in her eyes, each time he glimpsed her. In the stubborn set of her chin, the straight line of her shoulders. She'd been through hell, but she was a survivor, and she was determined to show the world exactly what she was made of.

There was such beauty in her courage. As though it were a light that shone from inside her, that beauty radiated over every inch of her.

She was a woman of strength. Such strength held a beauty that was all its own. It was a beauty he found irresistible in Risa.

"We'll carry on as though this were a botched attempt and you're a concerned lover. We'll use a private security firm to take you to and from the outings you have planned, and give Orion the impression you've hired a bodyguard because of the attempted kidnapping. We'll maintain your cover as a SEAL and work from there. If we play this as we started, then he may suspect an op, but he won't find proof of one."

Micah touched her hair again. "He doesn't flinch at the thought of going against an agent or agencies," he said softly. "Ariela was Mossad. Her husband was CIA and her son was Mossad. He doesn't worry about possible ops or complications."

"According to our source, his employer is pushing him hard as well," Jordan murmured. "We and our contact suspect the employer knows his identity. That's going to make him sloppy, Micah. Keep your mind on the operation we have here, not the woman. She's secondary."

His head jerked up. The rage burning inside him became a conflagration that threatened to burn into his soul.

"She is not secondary. Ever," he snarled. "Mark my words, Jordan, you risk her further than she's already being risked and you'll have a rogue on your hands. I won't tolerate it."

Jordan grimaced furiously. "Son of a bitch," he hissed. "I knew you were losing your head over her. You can't do that, Micah. When the mark becomes more important than the operation, shit happens. We saw that with Noah when that militia kidnapped his wife. Keep your head on straight or we'll lose Orion and Risa. None of us want that."

"I will not lose Risa to that bastard," he ground out between clenched teeth. "Get the items I asked for. I want her apartment checked again, now. If he managed to get more bugs installed during the commotion, then I'll move her. But mark my words, Jordan, he won't take her." *From me.* Micah bit off the words. He couldn't risk even the thought of such possessiveness toward her.

She was a woman of strength and courage. Such women should be protected at all times when they couldn't protect themselves.

"Everything is in place, I'll have the items you need," Jordan assured him. "But you better get a handle on those emotions, Micah. I thought I could trust the lack of emotion you've always displayed. Especially where women are concerned. You're going to make me start wishing I had put John in her bed instead."

Micah stared back at Jordan, knowing his emotions were throwing a kink in the cold, logical operation they were working within. At no time before had his emotions ever been displayed. He'd been cold, hard. Even before Orion had destroyed his life, Micah had known to protect his soul. Somehow, Risa had managed to break through that barrier, and now she held a part of him that he wasn't familiar with.

"Try to put another agent with her and we'll all regret it," he stated harshly.

Jordan's lips parted to speak when a choked cry drew his and Micah's gaze back to Risa.

Her eyes were open. Her face was sheet-white now, her body tense, her expression still dazed but bordering on complete horror.

Her gaze swung from Jordan to Micah. Micah had never seen such fear in anyone's eyes in his life.

"I want to get out of this bed."

Risa hadn't known such complete horror since her incarceration at the clinic where Jansen Clay had placed her eight years before, after the SEALs had rescued her, Emily, and Carrie from Diego Fuentes's cells. Risa had been unconscious during the rescue. But when she awoke, she'd been strapped to a bed, drugged, groggy. For nearly two years she had remained in a state of sedated hell.

She'd been sedated again. She could feel the grogginess, the inability to function as she wanted to, and it terrified her. Adrenaline began racing through her body, making the effects of the sedative worse. She felt the haze in her mind, the panic fighting to overcome it, and the knowledge that she couldn't help herself. She couldn't fight it. She had to get away from him, and she couldn't make her body move.

The scent of disinfectant wrapped around her senses, threatening to force her to throw up. She could feel the cramps in her stomach, the fear that battled with her efforts to make sense of what was going on.

Micah was with her. He wouldn't let her be harmed, she reminded herself. He'd promised to protect her.

"Risa?" Micah tucked a heavy strand of hair behind her ear as his thumb caressed her cheek. "Do you remember the wreck?"

She nodded quickly. She remembered it in that fuzzy, out-of-this-world way. "I remember it all. Now get me out of here."

She saw the look he exchanged with Jordan. God, they were going to make her stay. They couldn't make her stay.

His lips parted to speak.

"Micah, I can't function here," she rasped, breathing roughly. "Please don't make me try. I know I was drugged. I remember the wreck and the man trying to force me into his vehicle. I remember the injection. I know I'm safe." Her voice broke on a sob. "Don't make me stay here."

It was a hospital. It was filled with doctors who would lie to her and slide the needle into her arm no matter what she wanted. There were nurses who only followed orders, and who stepped away when they were told to.

She couldn't separate the present from the past. Bleak, black memories of the sedated hell she had lived within for nearly two years washed over her again.

A hard hand gripping her arm. The flesh was soft, so soft, but the hand was thick and heavy. A male hand. A needle punching into her arm, anger in his voice.

You should kill her and have done with it, the voice whispered through her mind. A cultured voice, almost foreign. It resonated with superiority and condescending hatefulness. *She's a weakness we can't afford.*

A man doesn't kill his own child. That had been Jansen's reply. *No matter how dismally ugly she is. For the moment she's of use to me. And to you. We need to know if your drug works.*

The drug was horrifying.

Risa shook her head, fighting against the memories as Micah's voice drew her back to the present. Something about staying, about letting the doctors check her.

She shook her head desperately.

"I'll be fine." She had to get out of here before the past overcame her and left her screaming in horror. "Get me out of here, Micah. Now. I can't bear it."

She watched his expression tighten for a moment as he stared down at her. There was a battle waging in his eyes, and she was terrified she was going to come out on the losing end of whatever he was considering.

"Micah." Her hand tightened on his wrist as she struggled to push away the fog wrapping around her senses. "I can't . . ." Her voice caught on a sob, and she hated that. "Please, don't make me stay."

Fear clawed at her stomach, sucked the oxygen from her lungs, and made it hard to breathe.

"Jordan, have the car brought around," he suddenly decided.

"Micah, she's in no shape to leave," Jordan protested quietly. "The doctor needs to examine her. We need to be certain she's not going to have a reaction to the drug she was given."

"Please," she whispered. "Don't make me stay."

He had sworn he would protect her, that he wouldn't let her

be hurt. She trusted him. The very fact that she wasn't locked in hysteria attested to her trust in him. But she knew if he didn't take her out of here, she would never trust him again. The knowledge of it seared inside her brain. She couldn't exist here, not even for another moment.

"Have the fucking car brought around," he ordered again as he tucked the sheet around her, then bent and eased his arms around her.

Risa wrapped her arms around his neck, buried her face in his shoulder, and fought the tears that wanted to fall. She shuddered as the scent of disinfectant disappeared. She could smell Micah now. His scent, warm and male, wrapping around her as he removed her from the room.

The sheet protected her against the chill that would have penetrated the hospital gown. His body heat seeped into her, wrapped around her, and eased the almost mind-numbing horror that threatened her sanity.

There were protests. She could hear the nurses, perhaps a doctor.

"She'll be looked after," Micah snarled to someone. "You are no longer required, Doctor."

She heard the swish of the door, felt the cool night air as it bit into the thin covering, then, seconds later, more warmth as Micah bent and moved into a car.

Her arms tightened around him.

"It's okay," he whispered against the top of her hair. "Jordan had a limo standing by. You're safe. Trust me, Risa. It's okay."

It was okay. Her mind was still groggy; the sedative she had been given made it so hard to think. She knew it was a sedative; she remembered it from the clinic. Strangely, she remembered the doctor arguing with her father over his choice of drug.

"Same thing," she whispered against Micah's shoulder. "The sedative. The same thing Jansen ordered at the clinic."

He stiffened against her. "Are you certain?"

She nodded. "I know how it feels."

She knew because the doctor at the asylum had always put her on another sedative after her father left. One that didn't cloud her mind so much, one that allowed her to retain memories, impressions of what was going on.

"I'll get on that, Micah," Jordan said. "We'll know exactly what the sedative was within twelve hours. It takes a while to complete those tests on the blood."

She shook her head. She knew the name of the drug. It was on the tip of her tongue. She remembered Jansen talking about it once.

"We have her records from the clinic as well as the hospital she was taken to after her rescue from there." Micah's voice drifted through her mind. "It should be in there."

"The drug they found in her system after her rescue from the clinic isn't the same," Jordan stated. "I already questioned the doctor tonight concerning that. The drug that was found in her system from the clinic was milder."

"Not always." Risa had to force the words past her lips, but it was getting easier to think, easier to make sense of what was going on around her, though she was still groggy. She would be groggy for a while.

"What do you mean, 'Not always'?" Micah asked.

She breathed in, out, tried to force her mind to clear enough to tell him.

"The doctor." Her voice was halting, a little slurred. "When Jansen wasn't scheduled in. He changed the sedative. The other, it would damage me, he said. He didn't want to damage me. Jansen didn't care."

She was still locked in that in-between place. Not really here, not really there.

"You had halperidol in your system when you were taken from the clinic," Micah said.

Risa nodded. "GHB before Jansen's visits." She frowned; why hadn't she remembered that before? "He injected me with GHB." She knew what GHB was. "The doctor called it GHB. Said he could kill me with it."

She heard their voices in her head, insidious whispers she couldn't escape. Jansen's laughter, the doctor's concern. And she heard the other man. Snide, his voice imperious but with an underlying accent.

"Don't take me back, Micah," she whispered, feeling the grogginess becoming darkness. "Don't let them touch me."

"I have you, Risa." His arms tightened further around her. "I have you."

She drifted off into that never-never land, aware of the tension that had invaded Micah's body. She would ask him about it later, she told herself. If she remembered.

Jordan stared at that girl in Micah's arms, aware of the way the agent held her, the possessiveness in his hold and in his eyes.

"Ariela Abijah was given GHB," Jordan said, watching Micah, knowing the tender spot he was pressing. Ariela had been Micah's mother, a woman of rare strength in Jordan's eyes. He'd met her once, just once, and she had impressed him when it was hard for anyone to do so.

"Orion always uses GHB," Micah said, his voice bleak. "It's easy to find, impossible to trace."

"She knows the difference." He nodded to Risa. "The doctor suspected it might be GHB from his initial tests."

"She came out of it early." Micah smoothed his hand down her arm as Jordan watched.

Hell, another perfect agent shot in the fucking heart, he thought. His Elite Operational Unit was going to hell in a handbasket. First Noah, now Micah? God help them all if John or Travis decided to bite the love bullet.

"How do you know she came out of it early?" Jordan questioned Micah.

"She drifted off again," he stated. "She would have never done that if she wasn't still under the influence of the drug. She would have fought it. I'd say six- to eight-hour dosage is what she was given. The tests on her blood should come back with that answer. That means he's most likely got a hole outside of Atlanta somewhere, perhaps further. The SUV had tinted windows. He could have dumped her in the back and gone for at least four hours before he had to get her secured. He has this planned down to the last second, from kidnapping to death. He'd be living close now that he can't depend on the bugs he had in the apartment. He took a chance today. He's being pushed to finish this and he's making mistakes."

"Then he'll make more before it's over with," Jordan decided with a nod. "He'll be pissed now. We'll get a plan together and get started on it."

He watched Micah closely. The other man didn't nod, he didn't agree. That was a damned bad sign. It meant that at any moment Risa Clay could end up on the missing persons list and only one man would know where to find her. The man who had claimed her.

Ex-fucking-Mossad-agent. Bastards. He'd never met a harder, more cunning agent than those the Mossad produced. Problem was with such men, once they lost their minds to a woman, then they were worse than lions protecting a cub. You took your life in your hands if you dared to endanger that woman.

Micah had that look. Noah had that look when his Sabella, or Bella, as most knew her. Yeah, that was the problem with hard-core black agents. They were only black until some damned female came around and decided to light up their friggin' lives.

Jordan pushed his fingers through his hair and started considering alternatives to each plan that he knew faced them. He'd have to make certain Risa wasn't just protected but had a damned bulletproof bubble around her; otherwise Micah would fight him.

He could enforce any plan he wanted to use. It would be simple enough to have Micah jerked off the unit during this op and replaced.

He rejected that idea quickly enough. He could jerk the agent off the case, but as Micah had warned him, he'd turn rogue. Risa would disappear and with her would go one of the best damned agents to be found on the face of the earth. Nope, that one wouldn't work at all.

"She remembered the wreck," Jordan suddenly pointed out as the thought tripped in his brain. "GHB affects memory and perception. She shouldn't have remembered."

"She shouldn't have remembered her rape or the fact that

her own father gave her to the bastard that hurt her." Micah cursed. "She remembered it. That was the reason why he had her placed in the private asylum. He was there when she first awoke, she remembered, and he kept her drugged and out of the way so she couldn't reveal what he was."

"Damned strange," Jordan pointed out. "Even Emily Stanton didn't remember exactly what had happened until after Jansen kidnapped her again. It took a catalyst, and full memory still hasn't returned. According to the psychologist, Risa's memories are amazingly intact."

"Intact enough that someone wants to die by striking out at her," Micah stated, his voice harder, colder, than before and savage enough that it pierced the fog that still wrapped around Risa's head.

She could hear them. She could feel Micah's tension, hear the murder in his voice when he spoke of the doctor her father had brought to the clinic with him. The doctor hadn't liked coming. He'd been angry. Her father had laughed at him, because he'd forced him to come, to inject her with what he called his creation. But the creation hadn't worked as they'd wanted it to somehow. It had been painful. And each time Jansen arrived, Risa had tried to fight to get from the bed, to get away from them.

She knows me. The voice crackled in her head. *She can identify me.*

She'd looked at him. Looked straight at him. But her vision was foggy; her mind was drugged, slow. Who was he? If she knew him, she should recognize his voice; she should know him if she saw him again.

"I know him," she whispered against Micah's chest.

Silence filled her head then.

"I can identify him." She felt Micah's arms tighten around her. "His hands are so soft. Like a baby. Such large hands, big and scarred. But his palms are so soft. . . ." She felt as though she was drifting away and fought to rise back to consciousness. Whatever she knew, Micah needed to know; she understood that. "But I can't see his face," she sighed. "I'm so sleepy, I can't see his face. . . ." Her voice trailed away.

Micah wanted to curse. He laid his forehead against hers and clenched his eyes closed for a long moment before he touched his lips to her forehead.

Strength. He could hear the strength in her voice. She was trapped somewhere between memory and reality, and she was fighting to remember both. He knew the effects of the drug, knew that the rare few whom it didn't totally work on were tormented by the distant quality of their memories.

She was strong enough to fight it, just as she had been strong enough to fight Orion when he'd attempted to take her. Strong enough that when she had awakened in the clinic, she had held on to her control, fought back her hysteria, and remained coherent.

"I want him dead," Micah whispered against her brow before lifting his head to stare back at Jordan. "I'll kill that bastard that helped Jansen Clay myself."

"To kill him, you have to identify him," Jordan pointed out, infuriating him. "We have to take Orion alive if we're going to identify anyone, Micah. You know that."

His lips thinned as he lifted Risa closer and watched the lights of the city as they headed back to her apartment rather than the hotel he would have preferred. John had checked the apartment; it was bug-free. The team was watching the corridor that led to her home, and two men were stationed in her room. Nik was still working on the surveillance tapes from the parking garage and trying to figure out how Orion had gotten past their defenses on the car.

They were close; Micah could feel it. Orion had made his first mistake. They now had his DNA and they had more of Risa's memories than ever before.

Almost there, Micah thought, stroking his hand down her back. They would have Orion, and when they had him, they would have his employer. Just a little longer, then Risa would be safe.

And when she was safe, he would walk out of her life and leave her to the future she deserved. One where she could name her dreams and go after them. Where she would know no more fear, no more danger.

She would be safe.

He would ensure she was always protected and he would start, he thought, by attempting to get her out of this game immediately. At this point he could have her sent to a safe house. There was always the chance that if Orion didn't see her coming or going from the apartment, he would suspect she was hiding inside and make a move for her when he thought Micah was away. Moving her to a safe house would ensure that her life, her dreams, survived.

But a woman couldn't have dreams with a dead man, he reminded himself. And Micah Sloane was no more than a borrowed name for a man who had died years ago.

David Abijah no longer existed. He had signed away his soul for vengeance. He had lost the right to dream.

Chapter 13

SHE WAS GOING to die of arousal.

Risa stared up at the ceiling as she brought herself awake, aware that her fingers were pushing beneath the loose band of her pajama bottoms, in the process of searching for her own satisfaction as she fought to pull herself out of the explicit, rousing dream that had filled her head while she slept.

She turned her head slowly, biting her lip as she made out the outline of Micah sleeping beside her. He lay on his back, one arm thrown over his head, the sheet pushed to his waist.

His breathing deep and even, he was clearly asleep. His hard abs and chest lifted rhythmically, his breathing heavy and deep. The darkness loved his body. It shadowed it, washed over it, and made him appear even larger, sexier, than he already was.

She wanted to touch him. Her hands trembled with the need, her fingers shaking as she curled them against her stomach to restrain the need.

She was worse than a nymphomaniac, she charged herself in an attempt to shame herself from watching him while he slept.

Her libido was cheering the accusation. God, she couldn't remember ever being so damned turned on. Not even the night she had humiliated herself in his bed had she been this hot.

She was going to get out of bed and change her panties if she didn't do something.

Think about something else. Something completely non-sexy. She couldn't think of a damned thing outside the need to touch him.

Root canal. Deeply rooted survival instincts kicked in with that one. But hell, she had never had a root canal; how was that supposed to help?

She turned slowly on her side, inching around until she stared more easily at his gorgeous body. And it was gorgeous. All hard muscle and male grace. She wanted to flow over him and lick every inch of his body.

She was so demented, perverted, she told herself as she reached out, wondering if just a little touch would wake him up. Just to feel his flesh. The warmth of it against her palm.

She kept it safe. After all, she didn't want to feel as though she were molesting him in his sleep. But dammit, he was in her bed. This was her bed, and he was pretending to be her lover.

Her pussy clenched violently at the thought of Micah as her lover. The memory of the night he had actually taken her slammed into her mind, and she almost moaned at the need that raced through her.

Her trembling fingers touched his abs, against the narrow band of hair that ran below the sheet. It was silky, warm. The flesh beneath seemed to flex, and her gaze jerked to his face.

His eyes were still closed. His breathing was still slow and easy. She didn't have the nerve to check his heartbeat, to see if it was slow and easy or thundering, as she knew it did when he was aroused.

Or did she?

Her fingers were moving, sliding up his chest, her heart in her throat as the hard, heavy beat echoed against her palm before she ever reached her chest.

Her eyes closed for a long second. When she opened them, her gaze slid from her hand, down his stomach, to the tenting of the sheet that covered his thighs. She could see his cock, hard and heavy beneath the light material, stretching along his lower stomach and sending a pulse of pure lust burning through her veins.

He was awake. She knew he was; she could feel it. Every muscle in his body was tighter now. Lifting her gaze, she looked up to his face again and saw the glitter of his black eyes through the narrowed veil of his lashes.

He didn't say a word. She watched as he swallowed, his lips parting to breathe.

God, she wanted. Just one more time. He tortured her by sleeping in her bed with him. Some nights he rolled against her; most nights he was touching her. Was she supposed to resist? Was she supposed to be a stone-cold robot that didn't ache? That didn't need?

"I'm sorry," she whispered, suddenly embarrassed, ashamed of the needs that rode her so fiercely that she would touch him in his sleep.

Her hand moved to lift away from him, only to find itself caught between his body and his hand. She stared at his hand as it covered hers, watched wide-eyed as he used his hand to push hers down, along his stomach. She swallowed tightly, almost whimpering as the sheet drew away from his thighs and he was curling her fingers around the thick, heavy shaft of his cock.

She moaned then. The sound that left her throat shocked her at the hunger in it.

"I'm sorry," she whispered again, even as her fingers curled around the pulsing flesh. "Oh God, Micah. I don't know what to do. I don't know how." Her breath hitched as she fought back a sob.

"Nothing you need to know." His voice was rough, hard. "My body is yours, Risa. Know only that. However you wish to touch it, wherever. Whatever you need, you have only to ask, love, and I'll provide it."

She wanted to cry. She wanted to scream with frustration as she fought to breathe. A part of her wanted to demand that he just fuck her and get it over with, to drive the need out of her so she could think again. Another part of her didn't want to rush a single moment. She wanted the memory. She wanted everything.

Her hand stroked down the shaft, watching the thick crested

cock head as it throbbed and glistened with moisture. Heavy veins pulsed beneath the flesh as it flexed in her grip, erect and powerful.

"I wish I knew," she whispered painfully. "Knew what to do."

"What do you *want* to do?" His voice was low, a part of the darkness, a part of the shadows that loved his body. "Tell me, and I'll help you. I'll guide you through whatever you want of me."

"Anything?"

"Anything, Risa." His voice sounded thicker, filled with lust and hunger. "There's no shame between us, baby. Only pleasure. Only the pleasure you want."

Only the pleasure she wanted. As though still locked within her dream, she let the sensuality, the sexuality, of the moment wash over her.

She rose, moved the sheet back, and moved from the bed. Feeling his gaze on her, she pulled off the long shirt she wore to bed, then shimmied out of the pajama bottoms and panties she had put on after her shower.

She was naked. Cool air washed over her body as a shudder of heat raced through it. She could feel the caress of his eyes, watched his body flex and shift as he lifted his hand to her.

Silently Risa took his hand, shaking as she moved to her knees on the bed, one hand pulling back from him to touch his hard chest, the other, his hard abs.

"I can do anything," she whispered, almost to herself, as she let her hand run down his body to grip the fiercely erect flesh of his cock again.

"Yes," the breath seemed to hiss from his lips. "Anything, Risa. Take what belongs to you."

What belonged to her. Had anything ever belonged to her? She couldn't remember if it had, but this strong, powerful man was giving her his body, however she needed to use it.

"I want." She swallowed tightly, lifting her gaze back to his. "I want to taste you, Micah."

She wanted his cock in her mouth. She wanted to suck it, taste it; she wanted to feel him throbbing between her lips.

She wanted to let free the sexual creature she could feel building inside her.

Whore's Dust or lust, she didn't know; she didn't care. All she knew was that it was only for this man. Only Micah made her hunger until she was dying for him; only Micah made her brave enough to try to reach out for what she wanted.

"Then taste me," he crooned. "Taste me, love, and when you're finished, I'll take my turn and taste you."

Risa swayed as she felt the punch of response that seemed to fill her pussy. The bare lips were already slick, wet, but more of her juices coated them now as the need for his lips against her flesh rocked through her.

"I dream of your tongue against the head of my cock," his voice whispered through the night as she moved to him. "Watching you between my thighs, your head lowering as you hold the shaft steady with your hand. Your tongue peeking out, licking over it."

She followed his hushed voice. Moving between his spread thighs, she gripped the stiff, heavy flesh at the base as his shaft rose toward her lips.

"You're beautiful," he groaned, reaching out to push her hair back over her shoulder. "Let me watch, sweet. Let me see you licking that taste of me from the head."

Micah was nearly insane with lust now. How he managed to lie still and not rush her, he didn't know. Never had he thought his patience would be tested to this extent, that his self-control would ever attempt to break so easily.

Her tongue was like a stroke of fire over the broad head of his cock. The too-sensitive flesh jerked with the pleasure, causing her head to lift in alarm.

"It's okay," he groaned. "It's pleasure, Risa. See how I enjoy your touch, sweet? Even my cock trembles for want of you."

A tentative smile seemed to touch her lips for just a second before her head lowered again and he was forced to bite back a shout of pure ecstasy. Heated and damp, her tongue licked over him, then curled beneath the crest, rubbing against the super-sensitive flesh beneath the head. It was exquisite. Never had a woman's touch felt so damned good.

"So good." He had to clench his teeth over the words, it was so damned hot. "Sweet Risa."

He was nearly panting as she licked, rubbed. Then, her lips slid over the head of his cock, taking it into her mouth and tightening as she began to suckle it tentatively.

He couldn't bear it. His hands fisted in the sheets beneath him. Her innocent caresses and tentative sucks were making him crazy.

"Lick," he gasped. "Use your tongue, baby, as you suck. Ah fuck." He nearly lost it as she applied her tongue in just the right spot, just below the flared head. She rubbed with her inquisitive little tongue, sucked with her hot, damp mouth, and his head nearly exploded.

"Ah, Risa," he groaned. "Cup my balls, baby. The sac is tight; roll them slow and easy. Let your fingers play, baby." He could barely get the words out.

He was teaching her each move that destroyed his self-control and he knew it. That pure eroticism of the moment was destroying her. He was teaching his lover all she didn't know. Complete innocence was reflected in her pretty face, in the gleam of her eyes. Hunger and curiosity lit her expression. The combination was erotic. Sexier than anything he had ever known.

Her moan vibrated around his flesh and he had to clench his teeth, fist his hands, and tighten every muscle in his body to keep from spilling between her lips. Lips that were stretched around the throbbing head of his cock, a hot little tongue that caught the spurt of impending release that slipped his control.

He couldn't do this. His body was straining, pushed to the limit as her nimble, gentle fingers played with his balls. Sweat popped up on his body, ran down his temple. He felt tortured on a rack of flames that was ecstasy and hell combined.

"Risa, sweet," he groaned, his hips jerking involuntarily against her mouth, driving his cock deeper. He wanted to fuck her. He wanted to bury every hard inch of his dick as deep as he could get inside her.

She moaned against him again, sank her mouth deeper on him, and he hissed in extreme pleasure. Have mercy on him, her virginal mouth was driving him crazy. Never had he had such a hair trigger with a woman. And he couldn't make her stop. He couldn't come yet, not yet; her mouth was still on him, and she was fucking enjoying him.

It was in her face, her expression, in the gleam of her eyes as she risked a glance at him. She was enjoying every lick, every suck, every stroke of her fingers against his flesh, and no doubt the feminine part of her knew she was fracturing defenses and shields he had spent a lifetime developing.

His hips surged again. He felt his balls tighten further, felt the rush of electric heat that raced up his spine.

"Risa, baby," he groaned. "I have a limit here. I'm going to come in that sweet mouth if we keep this up."

He watched her face, her eyes, and had to shake his head to fight back the urge to spurt inside her hot mouth then and there. Her expression became drowsier, hungrier, as her eyes gleamed in excitement.

Her mouth moved more firmly on his flesh, tightened; her tongue rubbed and stroked.

He couldn't do this, he told himself desperately. Coming in her mouth wasn't part of the deal. It was an intimacy she wasn't ready for yet. It was one he couldn't force on her. She had no idea—

"Fuck!" His hands flashed out, gripped her hair. His control was shattering. He could feel the pulse of release building in his balls, surging into his dick. "Risa," he breathed out roughly. "Baby. You're not ready for this."

He tried to pull her head back from the throbbing shaft. His fingers tightened in her hair and she moaned. Her tongue rubbed faster, her mouth sucked, and he was gone.

Never had control shattered so easily beneath a woman's mouth. Micah came when he was ready to come, not when his cock made the decision. But tonight Risa's sweet mouth was pushing him over the edge and making the decision for him.

"Risa." His voice was raspy, the protest faint as her tongue swirled around his cock head. "Sweet, I'm going to come. I can't hold back." His hips tightened, arched. "Fuck. Risa!"

Risa tightened her mouth on the throbbing head of his

cock and sucked him deeper, as deep as she could take him. Her tongue flickered over the little slit in the top of the crest; her fingers rubbed against his ball sac. She wanted his release. She wanted to taste him, luxuriate in him. She wanted to hold this part of him forever.

The harsh gasp he gave of her name was a warning. She wasn't letting go; she wasn't losing this. God knew she might never get her courage up for this again.

His hands tightened in her hair and the prickling at her scalp was another pleasure. His cock head throbbed again, a hard, violent flex of the flesh; then the first spurt of semen shot into her mouth.

The taste was dark, salty, sexy. Risa moaned around the taste and took more. Her mouth worked over the pulsing head as the male flavor filled her senses and sent flames rocking through her body. She took all he had to give, swallowing, drawing more to her eager tongue, and loving the shudders that tore through his body, the grip of his hands in her hair.

He was lost in his release. She could feel it; she gloried in it. Her femininity rose with a victorious shout as she moaned in rising excitement as the last pulse shot to her tongue.

He was strong, powerful, and in that moment Risa felt herself claiming him. Her heart, her soul. Parts of her she hadn't known existed rose inside her. Feminine, filled with an inner strength that she barely recognized. She lifted her head, licked her lips, and watched as he lifted his dark lashes and stared back at her.

Her hands rose, flattened on her belly, and moved up until she was cupping her swollen breasts, touching her hard nipples. She felt empowered. As though another woman lived within her body now.

"You're dangerous," he growled, his hands reaching for her.

"I'm yours," she whispered, feeling his hands cover hers, his fingers working hers against the sensitive flesh of her breasts.

"All mine," he agreed, rising, sitting up, his lips moving between her breasts. "Come to me; be mine, Risa. For this night, all mine."

Forever.

Her head tipped back as he pulled her hand from a breast. His lips covered the tight peak, sucking her inside with a hungry groan as she tightened in his arms and cried out his name.

She could feel that caress over her entire body. Her hand moved to the back of his head. Her other hand caressed her own flesh, following the direction of his fingers as he taught her how to pinch her nipples, how to make the pleasure hotter, wilder.

Sensation twisted over her, around her. Risa lost all sense of fear as the arousal became a conflagration of flames that left room for nothing but his touch.

"My turn," he growled.

His hands gripped her hips, lifted her, then lowered her until her back touched the bed.

Risa shuddered as he spread her thighs wide and moved between them. His head lowered, there was no hesitancy in his actions, no caution. His sexuality, his command, blazed around her until she was arching, lifting her hips to his devouring tongue and begging for more.

"Play with your nipples." His voice was rough black velvet stroking over her senses. "Let me see you pleasure yourself, Risa. Take your pleasure, sweet. All of it."

All of it. She wanted all of the pleasure. She wanted to explode in his arms again and again. Feel him thrusting inside her, coming inside her.

"Micah!" she screamed out his name as his tongue plunged inside the silky wet confines of her pussy.

He had never done that before, not with his tongue. The licking strokes were destructive to her senses. He lifted one leg, holding it high as he fucked her hard with the wet velvet of his tongue, rasped against sensitive nerve endings, and sent her senses spinning.

She writhed beneath him. She felt the edging darkness approaching and she welcomed it. There was ecstasy in the darkness, not fear. In the loss of control there was a rapture she could never have imagined.

"More," she cried out, desperate to feel him inside her. "Please, Micah. I need more. More."

She needed to feel him stretching her, burning her with the heavy width and length of his cock surging inside her. She wanted it now. She didn't want to wait.

He groaned as he pushed his tongue inside her again, lapping at the juices that ran from her as though the taste of her aroused him as much as the taste of him had aroused her.

"Micah. Please." She lifted closer, her fingers pulling at her nipples now, imagining his lips there, his teeth tugging at them.

Her head thrashed on the bed and perspiration covered her flesh. The room was too hot. There was too much heat burning inside her and around her.

When his tongue moved from the clenching inner muscles to her straining clit, she swore she would lose her mind. When his mouth covered the tight little nub and sucked it into his mouth, she exploded.

The darkness crashed in on her. Light sparkled in the inky darkness, then radiated and exploded around her as she tried to scream his name.

Her hips bucked in his grip, and she couldn't keep them still. Her nails dug into the back of his head, and she couldn't force herself to release him. She was locked in a cataclysm that she couldn't seem to escape.

She was twisting in the destruction of her senses, holding to him, keeping him to her, demanding, desperate for every ounce of pleasure she could experience, every touch, every cry, every spark of release that shuddered through her until she collapsed on the bed, panting and needing more.

"Now," she moaned, staring up at him as he came to his knees between her thighs and leaned over her, reaching for the drawer in the nightstand.

Where he kept the condoms he had never used. But he was prepared.

"No." She caught his hand, staring back at him as he watched her in surprise, his gaze narrowing on her. "I want to feel all of it, Micah," she pleaded. "I'm protected; I swear it. Please, I want to feel it all."

He froze, staring back at her for long, endless moments before easing back.

"You haven't tested your protection, Risa," he warned her.

"So test it," she whispered raggedly. "Please, Micah. I want all of you."

No condom, nothing between them. She wanted to feel him spurting inside her pussy as he had inside her mouth. She felt wild, wanton. She wanted everything she had never had. She wanted to be the woman she had craved to be in a lover's arms. In Micah's arms.

"You're going to destroy me," he groaned as she felt the head of his cock pressing against her. It was hot, pulsing, and iron-hard.

Her breath caught as he pressed inside her. She felt the full heat of his erection, felt him stretching her, working into her.

Risa moaned, pulled her legs back, and watched.

"Damn, Risa," he groaned. "Yes, love, watch me take you. Watch how sweet you stretch for me. How your pretty pussy sucks my cock inside you."

His explicit words were too much. Risa's breath caught as she felt a mini-explosion rocket inside the flesh he was taking.

"Oh, you like that, don't you, sweet?" He pressed in deeper. "You like being naughty, don't you, baby?"

Her lips parted as she fought to breathe.

"Do you like watching my cock take you, baby? The next time, I'll take you with the lights on. You can see what I feel. Your juices coating me, shimmering over my flesh. Fuck, I bet it looks sweet as hell."

Her hands locked on his wrists as his palms pressed beneath her thighs, holding her legs up as he worked deeper and deeper inside her.

And she watched. The room was dark, but she could see enough. She could see her juices shimmering on his flesh as he pulled back. Then he pushed inside her again, deeper, harder.

"Yes," she breathed out roughly. "I want all of you, Micah. All of you."

His body strained against his control. She could feel it. Sense it.

"Deeper," she whispered. "Fuck me deeper, Micah. Harder."

His hips bucked, driving his erection deeper, harder. Lifting to him, Risa cried out with the wash of pleasure consuming her. She bucked against him, thrust against him, her cries tearing from her throat as the pace he set destroyed her self-control.

"Please," she cried out, feeling the racing adrenaline in her veins, the violent need pounding in her pussy, pulsing through her womb. "Please, Micah. I need. Now."

He drove inside her, deep and hard, to the hilt. The blinding flash of pleasure and heat had her arching, her nails biting into his wrists as the breath seemed locked in her chest.

More. She needed more. Ah God, he needed to fuck her harder, deeper.

She was whispering the words, unable to scream them.

"Fuck me. Harder. Deeper." Like a prayer they fell from her lips, and his control shattered.

Hard. Deep. Faster. His hips surged against her, driving his erection inside her until she felt her pussy ripple, then tighten. The muscles through her body began to stiffen.

He thrust harder then, groaning her name, surging inside her, stroking nerve endings that burned, that screamed in pleasure.

When it came, she swore her spirit lifted from her body. She was flying, exploding into fragments as she heard her own wail echoing around her, joining Micah's fierce groan as he thrust inside her, buried to the hilt, and gave in to his own release.

The feel of him spurting inside her sent more sensation, another trigger of release, exploding through her. She arched to the breaking point, her muscles drawing her tighter as she flew higher, harder, and imploded with a violence that left her shaken to the core.

She felt Micah coming over her, his arms surrounding her, drawing her against him as she shook and shuddered through the echoes of ecstasy that flooded her body.

He held her close, an anchor in a storm she should have been frightened of. Her anchor, period. He protected her, held her; for the first time in her life Risa thought perhaps she had the courage, simply to be herself. Because if she fell, Micah would be there. His arms would hold her. His strength would renew her until she could strengthen herself and stand on her own again.

For the first time in her life, she thought maybe she knew, possibly, what love could truly be.

This. Held in his arms, unafraid.

Trust. Because she knew he would never hurt her.

Intimacy. She finally knew intimacy. His laughter, his silent confidence in her. His seed spilling inside her.

For the first time in her life, Risa felt complete.

Chapter 14

JORDAN ANSWERED his cell phone on the first ring, his gaze locked on the surveillance cameras tapped into the apartment across from Micah and Risa's.

"Jordan," he answered the call.

"We need a safe house," Micah's voice came over the line, heavy with regret and something more that had Jordan wincing. "I want her out of this. We have a chance of convincing Orion that I'm simply keeping her in the apartment and forcing him to make his move. I want her out of danger."

Jordan wiped his hand over his face. "That's what the FBI thought two years ago when they learned someone was gunning for a senator's wife. He killed the agent and the wife's bodyguards at the safe house. She ended up with her wrists sliced, Micah. You know that."

"The FBI didn't know who they were dealing with," Micah argued. "I want her out of this, Jordan. Now."

"Your emotions want her out of this," Jordan stated quietly. "You can't let your emotions affect an operation."

Jordan was aware of Tehya as she sat silently on the couch on the other side of his chair, watching him too closely.

"Are you going to fuck with me on this, Jordan?" Micah's voice was dark, dangerous.

At any other time, Jordan would have definitely fucked with him. Jordan was in command, not Micah. But in this case Jordan had a feeling Risa would have more to say in the matter than Jordan could come up with.

He'd seen her eyes at that meeting with the attorneys. She was stronger than anyone was giving her credit for. Risa would want to know the risks, she'd weigh them, and Jordan had a feeling she would give Micah a fight he hadn't anticipated.

"We'll discuss it," Jordan finally relented. "I'll be over there this afternoon. We'll let Risa know what she's looking at and see if she's willing to go to the safe house. We can't force her into it; remember that."

"She'll go." Micah's voice hardened. A second later the call disconnected.

Jordan closed the phone, laid it back on the table, and watched the surveillance videos thoughtfully.

"He has a weakness," Tehya said quietly. "You didn't anticipate this, did you, General Malone?"

He flicked her a cool look. He wasn't a general. He never had been. The mockery in her voice assured him that she was well aware of that.

"He'll get over it." Jordan shrugged, though he knew better. He'd seen Micah's eyes in the limo, seen how he held Risa. The man was a goner. He was so damned caught up in what he was feeling for Risa that he didn't know his ass from a hole in the ground.

"He'll get over it?" Tehya asked as she twirled a long strand of fiery red hair. "You don't just get over love, Jordan. Once it's there, it's there to stay."

"He's not in love; he's in lust," Jordan argued, even though he knew better.

Tehya's soft laughter was tinged with mockery. "You don't believe in love, do you?"

"Nope." He didn't believe in love. He believed in possessive instincts; he believed in a lust that sometimes went too deep. That was what was happening with Micah, he assured himself. Just a surfeit of lust.

"Then explain Noah," she challenged him.

"Noah was a Malone. There's no accounting for the insanity that runs in our family sometimes."

Noah had once been Nathan Malone, Jordan Malone's nephew. Now he was Noah Blake, one of the best damned agents Jordan had. Noah was also the man who had reclaimed the wife he had once known, and a soul Jordan had feared his nephew would never find again.

"But that insanity can't touch you, right?" Tehya pointed out.

He didn't take his gaze off the pictures displayed by the monitors set up.

"Have you known me to show insanity?" he asked her rather than answering her question.

She breathed out heavily. "Stone man," she muttered. "No, Jordan, you're never insane."

"Then you've answered your own question."

Now he had to figure out how to convince Micah that he wasn't insane, either. Because sure as hell Micah was falling into that emotional pit of darkness that men never seemed to claw their way back out of.

Love, my ass, he thought. He might as well blow Micah's head off himself, because there was no doubt in his mind it was going to explode before this mission was finished. And God help them all if Risa didn't survive Orion's determination to kill her.

"Yeah." Tehya rose, long gorgeous legs filling his peripheral vision as her voice echoed with anger. "I answered my own damned question. Good night, boss man."

He didn't speak. He didn't let his eyes follow her, but damned if it wasn't hard. If any woman had been created to be a weakness, then it was Tehya. And Jordan promised himself, *No weakness.*

FOR THE FIRST time in his life, Micah felt the knowledge that his heart was in danger. Staring into the dim light of the bedroom as dawn filtered through the heavy drapes, he felt his chest clench with emotions he wasn't entirely certain he was ready to face.

Tucked snug and warm against his chest, Risa slept on, exhausted and replete. Her body conformed to his, soft where his was hard, tender where his was tough.

He stroked his hand down her naked back, feeling the warmth of her, the tender flesh, the silkiness of her skin. As though he had never touched a woman's body before, he luxuriated in the feel of her. He committed each dip and curve of her body to memory, and reminded himself that dead men weren't supposed to dream.

That was one of the rules.

Dead men don't talk.

Dead men don't dream.

Dead men don't love.

Dead men don't have families.

Dead men didn't have memories.

And dead men definitely weren't able to have a weakness.

Micah had a weakness. A small, beautiful, passionate weakness that he feared could become the destruction of his soul.

Once, long ago, Micah had wondered if settling down, being a lover and a husband, would ever be a part of his future. Until six years before.

Until he had disobeyed the order that had come down through the chain of command in the ranks of the Mossad. The order that Orion was off-limits. All investigations into his identity were to be halted.

That order had come down just weeks after Micah's mother's death. It was an order he and his father had been unable to follow. And they had both died because of it.

His father at the hands of a suicide bomber.

Micah, or David as he had been, had died when Orion's bullet had grazed his temple and he had thrown himself overboard from the freighter he had tracked the killer to.

Somehow, the man Micah had been had been betrayed by his own. He'd made the mistake of calling in Orion's location and requesting a backup. Orion had found him instead.

Now, Orion threatened the woman who had managed to work her way into Micah's heart, when he had sworn he didn't have a heart to enter.

Dead men don't have a weakness, he reminded himself. He was a dead man, part of the Elite Operational Unit that existed in the dark, deeper than black ops, independent of government interference.

David Abijah no longer existed. Micah Sloane's identity could be terminated at any time and a new name, a new identity, could be created. A relationship, especially marriage or a family, could never survive the pressure.

His hand lifted to touch her hair, his jaw tightening at the silken warmth of the thick strands. Nothing, no other woman, had ever felt as warm in his embrace, nor as perfect.

"No one has ever held me like this." Her voice was soft in the twilight, a whisper of awe that had him blinking back a strange moisture from his eyes.

His Risa had never been held in a lover's embrace, and she had been born for a man to protect, to cherish.

"You could have had your pick of lovers," he told her, knowing it was true. "But I won't say I'm sorry to have been the first."

He turned to her, holding her against him as he stared into her upraised face.

The smile that curled at her lips was faintly disbelieving. "I'm not exactly beautiful, Micah."

He frowned at that statement. "This isn't true, Risa. Do you think I'd be perpetually hard for you if you weren't attractive? I can barely walk for the stiff cock torturing me."

Something gleamed in her eyes. An edge of hunger, perhaps the faintest hint of belief that she was indeed beautiful.

"You're odd, though," she stated with a hint of amusement. "Your opinion doesn't count."

"My opinion is the only one that counts." His arms tightened around her as he pushed his cock against the seam of her silky thighs. "My dick is the only one that matters, because it's the only one in this bed."

"That's true," she agreed somberly then. "Only you."

She would end up breaking his head before this was finished. He would end up hurting her before the day was out.

He'd already made up his mind what had to be done to finish this particular operation.

"Remember that, Risa." His hand tightened in her hair as

he held the back of her neck. "In the future, when you take another lover, remember, your beauty is unsurpassed. It's strong and wise, and it's a beauty that goes clear to your soul. Remember that, and whoever sees you will know it as well."

The thought of her taking another lover made him want to be violent. He'd have to mark Atlanta off his places to train, he warned himself. He'd never be able to come to the city without checking up on her. And he'd never be able to control his rage if he saw another man touch her.

"When I have another lover?" she asked, almost thoughtfully. "You don't intend to stick around for a while then?"

"You'll be safe soon. You won't need me after that." He kept his tone casual, kept the furious regret and unending hunger from reflecting in it.

Micah felt her breath catch, felt the tension that tightened through her body as she stared back at him.

He couldn't tell her he was sending her away, not yet. He couldn't make himself speak the words, couldn't force them past his lips.

"I see." She lay still against him. Micah couldn't feel a sense of anger from her, or even hurt. She was perfectly composed; whatever she might be feeling was perfectly hidden.

It infuriated him.

She was hiding again, even more than he did. Pushing her emotions so far inside her that even Micah couldn't sense them.

"What do you see?" He couldn't help but ask the question.

"That I had better enjoy what time I have with you then," she said quietly. "However you want to spend that time."

RISA FELT AS THOUGH she were breaking apart inside. She had told herself over the past week that Micah was nothing to her. He was just a man who made her feel wanted. One who wouldn't be staying long. She had known he wasn't committed to hanging around after Orion was disposed of.

But maybe a part of her had hoped. Maybe there was a fragile thread of emotion, something building inside her, that she hadn't wanted to acknowledge until now.

It wasn't that big of a deal; she would survive just fine when Micah was gone. And she was lying to herself. She knew she was, even as the thought drifted through her mind.

"I know how I want to spend this time with you," his voice whispered in shades of the desert. It was rare for the hint of an accent to slip free. Rare that the oddly fluid cadence was allowed to stroke over her senses.

She shivered at the sound, at the intent that suddenly tightened his body.

Risa licked her lips nervously, though why she was nervous she wasn't certain. She shouldn't have been. He'd touched her many times, he had taken her no more than hours before, and he had showed her the beauty and the pleasure of a touch that had brought her nothing but pain in the past.

He was wiping the past away, she realized. As she lifted her head, her lips parting for his kiss, she let the warmth of his touch steal over her.

She wasn't accustomed to his body yet, she told herself when his palm moving to her breast caused her to catch her breath in rising excitement. She was certain after a few more times it wouldn't be so cataclysmic, would it?

His kiss surely wouldn't steal her breath each time he kissed her for weeks on end.

Or would it?

A whimper left her lips as she arched against him, feeling his hand palm her breast, his finger and thumb as they found the stiff peak of her nipple and gripped it in a heated vise.

There was no place better to lose herself. The sensations were still a bit frightening, a bit surreal. As though this pleasure were forbidden, and she knew she was being allowed only a few moments of stolen time.

"My Risa," he whispered against her lips as he rolled her to her back and leaned over her.

He was a dim outline above her, the faint light of dawn barely pressing through the thick drapes that covered the windows. He was a warm shadow above her, around her.

He called her his, and yet he talked of leaving her.

But he was here now. She could memorize the taste and

feel of his flesh. She could let his rapid heartbeat sink into her, reassure her.

"Yours." She couldn't hold the word back as his lips stroked down her neck, igniting heated flames beneath her skin as he moved to her breast. "Micah," she sighed his name, and lifted to him as his tongue stroked over her nipple. "Touch me."

She loved his touch. The feel of his hands moving over her body, parting her thighs. The rasp of his body hair against her sensitive flesh, his lips, teeth, and tongue tormenting the hard tip of her breast.

"I love touching you, Risa." He lifted his head, his black eyes glittering in the darkness. A gleam of heat, lust, and pleasure that sent a thrill of awakening sensuality rushing through her.

He wanted her. She could feel it.

His cock was pressed at the juncture of her thighs, pressing against the tender bud of her clit as her legs spread wider for him.

"Look how pretty you are." He leaned back, spreading his legs wide between hers as his hands framed her breasts and plumped them up for her view. "Pretty, sweet nipples. They're hard and tight for me, Risa. Eager for my touch."

Her hands shook as she held on to his arms, staring up at him. His expression was intent with pleasure, as though touching her was more than a sexual act.

She was fooling herself with the feeling, and she didn't care. She'd been without touch, without emotion, for so long that she needed that illusion. She needed to feel it was more to him than just sex, just a warm and willing body.

"Risa, you make me lose my mind," he groaned as he shifted back.

He lowered one hand and gripped the base of his cock, moving it until it slid through the slick, moisture-rich folds of her sex.

Risa moaned in rising pleasure as she felt her body prepare itself further, felt her pussy grow wetter, slicker for his penetration.

Eyes wide, her breath harsh in the silence of the room, she watched as the broad, glistening head pressed deeper, against the flexing, tormented entrance to her vagina.

She was aching; a flaming need echoed between her thighs as she felt him working inside her in slow, tight thrusts. His hands moved to her hips and he lifted her along the incline of his upper thighs, pressing deeper as whimpering cries fell from her lips.

The feel of the broad, hot crest of his cock working inside her was exquisite. She could feel her muscles stretching, her flesh wrapping around him, revealing nerve endings that were otherwise hidden. They weren't hidden any longer. They were revealed, throbbing with awareness and so sensitive that each stroke had her crying out in pleasure.

She lifted to him, watching as his erection eased inside, pulled back, her juices gleaming on the heavy flesh before he entered her once again.

He rocked against her, into her. He filled her until she was certain she was overfilled, only to convince her body to take more, to move against him, to ease for him.

"See how pretty, Risa?" he groaned, his voice throbbing with the power of his lust. "I want to take you in front of a mirror. I want you to see your face as I work inside the hottest, tightest pussy I swear I've ever known." His voice tightened as he spoke, echoed with power and pleasure, and sent a rush of excitement spiking through her system. "I want you to see how pretty you are."

She was shaking, shuddering with the pleasure, with the look on his face, in his eyes. As the faint light of morning began to peek through the few cracks in the shades and drapes covering the window, it seemed to worship his face and the tight planes and angles of his tension-ridden body.

Risa stared up at him, her lips parted as she fought for breath, feeling the wonder of his touch, a gift she couldn't have imagined ever knowing before him. He gave her passion, he gave her a semblance of self-confidence, and he gave her touch.

Digging her heels into the bed at the sides of his body, she began to move with him. Thrusting into the slow penetrations as wild cries began to build in her chest. The slow undulations were killing her. She needed more. She was close to orgasm, so close. If he would take her harder, deeper, then she could find her release without battling that veil of darkness that tried to slip in, that rocked her senses with such a shock of sensation that she flew outside herself.

Desperation rode her now. She forced her hand from his arm, slid it down her body, and let her fingers find the swollen, tormented bud of her clit as he watched.

"Bad Risa," he breathed out heavily. "You're not allowed to cheat, baby."

But he didn't stop her. He watched her. His hands tightened on her hips, a grimace pulled at his expression, and his pace increased. Thighs bunching, his abs dewed with perspiration, he thrust harder inside her, working his cock into the flexing desperation of her pussy as Risa cried out in abandon.

She couldn't have imagined doing this. Stroking herself while he pumped inside her or the intensity of the wicked, erotic sensations that thundered through her veins.

Lifting to him, hips churning and thrusting, her fingers stroking faster over her clit as his cock pounded inside her with stretching, burning strokes.

She couldn't fight the pleasure. She couldn't fight the veil of darkness intent on rushing over her. It gathered inside her mind as the rush of pleasure became an inferno. Her fingers moved faster on her clit; her body tightened. The sensations tore through her until she slammed back at him, a wail parting her lips as her clit exploded in pleasure. The rush of orgasm peaked the little bud, then slammed into her pussy, her womb. The darkness rushed over her, then exploded into a cacophony of light and strangled cries.

Micah's groan sped through her mind as he moved over her. His arms wrapped around her, his elbows braced his weight. His hips quickened, his cock thrust inside her in furious, hard strokes, triggering a second, almost brutal release. A hard, throttled curse tore from his lips, and one deep thrust later she felt his release tear through him. It shuddered up his back as she held on to him. It tightened his muscles and locked him inside her as spurt after spurt of heated semen flooded her clenching sex.

Risa was certain she must have forgotten how to breathe for long, blinding seconds. She was gasping for air as reality began to seep into her mind once more. She held on to him, her arms and legs wrapped around him, locked into place as he jerked against her one last time.

Slowly, as the tension eased from her body, her legs slid from his hips. Her arms remained around his back, hoping he'd stay for just a few seconds more. That he would cover her and let her linger in the false sense of belonging that moved through her.

She felt as though she belonged here, in his arms, and she knew she really didn't. Risa had never belonged anywhere.

ORION STARED at the number on the ringing cell phone and grimaced before answering it. The bastard tried to hide his number, as though that could change the fact that Orion knew his identity.

"Hello?" Orion pretended he didn't know who was calling.

"I saw the news last night." Cultured, refined, his employer's voice dripped with sarcasm. "It seems there was an attempted kidnapping, from what several motorists saw, on the interstate. Security cameras on the overpass showed the entire fiasco in full fucking detail."

Orion winced. "No one can identify me. I made certain of it."

"I don't give a fuck if you could be identified," his employer ground out furiously. "You failed."

"Her boyfriend had a gun," Orion snapped back. "You neglected to inform me that she was sleeping with a damned Navy SEAL. Getting to her isn't exactly easy."

What the hell did this bastard know about his job? He pushed for instant results, never understanding that to kill as Orion killed took planning and exacting detail. It wasn't an overnight job.

"A dog wouldn't fuck that ugly-assed bitch," his employer fired back. "It has to be a bodyguard or something. You've given yourself away."

Orion smirked at the accusation. "I never give myself away, my friend, and you know this well. Trust me, he's her boyfriend." The few times Orion had managed to catch a glimpse of them, he'd known they were lovers. New lovers. She was still shy with him, still tentative, but she was definitely sleeping with the man.

"He's a friend of those SEALs' wives she's made friends with," Orion breathed out roughly. "Catching them off-guard won't be done quickly now, and I blame you for that. I told you it was too soon to try to take her. That was your attempt at a plan. I'll follow my own plan from here on out."

There was a seething silence across the line then. Orion knew his employer well, and he knew the other man detested failure of any kind.

"Orion, listen to me well," he snarled then. "If that bitch remembers who I am before you take her out, then remember, I can make a deal with any agency attempting to arrest me. My reputation and life will be shot to hell, but your identity will be revealed. I'll give them the key and the location to that little safe-deposit box I have, and you'll be dead. Are we clear?"

Orion stiffened. He was sick of being threatened with those pictures and the information this man held. It had been years ago, when Orion had first ventured into his present occupation. He'd been friends with this man, which hadn't been a very wise move.

A long time ago. It had been on one of Orion's first assignments with the CIA. The scientist he had been working with had a particular thirst for young girls. At that time, the scientist had been choosing women who looked and pretended to be much younger than they were. Unfortunately, one of those women had been threatening to expose him.

Orion had taken care of her in a manner that had thrown

all suspicion from the scientist. But the man had wanted to watch. Orion had wanted to show off. He had no idea there had been a hidden camera snapping pictures of the event.

It had been more than two decades ago, but Orion knew his features hadn't changed much from that time. They had aged, but he would be easily identified through the aging programs now available.

He was going to have to find a way to retrieve that evidence against him, and then he was going to have to kill his employer. The son of a bitch was getting too cocky, too arrogant, anyway.

"We are very clear," Orion said coldly. "I accepted the job." He really hadn't had a choice. "I told you, I'd make certain she was dead before she remembered anything. I'll take care of it."

"Make certain you do," his employer snapped. "Or I'll take care of you."

The line disconnected as Orion snapped his teeth in fury and slammed the phone to the bed beside him. He glared down at his foot. The bullet had passed clean through, but he had a broken bone and a fucking hole in his foot. He was wounded now, and he was pissed.

Reaching for the bottle of painkillers he'd had his handler procure (he couldn't risk his employer knowing he was wounded), Orion tapped two out, swallowed them with water, and leaned his head back before breathing in deeply.

He'd lie low for a week, perhaps two. If the bitch hadn't remembered anything by now, then chances were she wasn't going to remember in the time it would take his foot to heal. It would give her SEAL boyfriend time to get a bit complacent.

Orion frowned at the thought of the other man. He was a rather nice-looking individual from what Orion had been able to glimpse of him.

He'd studied the pictures he'd taken of her before and after the SEAL had arrived on the scene. Those later pictures were different. He was bringing something out in her that Orion hadn't expected—something that made her appear different.

Who the hell was he?

Micah Sloane was just a name. A Navy SEAL, according to the records that Orion's employer had managed to procure for him. Thirty-two years of age, he'd spent the past ten years in the Middle East and was now on leave from the Navy for an unspecified amount of time for medical reasons.

Orion knew his stats, his Naval record, which wasn't exactly perfect. Micah Sloane liked to be a bit insubordinate with his commanding officers. He'd barely slid past a court-martial once.

He'd been born in America, though. Parents were dead. No siblings. There wasn't a lot of information on him. He had a decent credit rating, a few late payments on the car Orion had totaled for him. There was a pitiful savings account, an apartment in Atlanta. Nothing noteworthy. He was Mr. Guy Next Door and he was pissing Orion off.

But there was one piece of information that gave him hope. Mr. Micah Sloane liked the nightlife. He liked the clubs and the bars and was known to frequent them often. He'd get bored, get antsy. He'd think he could protect his woman a night here or there if they went out.

Orion tapped his fingers against his leg as the painkillers finally began to ease into his system. Risa would be easier to take then. Orion would just stay back for a while. Wait. Watch. Then, when Mr. Sloane began taking his new lover out, Orion could strike.

It would work, he assured himself as he began to grow drowsy from the medication. He could make it work. It would just take a little patience. And he had plenty of patience.

Turning his head, he focused on the picture of his mark. The one from the mall where she walked with her new lover. To Orion's drug-hazed mind, the woman's tentative smile, the sparkle in her light blue eyes, and the sheer innocence in her expression were revealed.

She was pretty, he thought; then he frowned. It was the look in her eyes that always bothered him, and in that moment he realized why.

Ariela Abijah. Six years before. The Mossad agent who

had refused to beg. The only job that had ever haunted him. The young woman reminded him of Ariela. She had strength. Courage. She was a survivor and a fighter with an aura of endurance that few women possessed. And for a moment, for the second time in his life, Orion felt regret.

Chapter 15

MICAH DIDN'T LIKE the fact that Jordan insisted on Risa being present for the discussion of a safe house and the best place to move her. He knew that the man who headed the operational unit didn't agree with his opinion, and he could feel a stab of manipulation in the move Jordan was making.

Risa was quiet when Micah and Jordan entered the apartment after Micah had made the effort to hold the meeting in secret with Jordan.

She was sitting at her desk working on papers that had been delivered to her that morning. Nik had opened the door, cautious even though he knew who was on the other side, and stepped back.

"Hello Miss Clay." Jordan's smile was quiet, and the bastard was making the effort to be charming. Micah ground his teeth in frustration at the sight.

"Mr. Malone." She nodded back at him, though her gaze went to Micah. "Is something wrong?"

Nik closed the door, watching curiously. Micah wanted to warn the other man to take notes on just how calculating Jordan could be.

"We appear to have a problem," Jordan admitted. "Would you mind coming into the kitchen, where we can all talk comfortably? And perhaps I can convince Nik to make us a pot of coffee."

Nik grunted but moved in ahead of them to the other

room, where he proceeded to make the coffee Jordan seemed to live on.

Dressed in butt-hugging jeans and a soft light gray sweater, Risa edged in behind them, watching Jordan and Micah carefully.

There was a hint of confusion and of fear in her eyes as Micah caught her gaze. He almost grimaced.

"Everything's fine, Risa." He couldn't bear to see that fear in her eyes. "We're simply considering some alternative plans since Orion's attempt to take you yesterday. Jordan wants to discuss those with you."

"Okay." She nodded in agreement, but her eyes were still wary as she took her seat.

"Nik should have coffee in a minute." Jordan smiled again. Micah hated that damned smile. "We'll get this dealt with as quickly as possible so we can get on to the job of making certain you're no longer in danger because of Jansen Clay's activities before his death."

"That would be nice." Her voice was doubtful.

"We'll first go over a few things you mentioned while you were still sedated yesterday evening," Jordan announced as Nik set the cup of black coffee in front of him. "You mentioned remembering a few things about the man that raped you. Do you recall those memories?"

Jordan's tone was matter-of-fact. He didn't beat around the bush, and Micah watched as the approach seemed to give Risa the distance she needed to remain calm.

She breathed in deeply as though stepping back, mentally, from the fact that it was her rapist they were discussing.

"Large, soft hands," she said faintly. "I remember his voice; it was very cultured, very autocratic and arrogant. He wanted Carrie, but Jansen said he already had her sold." She swallowed tightly then. "He was a very large man. After I was transferred to the institution Jansen placed me in, he would come with Jansen during the visits he made. Jansen and my doctor would argue over the drug Jansen wanted used to sedate me. The doctor argued that the GHB would end up killing me. Jansen didn't seem to care. So the doctor only used that drug when Jansen made his visits. Otherwise, he used something he told the nurses was more acceptable."

"Halperidol." Jordan nodded. "That was what the doctors found in your system when you were taken from the institution by the team sent to rescue you."

She nodded.

"What do you remember of those visits Jansen made?" Jordan asked.

Micah watched her pale.

Moving behind her, he placed his hands on her shoulders, unable to stand away from her, from providing her some form of comfort as she was forced to pull those memories free again.

She hid from them, he knew that, and he hadn't pushed it. Had this operation worked out as they had anticipated, Orion would have been captured, her rapist in custody, and she would have been safe. There would have been no reason for her to remember.

"They were working on a drug," she whispered. "I don't remember the details, but it was supposed to replace the Whore's Dust. They would inject me, then watch my response to it."

"And you remember your response?" Jordan asked.

"I remember." Her shoulders were tight as tension sang through her body.

"Jordan, this isn't necessary," Micah protested.

Jordan's blue eyes slashed back to him. "But it is necessary, Micah," he stated, his voice cool. "If she remembers anything that could help us capture her rapist, then we'll ensure he doesn't hire another hit man once we've taken Orion out of the equation. That's our secondary mission, remember?"

Oh, he remembered, all right. But tormenting Risa didn't seem to be an acceptable course to catch the bastard. Orion would know who his employer was, according to their contact.

"It wasn't as bad as the original Whore's Dust," Risa stated, ignoring their argument. "It was more painful than anything else. Jansen was angry each time because it didn't seem to produce the effect he wanted."

"And what effect was he looking for?" Jordan asked as he made notes onto the legal pad he'd brought with him.

Micah watched as her hands clenched together atop the table.

"He wanted me to beg as I had the night he gave me to the other man," she stated, her voice quivering. "He wanted me to beg for . . ." She shook her head.

"For sex," Jordan finished.

Risa gave a jerky nod of her head as Micah glared at Jordan.

"I remembering thinking that I knew him." She breathed in roughly. "His voice and his hands. That I'd met him somewhere, but I couldn't remember." She gave a quick shake of her head. "That's so fuzzy, I can't remember it. I thought I could, while I was sedated yesterday evening. I was aware enough that the memories weren't hard to retain, but I can't seem to make the memory go far enough."

Jordan nodded at that.

"How will that information help you?" she asked him then.

Jordan lifted his head and stared back at her. "Micah seems to think you're not strong enough for this operation," he stated. "He wants you in a safe house. I need all the information I can get before we have you moved. Just in case Orion figures out what we're doing and manages to get to you."

The son of a bitch.

"Fuck you, Jordan," Micah growled as Risa tightened further, then with deliberate calm pulled herself away from him and rose from the chair.

When she turned to stare at him, he swore he felt a strike of pain slam into his chest. As though an invisible dagger had struck his body.

"He doesn't think I'm strong enough?" she asked, her gaze spearing into him, almost mesmerizing as he watched the anger that filled it.

"I didn't say that," he ground out between clenched teeth. "That's his take on it."

"But you agree with him?" she asked as though she couldn't believe he would and yet had irrefutable proof of it.

His jaw clenched. "You're not an agent."

"He's not trying to kill an agent," she pointed out, her voice burning with anger now. "He's trying to kill me. How will it make me safer if I'm not here? Won't he just follow me?"

"He won't know you're gone," Micah promised. "He should know I'll be more careful of you after the attempt. That I'd keep you at least hiding in the apartment. He'll make a move to get in and then we'll have him."

"Unless it works out as it did in Russia nearly five years ago," Jordan pointed out. "His mark was secreted to a safe house and a double placed in his home. Orion still found him. Orion killed a CIA agent and wounded another before taking the spy he was after. That spy was found in an abandoned warehouse two days later. The method of murder coincided with Orion's."

Micah stared back at Jordan furiously as he felt Risa's gaze slicing into him.

She turned to Jordan. "What do you believe would be best?"

Jordan leaned back in his chair and stared back at her with all the somber compassion and sincerity of a cobra preparing to strike, Micah thought.

"My opinion is that we follow our present plan. Orion's wounded. Traffic videos on the overpass close to where the attempt took place lead us to suggest he's wounded. It appears Micah's bullet caught him in either the ankle or the foot. Blood on-scene supports that suggestion. We have possibly one to two weeks before he'll consider himself in shape to make another attempt. That will give the two of you time to appear confident of your safety at this point. Micah will begin taking you out in public. His background states that he enjoys taking his women dancing and enjoying the evenings with other couples. It was our plan to give Orion a chance to strike or to penetrate your apartment once again in a controlled setting. I believe we should follow that plan."

"And what was yesterday?" she asked as Micah watched her fists clench at her sides.

"A fiasco." Jordan grimaced. "He got past our surveillance of the car. He can't get past an agent in your apartment."

She turned to Micah and he felt his entire body tense with the look on her face.

"Why doesn't your agent like this plan?" she asked. "If hiding a mark in a safe house doesn't work, then why attempt it?"

"I'm not certain," Jordan stated. "I could let you discuss this with him if you prefer. I have a meeting in an hour. I'll return this evening and see what the two of you have decided. How does that sound?"

Jordan was the dirtiest, most conniving bastard Micah knew, and that was saying a lot, considering Micah had once thought he had the corner on that particular talent.

Jordan rose from his seat, took a sip of his coffee, and turned to Nik. "I'll need you with me for this meeting."

Nik nodded and left the room as Risa continued to glare at them all.

"I'll make you pay for this one day, Jordan," Micah said coolly. "Be watching for me."

Jordan's answer was a slow grin. "I'll be sure to, Micah. I'll see you this evening."

Risa watched as Jordan left the room, her mind and her emotions thrown into confusion as he disappeared into the living room and a few seconds later the sound of the door heralded his exit.

There hadn't been a time that she had seen that man that it had been good news. She turned to Micah then, and felt that well of anger burning inside her reignite.

She couldn't remember ever being this furious, this hurt. Even Jansen Clay had never hurt her in quite this way. Her chest felt tight with the betrayal, tears locking in her throat as she pushed back the impulse to sob out in fury.

"I have work to do," she stated, moving around the opposite side of the table and heading for the doorway. "I'm sure you can find something to occupy yourself."

"Is that the only way you know how to deal with your anger, Risa?" he growled at her. His voice was deep, frustrated.

Poor baby, he was frustrated. Too damned bad.

"Last I heard, murder was illegal." The sound of her own voice was less than comfortable.

"And the last I heard, hiding from danger could be deadly," he stated, his voice oh, so damned cool. Superior. Arrogant. His arrogance lay around his shoulders like a particularly comfortable article of clothing. And it pissed her off.

"Who exactly has been hiding?" The rush of anger-powered adrenaline that surged through her had her fighting back the need to scream.

She didn't let herself get angry for a reason. Getting angry meant facing the fact that she was helpless against something. That something else in her life was controlling what she did, how she acted. It meant she wasn't in control of the situation and therefore her life. And she was sick of outside forces controlling her.

"You hide, Risa," he stated, his black eyes remote as he stared back at her. "You hide from the memories the same as you're content to hide in this apartment. It took you six years to get the courage to even find a lover."

"And just look at the prime piece I found," she had to snarl back in reply. "I waited all these years for a liar, a manipulator, and a coldhearted bastard. Lucky me."

It rose inside her then. The fact that she had been manipulated, that others had lied to her, that Micah had used her own arousal against her the night before she had been shocked with the fact that her life was in danger.

"I never claimed to be anything less." His eyes held her. They were cool, but there was a glimmer in the dark reaches, something that assured some primal sense she had that she was poking at a very dangerous creature.

Unfortunately, caution wasn't something she was in the mood for today.

He wanted her out of his life. That knowledge burned like a ragged flame inside her, searing her emotions. He thought she was too weak, that she couldn't see this operation out. That she couldn't participate in any way in her own protection.

"No, you didn't claim to be anything less," she agreed, hating the shaking of her voice, the tremor that rushed through her body. "And I guess I shouldn't have expected anything less, either, should I?"

She should have remembered, she told herself. She should have remembered he was an agent, not a lover. And he was a man. A man didn't have to feel anything to take a woman to his bed; all he needed was enough attraction to attain a hard-on.

God, she was so stupid.

She pushed her hands through her hair and fought back the bitter laugh that would have left her lips.

"You're making this into something it's not," he finally stated, his voice harsher now. "I want you safe; it's that simple. Orion wouldn't guess that you were at a safe house. The spy he killed in Russia was different. He would have expected someone to be watching for him. Everyone knew there was more than one contract out on the spy's head. He was a dirty bastard that pissed off too many people. Orion wouldn't expect your lover to send you to a safe house, Risa."

"No kidding." The bitterness showed then. It filled her voice and colored the anger surging through her. "He wouldn't have been alone."

"You're missing the point." His voice sharpened.

"I'm not a moron, Micah," she almost yelled back at him. "I know exactly what you meant. The fact of the matter is, you don't know what he knows at this point. He could very well be aware that this is an operation against him and expect me to disappear at any moment. We've been at this for over a week. You and Jordan both have assured me Orion would attempt to breach the apartment first. Well, he didn't. He nearly took me, in public, and almost killed you. Evidently you don't know him nearly as well as you think you do."

Her voice rose as anger and hurt clashed inside her, fueling emotions she had always shied away from simply because she didn't know how to handle them.

And he accused her of hiding? Accused her of fighting her memories and her needs so she could hide instead? As though nothing mattered to her but hiding. Damn him. There was a difference between hiding and healing. A difference between controlling herself and letting others control her.

"We're letting this get out of hand, Risa." His observation, carried out in that cool, distinct voice of his, had the power to trigger an explosion of almost overwhelming rage.

"You let this get out of hand." Her voice shook with the accusation. "You lied to me from the start. You manipulated me and now that things are getting too sticky, you're ready to opt out. Well, opt out, Micah." She threw her hand toward the door as her voice rose again. "Why don't you just go tell Jordan you're better at observation than you are at participation in this little mission? Maybe he can find another volunteer *to screw me over*."

He moved before she could anticipate his next action. He crossed the room, pushing her against the wall as his larger, harder body trapped her there.

And he was aroused. His erection pressed into her lower stomach, reminding her of the lover he had been, and the lies he had told even as he held her in the most intimate of embraces.

"You don't know what you're saying," he rasped, his hands catching her wrists as she tried to push against him and holding them against the wall. "Don't push me, Risa. I'm not the man you want me to be. I'm not gentle. I can't give you a future. And that's what you want."

And she hadn't even realized it until he told her he couldn't give it to her.

She wanted to curl into herself with the pain and the humiliation that he had seen something she hadn't realized herself.

"Let me go." She forced her voice not to tremble. Forced herself not feel.

She knew how to do that. She had learned at Jansen Clay's

knees when she had been a child begging for a father's love. He hadn't had it to give, and neither did Micah. That wasn't his fault, she reminded herself. She couldn't make him love her, couldn't make him want to try to love her.

"Risa, we're going to settle this, now," he warned her. "You're hurt, and I understand why. This was the reason I wanted you in a safe house, away from me. I don't want to hurt you, baby. I don't."

He was sincere. She could see it in his expression, in his eyes. And it made it hurt all the more.

"You haven't hurt me." She tugged at her wrists until he released her, then pushed against his body, forcing herself away from the warmth and the feeling of security that being close to him brought her.

He wasn't security, she told herself. His ability to catch Orion was all she needed. She didn't need a man to secure her life. For some reason, though, it had taken Micah to make her need one to secure her emotions.

"Jordan's options sounded much better to me than the idea of a safe house," she stated as she moved away from Micah. "At least this way, we know which target he's after and I have the entire attention of the team you're using. The safe house doesn't feel secure."

Micah didn't speak; he watched her. She could feel his gaze on her back as she moved back to the desk and the work that no longer interested her.

"His idea of public outings also seems the wisest course of action," she continued as she sat down in her chair and blinked back her tears as she focused on the accounting software pulled up on the monitor.

Control, she reminded herself. Releasing her emotions had never done anything but humiliate her.

"If you prefer not to see his plan through, then I completely understand," she stated as she tried to focus on her job. "I'm certain Jordan can find someone else. Maybe Jordan can find a double for you, Micah; that way Orion will never guess you couldn't stomach the job."

Silence filled the room behind her.

When Micah finally spoke, the sound of his voice sent a shiver down her spine.

"Jordan can risk his life in such a manner if it pleases him," he stated, ice coating every word. "Be warned, Risa, as long as this operation is in effect, any man that attempts to even consider taking my place in your bed had better take out life insurance."

She turned to face him then. He was watching her, his black eyes brooding, icy, dangerous.

"As you're no longer welcome in that bed, either, Micah, then it's not your choice to make."

Micah watched her stiff back as she turned back to the computer. His nostrils flared; his back teeth clenched.

Okay, he hadn't handled that so well, but then, neither had Jordan. The son of a bitch had sabotaged him as effectively as anyone ever had.

He moved to the couch and sat down slowly, forcing himself to remain in control.

He was Mossad, he reminded himself. Just because he was no longer a member of the elite force didn't change who or what he was. He was one of the most lethal killers, one of the most advanced agents, in the world. He'd killed for years. He'd faced opponents who had never made him sweat. Even his death had barely been a glitch on his radar. It had allowed him to exact revenge, nothing more. It allowed him to work with an autonomy and a security that Mossad hadn't given him.

The Elite Ops went beyond even black ops. They were privately funded but enjoyed a political backing that went beyond the American agencies.

He was one of the most advanced agents on the face of the earth, yet he couldn't handle one small woman with anything even remotely resembling grace.

He'd hurt her. The thought of that made him think of Ariela Abijah, the mother who had counseled him until her death. And he felt shame. She had taken the time to try to teach her son the intricacies of a woman's heart. With his father at her side, she had shown Micah the value of a loving, secure relationship. She had warned him to always remember that a woman's strength had little to do with how well she could fight physically but had more to do with where a woman's heart lay.

He'd forgotten that lesson with Risa.

She found her strength in pushing the memories aside and going on. He'd been unfair to her, and now he had no idea how to reach out to her. And perhaps that was for the best, he told himself. If she stayed angry, then she wouldn't lose her heart. If she stayed angry, then perhaps he wouldn't lose his, either.

One thing was for damned certain: She had torn him in so many different directions that at the moment, he had no idea how to deal with her.

He hadn't expected her fury or her hurt at the thought of going to a safe house. Honestly, he thought she would feel secure.

He'd known the moment Jordan had let the information out that Micah wanted her moved, that Risa wasn't feeling in the least secure.

Fury had pumped inside her small body, it had filled her eyes and her voice, and amazingly it had made his cock swell harder, tighter, than ever before.

The pure shimmering defiance in her expression had done something to him that he hadn't expected. It had made him want her more than ever before. As though he hadn't desired her enough. As though every time he touched her, kissed her, stroked her rounded curves, he didn't burn for her in a way that he had never burned for another woman.

She was a hunger he couldn't get control of, and that concerned him. It worried him.

And now, she thought that she could actually order him from her bed? Obviously she believed that her defiance was going to go unrewarded.

"The bed is not negotiable." He felt the need to warn her of that right up front.

She turned slowly, the office chair squeaking a bit as she faced him fully.

"No, it isn't negotiable," she promised with a smile so

falsely sweet that he wondered if it were possible to develop a sugar high from it. “My bed. Period. You, Mr. Sloane, can sleep on the damned floor for all I care.”

Micah propped his booted feet on the coffee table, laced his hands over his abs, and smiled back at her. “Bet me.”

Chapter 16

BET ME!

It was a damned good thing she hadn't bet him, because he had ended up sleeping in her bed. Right in the middle. His hand on her hip all night long.

Sleeping wasn't something Risa had managed much of that night, which left her crankier than normal the next morning. Cranky, angry, and hurt.

She couldn't believe he was that desperate to get rid of her. And if he was that desperate, why was he sleeping in the middle of her bed and touching her all night long?

She was greeted when she awoke to another replay of the newscaster going over the wreck and attempted kidnapping that had occurred, as well as phone calls from various news agencies. It seemed everyone was interested in Risa Clay again. Six years of anonymity shot to hell. Once again her face was plastered on the television screen.

To make matters worse, they were supposed to go out. Dinner and dancing, he had informed her over breakfast. Oh yeah, she was all up for dinner and dancing.

It was no surprise when a courier from one of the more expensive boutiques arrived that day with more new clothes, and Risa felt her temper rising that much further.

"You're staying, then you have to play the part," Micah informed her as she glared at the dresses, skirts, and tops laid out on her bed. "Trust me, Orion and his employer have run my background. They know the information we put out there for them to find. If you want his employer pushing him, then you'll play the part. The faster we finish this, the faster you can get on with your life."

He stared at her with that calculating look in his eye that he had held all morning. As though he were figuring out a puzzle, working the pieces and trying to make them fit.

She wasn't a puzzle.

"If they researched you, then they researched me," she told him between clenched teeth. "I wouldn't wear clothes like this."

"You wore clothes exactly like this the first night I met you," he pointed out, and Risa felt her blood pressure rising. At this rate, she was going to end up having a stroke. "But if you can't wear them." He shrugged philosophically as he eyed her with a mocking look in his eyes. "I'm sure we can make allowances."

As though she were too scared to wear them.

She stared down at the dresses. Maybe she was just frankly terrified of wearing them. Clothes like that made a woman feel daring; they made her feel as though she could conquer mountains. And Risa knew she wasn't quite up to mountains yet. She couldn't even conquer Micah.

The dresses were short; the skirts were short. The tops were sexy and the shoes were high-heeled and daring. She was going to so get in trouble wearing those clothes. Clothes she had once been terrified of. But not now. Not now because she knew she could wear them. She had worn the dress the other night, and the shoes. It wasn't the clothes that caused her to swallow tightly. It was the man and the look in his eyes as he glanced from the clothes to her.

"I don't need you to make allowances for anything." Damn her pride. "If you can stand to pay for it, then I can wear it."

His brow arched. "Don't let your mouth write checks your body can't cash, sweetheart. Because trust me, I know exactly how to dress a woman for prime impact."

Her smile was tight. "You don't scare me, Micah," she

scoffed. He terrified a part of her. Another part was ready and rearing to challenge him.

She was tired of being manipulated. She was sick of being worked. He wanted to use her and walk away later, fine and dandy, because she wasn't above using the security he offered her to gain a little self-confidence, somewhere. Maybe.

His smile curled a little wider, that luscious bottom lip tempting her even as the smile pissed her off.

"I should scare you." He leaned closer, those lips within inches of hers now. "Because what those clothes will do to that luscious body of yours will make me hard, Risa. Hard and hungry. If you take the kid gloves off and decide to tempt the tiger, baby, then expect to have a bite taken out of that lovely hide of yours."

"By you?" She sniffed as though in doubt when inside she was shaking. "I'm sure you can handle the pressure."

She doubted she blipped on his radar any more than it took to make him hard. Some men any woman could arouse. Maybe Micah was one of those men.

She picked up the closest outfit and just barely managed not to cringe. At least she liked the color. The chocolate brown silk would complement her coloring; the short length would compliment her legs. The matching shoes, high-heeled of course, were gorgeous. The scalloped bodice would be lucky to cover her breasts, and the thin straps didn't look strong enough to hold it up.

Micah's brows lifted at her choice. "I especially liked that one when I chose it from the website," he murmured. "Daring, Risa. Very daring."

With that, he turned and walked from the room, the door closing behind him as Risa let out a hard breath and looked at the dress again.

Oh, she was in so much trouble here. This dress was so outside the realm of anything she would have chosen to wear. Dreamed of wearing, yes. That fantasy Risa who was daring and unafraid would have worn it in a New York minute.

But the other Risa, the one who had learned to be cautious all her life, was shaking in her jeans and bare feet. That

Risa was certain lightning was going to strike and turn her to ash for wearing such a dress.

In for a penny, in for a pound. She laid the dress aside before going through the other choices. Short skirts and a few corsets to wear over shimmering thin long-sleeved blouses. There were snug blouses, a few more daring dresses. There were shoes to match everything. And she was in so much trouble.

"We'll be meeting at a small dance club in town with Ian and Kira. We'll have dinner at the attached restaurant and then drinks in the club," Micah informed her as she stepped out of the bedroom after putting the clothes away. "We'll be leaving here about seven."

"Are Kira and Ian part of this agency you're involved with?" she asked then. "The federal attorney said you were a private agency. What kind?"

He looked up at her from where he sat on the couch, his laptop opened and resting on the coffee table.

"A private group that sticks its nose in wherever it pleases," he told her coolly. "We're not an agency, Risa. We're a team."

"Perhaps I'd like to know exactly who my government has placed me in the care of," she told him, irritation flaring inside her. "Jordan Malone was a SEAL, so were Clint and Ian. Were you?"

"Close," he grunted. "What I was or what I am doesn't matter in your protection."

"Maybe it matters to me." Maybe she needed to know who or what she was sleeping with every night.

She should have questioned it before; why she hadn't, she wasn't certain. She had been curious, but she'd also been overwhelmed by other things. Those other things had exploded in her face and now she was beginning to wonder if this would as well.

"I can understand that it matters to you," he stated coolly. "Consider us a security firm. A group that goes in where other agencies can't and gets the job done."

"Mercenaries?" She couldn't see him as a mercenary, though he was tough enough, hard enough.

"If you want to think 'mercenaries,' then fine." He closed the laptop and gave her the full effect of his piercing gaze. "Do I seem mercenary to you?"

"You seem too arrogant and superior to me," she informed him. "That would suit a mercenary, wouldn't you think?"

"Met many of those, have you?" He rose slowly to his feet and moved toward her.

Risa remained still, despite the urge to retreat, to run from him. This wasn't the Micah she had gotten to know. This Micah was harder, more determined, and he did nothing to hide the extreme sexuality that moved through him.

She didn't know whether she should be turned on or scared to death. But her body was taking the decision out of her hands. It was burning for his touch.

"I've met you; wouldn't that be enough?" Her toes curled into the carpet beneath her feet as he stopped. He was almost close enough that the broad T-shirt-covered chest was within a breath of touching the hardened tips of her breasts beneath her own shirt.

His lips quirked. "I can be very mercenary when the situation calls for it," he assured her, his hand reaching out to tuck a strand of her hair behind her ear. "I can be so mercenary it would curl your little toes."

Her little toes were already curled. The feel of his fingertips against her cheek as his hand drew back sent a surge of longing racing across her nerve endings. Her nipples peaked, her clit felt swollen, and the sexual hungers he had awakened with her began to pulse through her system.

"Why doesn't that surprise me?" She had to force herself to remain in place, to ignore the heat flooding her system now.

His lips quirked; his black eyes watched her knowingly. "As well it shouldn't," he finally agreed as his fingertips trailed down her neck, creating a flood of sensation over her flesh. "It shouldn't surprise you, Risa. Just as it shouldn't surprise you to know that you can try to run all you want, but I'm going to end up fucking you again."

Her eyes narrowed. "Not even on a bet." But she was

breathless, almost panting for the feel of him moving inside her again. She could feel the heat flooding her body, dampening her panties.

The quirk of his lips became a full-fledged grin. "You enjoy lying to yourself?"

"Do you enjoy lying to everyone else?" she shot back.

The grin eased away from his face. His expression darkened, became harder, colder. "When I need to." He finally shrugged, but his fingertips were moving down her arm, gently, erotically. "Have no doubt, Risa, I have no problem lying when I need to."

And that put her firmly in her place. He wasn't above lying to her to catch Orion, but how far would the lies go? Her courage seemed to desert her at the prospect of asking that question, because she was afraid he would answer it. And he'd already proved he would lie to her. With his tender touches, his drugging kisses, and his too-experienced body.

"Do you know what I want to do to you?" he asked then, his voice lowering, becoming raspy as it stroked over her senses. "I want to push you against that wall behind you and pound into you while you're screaming my name. I want to feel your tight pussy convulsing around my cock and hear you screaming my name. And when we're done there, I'll slide you to the floor and take you again. You're within minutes of being fucked, baby. I'd move if I were you."

She couldn't move. She stared back at him, almost mesmerized by the black glow of lust that filled his eyes now.

His fingers moved from her arm to her thigh. His palm flattened, his hand angled and began to slide across her jeans-covered thigh, moving to the inside of it.

Her pussy pulsed and hummed. She could feel the flesh there swelling, preparing for his touch.

He was within an inch of the humid flesh when his cell phone rang, causing Risa to jerk in surprise as Micah's jaw clenched.

The tips of his fingers were so close. The needs racing through her were so hot.

"Saved by the phone," he murmured, moving his hand to

pull the cell phone from the small holster on his belt. "Go ahead and run, Risa; we can finish this later."

She was already running as he answered the phone, putting as much distance between them as possible and wondering if she would ever rebuild her defenses and have the control to simply tell him no. Even worse, she wished she *wanted* to tell him no.

COURAGE, STRENGTH, and sheer tenacity. Micah had seen each of those qualities in Risa that first night when she had sat at the club, battling her fears and the overriding certainty that she would be rejected.

It had taken her six years to get her nerve up to take a lover, but honesty compelled him to admit that she had taken that step far sooner than many women would have. She had the guts to do what she had to do. And she was doing far more than that when she stepped out of her bedroom in the chocolate silk tunic dress that whispered over her curves like a wet dream.

Matching four-inch-heeled pumps encased her small feet and made her legs seem to go on forever. Her skin shimmered with creamy translucence and the mounds of her breasts seemed in imminent danger of pressing out of the snug cups that made up the bodice.

Her long hair fell just below her shoulders, the multihued strands framing her delicate face as the subtle covering of shadow over her eyelids gave her a sensual, sleepy appearance.

Plump lips were covered with a hint of bronze lipstick, their natural pout intensified by the shimmering layer of color. It was enough to make a man pant in lust.

Hell, his cock was going to pound right out of his slacks and he swore his heart was going to tear through his chest as it raced in excitement.

She had a power over him that he couldn't have anticipated.

He watched as she moved across the living room, the little matching purse she carried gripped in her hands. She shoved a key and a small leather wallet into the bag, then turned to him.

The look in her eyes broke his heart. Beneath the glitter of anger there were shadows of uncertainty. Feminine uncertainty, as though she were unaware of her effect on him.

"Remember that wall sex I mentioned earlier?" He watched her face flush as a hint of heat filled her eyes. "If we don't leave, you'll find out exactly what it's like to grip my hips with those gorgeous legs while I pound into you."

It was no less than the truth.

She inhaled slowly, deeply, lifting those luscious breasts against the silk as her nipples tightened beneath the material.

"I have a wrap. I forgot it."

His teeth clenched as she moved quickly back to the bedroom. When she returned, it was with a thin silk wrap that covered her shoulders and breasts.

The whisper of silk was a seductive cadence as she moved past him and waited at the door.

Opening the door, he checked the hallway, aware of the backup weapon he carried at his ankle and the one he wasn't wearing beneath his jacket. The rest of the team would be more heavily armed, but for Micah, there was only the weapon strapped to his ankle.

Holding his hand out to her, he drew her into the hall, checked each end once again, then moved back as the door to the opposite apartment opened and John moved quickly into Risa's apartment.

"Have fun, kids," he murmured as the door closed behind him and the locks snicked into place.

"This is ridiculous," Risa hissed as Micah placed his hand on her lower back and led her to the elevator.

"No doubt," he answered just as quietly. "Don't worry, John doesn't take up too much space."

"No, he just cleans out the food in the refrigerator," she stated. "Doesn't Jordan feed him?"

"At least once a day," Micah grunted as he shifted until Risa was protected on the far side of the elevator as the doors slid open.

"Well, hello, gorgeous," Tehya murmured as she stepped into the hall, her long red-gold hair swishing around her as her green eyes filled with flirtatious humor.

Micah was aware of Risa stiffening beside him. She hadn't seen Tehya coming and going from the other apartment, and had no idea who she was.

Micah nodded to Tehya, aware that her presence signified the all clear downstairs.

He escorted Risa into the elevator, ignoring her little glare as he pushed the lobby button and stood slightly in front of Risa.

"You work fast," she drawled behind him, almost causing him to wince.

"Be careful, sweetheart," he warned her quietly. "Your pretty mouth is about to get you in trouble."

He was about seconds away from spreading those pretty legs and making certain she tasted just as good as he thought she did.

Thankfully, before she could say anything more, the elevator opened, depositing them into the lobby. The doorman, Clive, had a wide smile on his hangdog face as Risa walked toward him.

"Now look how pretty," he said, his eyes following Risa's every move. "It's good to see you out and about after that nasty wreck the other day. I couldn't believe the news report when I saw it, Miss Clay. There are sure some nasty people in the world."

"Yes, there are," she murmured as Clive held the door open. "Thank you, Clive."

"You're always welcome, Miss Clay." There was concern and curiosity in the older man's face as Micah passed by him.

Clive was the perfect doorman for the upscale apartment, Micah thought as he hid a grin. Cultured, his nose just a little in the air. His bald head and the goatee and mustache gave the perfect impression of superior standing.

The limo was waiting in the drive with Travis at the wheel. The ex–MI6 agent moved quickly to open the back door and closed it firmly after Micah moved into the interior.

"So we have a limo at our disposal now," Risa muttered. "What does your cover give for employment?"

"Navy SEAL and stock market analyst," he answered. "That's the work I do on the computer. It's actually a hobby of mine."

A hobby that had paid off in more ways than one. Micah had made some very interesting contacts through the few clients he had. Clients he had courted and now made use of in the interests of the team and the operations they took on.

Her lips pressed together as Travis moved into the driver's seat and put the vehicle in gear. Micah hit the switch at the side of the door and raised the privacy glass between them as he watched Risa with a knowing quirk to his lips.

The angrier he made her, the braver she seemed to get. It was a side of Risa he was certain he wouldn't have become acquainted with if he hadn't attempted to have her moved. He'd hurt her, and he regretted that. But he had also learned that she had triggers that could draw her past the fears and uncertainties he knew filled her. Anger was one of the triggers; arousal was another. Confrontation had an impact as well.

He'd tried to handle her with kid gloves, tried to treat her gently, but he was learning there was much more to Risa than he had ever imagined when he challenged her.

He wondered how much further she could be pushed before they reached the club.

"Come here." He lowered his voice, let it rasp along his throat, and wanted to crow at the slight tremor that raced over her as she stared back at him in surprise and anger.

"You must be joking." The haughty tone almost had him grinning. Damn, she made him hot when she looked down her nose at him.

"Actually, I'm not." He hardened his voice commandingly. "Come over here." He patted his lap.

And she laughed. The sound was filled with bitterness. "Not on your life, Micah."

Before she could evade him, he reached across the small

space between the seats, gripped her wrists, and pulled her quickly to his lap.

Before she could fight, he did what he'd been dying to do since the night before. His head lowered and he caught her lips in a heated, lust-filled kiss.

His tongue parted her lips and the sweet taste of her hit his senses like wildfire. He'd waited until now to taste her. It was the only way to hold on to his self-control, the knowledge that he had a limited time to touch her, taste her, before they'd be interrupted.

He held her to him, one arm around her back, the other over her hips. His hand clasped her thigh beneath the hem of the short dress.

Her struggles diminished, not that she had seriously fought to be free. Her lips moved beneath his, and a female cry of need tore past her hungry lips as he turned and bore her to her back beneath him.

She tasted like summer and sweet sunshine. Her arms twined around his neck and her thighs parted at the urging of his hand between her thighs.

And he was right. She was wet. So damned wet the silk panel of her panties was heated and damp against his fingertips. Her pussy was juicing, and for one insane moment Micah had to struggle against the need to tear the thin covering from her and plunge inside her.

Instead, his fingers pushed beneath the material, found her silken slick folds and the saturated flesh beyond. Heated syrup met the two fingers that eased slowly inside her entrance. She was snug, fist tight, and so hot as she gripped him that he wanted to shout in triumph.

Her hips arched to him as he kept her lips busy beneath his. Her legs fell farther apart, one foot resting on the floor as she arched and pushed his fingers deeper inside her.

His thumb found her swollen clit and rubbed against it with a subtle rocking motion that had wild cries echoing in her throat.

His lips slanted over hers to kiss her deeper, to draw her

as deep into the morass of sensations as he was being drawn. There was nothing as sweet, as hot, as Risa. She claimed a part of his soul with her innocent hunger and wild cries, and he prayed she never realized it.

Maintaining his distance was practically impossible when she wasn't in his arms. When he held her this close, felt the luscious heat of her body wrapped around his fingers, then all chance of distance disintegrated. She was heated honey, pure sensual female, and she was eroding his control into the dust.

She was a weakness, he knew. A weakness he could ill afford, and yet one he couldn't deny.

Lifting his head, he thrust his fingers deeper into the convulsive grip of her pussy and waited until her eyes fluttered open before he spoke.

Holding her, possessing her, he stared down at her with all the hunger, all the dominant needs, he could feel rising inside him.

"This is mine." His fingers owned her pussy now. "You're mine. For as long as I sleep in your bed and live at your side, this sweet, luscious body belongs to me, Risa. Don't attempt to deny it, because we both know it would be a lie."

Panting, her eyes darker, her face flushed, she tightened her muscles around his fingers and narrowed her eyes back at him.

"Bet me."

Chapter 17

RISA FELT THE eyes on her when she entered the restaurant Micah had chosen for his little night out. It was one of the most exclusive in the city. The food was excellent, the service beyond compare, and it seemed everyone she knew in Atlanta was there that night.

Before her mother's death, Risa had lived in Atlanta with her parents. It was only after her tenth birthday that Jansen had moved them to Virginia, then to Washington, D.C. It was only after her mother's death that Risa's life had seemed to turn into a farce compared to her life before.

Suddenly Jansen had become increasingly critical of her looks. Risa had retreated into a shell, spent more and time in her room or on the grounds of the small estate he had bought. Nothing she had done had pleased him.

The past six years, since her return to be closer to her grandmother and to put the past behind her, Risa had stayed well clear of the restaurants that she knew were frequented by those who had known her and Jansen.

Atlanta wasn't far enough away to escape the crowd Jansen and Elaine had been a part of, though. And their reactions to Risa varied.

She heard the whispers as she moved through the restaurant, her head held high when all she wanted to do was run and escape the furtive, pitying looks and gossipmongering.

Yes, the ugly duckling was dressed in silk, she thought as

she caught one woman's overly loud statement as they passed her table.

Risa didn't glance left or right; she followed Micah's lead at her side on autopilot, escaping within herself as she had always done as a child.

God, she hated this.

"Risa. Risa Clay."

She'd hoped to escape any sort of socializing with the people she had known before her kidnapping and rape. She wasn't that lucky.

She and Micah were halfway to the table where Ian and Kira were awaiting them when two diners rose from their chairs along the path they were taking.

Risa came slowly to a stop, her gaze moving from James Walters's long, aesthetic face to that of his wife, Corina. The couple had been acquaintances both in Atlanta and in D.C. James was one of the world's premier heart surgeons, his wife a nurse who worked by his side.

"James. Corina." Risa had a trick she used when she was forced to face people who had known her before. A way of staring at them while unfocusing her eyes and blurring the pity on their faces.

"Risa sweetheart." James caught her hands and bent to place a kiss on her cheek.

He never met his goal. Micah pulled her back gently until she was against his side, his arm curved possessively around her back.

An awkward silence filled the next second.

"James, Corina, this is Micah Sloane," she introduced him into the silence. "A friend of mine."

"Just a friend, love?" Micah asked under his breath as though they were indeed more than what they actually were. In the space of a second she wondered exactly what they were.

"Micah, this is James and Corina Walters. James is a premier heart surgeon, and Corina the miracle nurse that works by his side." Corina glowed at the compliment. "James, Corina, Micah's a SEAL with the U.S. Navy stationed here in Atlanta at the moment."

"A SEAL, how utterly exciting," Corina murmured. "Was he the gentleman with you the other day when that nasty character tried to kidnap you? The news said a shot was fired, frightening that vicious person away. We tried to call, dear, to make certain you were okay, but you weren't taking calls."

Risa swallowed tightly. "Micah frightened him off. If you'll excuse us . . ."

"Risa, darling, we were frantic to get hold of you and make certain you were well," James said, his tone sincere, though his gaze sparkled with pity and a hint of confusion as he glanced at Micah. "We couldn't believe someone was trying to harm you again."

"Risa's fine; aren't you, baby?" Micah's hand tightened at her hip. "But if you'll excuse us, we have a table waiting."

"Of course," James murmured, a frown touching his clear brow as he stared down at Risa. "Please call us soon, dear. We could have lunch and catch up."

"Of course," she muttered the lie. She wasn't about to call either of them.

Not that she disliked them or that there was anything wrong with them. James and Corina had been one of the few couples whom Risa had actually enjoyed talking to at one time. But that time was long ago and far away. She hadn't been an oddity then, or a topic of gossip and speculation. And she hadn't been submitted to their placating attention. She'd always pitied those who had been years before.

She turned her gaze away as Micah led her through the restaurant to the table where Ian and Kira were watching them curiously.

"Trouble?" Ian asked quietly as he rose from his chair.

"Nothing important," Micah answered as he helped Risa with her chair. "Acquaintances, I believe."

"Acquaintances are about it," Kira said softly so her voice wouldn't carry. "James and Corina can only be taken in small doses."

Risa lowered her head to her plate, wishing she had found a coat or a jacket to wear now. Anything but the skimpy dress and too-small wrap. She could feel the eyes on her; her skin crawled with the sensation of those looks.

"Risa, you're looking lovely tonight," Ian stated as he took his seat once again.

"Thank you." Her smile was stiff as she glanced at him.

Kira, as always, was a goddess of perfection. Her long black hair was pulled back from her face with jeweled combs, her smoky gray eyes were sensual and mysterious, and the stunning red slip dress she wore was both daring and elegant.

Ian was the perfect counterpoint to his wife. With his dark blond hair, brown eyes, and sun-darkened skin, he was amazingly handsome in a tough, masculine sort of way. And when he looked at his wife, his gaze softened with his adoration of her.

What would it be like, Risa wondered, *to be loved in such a way? To turn and see that look on a man's face?*

She pushed the thought away. Now wasn't the time to reflect on what she didn't have. She could do that later, after Micah was gone. If she lived that long.

She stayed silent as Micah, Ian, and Kira began to chat about Atlanta. Kira and Ian had a small condo they kept in the city for long visits. They were still close to the former SEAL members he had once fought with. They were a little more than close, Risa knew. They were also a working part of the group that Micah was involved with.

"Risa, that's a stunning dress," Kira commented, drawing her away from her thoughts.

"Micah has exceptional taste," she murmured a bit mockingly.

God, she was going to have to stop this. She shook her head. "I'm sorry, Kira. It's been a long day."

She kept her voice lowered so diners at the nearby table couldn't overhear her.

"And to top it off, you had to deal with James and Corina." Kira smiled in understanding. "Here's the waiter with our wine. A few glasses and a nice dinner, and you'll be in perfect form."

If only it would take no more than a few glasses of wine to put everything in perfect form.

She did drink the wine, and she managed to eat most of her meal. As Ian and Micah continued to chat over drinks, she let her fingers play over the stem of her empty wineglass. The wine had helped. She didn't drink often, and she rarely drank wine simply because of its mellowing effect on her.

"If you gentlemen will excuse us, Risa and I are going to go to the ladies' room." Kira rose to her feet and smiled back at Risa. "I hate going in there alone."

No kidding. It was like a cobra pit, Risa thought, barely managing to keep from rolling her eyes. She didn't patronize this restaurant for a reason. She and her grandmother had both agreed that only the snippiest, most condescending members of the community actually ate here.

But Risa followed Kira. She was amazed she did so without tripping over her feet as she felt the eyes following her. Thankfully, the wine had her just mellow enough that she, frankly, didn't give a damn who watched her.

Maybe she'd had too much. She frowned at that thought as she and Kira entered the surprisingly empty ladies' room. Kira followed Risa to the sinks where they washed their hands, dried them, and then looked around in amusement at the fact that the room was empty.

"And here I thought we'd have to fight our way in," Kira stated with amusement.

"I prefer the silence," Risa assured her. "So why did you drag me in here?"

"To give you a break," Kira sighed. "Even facing off a few dozen piranhas in the ladies' room is sometimes preferable to sitting in the middle of a restaurant and feeling their eyes on you."

Risa shrugged. "The wine has its own saving grace," she said with a smile.

Kira didn't smile back. "Are things going okay with Micah?"

"Fine." Risa nodded. She wasn't into sharing girlish confidences in the ladies' room.

Kira nodded. "Good then. I guess we better return before the stampede begins."

It began as they were leaving. Risa almost smiled at the group of women bearing down on them as they moved back into the hall. Several of those women frowned in consternation as Kira and Risa passed them. *Foiled again, ladies,* she thought a bit snidely.

She knew every one of them. This little outing was turning into a damned farce.

Taking her seat once again, she stared up at Micah with what she hoped was a pleasant smile and said, "Next time, I pick the restaurant if you don't mind."

"I'm not much into the local drive-thru," he murmured at her ear. "I have my manly form to think of, you know."

She almost snorted at that. "The local drive-thru is much more polite."

"No doubt," he agreed. "But not nearly as enjoyable."

He took his seat once again, his hand lingering on the back of her chair to play with her hair. Risa wanted to groan at the sensation of his fingers tugging restlessly at the strands. The sensual, seductive feel washed over her, tingling beneath her skin as she attempted to make small talk with Kira.

Unfortunately, the woman seemed to be well aware of what Micah was doing to Risa.

"Gentlemen, I'm ready to dance," Kira finally announced. "And I'm certain the band is just waiting on me and Ian to add some excitement to the dance floor."

Ian chuckled at that, but both men came to their feet, helped the women from their chairs, and led the way from the restaurant to the small arched tunnel that led to the connecting nightclub.

The music pulsed around her. Risa was certain she could feel the rhythm of it filling her blood.

She had once loved to dance. She had danced with her friends, other young women considered the less acceptable or less pretty of their social set. They were always invited to the parties, but they were always the ones huddled along the wall in boredom.

It had been Risa's idea that last year, for them to hit the dance floors together. They had all loved to dance, and they had been able to enjoy the hours they were stuck at those parties that way.

For once, Risa had enjoyed the parties as well. Until the kidnapping. Until Jansen had laughed at her during that plane ride where she had found hell.

The ugly little bitch, she can't even get a man to dance with her, he'd sneered, *let alone actually fuck her.*

She'd been eighteen. She had never had a boyfriend, never had a date. She'd been a virgin, and that night she'd learned how evil a father could be.

The wine was still affecting her, Risa told herself even as she crossed one leg over the opposite knee and twirled her foot to the club beat.

She wanted to dance. She wanted to give herself to the music. She didn't have to worry about what her face looked like then, or why her lover wanted to be rid of her. She didn't have to worry about dying; all she had to do was live within the music.

She rose to her feet, felt Micah's hand slide down her arm until his fingers were loosely gripped around her wrist as he stared up at her.

"I want to dance," she told him, hungering for the freedom the music had always given her. The freedom to be more than the ugly little girl she had always been.

His expression tightened, his black eyes grew impossibly blacker, sexier, as he rose from his seat. He shrugged the leather jacket he wore from his shoulders and laid it on her seat, atop her purse and wrap, as though protecting them, hiding them from view. Then he took her hand and led her to the dance floor.

MICAH HAD KNOWN that the day would come that Risa would find a way to completely blow his little mind. She'd already taken control of his cock; it stayed hard for her, and for her alone. But on the dance floor, amid dozens of dancers vying for attention, she stole another part of him. He had a feeling there was going to be very little of himself that he owned by the time this mission was over.

She danced liked a dream. The chocolate silk tunic dress shifted and shimmered over her gracefully as she moved. It did nothing to hide the heat of her flesh as he touched her, did nothing to hide the sensual, sensuous woman who lurked beneath her quiet exterior.

He watched her nipples bead harder beneath the silk, watched as her light blue eyes became leaden, sensual. Her face flushed, her lips parted, and he knew she was the center of his world at that moment.

He would die to protect her. There had been no one in his life, outside of his parents, whom he would have consciously walked into death for. For this woman, he would.

She swayed before him like temptation itself. Her arms lifted, her hips moved, and all he knew was the remembered feel of her moving beneath him.

His hands touched her, stroked down her back, along her hips. He turned her and her back rubbed against his chest as his hand flattened on her stomach, pressing the sweet curves of her ass into his cock.

She twirled with an exotic allure.

She owned him.

He could have danced with her forever. He was perfectly content to remain locked in time, right there, with the vision of her dancing just for him.

And he would have until the moment she collapsed against his chest, laughter falling from her lips as her light brightened with self-amusement.

"My legs are giving out," she laughed. "I don't think high heels were made for this."

Laughter. It was the first time he'd heard her laugh, the first time he had seen that happiness shining in her eyes, and he felt his heart clench. It was the most beautiful sight in the world. A gift he would always remember.

"I'll hold you up." He held her against his chest, moving

more slowly to the music, taking her weight and cuddling her against his chest as her arms moved to wrap around his neck.

She rested against him, swaying with him as his head bent over hers and he closed his eyes at the sneaking suspicion that walking away from her was going to flay his soul.

Her fingers played along his neck, a finger twining through the short strands of hair at the back of his head. Her nails scraped his scalp. She was a flame in his arms, seeping into his pores, chaining him when he had no desire to be chained.

"I need you." He brushed his lips over the shell of her ear and felt her shiver. "All of you."

"Hmm." Her head lifted. "You had me and wanted to send me away," she reminded him. "You're not the weather, Micah. You can't change from day to day on me."

His lips quirked. "Do we want to fight tonight, Risa? Or do we want to love?"

He hadn't meant to whisper the *l* word against her lips. But at the sound of it, he felt her body tighten; he swore he could feel the wash of her need singeing his body, cutting into it like dull knives as he fought the sensation.

"Love?" His shoulder cradled her head as she looked up at him. "I'm certain that wasn't the word you meant to use, Micah." There was a subtle, almost hidden vein of bitterness in her voice.

His lovely Risa. She had never been loved, not truly. She'd been used, she'd been hurt, but she'd never had love to balance the darkness that had filled her life.

He couldn't answer her. He couldn't give her hope where no hope should exist. He had to remember what came after the mission. And what came after was another mission, another danger, perhaps another identity. There was no place for love in that life.

Noah had done it, another part of him reminded himself. Noah had a home, a wife, he would soon have a child, and he balanced that life. But Noah was the nephew of the unit commander. It made a difference.

"Does the word I use matter?" Micah's hand framed her face as he bent his head to her. "I won't wait much longer,

Risa. You don't give a man a taste of paradise, then jerk it away from him."

"Really?" Her head lifted, her arms slid to his shoulders. "But you can give it to a woman and then tear her away from it without a thought, can't you, Micah?" She stopped moving and tried to draw back.

Micah held her to him, frustration and arousal biting into him as she tried to put distance between them.

"I think I need a drink—"

"Risa, is that you?"

Micah's head jerked up; his nostrils flared in primitive anger at the sight of the man standing at their side. He wanted to push Risa behind him, wanted to get her as far away from this primal threat as possible.

"Mac?" Amazement and laughter fell from her lips as she turned to the other man. "Oh my goodness. Mac Knight? Look at you." Her hands reached out for his, large hands that gripped her smaller ones before the other man pulled her close for a hug. "Look how you've changed," she breathed out in surprise.

Micah's teeth almost snapped together as the younger man's chest seemed to puff out. Dressed in jeans and a cotton shirt, he was military; there was no missing that. The way he held himself, the look in his eyes, screamed Special Ops.

"How I've changed?" Mac's smile was amazed as he stood back and stared down at Risa. "Damn, Risa, you look like a million bucks." He shook his head as though amazed before asking, "Dance with me? Just for a few minutes?" He looked to Micah as though in permission before his gaze turned to Risa again.

Micah wanted to slam his fist into the bastard's face.

"For a minute." Risa turned to Micah. "He's a friend of mine. He's been in Iraq forever. I'll be fine."

The hell she would be.

Micah nodded stiffly before moving back and placing his back against the thick support post at the edge of the dance floor. He hoped neither of them expected him to just tuck his tail and slink back to the table, because it wasn't happening.

The dance mix had moved into a slower tune, a soft ballad that required the other man to take her into his arms. At least she wasn't rubbing against him like the sensual little cat Micah knew she was. But she was too close to the other man, and for a moment Micah knew complete bloodlust.

"YOUR BOYFRIEND is upset," Mac said as they moved to the music, his topaz eyes watching her assessingly.

That was Mac, always thinking about things, she thought fondly.

"Micah will be fine." She gave her head a little shake before the impulse to look over at him got the better of her.

"I heard about the abduction, Risa." Mac's statement had her head jerking around as humilitation flared within her. "I was in Iraq with Reno when they pulled the rescue team together, and I asked to transfer to the rescue team. They denied the request. I would have found a way to get you out of that clinic if I had known."

It was a statement. It was an acknowledgment that she had needed help then. The humiliation drained out of her, but weariness seemed to set in.

"I made it out." She didn't want to talk about it. "And I don't want to discuss that, Mac. But look at you. You filled out."

He grinned. He was a few years older than she was, maybe seven years, she thought. That would make him thirty-two maybe. The last time she'd seen him she'd been sixteen and he'd been a wise, older twenty-two-year-old who had just joined the Army.

So many years. And they'd both changed.

"I'm not the only one." He smiled down at her with wry amusement. "You're looking beautiful. But didn't I always tell you you would?"

"Yeah, after you made me cry by calling me the ugly duckling," she pointed out without bitterness. It was impossible to stay angry with Mac for long, even then. He'd had a shy, touching smile and a way of telling you the way it was, no matter what you wanted to believe.

"I was right." He nodded briskly. "You turned into a beautiful young woman, Risa."

She shrugged, uncomfortable with that thought. She still saw the plain features; if there was any beauty there, it hid from her in her mirror.

"So what do you do in Iraq?" she asked, desperate to know more about one of the few friends she had had as a child.

"I work in Special Ops," he stated. "We coordinate many of the missions that go out among the SEALs and Special Forces in the Middle East. Most of them make it through our command center eventually."

"You should have met Micah somewhere then," she told him. "He was a SEAL before returning to the states."

He glanced at Micah, then back at her. "He's not a SEAL, Risa," Mac stated.

"Yes, he was." Risa stared up at him in confusion. "He worked primarily in the Middle East."

Mac shook his head as a touch of worry entered his expression. "I don't know what he's trying to pull on you, but I know damned good and well he's not a SEAL," he said again. "Not just because I don't know him, but because SEALs carry themselves a certain way, even after they leave the Navy. If they ever do. That man has never been a SEAL. An agent somewhere perhaps, definitely not someone you want to mess with." His gaze sharpened on her face then. "Riss, are you in trouble? Do you need help?"

Risa felt an overwhelming surge of affection fill her. That was Mac, always trying to look out for someone else.

"I'm fine." She shook her head. "But trust me, Micah's a SEAL." Wasn't he? She was desperate to convince herself that at least that much was the truth. That Micah's entire personality couldn't be false.

Mac shook his head again. "You trust me, Risa, if that man was a SEAL, then I would have met him. And I know SEALs. He's nothing—" He broke off. "Riss, is that Ian Richards with him?"

She nodded; she didn't have to look.

"Riss." Concern colored his voice. "Sweetheart, what are you involved in?"

"WHO IS HE?" IAN moved in close to Micah as they watched Risa dance with the other man.

"Mac Knight, Special Ops in Iraq," Micah answered. "And whatever he's telling her isn't setting well with her."

"Fuck, I know Knight." Ian grimaced. "Special Ops my ass, he's deep level. Every damned mission over there goes through his office one way or the other. He could blow your cover sky-high."

"Get Jordan on the line," Micah ordered him as he straightened from the post. "Have him pull Mr. Knight out, ASAP. I want him unable and unwilling to open his damned mouth."

Ian flipped open his cell phone as Micah tensed. Risa looked worried. She kept her expression turned from him, her body was tense, and Mac Knight looked thunderous.

Micah watched them, frowning. He didn't like that proprietary look Knight had in his eyes any more than he liked seeing Risa in the other man's arms.

"Give Jordan one minute," Ian murmured. "He's having him called into base. Jordan will be waiting there on him along with his CO."

"If it's not too late," Micah growled.

They watched, and almost to the minute later the other man paused, his gaze slashing to Micah and Ian as he pulled his cell phone from his jeans, spoke into it, then glared back at them.

Micah smiled, a slow, triumphant curve of his lips that he made certain wasn't there when Risa turned back to him.

The look in her eyes assured him that she had heard something that had upset her. Something that had most likely pissed her off.

"Ian." Mac's gaze was cool as he faced both Micah and Ian. "It's good to see you again."

"Mac." Ian nodded, then looked at Risa before lifting his gaze back to the other man. "Leaving so soon?"

A mocking glint filled Mac's eyes as Micah curved his arm around Risa's stiff back and pulled her against him.

"Duty calls," Mac stated, the mockery fully present in his voice. "I hope you're looking after Risa," he warned Ian then.

Ian tilted his head, looked at Risa, then at Mac, and let a smile tip his lips. "I let Micah take care of that, Mac. Since he's living with her, I'd consider that his job, wouldn't you?"

Mac didn't answer. His yellow-brown eyes stared into Micah's as Micah felt the overwhelming urge to show the little pup exactly who the big dog was where Risa was concerned.

"I'll be talking to you soon, Ian." It sounded like a warning as Mac turned to Risa, bent, kissed her cheek, and nodded in farewell before leaving.

"How very interesting." Risa looked up at Micah with false brightness. "You're a true man of mystery, Micah." Then her eyes hardened as she stared at Ian. "I'm ready to go home. I've had enough for the night."

She didn't give either of them a chance to respond but moved away instead, her hips twitching with a snap. Micah grimaced. She was pissed.

"We're in trouble," Ian murmured.

"No," Micah sighed. "I am. You're not the one that has to live with her when she's pissed."

"True," Ian grunted. "But I have to live with Kira. Ex-agent. Remember?"

"She'd just kill you fast," Micah sighed. "I get to die slow."

"There is that." Ian was almost laughing. "There is definitely that, Micah."

Chapter 18

BY THE TIME THE limo pulled up at the apartment building, Micah could feel the tension humming around Risa. She was silent, deadly with feminine rage. He could feel it pulsing in the air around them.

Ian and Kira pulled into the parking lot in front of the building, there more or less on Risa's orders. With a sweet smile and a firm command she had posed it as a request, but Micah and Ian knew better. The invitation she had made for the other couple to return to the apartment was couched in gentle words, but they'd all seen the look in her eyes.

Kira had been amused but questioning as she looked from Micah to Ian, as though they should know exactly what Knight had said to her.

The hell if Micah had a clue, but he made a mental note to find the bastard himself soon and find out exactly what had happened.

"I'm surprised you wanted company tonight," Micah observed as Travis opened the door and helped Risa out.

He noticed she released the other agent's hand as quickly as possible.

"I'm sure you are." Her voice was as tight as her body; a few times during the ride he thought he'd caught a shimmer of tears in her eyes.

"Risa?" He cocked his head and stared down at her as Ian

and Kira moved across the parking lot. "Is there something I should know?"

Her smile was brittle. "I don't know, Micah. Is there something *I* should know?"

He controlled a frown as Ian and Kira reached them.

"Risa, everything okay?" Kira looked around at the well-tended grounds, the small park across from the parking area, and the well-lit exterior.

"I'm fine." Risa shrugged as she turned and walked through the door that Clive held open for her.

He nodded at them as she passed. Risa took the time to thank him, to bestow a sweet smile on him. She hadn't smiled or even chatted since her dance with Mac Knight.

They moved as a group to the elevator. Risa remained silent on the ride up, the tension humming through her reaching out to the rest of them.

She moved up the hall, glared at the door opposite hers, then waited for Micah to unlock the door, check inside, then cover the hall as John moved quickly into the opposite apartment.

Risa stepped inside the apartment, wondering if she was going to strangle on her anger as she turned to the others and pasted a smile on her face. "I'm not much on wine," she informed them. "I do have beer, though."

"Beer's fine, Risa." Ian nodded, his gaze questioning.

"Great." Okay, her smile was overly bright, but she wasn't screaming at them yet. "I'll get them."

She moved into the kitchen, took four beers from the refrigerator, popped the lids, and returned to the other room.

When everyone had a cold brew and had found seats, Ian and Kira on the couch, Micah in one of the two easy chairs, Risa perched on the seat of the remaining chair and smiled back at Ian.

"So, how long have you known Micah, Ian?" she asked him.

"About five years." His look was mildly curious. "Why?"

Why? As though he hadn't been lying to her, as though he

hadn't been as much a part of the deceit as the others had been.

"You met in the Middle East?" she quizzed him, feeling the tension that threatened to tear her apart from the inside out. "Jordan mentioned that the morning I was told of this little operation. That Micah was a former SEAL. He'd worked with your team."

Ian stared back at her for long moments before he leaned forward and set his beer on the table.

"Risa, why don't you just say what's on your mind?" he said gently. "Don't beat around the bush with me."

Her lips nearly trembled. She had to tighten them to hold back the need to cry. Jansen had told her that she was nothing but a crybaby. That she didn't know how to handle reality or how to be an adult. That she would always deal with her problems by crying.

It seemed he was right. At least in this case.

"You were there," she whispered. "In that hellhole Jansen let them take me to. You helped rescue me, Ian."

He nodded as Micah cursed under his breath.

"I was there, Risa," Ian agreed. "And I wanted to kill those bastards for what they did to you, Emily, and Carrie. If I'd known what happened later, I would have taken you out of that clinic and made certain you were protected. I would have killed Jansen myself."

She nodded. She knew that. Ian was like that. He would always try to protect others; it was a part of him.

"I trusted you, Ian. You, Reno, Kell, and Macey. I trusted all of you with my life, because you were there." Her breathing hitched as Micah jerked from his chair and paced closer to her.

"Risa, why don't you just tell us what Knight said," Kira stated then, her voice compassionate but matter-of-fact.

Risa turned to Kira and wanted to scream in rage. The tears were tearing her chest apart. They burned behind her eyes; they choked her as they rose in her chest.

She wanted to fold up into herself and escape. To hide as

Micah had already accused her of doing. But surely hiding wasn't as painful as facing the lies.

She wished she were as strong as Kira. As confident. For six years Risa had been so envious of the other woman. But she wondered at the hell it would have to take to find such confidence in her ability to survive. Risa didn't imagine she could survive worse than what she had known herself, yet she had found no confidence in her survival.

"You didn't have to lie to me to convince me to meet him," she whispered, staring back at Ian. "And you didn't have to lie to me after that, that he was a friend of yours. That he was a SEAL. I wouldn't have fought this operation you wanted to use me for. All you had to do was tell me he was a friend, Ian. That was all."

Silence filled the room as she rose to her feet and turned her back on the three of them. She felt as though she were going to shatter.

"You'd think I'd be used to the lies," she mused roughly. "I should be by now, shouldn't I? It shouldn't affect me so much, that you had lied about something so small."

She turned and faced them. No one said a word. They were watching her cautiously, as though they still weren't certain exactly what she knew. Even Kira seemed to be on alert, watching her intently. Micah's black eyes were penetrating, his brows lowered heavily as he watched her.

"Is he even American?" She turned to Ian as though she were only curious. "I could swear at times that he's not. Can any of you even tell me the truth there?"

"Risa." Ian cleared his throat.

"Please don't lie to me again, Ian," she said conversationally, as though the tears weren't ripping into her soul. "I counted you and Kira both as friends. People I could depend on." She almost snorted at that thought. "Perhaps I should have known better. The operation is more important, correct?"

"I warned you," Kira said softly to her husband as her gray eyes stayed on Risa.

Risa hated the look in her eyes. She hated being watched as though she were a bug under a damned microscope.

"Why did you lie to me!" she screamed back at them, barely aware of the subtle flinch that jerked through Micah's body as she glared at Ian and Kira.

"Because you needed to trust the man that was going to be sleeping with you, Risa." Kira was the one who answered her.

The other woman rose to her feet, her look so damned pitying that Risa had to curl her fingers into fists to keep from going for her face.

"Look at you," Risa accused roughly. "You feel so damned sorry for me, don't you, Kira? I get sick of the pity in all your eyes. Try telling me the damned truth for a change and you wouldn't have to feel sorry for poor little Risa."

Kira winced. "Guilty as charged." She nodded. "And you're right: We should have been honest with you. But in our defense, Risa, we could never be certain how strong you were, or how you would have accepted the unvarnished truth."

"And that truth is?" Risa laughed bitterly. "Let's see." She turned to Micah. "That first night he was your good and dear friend who fought with your husband in the Middle East. The next morning he was one of Jordan Malone's agents committed to protecting me." She turned back to Kira. "What is he now?"

No one answered her. They stared back at her as though she were demented, but there were no answers forthcoming. She could feel the bitterness tearing through her. It cramped her stomach, ripped at her chest. She felt as though her knees were going to give out on her and leave her clawing at the floor in pain.

She turned to Micah. "No explanations? No answers?" Her voice was grating as she shuddered at the look in his eyes. Part torment, part complete impenetrable male arrogance.

"I can't tell you what you want to know," he finally stated. "But know this, Risa: I didn't lie to you. Nothing I've done, nothing I've given you, has been a lie."

"Liar." She wanted to scream, but the accusation was torn, ragged, instead. "You lied every time you touched me, Micah. You lied to me with every word out of your lips so you could see this mission through. At least admit that."

"I didn't have to lie, Risa," he stated somberly. "Because you didn't ask questions. And now, you're asking questions I can't answer."

"Of course you can't." Her stage whisper was bitter and filled with pain. "Super-secret agents don't answer questions, do they, Mr. Sloane?"

"This is ridiculous, Risa," he accused her, his gaze snapping with ire now. "You knew this was a mission. You knew what we were trying to do. You can't cry foul now. And you can't expect me to endanger that mission by answering questions that contain information that could be dangerous in the wrong hands. Information that could only end up hurting you."

She flinched at the anger in his voice and his refusal to answer something as simple as what the hell he was.

"Well, I guess I'm asking the wrong person." She turned and swung for the door. "Let's see what Jordan has to say."

"No, Risa." Micah jumped for her, but he was too late. She was out the door, across the hall, and pounding on the door where she knew the so-called agents lodged.

She wanted answers. She didn't want more lies and she didn't want more cover-ups. She wanted to know exactly whom she had given her body and her heart to. She wanted to know the man she was going to lose.

"Risa, not right now," Micah growled, his fingers curling around her arm.

"Now." She jerked out of his grip as the door swung open.

Jordan stared back at her, his blue eyes glowing with anger as he glared at Micah over her head. But Jordan wasn't the one who held her attention.

She heard Micah's vicious curse behind her, Ian's "God, Jordan, what the hell are you doing?"

Her eyes were held by the man who stared back at her, his topaz gaze shattered as his head lifted from the pictures scattered over the table.

Mac Knight.

He had been her friend when so few young men would even take the time to speak to her. He had danced with her when she would have been humiliated at not having an escort for a particular part of an event.

He had been like a brother. He and his parents had lived on the estate next to the Clays', so they had socialized often. He had taught her how to play poker one summer. He had slipped her her first bottle of beer.

He was one of the few good memories she had from her youth.

"Risa." Mac rose slowly to his feet, his oddly colored eyes damp, filled with horror as he stared back at her with pity. "I didn't know. God, Riss, I didn't know."

His voice was thick with anger, regret. And pity.

"I would have done something." His voice was thick with emotion, with regret.

Risa ignored it. Her gaze was captured by the pictures spread out on the table.

Pictures of her.

She remembered the flash of lights as someone had taken pictures in the plane. She also remembered something about video. They always took pictures and video of their victims, she remembered distantly. Diego Fuentes had insisted on it. He'd had a very small supply of Whore's Dust, so it was only used on victims who could benefit him. The sons and daughters of powerful men. Women who worked in sensitive or classified areas. They were predominantly the victims he'd chosen himself.

Sometimes, his associates had bought the Whore's Dust from him and used it in other ways. But always there had been pictures and videos.

"It wasn't exactly my best pose," she said, staring at the top picture.

Her face was red, her eyes wild and filled with tears. There were more under that one. Vivid, shocking, explicit pictures.

She heard Micah behind her; it sounded as though he were ready to kill, but her gaze was held by the pictures.

"Riss," Mac's protest was swallowed by the roaring in her ears.

She hadn't seen the pictures. She'd had no idea Jordan had them.

"They made you look at these," she said as she gestured to the pictures, feeling the numbness in her lips before it moved through her body. "I guess you were being berated for telling on Micah."

She slid a few more pictures free. They were grainy but explicit. Nothing was hid from the eye of the camera that night. It was all there in glaring detail. At least it wasn't in color, she thought faintly.

She had to put her hand over her mouth to hold back her screams, to hold back the need to gag as she was greeted with the sight of her own nude body. Bruised, filthy. The canvas beneath her was smeared with her blood.

"How tacky, showing these to you." She couldn't breathe. She could feel the need to draw oxygen into her lungs, but she couldn't seem to get enough inside her. "You should have shredded them for me."

She could hear herself screaming. In the back of her head, she was screaming and begging Jansen. *Daddy, please. Please make it stop.*

You damned crybaby. Big girls don't cry, you little bitch, he had accused her.

And she could hear his laughter. It raked through her mind like diseased talons and left her feeling feverish, weak.

She could hear voices behind her. She could hear Micah cursing Jordan, Ian, Mac, and anyone else he could curse. She didn't see the tears Kira had to hide, or the redhead who had turned her face to the wall as her own tears began to fall from her eyes.

Risa lifted her gaze to Mac. "How sad," she whispered. "Definitely the ugly duckling, aren't I?"

Her expression was twisted in those photos. She was ugly, blemished, dirty. She had been a creature, an enraged animal, and it showed in the grainy photos that had been printed out.

"Stop this." Micah jerked her around.

Risa stared up at him in shock. His black eyes were primal, sparking with bits of white light that almost held her entranced.

"Did Jordan show him the video as well?" She told herself she was merely curious. It wasn't as though the video could be any worse than the pictures.

"Risa, stop." Micah's hand framed her face, his long fingers pushing into her hair as he stared back at her, his gaze tormented. "Knight refused to listen to Jordan's explanations. He wanted proof. He wasn't backing down without it, honey. It was give him proof or kill him."

A smile curved her lips. She felt it. An automated response as something began to tear loose inside her soul.

"I think I would have preferred that you kill me," she stated. "Have you seen them?"

"Risa," he objected roughly. "Let's go back home; we'll talk about this there."

She jerked her head from his grip and stared around the room. Ian and Kira; there was the agent John who stayed in the apartment. How interesting, the chauffeur who had driven them earlier stood in the doorway to a bedroom. Nik watched her with icy Nordic blue eyes. There was the redhead from the elevator. And lo and behold, why, there was Risa's good friend Emily's husband stepping into the room, Kell.

"Have all of them seen those pictures?" Risa turned back to Micah. "Did you have like a meeting? What do you call it? A mission objective where you looked at the gory evidence first? Did you get to see the video? I can't imagine it was very interesting."

She was talking too fast. Risa felt cut off, disconnected with herself, as voices echoed in the back of her head.

"No, Risa," he bit out roughly. "The pictures were part of the file we had. I didn't look at the pictures and neither did the others. We knew what had happened to you."

"And you're not a SEAL." She knew he wasn't. She leaned forward almost playfully; she felt like a wooden doll with no soul. "I bet that was Emily's idea, huh? She knew I used to dream of a SEAL slipping into my bedroom and rescuing me when I was a child. Did she tell you that?"

"Risa. Baby." Micah's voice lowered, and she wondered if that was his hand that shook as he touched her cheek or if she was simply shaking that hard.

"No answer?" She felt weak. She felt as though she were being ripped apart inside and she couldn't even let the rage escape. She couldn't hit him; she couldn't hate him. She stared up at him, and in that second of agony she actually realized she loved him.

She almost laughed at that thought. Poor ugly Risa. She thought she'd found a SEAL, and now she didn't even know what stood in its place.

"Micah is former Israeli Mossad, Risa." That was Jordan's voice. It was low; it was wicked dark. Funny, she shouldn't even care that he sounded as though he was in pain.

"Mossad," she said faintly. "Yeah, it fits. Jewish. No bacon."

"Risa, stop this." His expression was worried, filled with pain. Tormented.

She turned her head and stared at Mac. His eyes were darker than she had ever seen them. "We were friends," she whispered.

"We're still friends." He swallowed heavily. "We'll always be friends, Risa. Do you think I'd blame you?"

She shook her head. "No friends, Mac. Don't have friends, they just lie to you, don't you know that?"

She heard someone sob and thought maybe it was the redhead.

"Micah, get her the hell out of here," Jordan cursed. "I'll call her psychologist and get her over here."

Risa wanted to laugh at that.

She whirled on Jordan instead. "Don't worry, Mr. Malone, I have medication, and I know how to take it if I need it." She stared at him with cold, brutal anger. "Do you know, every time I've seen you you've been like the Grim Reaper of goodwill and cheer. You should find another profession."

Surprise glittered in his eyes.

Risa shrugged off Micah's hold and moved carefully, deliberately, across the room. She wasn't going to cry here. As she reached the door, she turned and looked across the room to Kell. His green eyes were filled with regret.

"Tell Emily I love her anyway," Risa whispered, as she had to clamp her lips together to keep from sobbing. "She lied to me, Kell. Both of you lied to me."

She felt loss, and she felt alone. She stared around the room, realizing that everyone she loved had lied to her as though she were a child who couldn't handle the truth, who couldn't handle reality.

"All you had to do was tell me the truth." She stared at Micah, her heart breaking as her first tear fell. "Just the truth."

She opened the door. Micah was behind her, silent, as icy as death, as he walked her across the hall and back into her apartment.

The door closed behind them and she kept walking. She moved through the living room and into the bedroom before closing and locking the door behind her.

She moved through the bedroom and into the bathroom and closed the door there.

She looked different.

She stared into the full-length mirror.

She didn't see the ugly duckling.

She didn't see the woman enraged by Whore's Dust or the desperate child who used to sit in front of her bedroom window and dream of a SEAL to rescue her.

She saw a young woman. She wasn't ugly, but she wasn't beautiful.

She wiped at her tears, but they refused to stop falling. She was a little plain maybe, but Micah didn't need to put a bag over her face to fuck her.

He just needed to lie to her.

Her mascara was running, though. And the tip of her nose was red.

She reached out, touched the mirror that had followed her through her childhood into adulthood. The same mirror on its heavy dark stand.

She reached out, gripped a bottle from the cabinet, and with an enraged cry, threw it into the mirror.

She watched it shatter. Glass rained around her as she heard the bedroom door crash. A second later the bathroom door slammed into the wall behind it.

"There." She turned on him.

Shaking in rage, the tears falling from her eyes, she faced him. "There's your damned mirror. There's your ugly duckling. I need you just about as much as I need that fucking mirror."

Her fists slammed into his chest as she began to sob. She struck out at him. There was nothing else to strike out at. All the pain and rage of six years rose inside her until she was screaming with it, her head buried in his chest as he picked her up, holding her close to him, and carried her to the easy chair that sat in the corner of her bedroom.

He held her. One hand against her head to hold her screams against his heart. The other wrapped around her upper body as he tucked her close to his chest and rocked her gently.

She couldn't hold it in. She couldn't fight it. She'd fought for six years. She hadn't cried; she hadn't lost control. She had made certain she wasn't the crybaby Jansen Clay had accused her of being over and over that night.

"Risa, baby." Micah's hand stroked down her back. "I have you, love. Right here against my heart. I have you, Risa."

She felt his heart beating against her cheek, strong and sure, a heavy throb that had soothed her the only night she had allowed herself to sleep against him.

Into his chest she poured eight years of rage, grief, and pain. She poured the child she had been against his chest, and the woman who didn't know how to be free. She held on to him with desperate hands, and she let herself be weak.

She let herself accept.

Friends would lie.

Sometimes, there was going to be pity.

She couldn't always be strong.

And one day soon, Micah would leave.

She never saw the tears Micah shed as she sobbed against him. And she never saw the pain that burned in his soul for the woman he couldn't have. The woman who was strong enough to cry, and strong enough to survive.

Chapter 19

SHE SHOULD HAVE slept the night and the morning away. By the time Micah stripped the beautiful silk dress from her and tucked her beneath the blankets, she was exhausted from her weeping.

She was aware of him undressing, and when he slid naked into the bed, she couldn't help but curl against him.

"My mother once told me that when a woman sheds tears, the angels bring her strength," he whispered into the darkness as he held Risa against him. "You're not weak, Risa. And I have never pitied you. Not even once. I have always been in awe of your courage and your tenacity to survive."

"I've hidden," she whispered hoarsely.

"Yes, you hid." He sighed. "From yourself. From the beauty that shines from inside you and fills the gentle curves of your face. You've hidden from a past that no one can blame you for not wanting to remember. And you've hidden from yourself, Risa. But you didn't hide from life, and you didn't hide from the knowledge of events you wanted to forget. You've always handled that with grace."

"I'm tired." She let her eyes close. "I just want to forget for a little while, Micah."

His hand smoothed down her back before he tucked the sheet and comforter closer to her neck.

"Sleep, love. I'll be right here."

She was silent for long moments, staring into the darkness.

"I didn't want you to see those pictures," she said then. "I wanted to forget they existed."

She felt his arms tighten around her and realized in that moment that she had never been held when she had cried. She had never been held, period, other than the few times her grandmother had hugged her.

"They won't exist much longer," he promised her. "The video was destroyed, though, years before. Jordan made certain that all the videos that were confiscated were destroyed. There's no video out there, Risa. And I promise you, there won't be any pictures much longer."

She nodded, her lashes drifting over her eyes.

Sleep came over her swiftly. She should have slept for hours. She slept dreamlessly at least. There were no nightmares plaguing her as they had in the past nights. She slept, warm and comfortable against Micah's chest, and came awake as morning light filtered through the bedroom curtains.

She was warm, cuddled close against his chest, her leg thrown over one of his as he wrapped himself around her.

Protecting her.

Her hand rested against his heart, just below her cheek. The slow, steady beat soothed her, relaxed her.

She had always wondered what it would be like to have someone to awaken to every morning. It should have cut at her, knowing he wouldn't be there any longer than it took to catch a killer, and the pain was there. But it resided with weary acceptance.

Yes, he would be gone, but she knew now what it meant to love. She might not know what it meant to be loved, but loving was almost as good.

And loving meant wanting.

She could feel her body, each nerve ending awake and pulsing for his touch. Hunger gnawed at her senses, the memory of his possession heating her until her clit became swollen, her pussy wet and aching.

"You're awake." Micah's voice wasn't in the least drowsy.

It was dark and hot with need. His cock was a thick wedge of flesh pressed against her stomach, throbbing with the same heady pace as his heartbeat.

Was that what had awakened her? The knowledge that he was waiting for her, hard and ready to pleasure her?

"I broke the mirror," she whispered, horrified that she had done such a thing. "Grandmother is going to cry. She gave me that mirror when I was a little girl."

As she spoke, she couldn't help but rub her fingertips against his flexing abs, to feel the strength and the power that resided there.

"We don't need the mirror."

The sheet shimmied over her flesh, dragged carelessly from her body. A shudder rushed through her.

She couldn't resist his touch, not when she needed it so desperately. When the pain and humiliation, the lies and the fears, twisted in her stomach like a feverish fist.

"*Ahuvati*," he whispered, the desert-dark heat of his voice stroking over her as his palm caressed her stomach to her swollen breast. "My Risa. How I hunger for you."

He rose over her, his head tilting, his lips settling over hers in a butterfly kiss that sent waves of heat shuttling through her body.

"Kiss me, Risa," he crooned against her lips. "Take me."

A whimper left her lips. Her arms circled his neck, her fingers burying in the short length of his hair to pull his head to her.

Her tongue stroked over his lips as an earthy male groan met the caress. He tasted of male heat and dark desire, an ambrosia she craved.

As she moved closer to the warmth of his body, her breath jerked in her lungs at the feel of his cock, heavy and hard against her thigh.

"My beautiful Risa," he groaned against her lips as his head lifted from their kiss. "Sweet love. *At yafa*. You're beautiful."

She shivered beneath the midnight cadence of his voice, and the feel of his palm curling around her breast, his fingers moving to the distended peak of her nipple.

"The taste of you heats me." His head lowered, his tongue stroking over the opposite nipple as his fingers plucked at its mate. "You make my blood heat with my hunger for you."

She arched, the sound of his voice almost a physical caress over her senses before his lips parted farther and he drew the tight bud into his mouth.

As she pressed her head back into the pillow, her eyes flared wide at the feel of his teeth raking the tip, then closing on it, tugging it gently.

Little flares of pleasure that bordered pain tore through her and raced to her sex. Her vagina pulsed and spilled its slick dampness, while her clit swelled and throbbed with imperative need.

The feel of him, his lips drawing at her nipple, his hands stroking over her body, was life. It was the essence of pleasure. He touched more than her flesh, and she wondered if he knew. Did he know that when he touched her, he touched her soul?

"Micah," she whispered his name, desperate to give voice to the sensations as they washed over her like a warm, silken wave. "Touch me. Let me feel, Micah. Just for now, let me feel." Feel his body, his heart, his soul.

Just for this moment she wanted as much of him as she was giving him. She'd return it, she promised silently. She wouldn't hold him prisoner to the needs or the emotions rising inside her. She'd give him the freedom he needed to walk away from her.

"Please." Her head lowered until her lips could caress the hard muscle of his shoulder as his lips drew at her breast. "Let me feel you."

"*Ahuvati*." *My love.* The words slipped from Micah's lips again as the throb of her need speared through his senses. He could feel the power of her desire, not just her sexual desire, but the bond he'd always sensed, even before he'd touched her. The desire to feel it, to touch it, even as they touched physically.

He was reminded of those visits to Atlanta when he would only glimpse her coming or going from one of the Durango team's homes over the years. Her head had always been down, her hair shielding her face. But he'd felt her. He'd felt the glow of her spirit, a part of her reaching out to him even as he'd held back from her.

There was no holding back from her now. He was giving himself to her. He was aware of it. He couldn't stop it.

She was his heart. She was every emotion he had never allowed himself to have. She was every touch he had never given another woman.

Silk and satin, heat and longing. All things he had never thought he would ever possess.

He cupped her breast in his palm, his mouth suckling at the hard tip of her nipple as his other hand caressed down her stomach, feeling the ripple of response just beneath her soft skin.

His fingers met the bare flesh between her thighs and he groaned at the sensation of heated, slick silk. Like syrup, sweet and hot, spilling from her body to coat the swollen folds of her pussy.

Micah groaned at the feel of her response. So unabashed, so innocent. She arched to him, obviously lost in the pleasure he brought her.

He sensed no fear, and the knowledge of that dug restless claws into his soul.

She gave to him without reservation. She came to him without motive, with emotion and with pleasure.

"I could spend eternity here, touching you," he groaned against her breast as the need to taste her grew overwhelming.

Risa felt pleasure and need as it restricted her breathing. She stared into his dark eyes, mesmerized by the subtle flames that lit the black depths.

Her hands shook as she clenched her fingers against his shoulder and watched as his lips smoothed between her breasts, dropping little kisses along her flesh as he worked his way down her body.

"Micah," his name sighed past her lips. "Don't stop. Please don't stop." For eternity. She wanted his touch always.

Flares of searing sensation rocked her body as his fingertips glanced over her clit. He parted the sensitive folds, caressed through the narrow slit, and drew a startled cry from her lips as her womb flexed in response beneath his lips.

Their breathing was ragged. Risa could hear their breaths, her strangled moans as well as his. The room heated until perspiration seemed to drench her body.

"Micah." She twisted beneath his hold, her hips arching as he rimmed the entrance to her vagina. His fingers were wicked, knowing, as they stroked the flexing entrance.

"Easy." His teeth nipped at her thigh as he eased her legs farther apart with his free hand. "Let me taste you, love."

The endearment had an involuntary cry leaving her lips. It seemed to stroke inside her, to stoke the flames of response burning through her system.

"I want to taste you," he whispered against her thigh. "All that sweetness spilling for me. I want my tongue on you. Inside you."

She shook her head desperately as she fought to hold on to enough of her senses to remember every touch, every sensation.

Her hands fisted into the sheet beneath her body as she strained to be closer to him.

His head moved, his tongue licked over her clit, at the same moment that he pushed two broad fingers into the needy depths of her body.

Risa arched and screamed with the pleasure. It was a bolt of lightning striking in a never-ending pattern, firing tiny explosions through her system as his fingers filled her, his mouth possessed her.

The pleasure was violent. The need for release was a driving, overwhelming sensation all its own. She strained toward it, fought for it.

"I love the taste of you," he groaned before he licked around the throbbing bud of her clit again. "So warm, so sweet."

He was patient. He took his time. He licked as his fingers stroked inside her slowly, stretching her, parting her until the wicked bolts of pleasure raced through her with unrelenting sensations.

She wanted him. She wanted more than simply lying there and taking her pleasure. She wanted to give pleasure.

Her head lifted, her eyes took in the sight of him, his eyes closed, his tongue working around her clit with delicious strokes.

"I want to touch you." She struggled against him, the need destroying her. "I want you, too, Micah. I want to touch you, taste you."

His forehead touched her lower belly as he took in a ragged breath, his head shaking slowly, his fingers pausing inside her.

"Please." She pushed against his shoulders. "Show me how to touch you, too."

"Risa," he groaned. "Let me love you. Lie beneath me, love, and let me pleasure you."

She shook her head. She wanted it all. This morning, as the room brightened around them, she wanted all of him. His touch, his hunger, even as she touched and hungered. She wanted to spill as much into him as he gave.

"No." She shook her head. "Please, Micah. Show me. I want to touch you, too."

Show her how to touch as she was touched.

His fingers slid from her snug grip. Eyes narrowed and glittering, he lifted himself from her.

"Are you sure, Risa?" His voice was dark, sexual, as he stared down at her with a dominance in his expression that should have frightened her. "The pleasure can get out of control, love. You can lose yourself in it." His voice dropped to a whisper as the need for it seemed to glitter in his eyes. "You could get more than you may be comfortable with."

It was a dare. A male-centered sexual challenge that filled her with excitement rather than fear.

"What will you do that you haven't already?" She let a teasing smile tip her lips as she gave her own challenge.

A rough chuckle washed over her. "Your pretty ass will be bare to my hands, my fingers." And hunger tightened his expression. "Give me a taste of power, Risa, and you may be surprised at the animal you release."

Her lips parted. She drew in a ragged, rough breath. "Show me."

She hungered to know. She craved each touch, each adventure she could find in his arms. She craved the man she could sense he held back.

"You're going to steal my mind," he groaned, but he moved, lifting himself along the bed until he lay back as she moved to sit beside him.

"Come to me, love." He lifted his arms to her. "Take me, and I'll take you."

Could she? Did she dare not? These were the memories that would sustain her when he left, when it was all over. And if the worst happened and Orion won, then she would have her memories in death. She wouldn't die regretting that she hadn't taken every touch, every adventure.

Rising to her knees, she swallowed tightly, pushed back the hesitancy, the instinctive fear of the unknown. No matter how powerful the sensations, she knew Micah would ground her.

"Like this, baby." He guided her. His hands on her thigh, her hip, until she straddled his face and stared down along his body.

Risa shivered at the unfamiliar position. Longing, excitement, and wariness surged through her at the sight of his erection, fully engorged and heavily veined as it rose along his lower stomach.

Exhilaration surged through her as well as tingles of awareness that not only had he opened himself to her touch, but she was more fully exposed to his as well.

"Go slow," she panted as she leaned over him. "Let me pleasure you, Micah."

His hips shifted, lifting to her as she gave in to her first impulse and licked down the long shaft.

"You'll destroy me." His arms curved over her hips, his hands gripped the cheeks of her rear and pulled her lower.

But he was destroying her. When she had asked for "slow," she meant to ask for mercy, because his caresses had the ability to steal her mind. She should have asked him to have mercy.

She should lift her head and ask for mercy now, but each time her tongue stroked beneath the crest of his cock, she could feel the response of his body. His tongue grew bolder, his hands clenched her rear, separated the cheeks, and she felt a flare of response in nerve endings that should never be responding.

Gripping the heavy length of his erection with one hand, she lifted it until her lips could cover the throbbing cock head. He retaliated. His tongue speared inside her vagina, flexing and licking as a startled cry tore from her lips.

His fingers eased the dampness spilling from her pussy back along her rear crevice to the tiny entrance there. They caressed with diabolical precision until Risa became lost in the sensations, mindless to anything but the pleasure consuming her, even as she consumed him.

Risa filled her mouth with the heated male flesh, suckled the broad head, and caressed the shaft with her fingers. She worked her mouth along it, feeling him tighten, hearing his groan as his hips shifted sharply, burying a fraction more between her lips.

She felt the first clench of the hard flesh and knew he was close. She was affecting that amazing control he had.

She could have broken it, but at the moment she sensed he was ready to break, his hand landed on her upturned rear in a heated, heavy caress.

Her mouth jerked back to draw in precious oxygen as a cry tore from her throat. Every muscle in her body tightened as his lips covered her clit, sucked it inside with devastating results as his hand landed again.

Dazed, motionless, she let the sensations wash over her, through her. She accepted the results for the striking pleasure-pain now tearing through her.

As the fourth light slap sounded against her flesh, and fire poured through her senses, she heard the muted wail that fell from her lips. Ecstasy was so close. She could feel it pulsing through her veins, building in her womb.

"Damn you." His lips jerked back from her clit as one hand slid up her back and pressed at her shoulders. "Suck me, Risa. Take my cock back into your sweet mouth, love, or we stop this here and now."

Stop? If he stopped, she might die.

Her head lowered, but her hips did as well. She pressed the too-sensitive folds against his mouth, writhed her hips, and cried out around the flesh filling her mouth as his tongue sank inside the greedy depths of her pussy.

She was awash in sensations now. Waves of them rushed over her, through her. His hand landed against her rear again and sanity became no more than a memory of who and what she had once been. Frightened. Untouched by pleasure. She wasn't the woman she had been then. She was Micah's woman. She belonged, in this moment, for eternity, to this man.

Her hips churned into his caresses as her mouth sucked at the throbbing cock head. She tasted his essence as a sharp burst of it filled her mouth. She sucked him deeper, harder, and as he eased more of her juices back, she felt the tip of his finger enter her, working inside her even as his other hand landed on the cheek of her rear again.

Too many sensations rushed through her at once. His tongue pumped inside her in hard, driving strokes. His chin caressed her clit, his hand landed against her rear, and a finger slid inside the tiny untouched entrance he had found between the cheeks of her ass.

Her screams were muted around his cock. She tightened until she felt as though she were going to break. When she was certain she could bear no more, it exploded inside her.

Her hips bucked until he wrapped one arm around them, holding her to his mouth as his tongue pumped harder inside her and his finger delved deeper. Explosions of fire, sensations so sharp, so violently pleasurable, tore through her until Risa swore she felt her soul explode with the ecstasy of it.

Her mouth was filled with the taste of him. His release spurting inside the suckling confines as his hips arched to her.

She was lost in the wonder of him. Lost in the sharp, mindless explosions that tore through her own body until he finally eased her free of them and left her limp and panting as he shifted his hips and drew the still-engorged flesh from her lips.

She moaned as he moved her.

Opening her eyes, Risa watched as he laid her back against the pillows, his black eyes gentle and still filled with heat as he spread her thighs and moved over her.

A sharp inhalation jerked through her as the head of his cock pressed inside her pussy. His expression tightened, a grimace covering it as he worked his erection inside her.

This was more than simply pleasure. Watching him, feeling his hunger meld with her own, feeling his body become a part of her. The sensations wrapped around her, flooded her senses, and left her gasping with the sheer power of it.

"Just a little more," he groaned, his hips thrusting slow and easy as he filled her with his cock. "Sweet Risa. I can't get enough of you. I'll never get enough of you."

It was like flying. Risa had never known such freedom of pleasure, just intensity, as she felt in Micah's arms. She watched, her gaze centered between their bodies as he took her. Her flesh parting, hugging the hard, flushed shaft as he filled her, then left her empty, only to fill her again.

Her hands gripped the hard biceps as he held himself up by his powerful arms. Thrusting against her, filling her with the heated power of his hunger, his thrusts.

The pleasure was never-ending now. She arched to each thrust, watching as he retreated, gasping each time he filled her. She was dying in his arms and she didn't care. Flying until a ragged cry tore from her chest and she exploded around him again.

He lay fully over her then, his arms curling beneath her, his hands holding on to her as his thrusts increased, each driving stroke pushing her own orgasm higher until he gave a hoarse groan and spilled his release inside her.

Satiation held its own moments of peace. Those minutes spent drifting back to reality, where nothing mattered but the sensation of fulfillment, completeness.

Risa let herself luxuriate in that feeling. In the satisfying sense of being bound to someone else, if only for this moment.

She didn't want to lose it. She didn't want to let him go until reality and the danger surrounding her forced her to.

She wanted to lie, just like this, forever. She wanted to capture this moment within her soul and know that when the loneliness came, she could take it out and relive the feeling.

She let her fingers test the resiliency of his shoulders; she felt the morning shadow of a beard against her cheek.

"You make me damned weak, Risa," he finally groaned, shifting from her but going to his side as he dragged her against his chest.

"You're always strong," she said softly, and she knew it was the truth.

But she had her own strength. A strength she hadn't known she had. One she had found in the realization that nothing was as it seemed.

Perhaps, she thought, she had grown up last night when she had stepped into that room, seen her friends gathered there and the pictures that were laid out.

They had all seen the pictures. They had known her shame, and they felt pity for her. But she didn't pity herself, at least not any longer.

"When you leave," she whispered against his chest, "will I ever see you again?"

And she knew the answer to that.

"No."

She hadn't expected the truth from him.

"Risa."

She moved, covering his lips with her fingers and staring back at him soberly.

"No excuses," she said firmly. "No apologies. And no lies. Thank you for that."

But she had to force back the tears, because a part of her had dreamed of hearing the lie.

Micah kept his lips closed; he kept his thoughts to himself when they threatened to spill from his lips with all the dreams he knew he wasn't supposed to have.

Instead, his hand lifted, his fingertips caressing over her silken lips as he stared down at her. *No promises,* he reminded himself. *No lies.* From here on out, from this moment on, he could never lie to her. He could never do anything to make her pain greater.

He had to leave her. Soon, the day would come that he would walk from his other half.

That knowledge tore into him like dull knives. It ripped at his soul; it shredded the man he was and left only Risa's man in its place.

"*Belibi tamid.*" *In my heart always.* He couldn't give her what she needed, he couldn't be the man she needed, but he had given her his heart. He knew it. He accepted it. Just as he knew he could never reveal that to her.

A smile trembled at her lips, a saddened curve as her blue eyes moistened with tears. As though she knew what he couldn't speak.

Her hand cupped his cheek. "It's day," she said then, her voice rougher; the emotion that filled it had his jaw clenching with such pain that he wondered how he breathed through it.

"It's day," he agreed.

She nodded slowly, slid her hand from his cheek, then turned away.

Micah watched as she moved from the bed, her naked body graceful, beautiful.

"I'll shower first," she told him. "I promise to save you some hot water."

Not that she had ever used it all. But he knew what her escape hid. It hid her tears.

CHAPTER 20

IT WAS NEARLY noon before Micah received a call from Jordan to meet with the team in the other apartment while Emily Krieger, Morganna McIntyre, and Kira Richards took bodyguard duty.

Risa watched as her friends stepped into the room and the door closed behind them.

"It's too early for wine." She shrugged negligently as she moved to her desk and began arranging the accounts still awaiting her. "There's coffee though."

She turned back to the other three women and felt her lips tremble at the sight of the tears on Emily's face.

Damn, she loved Emily like a sister. Several years older than Risa, Emily had been kidnapped the night Risa had. She had been drugged. She hadn't been raped, but Risa knew the scars ran deep in Emily's soul from that night.

"You're not allowed to cry." Risa felt a tear track down her own cheek and swiped at it hastily. "The time for crying is over for me, Emily."

Risa wanted it to be over. She needed these three women to believe it was over. When Micah was finished here and he left, then she would want solitude. She would need time for her tears, and she would need it alone. She wouldn't shed any more before then.

"Does that mean we're not friends any longer, Risa?" Emily asked, her voice strong despite her tears.

That was Emily. She was one of the strongest people, on the inside, whom Risa knew. Emily's confidence had always been something Risa was in awe of, her inner strength something Risa envied.

Risa turned and braced herself against the desk.

"We're friends," she said simply. "Nothing's changed."

"Even though we lied to you about Micah? We set you up?" Yeah, that was Emily. She could go for the jugular when she needed to.

Risa's lips quirked. "Yeah, well, I'll just be sure to remember this the next time you try to fix me up with one of your husband's friends."

There wouldn't be a next time.

"Coffee." She cleared her throat as she turned and headed for the kitchen. "Micah drinks it faster than I do. He finishes the pot before I've finished the first cup."

She was uncomfortable, and Risa hated feeling that way with the friends who had helped through the horrors of readjusting to life after nearly two years of drugged captivity in a private asylum.

She moved into the kitchen and begin preparing the coffeemaker. She wanted to turn back to them, to joke as they once had, but the time for joking was past and the future undecided.

"How long was this operation in its planning stage?" she asked the women as she finished and turned back to them.

She kept her fingers curled over the counter's edge behind her as she watched them.

Emily breathed in deeply. "Kell told me when the information came in that you were in danger. They had a week to get a plan together."

Risa nodded at that as her throat burned with a mix of humiliation and despair.

"Why wasn't I told the truth?" She wasn't angry now. The anger had been burned out of her by the truth that when this was over, Micah would be gone forever. "Did you think I couldn't handle it?"

"We didn't have time," Kira stated as the three women moved to the kitchen table. "We got a workable plan together and arranged for you to meet Micah. Just meet him, Risa, to see if you could tolerate being around him. You've not exactly been agreeable to dating in the past six years."

Risa's gaze sliced toward the other woman as she smiled thinly. "Yeah, being the belle of the ball wasn't high on my list of priorities. Could have had something to do with all those nasty little nightmares that kept plaguing me."

Kira nodded at that. "You're stronger than I ever believed you were. But we couldn't risk telling you before you met Micah. We weren't certain of your strength or your ability to handle what you were facing. That's why it was agreed that we'd wait and have the federal attorney meet with you instead."

"Probably a wise move." Risa nodded.

"Risa, we lied to protect you," Emily said then. "Micah truly is a friend, as you're aware; he's just not an active or retired SEAL."

"Why Micah?" She stared at the three women then. "What did they do, draw straws to see who got to babysit the neurotic mark?"

She didn't ask the question in an angry manner. Anger wasn't simmering; it wasn't even lit. She was curious, but the truth of the answer frightened her.

"Micah demanded this assignment," Kira told her, a smile curling her lips. "After a few choice phrases in Hebrew concerning Orion's parentage. He wouldn't let anyone else take the job."

"You know Hebrew?" Risa asked then, her heart pounding, the words Micah had whispered to her that morning still resounding through her head.

Kira nodded. "A bit. Not a lot. Enough to know that Orion's parents are likely lame camels lying in their own waste. Or something to that effect."

Risa grinned at the thought of that. For a moment, a brief moment, she considered asking Kira what the phrase Micah had whispered to her meant, then changed her mind. Whatever it was, it was something between the two of them alone. Maybe later, after he was gone, she would figure it out. Until then, she would let Micah hold his secrets.

"Risa, the lies weren't so bad," Emily said, her blue eyes somber and filled with regret. "It was for your life."

Risa stared back at her friend for long moments before she nodded slowly.

"I would have done the same for any of you," she finally whispered, knowing it was the truth. "The friendship wasn't in danger, Emily."

No, only her life was in danger from a killer who had never been caught, and one who had never failed.

"Coffee." Risa turned as the timer went off. "We could have used the wine, but it's a little early for it."

"Hey, it's five o'clock somewhere," Kira drawled. "I say we do the wine first, then the coffee."

"We're her bodyguards," Morganna reminded the older woman with a laugh. "We can't have wine."

"Sure we can." Kira grinned. "We just can't get tipsy. Well, except for Risa. And I think a little tipsy wouldn't hurt her in the least."

Risa laughed at that, though she got the coffee cups down rather than the wineglasses.

Tipsy wouldn't hurt her, but she didn't want to be tipsy now. She didn't want to miss a single moment that she could spend with Micah by shadowing it with alcohol.

"So, what was so important that Jordan needed Micah?" she asked as she set the coffee on the table, grabbed her own cup, and took her seat. "He doesn't normally call this early."

"A CIA operative has been watching you and Micah," Kira told her. "Nik managed to capture her just before daybreak, and they're questioning her at the moment. Micah's their interrogation specialist."

Risa inhaled slowly. "The CIA? Why would they be watching me?"

"I guess we'll find out when Micah's finished." Kira

shrugged, though her gaze was distinctly wary. "Are you sure you don't want that wine?"

At the moment, she really wasn't sure.

MICAH RESTRAINED a sigh as he walked into the spare bedroom and stared at the captive bound, gagged, and blindfolded in the wooden chair that sat against one wall, devoid of the disguise she had used while watching him and Risa each time they left the apartment building. He was the team's interrogation specialist. This was his job, and he had to do it in a way that would hide his identity from this woman—a cousin he was fond of.

They were all screwed now.

"Bailey Serborne." He almost grinned as she remained completely motionless. "You're slipping."

He nodded to John; good old Heat Seeker grinned rakishly before pulling the tape from her mouth.

"Bastards!" The insult was a snarl of fury. "Do you think I don't know what the hell is going on here? Every one of you will fry for this."

Micah held back a chuckle. She was a wild one. She was enraged and with good cause. He had no doubt Nik didn't play up the big bad Viking image that fit him like an old pair of jeans. Real comfortable.

Micah straddled the chair he had placed six feet in front of her and crossed his arms over the back.

"We're in trouble here, buddy." He looked up at John.

"Oh really?" Sandy blond brows arched in question. "How so? She looks dainty enough to me. I bet we could skin her out, chop her up in bite-sized portions, and sell her to the local dog food company. They're always looking for cheap meat, you know."

Micah winced. *Cheap meat?* he mouthed in amazement as he nearly laughed.

John grinned and shrugged.

"Cheap meat, your scrawny asses." She fought the ropes holding her.

"Scrawny asses? She must be talking to you, Seeker," Micah stated as he shook his head. "I have it on rather good authority that I have a nice ass."

"Yeah, but your authority is prejudiced," John snickered. "She's not seen mine yet."

"If you want to keep your ass, you'll make sure it stays that way." Micah frowned back at him. He didn't consider that much of a joke.

But Heat Seeker only grinned.

"I'm talking to both you morons," she screeched. "Let me the hell go."

"Keep your voice down or the tape goes back over your mouth," Micah warned her sharply. "Don't forget, Ms. Serborne, you are the captive here, not the other way around."

"Yeah, and the boss wouldn't let me tie her down on the bed," John grunted. "What kind of captor doesn't tie his pretty captive to the bed, hm? I think we should file a complaint."

While he spoke, John lowered his head until he was speaking against her ear, the smile on his face decidedly playful. One of these days, John Vincent was going to be forced to take something or someone seriously. Micah wanted to be there to see the fireworks.

"I'm not working alone." She tried to slam her head into John's. "I'll be found."

"Your partner's dead," Micah informed her. "He died in Russia in that little trap you laid for Orion. You haven't been assigned another partner. Actually, you're in rather a lot of trouble with your boss these days. Didn't he tell you to back off in locating Orion?"

Micah knew the director had ordered her off the investigation she had taken upon herself.

She froze. "Sons of bitches," she cursed. "Who the hell are you?"

"Tsk-tsk now, we're asking the questions," Micah chided her.

She snarled. Her lips pulled back from her teeth and the sound that came from her throat was pure throttled rage. He grinned at that. He knew how to push her buttons.

"I'm not answering your damned questions." She struggled against her ropes again.

"I still say we sell her for cheap meat," John reminded him. "We could get a few bucks out of her."

"It would be tough for a Rottweiler to gnaw on," he finally chuckled. "Our Ms. Serborne is rather stubborn."

She was still now, her jaw working as she clenched and unclenched her teeth. He swore he could hear her molars grinding.

"She's a pretty little thing," John crooned, grinning wickedly as a growl sounded in her throat. "And she just makes the cutest little noises."

Breathing roughly, shaking with anger, she remained still this time.

"You know, she took me away from a rather important day that I had planned," Micah sighed. "I'll tell you what, if I don't get what I need in the next, oh . . . let's say ten minutes, then you can skin her out and see what the going rate on cheap meat is today. How's that?"

John laughed as he squatted next to her chair and checked the ropes holding her.

"Yeah, some old lady's terrier will have a hell of a time chewing her up."

"He'd just spit her out," Micah laughed.

John wagged his brows and mouthed, *Not me.* Micah could only shake his head in amusement.

"Now, Ms. Serborne, I'm sure you wouldn't enjoy the preparations to make you a dog treat. So why not just tell us nicely who you're looking for? You're threatening our own little op here, and we don't appreciate it."

Her mouth remained a straight, stubborn line. Micah knew that line. Strangely enough, his father had once had the same determined, hardheaded set to his lips when he was pissed off.

She was family, sadly enough.

Micah's father, Garren Abijah, hadn't been Israeli. He'd been adopted by the Abijah family when his parents had been killed visiting them.

Garren Serborne had become Garren Abijah, with no

objection from the American branch of the family. The blond-haired Nordic giant who Garren Abijah had later become, raised amid a Mossad family, had been recruited by the CIA with Mossad's blessing and worked primarily in Israel.

Bailey Serborne, the little witch sitting in front of him, had been the daughter of Garren's favorite cousin. Once they had become adults, the two men had made certain they visited often.

Ben Serborne, Bailey's father, Bailey, and her mother had been the only American family in attendance at both Ariela and Garren Abijah's funerals.

Bailey had cried on Micah's shoulder. Already an agent with the CIA, she had vowed to kill Orion. He had nearly killed her instead. Orion had killed her partner, then knocked Bailey unconscious and sliced her wrists. Not enough to bleed her out, just enough to scar her for life.

The bastard was taking a toll on his family, Micah thought furiously.

"Psst, I don't think she can answer questions if you don't ask them," John reminded him long moments later.

As John spoke, he was rubbing a long swath of Bailey's thick black hair between his fingers, pulling at it just a little and causing her to make another of those enraged little snarls of fury.

"You're here for Orion," he began.

"I'm not worried in the least about fucking Orion," she snarled. "Not now."

Micah's brows lifted. "Why not now?"

"You're the bastard sleeping with his mark, aren't you?" A satisfied little smile curled at her lips. "I've been trying to figure out who the hell you were for a week. I finally recognized your voice. Where did you pick up your buddy?" She tried to slam her head into John's when he blew into her ear.

"And you heard my voice where?" Micah asked, neither confirming nor denying the charge.

"At the nightclub the night you picked up the Clay girl," Bailey sneered. "She was rather easy, wasn't she, bub?"

It was a damned good thing Bailey was family; otherwise, he might have to kill her for that.

"Now, you should have warned me that you wanted to play hardball," he said coldly. "I could have let my friend here take some hide off your arm just to prove he could do it."

She stilled as John ran a finger slowly down her arm.

He was going to have to have a talk with John about his chair-side manner here any moment.

"Sorry. Maybe she wasn't so easy after all." Her smile was tight. "But you are the man that moved in with her. I know you are. You're after Orion, aren't you?"

"So what makes you think you shouldn't have to worry about Orion now?" he quizzed her curiously.

"Micah Sloane, age thirty-two, Navy SEAL, my ass," she snorted. "You're a nobody, Mr. Sloane. You have a very impressive record, and you just happened to be listed as working with the Durango team in the Middle East. Sorry, sweetcheeks, that doesn't jife with me. You're no SEAL."

"Then what am I?"

"A nightmare," she said with a strange sense of private satisfaction. "I wondered if you were with Orion, or Orion himself having fun. But Orion doesn't work with a partner."

"Ow. Shit." Score one for Bailey; her hard head met the equally hard forehead of Heat Seeker. "Now dammit, you didn't have to do that," the other man laughed as he backed away a safe distance.

"You're working with a moron," she sneered. "Couldn't you find anything better?"

"Not on such short notice," Micah said coolly. "Why were you checking me out?"

Bailey remained silent.

"Let's not go through the whole song and dance again," he sighed. "Just tell me."

"Orion killed family," she finally stated. "I want a piece of him."

"You and about a dozen other families," he grunted. "What makes you so special?"

"What makes you so special?" she countered. "How did you figure out where to get in and how so quickly?"

"My business," he informed her. "Answer the question."

Her teeth snapped together as John blew another puff of air at her ear.

Bailey had some damned sensitive ears, and Micah knew it. He'd watched her nearly break a man's neck ten years before when he'd dared to blow in her ear.

"He killed my family, my partner, and he scarred me," she raged. "What other excuse do I need?"

Did she need more? She had more than he did, but he knew Bailey. She had more.

He shook his head again. "I'm going to start skinning you myself," he told her. "I'm running out of patience. Why do you want Orion?"

"Because he knows the identity of a monster," she spat. "The doctor that worked with Clay's father. A scientist. He's responsible for the rapes and horrific mutilations of several teenage girls in Ukraine. Girls I knew." Her voice dropped to a whisper. "Girls I promised to protect."

Micah closed his eyes and breathed out roughly. He'd had no idea that Bailey had been part of the group of agents that had escorted four teenage girls to a private clinic on the Ukrainian border. Those girls had been taken from the clinic that night by a doctor who had "bought" them from the nurses there. The girls had been found three weeks later in St. Petersburg in a cold dark alley, naked, mutilated, tortured beyond belief.

"I'm sorry about that," he said softly.

"We were supposed to protect them," she breathed out roughly. "We swore we would. One of those girls was a damned genius in math. Another was an artist. The youngest wanted to be an astronaut; the oldest just wanted to be safe."

Risa's rapist definitely got around. "And how will killing Orion help you to find him?" Micah asked. "He was no more than an employer if he's involved with Orion."

"He's involved," she answered wearily. "It's the same doctor one of my family members was tracking. Orion killed her."

"Ariela Abijah," Micah said softly.

Bailey stilled as John watched curiously.

"Yes." She finally nodded, swallowing tightly. "He killed Ariela. Six weeks later my cousin Garren all but killed himself when he rushed a suicide bomber. Two years later, their son, David." She pronounced his name "Da-Veed," a sound Micah hadn't heard for six years. "He was killed two years later when he tracked Orion down to a freighter off the coast of Tel Aviv. Two years later, Orion was hired to kill a Russian double agent I was protecting. He killed my partner and nearly killed me."

"And six months later you lost the girls from Ukraine," he stated.

She nodded wearily. "It's the same man," she breathed out roughly. "The doctor that hired him to kill Ariela is the same one that tortured those children. And Orion can lead me to him. I've been following rumors for two years. It led me here. I almost had him when he attempted to kidnap her." She shook her head. "In the confusion another vehicle sideswiped mine and I lost him."

Talk about the mother of all fuckups.

Micah wiped his hand down his face before turning and staring at Jordan where he stood in the open doorway. Jordan shook his head slowly. There was no pulling her in on this, but Micah knew there was no keeping her out of it, either. Bailey was as damned stubborn as her cousins were. She'd die herself before she gave up. Orion had taken too large a piece of her. He'd wounded too much of her for her to ever walk away.

"You're going to have to let the doctor go," Micah informed her coldly. "As well as Orion. I'm here to kill him, not question him."

She laughed at that. A strangely hollow sound that sliced across his senses, it was so filled with pain.

"Liar," she whispered. "You want both of them, Micah Sloane. Because I know what you don't want anyone to know. You're in love with the mark. That doctor raped your woman. Everyone in the community knows that Orion's main employer worked with Jansen Clay and that he was there the night Clay had his daughter and the other girls kidnapped. He raped her, and you won't rest until he's dead."

"Wrong." It was the truth. Both of them would die before this finished; Micah would make certain of it. "You, Ms. Serborne, will be picked up by two of your fellow agents come morning. Your director will have you locked up for your own protection until this is over."

He rose to his feet.

"No!" She tried to come out of the chair. Rage tore through her voice, flushed her face, and caused her to nearly topple to the floor as she fought the ropes. "You can't do that. Don't you dare. Let me help. I can help you."

"I don't need your help."

"You need me," she cried out roughly. "I know what you don't know."

Micah paused. He knew her voice; he knew when she lied, when she told the truth. He had known her since she was a child, and he knew she wasn't playing games this time.

"What do you know?"

"An exchange," she bargained, her breathing rough as she turned her head to his voice. "Let me in on this."

Micah shook his head. "I'm sorry, Ms. Serborne. The family of Abijah has lost enough of its children. I'd just as soon see you live. You don't know his identity, or you'd have already struck."

"He wears a wig." She spoke quickly, desperately. "I know this. I know how to tell. I've seen him twice. I know how he walks; I know his voice. Don't you cheat me out of this!" she screamed.

"I can find him without your information," he told her. "Give your director my regards when you see him, Ms. Serborne, and if you want to save your career, you'll make certain you follow his orders while you're with him. Because I can and I will have you taken out of that agency, are we understood?"

"I'll kill you." She jerked, fought her bonds, and forced John to catch her chair. He received another harsh head butt for his efforts.

"Hell!" John cursed, letting her go. The chair bounced, rocked, and tipped to the floor as she screamed out in rage.

"Gag her," Micah ordered. "Take her to her friends. And make damned sure they know the consequences of allowing her out of their sight."

He turned away from her, and turning away tore at him. If she ever learned who he was, she would never forgive him. David Abijah would indeed be dead, because Bailey Serborne just might end up killing him.

Chapter 21

HE WAS BALD.

Bailey knew his voice.

She knew his walk.

She knew how he moved. Bailey was the only person to have come against Orion and lived to tell the tale.

"She could be helping him," John stated, keeping his voice low as they met in the living room of the apartment.

Jordan was silent, as was the rest of the team. Micah stood by the heavily covered windows, his arms crossed over his chest as he considered the suggestion.

He didn't have the proof to veto it.

"She knows something about the doctor," he said quietly. "She was too evasive. She kept attention focused on Orion. Whatever she's hiding, though, we'll not be able to extract short of drugs, and she's trained to resist those."

"How far could she resist them?" Jordan asked, and Micah knew what he was considering.

Micah breathed out roughly as he shook his head. "She was weak in that area. Garren Abijah oversaw a lot of her training. She tested in Mossad laboratories in that area, and we broke her within an hour."

He watched John wince. They knew the training Mossad went through to resist drugs and their effects. It wasn't pretty and testing was never easy. The fact that she had broken so easily wasn't a sign of weakness, but it was a sign that she could be broken. The CIA had known that. They had kept her on assignments with the least amount of risk in that area. There were a lot of CIA agents who broke easily under Mossad testing, though. It was rigorous, and at times it had been deadly.

"It's an option then," Jordan suggested. "You could oversee it."

Micah shook his head. He couldn't oversee it. It just simply wasn't in him at this point.

"She's the last of my family, Jordan," he told the other man roughly. "There's not a chance in hell I could do that to her."

"Were you there during the testing?" Jordan asked, his eyes narrowed.

Micah nodded. "I walked out halfway through it. Even Garren couldn't stay for the full session. She's like a sister. I won't cause her to suffer in the ways it would take to break her and extract the information when I'm almost certain that what she's hiding, she's hiding so she can take down the doctor first."

"What if she's a liability?" Travis stepped forward, his brooding expression darker than ever as his blue-gray eyes flicked to the closed bedroom door.

"The CIA will control her until this is finished," Micah stated. "Her director can determine after that what she is. I won't be a party to her torture to find out one way or the other. Hold her until we're done."

"She knows more, Micah," John argued. "You said it yourself: She kept the focus of the questioning off the doctor. What if she knows who Orion's employer is? What if she's in league with them?"

"Travis." Jordan addressed the former MI6 operative though he kept his gaze on Micah. "Take her to our secondary location and get the information we need."

"Jordan." Micah stepped forward warningly.

"Is Risa's life worth this risk, Micah?" Jordan asked, bringing him to a full stop. "Travis won't kill your cousin, but he can and will get that information. It's too important."

Micah's jaw clenched. Was it worth Risa's life to let this go? It wasn't. Risa's life was everything to him, but Bailey was the last of the family of Serborne. Her parents were dead. Micah's parents were dead. They were all gone but Bailey and Micah, and he could never claim that relationship again.

"Travis, John. Go," Jordan ordered them. "Transport her to the secondary location and see what you can find out."

"Travis." Micah stepped forward, then stopped. His jaw clenched because he knew he was about to go against every iota of training he had ever been given with the Mossad. He was going to ask for mercy.

And he couldn't.

"When this is finished," he said instead, "if she carries more nightmares than she carries now, then I'll know who to blame."

Travis shook his head. "If she carries more nightmares, then it will be her own fault, Micah. She's an agent. She knows what we need. I'll make certain she's given every chance to understand we're on the same side. After that, whatever comes down on her is on her head, not mine."

Jordan continued to stare back at him. Micah was the interrogation specialist. He knew the drugs needed. He knew her breaking point. What was more, he knew the drug required to break her.

He inhaled roughly.

"Now is the time to speak, Micah," Jordan warned him.

"Traditional drugs won't work," he told Travis quietly before giving him the name of the hallucinogenic guaranteed to break her. She couldn't fight its effects. She was particularly susceptible to the drug. It was her weakness.

Travis stared at him for long moments. "It's a hard one," he finally said. "Are you sure?"

Micah nodded. "Mossad doctors are damned good. It took them a week to come up with the drug that would break her the fastest. As I said, it took less than an hour."

Travis nodded.

"John, call her director. They can pick her up when you're

finished at a location of your choosing. Get what you can as fast as you can." Jordan turned to Micah. "You're going out tomorrow. Risa has an invitation to a ball being thrown to raise money for area hospitals. She and her grandmother have yet to attend one of these parties because of Risa's reticence. The two of you will be there. See if she recognizes anyone."

Micah nodded. He dreaded it, but he realized the importance of it. There was no way to shield Risa from this, as much as he needed to for his own sake. When this was over, his time with her would be over.

"Micah." He turned back to Jordan as the other man continued. "You're getting personally involved here." Jordan glanced at a silent Noah. "I thought we all agreed the rest of you were going to keep that from happening?"

Micah glanced at Noah as he watched Jordan silently. The commander's nephew was no one's fool, and he was one of the few men who had a chance of influencing Jordan.

"Dead men don't have a weakness," Micah said tonelessly. "But even dead men have a conscience, Jordan."

With that, he left the apartment. There was no argument here, just as there was no denying the guilt Micah knew would lie against his soul for what Bailey would endure.

He stepped across the hall, knocked softly, then used his keys to let himself in.

He stepped inside, closed the door, and came to a stop. Kira was watching television, her weapon lying on the arm of the chair at her side. Risa was asleep on the couch. Morganna and Emily were stretched out on the floor.

"One of us should call Clint and Kell," Kira said softly as she rose to her feet.

Micah nodded as he felt his throat constrict. Risa slept with comfortable innocence, her expression serene as she lay on her side, her head propped up on one of the small couch pillows.

As Kira made the call to the two men on backup, Micah moved to the couch, picked up his woman, and carried her to her bed. He tucked her beneath the blankets before returning to the living room in time to see Morganna rising groggily from the floor while Kell lifted his wife in his arms.

The two men nodded back to Micah soberly as Kira went to the door, checked the hall, and gave the all-clear nod. They moved from the apartment as Micah caught the door. Closing it behind him, he checked the locks, then made his way through the other rooms to test the windows and the security there.

He couldn't still that ragged voice inside him that reminded him of Bailey's grief at his parents' funerals. He couldn't still the memories of the child she had been or the decision he had made tonight.

He was getting old, he decided as he moved back to the bedroom and stripped his clothes off wearily. He had just spent the past eight hours tracking Bailey's movements over the past few years, as well as any connection she could have had to Orion other than the Russian mission. Then, Micah had questioned her. His sin was in allowing another man to break her reluctance to tell them what they needed to know.

Why would she hide it?

Micah crawled into the bed, his eyes closing as Risa rolled to him, reaching for him even in sleep.

His arms surrounded her, his hold almost desperate as he buried his face in her hair and fought every instinct he could feel rising inside him to take her and run. He could hide her, he told himself. He was Mossad. He wasn't just an agent; he was every second of training he had absorbed during those years. Every instinct honed to lethal sharpness. He could protect her.

Unless something happened to him. Unless he blinked and the worst happened. And then he would be without her.

He kissed her hair.

"*Ani ohev otach, Risa,*" he whispered on a nearly silent breath. *I love you, Risa.*

He loved her.

She was his heart.

And Micah feared he would never survive when he was forced to walk away from her.

"Micah." She breathed his name against his chest.

Her hand smoothed down his torso until it lay on his abdomen, inches above the thickly erect cock that rose from between his thighs.

He ached for her; he hungered for her. But as much as he wanted her physically, tonight he simply needed to hold her.

There were things he had never expected to face when he had signed his life away to the Elite Ops. He hadn't expected to find a woman who touched his soul, just as he hadn't expected to face the last remaining blood relation he had or to allow her interrogation.

Now he had to face what he was losing, and he admitted the cost was much too high.

"Make it stop." A whisper of fear in Risa's voice drew him back to her.

She didn't scream the words; she didn't cry out in fear or in pain. The sound was broken instead, a drugged hiss of agony that tore through his soul. "Daddy, please, make it stop."

Micah tightened his arms around her, desperate to awaken her but knowing that each dream could hold the key to saving her.

He clenched his eyes closed, held her closer to his body, and swore if he ever got his hands on the last living demon that had touched her, then he would kill.

Risa hadn't dreamed much once Micah had invaded her bed. But as she slipped into the warm soothing tide that came whenever Micah held her, she felt her defenses against those dreams slipping.

She was safe in his arms. She could feel them surrounding her, his presence almost a shield between herself and the pain.

This time, when the dream came, it was as though she were watching herself, rather than being herself within the dreamscape.

She stared at the girl strapped to the gurney. Wild light blue eyes were wide, panicked, as the two male figures stepped to the narrow bed.

She saw Jansen Clay, his blond hair perfectly styled,

amused derision on his face as he glanced at the man on the other side of the bed.

Risa couldn't see his face from where she stood. Only his back. And no matter how badly she wanted to stare at him, to memorize whatever she could of this dream, still her attention was held by the woman who whimpered in distress.

"I don't know why you don't just kill her." Risa flinched at the cold disgust in the other man's cultured voice. He spoke as though his mouth was pursed and wouldn't stretch around the words.

"She serves a purpose for the moment." Jansen shrugged. "Besides, if I kill her, I'll no longer have access to the trust fund her mother and grandfather left her. She does have an incredible amount of money. It returns to her grandmother if anything happens to her."

"So kill the grandmother," the other man ordered callously. "What good is she to you?"

"Matricide?" Jansen mused. "I'm not quite ready to step over that line as of yet."

Yet he'd had no problem in his attempt to slowly kill off his daughter.

"Matricide would be the least of your crimes, Clay."

Jansen laughed. "And what of your crimes, my friend? I may have no love for my daughter, but neither have I allowed her to become part of the horrific experimentations you so enjoy with the little girls you buy. Really, one shouldn't cast stones."

The other man's back stiffened. "Science," he stated. "I've made breakthroughs with those girls. They've contributed to science. Your victims have only contributed to your own wealth."

Jansen's expression was filled with skeptical mockery.

"Spare me the condescension and get on with this little experiment," Jansen ordered. "I have a party to attend later and I'd prefer not to be too late."

Large hands reached for her arm. Risa focused on those hands even as she tried to stare up into his face. She whimpered desperately as the girl in the dream tried to fight those beefy hands as they lifted her arm.

"I'll remember you." The dream Risa stared into his face. "I'll remember you."

He snorted as he laid the needle of the syringe against the vein in her wrist. "You'll be lucky to remember your own name once we've finished this."

"I'll remember you." Risa felt the words coming from her own lips even as she watched her dream self. "Your hands hurt me. They're too big for surgery. Do you kill your patients?"

The hand paused. The syringe pricked at her flesh as the dream self glared up at him.

"If you do your job right, then she'll never remember who you are," Jansen chuckled.

"Do your job right," Risa whispered as she stood behind him and focused on the hand, on the nipple. "Scars, like tiny lines in your hands. I know your hands. I've seen them before. They frighten me. I'll remember you."

She watched as her dream self tugged at the hold he had on her arm. The flesh trembled with the effort she exerted.

Yet she couldn't escape. The syringe bit into her flesh and a second later boiling lava was fed into her veins.

She tried to scream. Risa watched herself. She didn't feel the pain, but she saw it in the light blue eyes that suddenly rolled back in the dream Risa's head. Her body jerked against the restraints that held her to the gurney as a strangled scream tore from her lips.

Risa watched herself. She watched as she bucked and heaved against the thin mattress. She couldn't scream, but her lips parted as she tried. She fought to focus on Jansen. Risa knew she was fighting to beg, to plead with him for mercy.

"Daddy, please," she wheezed. "Please, Daddy."

And he laughed at her.

He was her father. He had never been a loving father, or an affectionate one. But until that kidnapping, she hadn't thought he was truly a monster.

She watched, unaffected as her dream self writhed on the

bed, trying to scream, lost in an agony Risa only dimly remembered.

"She's in more pain than arousal, my good doctor," Jansen drawled as they stood there forever, their attention going between her and the monitors that electrodes were hooked to. "You still have some adjusting to do, it seems."

"Her heart is at critical level," the doctor mused as he tapped her heart monitor. "You should allow me to open her heart, to see the damage it's causing."

"Much too messy." Jansen shook his head.

Risa shook her head as she watched herself buck and struggle against the pain. She wanted to scream, to give voice to the silent agony her dream self was enduring.

"So much pain," she whispered at the doctor's back. "Why did you hurt me?"

"Adjusting the drug isn't going to be as easy as we first assumed," the doctor commented thoughtfully. "Fuentes's scientist was rather advanced in the synthetic qualities used to create the Whore's Dust."

Jansen stepped back, a scowl on his face as the doctor shook his head. "Too bad she's so damned ugly, Jansen. You could have at least sold her off. At this point, she's only a liability to you."

Risa turned then, her gaze lifting until she could see the back of his head. His hair. Dark mixed with gray. Her vision was suddenly fuzzy; she felt light-headed, so frightened.

Shaking her head, she jerked her gaze back to herself, only to find her eyes locked with her own.

"You know him," the bound Risa cried out in agony. "You know him. Don't trust him. You know him."

She fought to regulate her breathing, her fear. She tried to look at him again and a flash of disorientation assailed her.

"Look at him," the dream Risa cried out. "You know him. Stop him. Oh God. Please. Please make it stop!"

Risa could hear the screams now. They echoed around her, resounding with torturous pain as she moved slowly around the bed, her hands gripping the metal rails that shook with the force of the dream Risa struggling against them. She moved in front of Jansen and lifted her eyes—

"Wake the fuck up, damn you!"

Her eyes jerked open.

She was no longer in the dream. She was struggling against Micah, her own screams still filling her head as she fought him.

She was on her knees facing him. He was kneeling in front of her, a bloody scratch running down his cheek. He was dressed in jeans, his bare chest was damp, a smear of blood on his shoulder, and he wasn't alone.

Panting, fighting to breathe, Risa stared wildly around the room. There was Jordan and the redhead. Risa couldn't remember her name. Had anyone introduced them? Jordan and the redhead were watching her as though she were crazed. His eyes were narrowed; the redhead's green eyes were damp, as though she was on the verge of tears.

"Why are they here?" Risa's throat was scratchy, her voice rough.

"You were having a nightmare," Jordan stated as Risa saw Micah's lips part to answer her.

Micah didn't appear pleased that Jordan had jumped in. Handsome, hard, cold. Jordan Malone had the ability to frighten her.

She turned her eyes back to Micah. "Can they leave now?"

She wanted Jordan out of her bedroom. She didn't like strangers staring at her as though they were dissecting her and whatever she might have said or dreamed.

She was too shaken by what she had dreamed this time, the way she had dreamed it. For the first time she hadn't relived those nightmarish memories; she had merely observed them.

"You saw the man that came to the clinic with your father," Micah said, his own voice rough. "What did you see, Risa?"

Her gaze moved back to Jordan. He was still dressed in perfectly pressed black slacks and a gray, starched cotton shirt. Did the man ever have a wrinkle anywhere on him?

"I saw me." She shook her head as she pulled away from

the warmth of Micah's hands and struggled to sit on the bed, her feet flat on the floor, her back to the others. "Tell them to leave, Micah. I'm not in the mood for company at three o'clock in the morning. For God's sake." She turned her head and glared at Jordan. "Don't you ever sleep?"

A heavy black brow arched with a hint of mockery. "I just replace my batteries when they run down," he remarked laconically. "It's more efficient."

She snorted at that, shaking her head as Micah moved from the bed.

"Tehya, get Jordan the hell out of here," Micah ordered her roughly. "And next time he wants to barge in, do me a favor and chain him to the bed or something."

"He would have to be in the bed first," Tehya commented. "I think he's frightened I'll join him."

Risa could only shake her head at the teasing going on behind her. She inhaled slowly and closed her eyes. She could almost see him, the man who had raped her, the one who had accompanied her father to the clinic and pumped her with that drug.

She knew him. Her dream self had screamed that knowledge at her. She knew him.

She knew his hands.

Those hands flashed through her head. They were large, dark. They looked rough, but the palms were baby-soft. So soft, it was creepy.

She shuddered at the remembered feel of them, holding her wrists to the floor of the plane as he raped her. Strange, she remembered the feel of his hands more than she remembered what he had done to her.

"Risa?"

She opened her eyes to see Micah kneeling in front of her, his expression concerned despite the glow of anger in his eyes.

"They're gone." He pushed her hair back from her face, looping one thick strand behind an ear. "Jordan called while you were dreaming. He heard your scream."

"He was being nosy." She shook her head. "What? Does

he think you won't tell him anything I remember in my dreams?"

His lips quirked. "He's an impatient prick."

She almost laughed, because that was just about the truth.

"Risa." He cupped her cheek with his palm. "If I could wipe away the nightmares, then I would. If I could save you this pain, this fear, then I would take it all away."

He would. She saw it in his face, in his eyes.

"It will be over soon," she whispered, and regretted that it would be. She would live with the fear, she thought, the danger to herself, if it would mean holding Micah to her just a little bit longer.

"It's almost over." One hand threaded through her hair as the other tightened at her waist. "You'll be safe soon."

She would be alone soon.

Her hands lifted from her lap to his shoulders, her fists uncurling so her fingers could grip the hard muscle, feel the warmth and power beneath his skin.

"Why are you in jeans?" she asked breathlessly. "You were naked when you got in the bed."

A smile tugged at his lips. "I pulled them on when I heard Jordan and Tehya enter the apartment. Couldn't let them see my bare ass, darling. Tehya's frisky. She would have patted it."

Risa wanted to smile at his teasing. "I'd break her hand," she promised.

"I knew I could trust you to help me hold on to my dignity." His eyes smiled. She loved that. The way they lit up with amusement, with warmth.

She loved him. Loved being with him, touching him, the way he held and protected her.

"Thank you for keeping me safe." She stared back at him, watching his dark eyes as they seemed to darken further. The pupils blended into the irises as her hands stroked over his shoulders. "Keep me warm tonight, Micah."

Her hands lowered to the band of his jeans, where she pulled the snap free, then gripped the zipper and eased it over the erection swelling beneath the denim.

"Are you cold?" His voice was a rough whisper through the room.

"I'm very cold." She lifted against him to brush his lips with hers. "And I'm very needy."

"Needy, are you?" he asked as the hem of her shirt was pulled up, his hands gripping the cloth and easing it over her arms as she lifted them.

Her breathing was ragged now, rough.

"How would you take me, if you could take me however you liked?" she asked him then.

"Slow and easy," he answered her without delay. "I'd lay you down and spend hours, days, years, learning your passion."

A sob caught in her throat. She wanted years. She wanted the rest of her life spent in his arms, in his bed.

She lifted her hips as his hands tugged at the waist of her cotton sleep pants. He pulled them, along with her panties, over her hips and down her legs. As he tossed the material away, he rose to his feet and removed his jeans, revealing the hard, fully erect flesh her body was so eager for.

She couldn't deny herself the needs rushing through her. She knew, sensed with every fiber of her being, that soon Micah would walk out of her life. She had so precious little time to store the memories she needed to carry inside her.

"I love touching you, tasting you," she sighed as she smoothed her hands up his hard thighs.

"I love your touch," he groaned. But the sound could have been caused by the sensation of her hand stroking down his cock.

It was heavy, thick. The broad head was tapered at the tip and broad at the flared base before it curved into the shaft. The flesh was dark, with thick veins pulsing beneath. As she stroked him, a pearly bead of semen formed at the tip, drawing her mouth.

"Ah, Risa. Sweet, sweet Risa," he crooned in that desert-rough voice of his as her tongue licked over him. "Sweet love. How will I ever survive without this?"

How would she survive without it?

Her lips followed her tongue, covered the heated cock

head and drew it into her mouth. He tasted like summer in the middle of winter. Addictive. Powerful.

Her tongue flickered over the underside as she sucked him in, loving the feel and the taste of him in her mouth. She hungered for him. It was a hunger she could only associate to Micah. Not to a drug. Not to anything unnatural. Needing Micah was as natural as the land needing rain, or flowers needing sunshine. It was imperative. It was the key to survival.

Drawing back, she surveyed the slick wetness she had left on the tip, laved over it again with her tongue, and gloried in the hard groan that echoed from his chest.

"I'm wet." She lifted her head and stared up at him, aroused past the point of sanity. "I need you inside me."

"Hell." He knelt in front of the bed again.

The position was perfect. His hips were aligned with hers as he pushed her thighs apart. His cock pressed against the swollen bare folds of her pussy. The head of it had more of her juices flowing, her muscles convulsing in anticipation.

Risa watched, eyes wide, fighting to breathe, fascinated by the sight of that thick crest parting her folds and nudging against the entrance to her body.

For one incredibly insane moment she wished she weren't on birth control. She wished for things she couldn't have. She wanted his child. A part of him that couldn't be taken from her.

"Slow and easy?" His rough voice distracted her. "Or fast and hard? Which do you want, baby?"

His hands framed her breasts, lifting them to allow his mouth to stroke over them. Fire erupted in her nipples and streaked to her belly. Her breath caught at the pleasure, at the incredible need surging through her.

"Fast and hard. This time," she panted.

His lips quirked, an almost-smile that charmed her, that warmed her.

"Slow and easy next time?" He pressed in, the width of him stretching her opening, sending flares of liquid heat to streak through her veins.

"Oh God yes," she cried out, leaning back on her elbows because she didn't have the strength to sit up and she wanted to watch. She wanted to see him take her. "Next time, slow and easy."

He paused, the heavy head alone lodged inside her as she felt her inner muscles suckling at it, trying to draw it farther inside her.

"Fast and hard?" he asked again.

She lifted her head, licked her lips, and said, "Fast and hard, Micah. Fuck me like you'll never fuck me again."

Chapter 22

MICAH PAUSED as Risa allowed the words to pass her lips. His eyes narrowed. "Naughty baby," he crooned with a sensual little grin.

"I've said that word before," she gasped as she felt his cock throbbing inside her.

"Do you want to get naughtier, pretty Risa?" His hands slid from her thighs to her breasts. He cupped them, shaped them, tweaked her nipples, then rubbed the little pain away.

"With you? I think I could be very naughty, Micah," she breathed out roughly.

He rewarded her. One hard thrust buried his erection halfway inside her. It stole her breath, had her head tipping back and her hips writhing as her legs lifted, knees bending to clasp his hard hips.

"Ah, pretty Risa. Your sweet pussy is so tight, so hot around my cock." His voice was darker, rougher, that hint of desert stronger.

"Oh God, Micah, you're going to make me crazy." Her eyes opened as her head lifted.

She stared down her body, her breath catching at the sight of her pinkened flesh parted and hugging the stiff shaft buried only halfway inside her.

"Is that all I get?" she breathed out in disappointment.

Micah groaned.

As he pulled back, Risa caught a strangled cry in her

throat at the sight of her slick juices coating and clinging to the hard flesh.

"So hot and wet for me." Micah ran his finger over the wet flesh, collected the moisture, and as she watched, brought it to his lips.

His hips slammed forward as he licked her taste from his finger.

Risa screamed out with the pleasure. The sight of him tasting her, the feel of him plunging full length inside her, was nearly too much. She could feel her orgasm swelling inside her, building, taking her over.

"Do you know what I want, sweet Risa?" His hands gripped her hips as she stilled, him buried inside her to the hilt, his cock throbbing against the tender tissue gripping it.

"What do you want?" she moaned. She knew what she wanted. She wanted him to move, to thrust, to stroke until she was screaming with the pleasure of it.

He leaned closer. His cock went deeper, flexing and throbbing as she fought to breathe from the pleasure of it.

"I want you to let me behind you, Risa," he crooned. "I want to stoke your pretty ass as I fuck you. I want you to give me all of you, baby."

She stared back at him in surprise, with a tingle of uncertainty and fear.

"Behind me?" She tried to think, to assure herself she could do it, but all she could do was feel him inside her.

He moved, pulled back, pressed back, and she moaned at the tingling rush of sensation.

"Behind you, Risa. It will be so damned good. I can stroke your pretty clit while I fuck you hard and deep, or play with your tight little nipples. You'll love it."

She shook her head. Could she bear it? Would the nightmares flood her? Would the fear rush in and overtake the pleasure?

"Micah." She stared back at him in distress. She didn't know if she should be turned on or terrified of what he wanted.

Then, he pulled away.

"No. Don't stop." She reached for him, desperate to bring him back to her.

"Come here, baby." He pulled her up and turned her, pressing her knees to the bed as he placed a hand against her shoulders. "Just there," he crooned as his hand slid over her shoulder and under her chin. "Now look up. See what I see?"

What she saw was her face, flushed with arousal, her eyes too large, darker than normal, as she stared into the mirror over the chest of drawers at the side of the wall.

Behind her, Micah looked like a conqueror. His dark face tight and honed with lust, his black eyes glittering in approval as he caught her eyes in the mirror.

Her lips parted in shocked surprise and wonder. She wasn't ugly here. She looked like a woman, she looked unlike herself. The mask of passion and need that covered her face gave her a softer, gentler appearance.

"Fucking beautiful," he groaned.

Risa stared at his image. The way one hand gripped the thick, dark cock as he held her hip with his other hand.

"Now, let me show you how to get naughty, sweetheart."

He tucked the head of his cock between her thighs, pressed it against the swollen folds, and eased it just inside.

"Take me, Risa. Work your pretty pussy over my cock. Show me how naughty you want to get."

How naughty she wanted to get.

Risa stared into the mirror, her gaze fixated on Micah. His shoulders flexed with power; a small rivulet of perspiration ran down his chest to be absorbed by the spattering of rich black hair that grew across it.

His abdomen flexed. His hands tightened on her hips, and Risa moved.

She watched her hips press back, felt the full width of his cock stretching her, overstretching her, taking her.

"Micah," she breathed his name in a rush of exquisite pleasure.

She pulled almost free of him and watched the tight grimace of hunger that twisted his face. His lips were drawn back from his teeth; he looked wild, primitive. He made her feel wild.

"Touch your breasts, Risa," he groaned as she stroked back on his erection. "Let me see you play with those tight little nipples. I love your nipples. Sweet little berries that taste like nectar against my tongue."

She moaned and lifted one hand to play with a nipple. She gripped it, tugged at it, and worked herself on the stiff flesh impaling her.

She was becoming lost in the pleasure. She could feel it. With her eyes locked on his, she let her fingers trail from her breast to her stomach. Curiosity consumed her as deeply as the passion. Her fingers moved between her thighs, and she moaned at the feeling of her hot juices against her fingertips. Her lips parted on a silent cry as those fingers encountered the iron-hard flesh she was moving on.

A silent snarl curled his lips as his head tilted back on his shoulders, his eyes closing as pleasure tightened his face. The sight of it weakened her, threw her closer to orgasm, and strengthened her in the same wash of sensation.

Her shoulders collapsed to the bed as her fingers found her clit. The fingers of her other hand found a nipple and she knew he was watching. She could feel his eyes on her as she twisted her hips, pushed back, and took all of him.

She eased along his cock, pulling free of him only to push back with a desperate cry as her hungry flesh sucked him back in.

She was lost. Moaning, crying, filled with him and desperate for more.

"Open your eyes," he ordered roughly as she felt him move over her. "Look at me, damn you. Look at me, Risa. See me loving you."

Her eyes opened. His face was next to hers as his knees rested between her thighs on the bed now. He was taking her, his hips moving, churning, powering his cock inside her in hard, repeated strokes that pushed her higher, pushed her closer.

"Micah," she whispered his name, feeling the explosion building inside her. "Oh God. It's too good. It's too good."

"Always," he groaned. "Ah God, Rissa. *Ani ohev otach. Ani ohev otach, Risa.*"

I love you. He loved. He was torn apart by the emotions pouring through him, tearing at him, whipping through his mind as he felt his balls tighten, felt the onslaught of release at the moment he felt Risa explode in his arms.

"Micah," she screamed his name. "Oh God. Love me, Micah," she cried the plea. "Oh God, please. Please, Micah."

She bucked, then tensed; then Micah felt her. Her juices rushed around his cock as he felt his release crash inside him. Sensation raced along his spine, then back to his balls. His semen spurted from the tip, spilling inside her in a rush of heat as his hand gripped her head, turning it closer so his lips could cover hers. So he could hold back the vows that rocked him to his soul.

She was his forever. He would always be hers. Into eternity he would love her. And if he didn't know to his soul that she was protected, then he would have sworn that a pleasure this deep, this profound, could have only one conclusion.

Shuddering against her, Micah released her lips and groaned at the final pulse of release that jerked from the tip of his cock.

He was breathing hard, heavy. He couldn't seem to get enough oxygen to his brain; he couldn't still the thunder of blood enough to make sense of all the emotions, all the sensations, that had crashed inside him in a wave of ecstasy.

She lay beneath him, sated, the tension slowly easing from her body, covered by him. The trust the position had taken rocked him to the core. He hadn't expected it. He had expected her fear, perhaps a denial. But he hadn't expected the trust she had given him.

"*Ani ohev otach*," he whispered again. The words of love in his native language, in a language as old as time, with a love that filled his entire being.

He had never known love outside a parent's love, or his

love for his parents. He had never known the love a man felt for that one woman who would complete him.

"I love you, Micah." He barely heard the words. Her face was pressed into the blankets; it was no more than a whisper of sound, but it crashed inside him with a power that rocked him clear to his soul.

God help him, how was he to let her go when this finished? And he knew, clear to his soul, in the warrior part of his subconscious, the end was coming. Risa would be safe. He'd have his vengeance, but when it was over, there would be nothing left to hold on to. Vengeance would be ashes in the wind, and his heart would always linger in the darkness, always following one woman, a shadow of her shadow.

"I could stay here, covering you like a blanket meant to protect, forever," he whispered at her ear. "You are a light that will always guide me, a whisper I'll always strain to hear."

Her slender body shook on a sob as he felt her fingers digging into the mattress.

"Know that, Risa." He kissed her neck, her shoulder. "Always remember, in my life I will never know a warmth as sweet, as giving, or as beautiful as you are."

She shook her head as he eased from her, but she curled against him eagerly when he lay beside her.

"Talk to me." Her voice was filled with tears. He felt the dampness of them against his chest and felt them in his soul.

"What should I talk to you about?" He let his fingers comb through the silken strands of her hair.

"What makes you happy? What memories are best to you? Just talk to me, Micah. Tell me about you."

He breathed out heavily. She made him happy. The memories of being with her would always be the best to him.

"I remember the desert," he whispered. "Israel is a place of many people and yet many beauties. The desert can bake a man in the day, freeze him when the moon rises high. It's a place of brutal beauty and enduring strength. It nourishes a man, even as it challenges him."

"It's very violent," she whispered. "I was there once, a

long time ago with Jansen. I wasn't allowed out of the protected house he'd been given use of."

"You would love Israel if you had the chance to experience her," he promised Risa. He would love to see her there beneath the blazing sun. To show her all the secrets Israel held, as well as the vast richness. "There can be violence; that part of Israel is splashed across television sets around the world. But you rarely see them show the ocean as it caresses a moonlit beach. Or the desert that shifts and changes on a daily basis. It's secretive and resourceful. It respects strength and power, and gives it in turn."

"What is the breeze like?" Her voice was honey and sweet pleasure. It was a light in the darkness, the promise of warmth in the winter.

"The breeze can be gentle with the heat of the desert filling it, sinking it into your pores as though it would sustain you with its earthy gift alone. Or it can be sharp and wicked; it can tear at the flesh and slash at the bone as though it were a woman displeased with her lover."

He chuckled at the light pinch she gave his hard abs.

"See what I mean?" He caught her hand in his. "Wicked woman."

Her soft laughter flowed over him like the desert's gentlest caress.

"Do you have family that you left there?"

Micah stared at the ceiling before he shook his head. "I have only a cousin. A rabid little female as stubborn as the desert itself."

"And you love her," she said softly. "I can hear it in your voice."

"Yes, I'm quite fond of her." He would have smiled at the thought if he weren't well aware of what he had left her to. The need to choose between Risa's safety and Bailey's comfort wasn't a simple one. He consoled himself with the fact that both would survive in the end. They would have their lives ahead of them; whatever they desired could be theirs.

"When you leave, will you remember me, Micah?" Risa asked then, her voice in the darkness stroking over his senses.

"Even death could not steal your memory from me," he promised her.

Silence filled the room. Dawn was coming and with it the knowledge that he would have to hurt her again. Her grandmother had told Noah that Risa had flatly refused to attend the medical banquet thrown each year. Medical professionals from around the world would be in attendance. The best and the brightest in the medical field would don their evening finest and mingle in an event created to allow each to make the contacts needed to access the myriad funds made available for medical research.

The ball would be held in a week, and until then, there were several parties thrown as individual scientists and doctors arrived in the city.

The first of those parties would begin later in the night. He would attend as Risa and Abigail's guest, as would Ian and Kira Richards. Jordan and Tehya would be there as well, with the rest of the team providing backup and security.

And Micah knew Orion would make another move soon, most likely at one of those parties.

"I'm cold," Risa's soft voice dragged him from his thoughts.

Micah let his hand caress down her back before he dragged the comforter from their hips to her shoulders. The air was a little cool, he admitted.

She snuggled closer to his chest and was silent so long that he wondered if she had fallen asleep.

"I would have liked to have seen your desert with you." When she spoke, the emotion in her voice seared his heart. "Will you think of me if you ever visit it again?"

"Always," he promised her softly. "I will always think of you when I think of the desert."

He would always think of her, no matter where he was, no matter what he did. He would always carry his memories and his loss along with him.

"Maybe one day I'll see your desert," she said softly. "And I'll think of you, Micah."

He stared up at the ceiling; he saw into the past, and he

saw into the future. He saw the bleak darkness he had known before she came into his life, and he saw his return to it once she was safe.

And he saw himself, always watching her from afar. Always craving her.

Letting her go would be the hardest thing he had ever done.

RISA WAS SURPRISED that she was able to sleep at all. But sometime before dawn she drifted off in Micah's arms and slept without nightmares.

She was aware of him, even in sleep. She knew when his breathing evened out; she dreamed he kissed her forehead and whispered, "I love you," in the gentlest voice.

She dreamed of the desert awash in warmth, the sun shining down on them, and she dreamed he disappeared from her side to become a part of that desert.

When she awoke late the next morning, she showered, ate the breakfast he prepared, and went quietly back to work at her computer.

She couldn't think about tomorrow today. She couldn't let herself imagine him walking out of her life, even though she knew it was coming much more quickly than she had envisioned before.

"I have a couple of meetings scheduled today," she told him as she booted up her computer and the reminders popped up on her monitor. "Several clients are stopping by to drop off some information I need for their accounts."

"I remembered," he told her. "Jordan completed their dossiers several nights ago. They all came in clean, so we're good to go. I'll be here with you just in case."

She turned back to him with a frown. "Clients don't like discussing their information in front of others," she told him worriedly. "If you hang around here, they'll be suspicious why. They're regular clients, so they're used to meeting with me alone."

His hands propped on his hips as he glanced at the kitchen door. Risa knew she should be focusing on the problem of those clients rather than the jeans and T-shirt he was wearing or how sexy those jeans looked when paired with boots.

The man was definite eye candy. He wasn't traditionally handsome; he was rugged instead. Rugged and sexy as hell. And right now, he had that dangerous glint in his eye that assured her that he was focused solely on ensuring her protection.

"I can go to the kitchen." He nodded. "I'll let them in, then retreat just inside the entrance. I'll be close enough in case any of them pose a threat."

A shiver raced up her spine as a surge of wariness raced inside her. She should have canceled the meetings. It was too late now, but she should have followed Jordan's advice there rather than insisting that she had to keep those appointments.

"Don't worry, Risa." Micah soothed those nerves with his silky, dark voice. "Jordan and the others are just across the hall. There's a listening device we'll activate before the first meeting so Jordan will be aware of everything that's going on, and I'll be just inside the kitchen. You're completely protected."

She nodded firmly before turning back to the computer. She was protected, she assured herself. Everything would be fine.

IT WAS ALMOST time.

Orion surveyed the healing wound on his foot before shaking several pain pills into his palm and washing them down with water.

The medication helped dull the pain, but his senses felt fine. He was still in control; that was all that mattered.

Replacing the pills in the bedside table drawer, he pulled his laptop across the bed and clicked through the pictures that had come across through the night.

The camera he'd installed just across from the elevator on Risa's floor ensured him the opportunity to at least keep track of her comings and goings.

She didn't leave often. Traffic was amazingly light for the past few days. Risa's lover was keeping her fairly close to home. Other than a night out at a club, they had stayed inside.

Mr. Sloane was on alert. He was a SEAL, which meant he could be a problem if Orion didn't play his cards right.

He smiled at the thought. He had several aces, and he would play them.

Tonight was a swanky party she was to attend. A small ball for a scientist coming in from Germany. Orion almost laughed at the thought of it. The moment she saw his employer, all shit was going to hit the fan, and he knew it. He could feel it. And he had planned for it.

This was much better, he assured himself as the painkiller began to ease the ache in his foot. A man couldn't plan his pinnacle job before retirement while in pain. He might miss something, or he could misjudge his timing. Orion couldn't allow that.

In the past days he'd had to rework his original plan just a bit, but he was confident he could make it work. Whistling silently at the thought, he pulled up his e-mail and let a smile curl his lips.

Contacts. It was all in the contacts a man made throughout his lifetime and what he knew about them.

In the secured in-box was the e-mail he had been awaiting since beginning this assignment. The security code he needed to get inside.

He pulled up the e-mail, memorized the code, and then deleted it.

Soon. Another day or so and he could make his move.

This plan was much better than the last one, and it would afford him the security he had dreamed of having in his retirement.

He had even chosen the perfect little island to buy. It was nearly deserted; the previous owner had built a rather imposing mansion on the single mountain that graced it. The lagoon was the only access to the island. The cliffs that ringed it would make it impossible to breach any other way.

Orion would be safe there. He could play all he wished.

And Orion did so like to play.

He sighed at the thought of retirement. He wouldn't miss his job, he told himself. He'd grown bored with the ease of each assignment. There was no challenge anymore. Until this one, his final job, everything had come so easy to him. Defeat wasn't even a thought.

Until that SEAL had pinned his foot with a bullet.

Orion chuckled at the thought of the man. Micah Sloane. He still didn't have enough information on the SEAL. He had definitely been in the Middle East, though. A little hack and look-see into security command in Iraq assured Orion of that. But even more, he had a few strings there he could pull. He'd called a certain friend who was aware of any and every SEAL that came through. Mac Knight. The bastard had a hell of a name. Orion had established that connection through a friend of Mac's during one of his leaves several years before.

A friendly little call a few hours before had yielded quite enough information to assure Orion that his SEAL was no more than a SEAL. And not even one as effective as Orion had feared.

It seemed Micah Sloane was in a bit of trouble with his commanders because of insubordination. He might not even be a SEAL for much longer.

Yes, connecting with Knight had been a hell of a thought at the time. A man never knew when he would need information on a mission in the Middle East or a particular soldier. And Orion had arranged it so the somber Mr. Knight would owe him enough favors that he couldn't exactly say no. It had paid off. Especially when Orion and his employer were required to travel there occasionally.

Orion breathed in with satisfaction.

Micah Sloane wouldn't be a problem here. It was all in the timing and in the execution.

Orion pulled up his most recent picture of Mr. Sloane and Risa Clay. She had a pretty little glow about her. She was a woman being well loved, Orion mused. And Sloane was obviously enamored of her.

Beside Sloane's picture was another picture. The face recognition program Orion used had consistently pulled up David Abijah's face when the picture was placed in the search criteria.

He tapped his fingers against the bed. Micah Sloane couldn't be two different men, could he?

Orion pursed his lips and shook his head. It shouldn't be possible. He was going to assume it wasn't possible, simply because he was very well aware of the guilt that raged inside him over the Abijah family.

Then, he pulled up the picture of his employer and grimaced.

Hurry. Hurry. It was the daily demand fracturing Orion's nerves. He was going to hurry. It would end this week.

He pulled up the picture of his little island. Yes, by the middle of next week he'd be having fun in the sun. It was all coming together just as he had always dreamed.

JORDAN ANSWERED his cell phone on the first ring.

"It's Knight." The major's voice was a furious growl across the line. "The call came."

Jordan smiled. He'd known it. The moment he'd realized the threat Knight was to this particular operation, Jordan had known to pull him in.

"The name I know him by is Paul Blade," Knight stated. "He's CIA. Came through on a mission with another group a few years ago. A few months later he was in a little bar we had set up on base. We had a few drinks, talked shop. Couple of weeks later he started smuggling whisky in for me. My brand. He called in the favor tonight. Wanted to know about a SEAL named Micah Sloane. I gave him what you gave me."

"He was able to track you down in the states. Interesting," Jordan mused. "When do you return to duty?"

"Four weeks, and I want in on this," he stated, his voice cold. "If he's Orion, then Risa is in more trouble than you thought, Malone. The guys he went in with on that mission say he's bad damned news. They were all scared as hell of him, and they were some tough-assed mothers."

Jordan grunted at that. "Give me stats. I'll contact my source and see if I can get an ID on him."

"Last time I saw him, I'd guess forty or older, probably closer to forty-five. Stocky but muscular. A mustache and goatee sprinkled with gray. Shaven head. Broad face. His eyes were a little narrow, a little longer than normal. He gives off a very professorial air. Studied bastard."

Jordan nodded as he made notes. "His cover was Paul Blade?" he verified.

"Definitely a cover," Mac said firmly. "He's deep cover, too. I knew his handler for a while before he was killed. I mentioned Paul to him once and his expression was very uneasy. Told me to steer well damned clear of him."

"And did you?"

"Hell, Malone, I steer well damned clear of everyone. You know where I'm stationed. All I see are the teams going out or coming in. Not a lot of chances to get into trouble there."

No truer words were ever said. And what a stroke of fucking luck. "Get over here," Jordan decided. "I'm not going to risk tipping him off. We have pictures taken of every figure that's passed the apartment building or entered it. We have stacks of the damned things here as well as pictures of everyone Risa associates with or will associate with. Let's see if you can ID him for us."

"On my way," Mac promised.

"Use the stairs, not the elevator," Jordan warned him. "We know there's a security camera there that's been wirelessly hijacked several times. We're trying to get a GPS on the signal, but he haven't managed it. We have more intel coming in and might have to move fast."

The line disconnected as Jordan lifted his head and grinned at Tehya where she watched the monitors trained on Risa's apartment door.

"Bingo." He grinned with a show of teeth. "He contacted Knight wanting intel on Micah. Knight's done drinks with him, talked to him. He's in the bag."

Tehya's brow lifted. "Counting your chickens, Jordan?" she asked cynically.

He couldn't help but laugh at her reply. "Praying the chickens are laying is more like it." He pushed his fingers through his hair and repeated the prayer that the eggs all dropped in one place and that he was there to crack them.

"Call in backup. Let's get a game plan together. Whoever he is, he's CIA. That explains the leak in Russia. It also explains his employer's ability to track investigations against him. A sweet little network, don't you think?"

"Very sweet," she agreed, her chin propped in her hand as she continued to watch the monitors.

Jordan glanced at them, then back at her. "Call in the backup, Tehya."

She rolled her eyes, pulled out her cell phone, and made the call, all without taking her eyes off the door to Risa's apartment.

"What the hell do you see?" He frowned at the monitors, then back at her.

"A casualty," she sighed, and shook her head before turning her gaze to Jordan. "Are you going to tell him he doesn't have to leave her?"

Jordan stilled and stared back at her. "He has no choice but to leave," he told her, his voice turning cold. "You know the rules. He's dead. His life is property of the Elite Ops."

"Noah has a wife, a child," she said softly. "Morale is going to seriously suck around here if Micah has to leave her."

"He's a dead man," Jordan reminded her. "He knew what he was doing when he signed those papers. Noah's case is different. It always was and they've always known that."

She shook her head. "Big mistake, boss. Very, very big mistake."

He waited until she rose from her chair and turned her back on him before he let a grin twitch at his lips. They'd see whose mistake it was, and Jordan was betting it wasn't his.

Chapter 23

RISA STARED AT the gown laid out on the bed, then lifted her gaze to Micah.

"You should have warned me," she said carefully. She was furious. He had sprung the information that she had to attend the ball on her. Micah had merely stated they were going; he hadn't given her the option of refusing.

"You've avoided this party every year that you've received an invitation," he stated. "Why?"

"Because I don't like doctors," she said between clenched teeth. "Maybe a better way of saying it is that I despise the bastards. I can barely tolerate my own. How's that?"

"Not a good enough reason." His smile was tight and cool, his black eyes flat and hard. "But no one else will expect you to be there either, especially the doctor determined to kill you."

It was his determined expression, and she was growing to highly dislike it. It usually did not bode well for her.

"You're trying to force me into remembering who did it," she said angrily. "You're trying to make me identify him."

"Identify your rapist and we identify Orion when we question him. The most elite of the medical field in the world will be at these parties. Orion's employer and your rapist was rumored to be one of the most advanced scientific minds in the world. He'll be there."

"Then why should I be there?" Risa could feel the panic

building in her chest, along with the fear. She avoided doctors like the plague, just as she avoided anyone who had been associated with Jansen Clay. "You said it yourself; all you have to do is capture Orion. He'll tell you who his employer is."

"Or vice versa," he said quietly. "If we identify the scientist quickly, then he can't escape if he's not American."

"He's American." The words burst from her lips before she even realized the truth of them.

"You're remembering more." He stood across from her, watching her closely. "What have you remembered since the dream, Risa?"

She pushed her fingers through her hair as she turned from him, tightening them in the strands as she fought against the fear trying to overwhelm her.

"I don't want to go to this party," she breathed in roughly. "You can't make me go." She swung around to face him again, glaring back at him fiercely.

"No." He shook his head. "I can't force you to go, Risa. But if you let fear control you, then you're never going to have the life you've dreamed of having."

"What do you know about my dreams?" she charged him, her voice rough. "As far as you know, Micah, I don't have a single dream."

His lips quirked in an oddly sad curve. "I know you dream, Risa. You have the pictures and plans of the home you want one day. It even has a white picket fence around it. You keep the picture on your desk. I know you don't splurge in your money, but you want to. You want the pretty, sexy clothes, but you're afraid to wear them. I know you dream of a family. A husband and children." Something flamed in his eyes then; some emotion flashed across his face that she couldn't decipher.

"Every woman's dreams." She shrugged his perception off.

"You want to go to the desert," his voice lowered. "You want to feel the caress of a breeze that feels as though it's come from the sun itself."

She turned away from him. That dream had come to her in the middle of the night as she heard him describe Israel to her. But it was only a part of the dream. She dreamed of being by his side as she felt it.

"You need to do this, Risa. You need to take your life back. Are you going to let Orion or the man that tormented you rule your dreams and hold them back forever?"

She hated his logic. She hated that look in his eyes, the one that said he knew she would do what she needed to when she wasn't so certain herself.

She looked at the evening gown again. It was simply gorgeous. The dark gold and bronze beaded color shimmered beneath the light. There were bronze heels and a small clutch purse. There were even bronze panties.

The fabric of the dress shimmered with the tiny beads as it ran from dark gold and bronze, steadily darkening to a rich, vibrant black at the hem. It looked as though it glittered with stardust.

"You definitely intend to make me stand out," she murmured.

"A woman learning her own sexuality and her effect on her lover would want to stand out," he said, his voice dark, rough. "A woman of your courage, healing from the trauma you suffered, would become bold, adventurous, when her lover encouraged it in her."

"You're daring me," she sighed. "I hear it in your voice."

"Daring you to live?" he asked. "Yes, Risa, that's exactly what I'm doing. I'm daring you to live."

She wrapped her arms across her breasts and stared at the dress again.

"And if I break down?" She couldn't look at him now. "If I see him, know him, and I break down?"

"I won't let you break down. You'll hold on to me. You will know you're safe, in my care, and protected, Risa. You won't break down. You'll tell me who you suspect, and later he'll be investigated and questioned. That simple. And he'll break. Then it will all be over."

Just as Bailey had broken, Micah thought sadly. His cousin was currently resting in a secured location. Jordan was reluctant to call her director now. The news that Orion was CIA changed many of the team's options in regards to the assignment.

Bailey hadn't broken easily. It had taken her longer to break than it had during her training. She had fought the drugs, she had cursed Travis. But in the end, she had revealed what she knew and why she was there.

She was definitely there for Orion, but only because she believed her cousin, David Abijah, would be tracking him. She was searching for her last blood relation. The one she had never believed to be dead.

His past was coming back to bite him on the ass, he thought as he watched Risa run her fingers down the shimmering material of the gown.

She nodded slowly. "What time do we leave?"

"We leave here at eight along with Tehya and Jordan. We'll meet your grandmother, along with her escort, and Ian and Kira at the hotel where the ball is being held."

"A matter of hours," she murmured. "You didn't give me much of a head start, did you?"

Micah moved around the bed then. His hands cupped her shoulders as he turned her to him.

"I didn't give you time to worry over things that you shouldn't worry over," he said quietly. "You have time to dress. There will be a buffet dinner at the ball if you're hungry."

She shook her head; the multi-hued streaks of silken blond colors rippled around her shoulders. "I won't be hungry."

"Risa." He lifted one hand from a shoulder and cupped her cheek.

Raising her head, he stared into her worried eyes.

"Do you believe I'll protect you?"

She nodded. "You won't let him take me."

"I won't let him take you," he promised. "We're going to make this work, you and I. And you're going to shine at that ball like the beautiful, vibrant woman you are."

"Beautiful to you," she whispered.

"Beautiful, period." He stroked his thumb over her lips. "You are pure beauty, Risa. And tonight, you're my woman. My beauty. The woman who holds my entire attention."

It was no less than the truth. She held every fiber of his soul.

"I need to shower." She inhaled deeply, but her face was still pale, her expression tinged with fear.

How had she survived? he asked himself as she pulled away from him and headed to the bathroom. How had she endured the past eight years and still managed to retain that air of innocence and unaware beauty?

She wasn't cynical. She wasn't a coward. She was facing her fear, her demons, and the danger surrounding her with a grace that amazed him.

Breathing out roughly, he flipped open his cell phone and placed a call to Jordan.

"Yes?" Jordan answered on the first ring.

"She's agreed to go," he stated.

"Good," Jordan murmured. "We have everyone in place. Mac Knight secured an invitation as well. He'll let me know if he sees Orion. We have the information Bailey gave us on the doctor. It was scant. American, broad, large hands, according to a few reports of surviving victims. But she did remember the names of several doctors that the Russian double agent had been in contact with. James Walters was one of them. We managed to get confirmation from our contact, the man we suspect is Orion's handler, that he has made plans to attend the party tonight. Everything will be in place."

Micah shook his head. "It's not Walters. She was too calm. Her subconscious knows who her rapist was. She hasn't seen him or she would have remembered him already. We're looking at a potential mess with Orion and the rapist in the same ballroom as well."

"I agree," Jordan stated. "But this is our best chance to acquire at least one of them. That's all we need. Tehya and I will leave ahead of you. Travis will have your limo; Nik will be following behind you. We'll meet in the lobby of the hotel along with the grandmother, and Ian and Kira Richards."

"Check," Micah murmured as he watched the bathroom door.

He wanted to shower with Risa. He wanted to watch her curvy body, love her to distraction, and ease the fear filling her. But there was no time. There was simply no time.

He had run out of time.

He disconnected the call before moving to the closet and pulling free the silk suit that had been delivered along with Risa's dress.

He took it and the hunger to shower with her and left the room to retreat to the spare bedroom where he would shower. Alone.

He needed to remember what being alone was like. Soon he would be without her, and he needed to prepare himself for that. If tonight went as planned, then by tomorrow night, Risa would be safe.

And he would be leaving. Without her.

Without her.

It echoed in his mind, his heart, and his soul.

He would be leaving, without her.

THE GOWN WAS gorgeous.

Risa felt the swish of the skirts around her as she and Micah walked along the hallway to the elevator. He held her hand and kept her close to him. She could feel the warmth of him, the power, and the tension that radiated in his body.

It was a tension that seeped into her as well. She could feel her stomach tightening with fear, her heart racing with it as the elevator doors opened and they stepped inside.

The moment the doors closed, she found herself in Micah's arms, against his chest, his lips on hers as he kissed her with a hunger that seared her to the bone.

"You're making me crazy," he groaned as he lifted her against him, pressing her hips into his so she could feel the erection raging beneath his slacks. "You look like a banked, glowing flame in that dress, Risa. So beautiful you take my breath."

Her lips parted as she saw the hunger in his eyes, his expression.

"You should have built some time in for a nap before we left," she murmured.

"Just a nap?"

"Well, we'd have found something to do in that bed if we didn't sleep." She tried to tease him; she tried to ease her fear and his tension.

"Many things," he agreed as the elevator beeped a warning that it was reaching the lobby. "Things that would have made us incredibly late."

He released her as the elevator doors opened, though he kept his hand on the small of her back.

"Ah, Miss Clay, you shine like the brightest star." Clive Stamper was standing in the lobby, his smile beaming as she walked toward the door.

"Thank you, Clive." She smiled back at him nervously as he held the door open.

"Have a very nice night, Miss Clay, Mr. Sloane." He nodded as they passed.

"I don't know if I can do this," she whispered as the chauffeur opened the door and Micah helped her into the passenger area.

He moved in beside her, his arm going around her as he pulled her into his lap. The door closed behind them, and seconds later the limo was pulling away from the building.

"I'm here with you, baby." He held her close to his chest, his hand stroking her back as he pressed a kiss to her neck. "Nothing or no one will touch you tonight but me. Okay?"

She pulled in a hard, nervous breath. She wanted to scream at him. She wanted to fight. She wanted to demand that he turn around and take her back home.

"Do you remember the night we met?"

She felt his breath against her neck and shivered with the pleasure. She nodded.

"I watched you walk into the nightclub. I was sitting at the bar when you entered. You looked around nervously. Your eyes were wide with fear, but you forced yourself to walk across the room. Your courage amazed me. Awed me."

She shook her head. "That was different."

"How could it have been different?" His nose brushed against the lobe of her ear in a curiously gentle caress.

She almost grinned. "I already knew I was going to go to bed with you. I decided before I ever arrived at that night-club."

He stilled against her. "You had already decided? You didn't know me, Risa." There was a warning edge to his voice that had the grin tugging at her lips.

"Emily told me you were completely handsome." She looked up at him, her hand curling around the side of his neck as she took in his black eyes, his black hair. "She was right, Micah. You're devastating to a woman's senses."

He grunted at that. "And you decided to sleep with me based on that?"

"Sorry." She gave a small laugh. "I did. But when I saw you—" She swallowed tightly at the memory. "When I saw you, Micah, I knew I had to. I didn't want to change my mind. I didn't want to run from you. I just wanted you."

She wanted him to hold her, to kiss away her fears, to show her what pleasure was, rather than pain.

"You terrify me with your courage, Risa," he sighed as his lips whispered over hers.

"I don't know about the courage part." She looked out-side; they were only minutes away from the downtown exit and then would be even closer to the hotel where the ball was being held. "I'm so scared, Micah."

"There's no reason for fear, sweet." His fingers brushed back a few loose strands of hair that had slipped from the loose upswept style she had chosen. "Tonight, we're going to mingle with our friends, we're going to dance, and we're going to people-watch. Nothing more."

"Monster-watch," she breathed out roughly.

She could feel it. She knew the truth. He would be there tonight. The man she fought not to remember. With his large, hurtful hands. His cold, precise voice. He would be there.

"We'll monster-watch then." He sounded unconcerned.

"But it won't touch you. He won't touch you. We'll identify him if he's there; then you and I will leave him to the others. Agreed?"

She looked into his eyes. "You're lying to me," she accused him. "You won't leave him to the others. You'll kill him first."

He stared down at her, his expression stilling before he nodded slowly. "I will kill him first," he stated. "For daring to lay a hand on you, Risa. For that alone, even if there was nothing more, I will be the one to kill him."

But there was more. There was the history he had with both Orion and the scientist. His friends who had died because of them. Or was it his friends? She watched him closely, saw the flicker of guilt and of pain in his eyes, and she knew the truth. She knew her lover. She knew he had once been Mossad. Mossad didn't walk away from their culture or from their vision to work for an outside agency.

"They were your parents," she whispered. "Weren't they? And the son, he was your brother?"

He shook his head slowly as he watched her. "There was no brother. There was only a father, a mother, and a son. A man so bent on revenge that he accepted a life of the walking dead to draw the blood of his enemy." He lowered his head, brushed her lips with his own. "And when this is over, he will be alone again, with more than the memories of the desert to sustain him. He'll have the memory of a woman. A touch that burns with passion. A kiss that sustained his soul. He'll have his memories of you, Risa. More than he ever believed he would or could have."

She stared back at him in shock. He was David Abijah. The son who had supposedly died at Orion's hands when he stalked him.

She felt her throat tighten in remorse, felt her heart ache for everything he had lost.

"You don't." She swallowed tightly. "You don't have to leave, Micah."

He laid his finger against her lips. "I'm a dead man, Risa. I made a vow. A promise. And I forsook any dream I may have wanted at a later time. I made a vow that I can't walk away from now. Even for the most beautiful, the most courageous woman I've ever known."

She felt her lips tremble. At least he didn't love her, she thought. As much as she loved him, if he had breathed those words to her, she would have shattered apart. She could love him and lose him, but the thought of Micah throwing away a chance at love would have broken her.

"I'll always be here," she told him. "You can visit."

He could hold her whenever he wanted to. She would be there for him. She would await him.

But he was shaking his head. "You have a life awaiting you, baby. I signed mine away. Live your dreams. Breathe in the desert air. Build the home of your dreams and fill it with children. Be the woman you dream of being."

But she dreamed of being his woman.

She looked out the window and watched as the limo turned off the interstate and headed into town. They were almost there. She wanted to scream at him to turn around now, to take her home. Because when the mission was over, there was nothing left to hold him with her.

Instead, she slid from his lap, gathered the tattered remains of the courage he thought she had, and forced herself to be silent. To be dignified.

Only children threw tantrums, she told herself. But she wanted to throw a tantrum. She wanted to scream and rage. She wanted to fight whatever fate had decided that she couldn't have the man she dreamed of having.

"We're meeting Jordan and Tehya, as well as Ian and Kira Richards with your grandmother and her escort, in the lobby of the hotel," he told her again. "We're going to enter the ballroom, get us some drinks, and mingle. You'll know many of the people there. You'll introduce me as your friend. Look for the doctors you know. If you recognize the man that accompanied your father that night, and later to the clinic, then turn in to me. Don't stare at him. Simply tell me you're ready to leave, and we'll leave. You can give me his name after we leave the ballroom."

"Then what?" She watched as the lights of the hotel came into view.

"Then I'll return to your apartment with you and the others will meet with me. We'll work up a plan and we'll go after him. That simple."

"You'll leave me alone?"

"Never." His look was possessive, fierce. "You'll be protected, love. I swear it. Are you ready now?"

The limo pulled into the front entrance of the exclusive hotel.

"As I'll ever be."

It came to a stop as the doorman stepped to it and opened the door with a practiced swing of his arm.

Micah stepped out, then reached in and took her hand to help her step free of the limo.

Risa drew in a hard breath.

She could do this, she assured herself. Micah was depending on her. Orion and the doctor he worked for had destroyed Micah's family. For whatever reason, it had caused him to sign away his future. He deserved his chance for revenge.

She felt his hand on her lower back, a warm, comforting weight as he led her into the hotel.

Bright lights assaulted her eyes. She clutched at the small purse she carried and looked around frantically at the guests gathering outside the nearest ballroom. Faces blurred; the music seemed distant and far away. She felt as though she were suddenly outside herself and scrambling to find purchase.

"Risa. There you are."

Her head jerked to her left. Her grandmother Abigail was moving across the lobby, her escort behind her. Dr. Oswald Heinrick was a family friend. She had tried to get Risa to let Heinrick see her after she was released from the clinic, but she had refused.

Heinrick, like James Walters, had been a friend of Jansen Clay's.

Ugly little girl. The words clashed in Risa's head as her grandmother's voice seemed to fade. *Damn you, Jansen, you promised one of these girls to me. I've risked my entire reputation for your fucking drug.*

Risa shook her head.

"Risa, dear, are you okay?" Her grandmother hugged her.

Abigail's now short, spiked hair brushed Risa's jaw. She glanced behind her, looked up, and encountered Oswald Heinrick's cold green eyes.

I know you! I know you! Her own screams echoed in her head.

"Risa, you look simply beautiful." Her grandmother drew back and stared at Risa with a beaming smile before looking over her shoulder. "Isn't she gorgeous, Oswald?"

"She's simply beautiful." *His voice.*

Risa shook her head. It wasn't the right voice, was it? She remembered a colder tone. Didn't she?

God, she couldn't breathe. There were too many people surrounding her, too many voices. She couldn't think.

"Risa, darling?" She felt Micah's arm around her back as she stared up at Oswald Heinrick. His smile was warm and friendly. His eyes were cold. The thick beard and mustache that covered the lower part of his face distracted her.

It shouldn't be there, she thought.

"You grew a beard," she whispered faintly.

His eyes narrowed on her. Snake's eyes. Small and mean. She remembered those eyes. Like ice. Hatred and disdain filling them.

"Actually, I did." His smile was wide, disarming, as he ran his hand over his lower face. "Abigail isn't quite used to it yet."

Abigail wasn't the only one.

"Micah, please meet Oswald Heinrick," Abigail introduced them. "Oswald, this is Risa's gentleman friend I was telling you about, Micah Sloane."

"Mr. Sloane." Oswald lifted his hand. "It's good to meet the man that finally broke through our Risa's reserve. Her grandmother has been worried about her."

Risa's heart was racing in her chest as she stared at his hand. It was large. Broad. It would be rough on the back. She wanted to know about his palm. Was it soft?

She could feel her stomach trembling. Her hand reached out, her fingers shaking as she gripped his wrist.

"Risa?" Micah's voice was at her ear. She heard him, the tone dark, warning.

She wouldn't break down. She was to turn to him.

She turned Heinrick's hand over.

"Risa?" Oswald questioned her.

His palm was soft. She stared at it. She couldn't bring herself to touch it. It was pale and white, without so much as a callus.

Against her hand she could feel the back of his. She felt the fine, almost invisible scars.

"I'm fascinated with hands," she said faintly as she released him.

"Really, dear. You're being a bit odd tonight, even for you."

She tilted her head. There it was. The derision. The mockery.

She stared into his eyes.

I know you. She spoke the words silently and watched his pupils flare.

Yes, she knew him.

Her nails were biting into Micah's wrist.

"I need to leave," she whispered. "I'm not feeling well, Micah."

That simple. That was all it took. His arm went around her and they were moving for the doors. She looked behind her to see Oswald's eyes narrowed on her. Hatred flamed in them before he could hide it.

It was him. She knew it was him.

She heard Micah talking, but she didn't know who he was talking to. She was filled with the images from the past. Those hands holding her wrists to the floor of the plane, his voice at her ear, telling her how ugly she was. How it behooved him to rape her. How she should thank him for teaching her how to be a woman.

"Because I was born to be used," she whispered as Micah rushed her back into the limo. "I was born to die."

"Stop it, Risa." The door slammed behind them as Micah pulled her against him, holding her against his warmer body. "It's over. You don't have to remember this."

"I should thank him," she said tonelessly, repeating the words Oswald had thrown at her the night he raped her. "I should thank him for lowering himself to settle for me. At least I was a virgin." She flinched at the sensation of tearing, ripping pain.

She could feel the sickness gathering in her stomach. It boiled and threatened to gag her as she fought it back.

"Stop it." Micah jerked her face up to meet his black, enraged gaze. "It's over. Do you hear me? It's over. He'll pay for what he did to you, Risa."

"Jansen paid him." She smiled mirthlessly. "He had to pay someone to fuck me after all."

And he wasn't the only one. Micah had fucked her to gain his way to the man who would lead him to Orion. Even Micah had an agenda.

She loved him, but there was no love for her.

She lowered her head and stared forward. She pushed back the emotion, the fear. She pushed away the pain. But nothing could still the betrayal.

Oswald Heinrick was a family friend. He had dated her grandmother for years. He had always been kind to Risa. Until the night he was with Jansen for the chance to molest a child. He'd wanted Carrie. Jansen had forced him to settle for Risa.

Micah wanted revenge, and he had taken Risa to get it.

She stared into the darkness, and for the first time, oddly enough, despite the rape and her confinement for nearly two years, Risa finally felt defeat.

CHAPTER 24

"HEINRICK IS IN the house." John's voice came across the receiver Micah had tucked at his ear as Jordan, Travis, Nik, Noah, and Mac all gathered in Risa's apartment along with the Durango team.

Morganna and Kira were sitting in the living room with Risa. Micah stood at the doorway watching her, his brows lowered in a frown as he took in her pale expression, the dazed look in her eyes.

"Observation only, Heat Seeker." Micah lifted his wrist and spoke into the small mic attached to the strap that surrounded it.

"Observing impatiently, Maverick. The bastard is getting ready to run."

"If he tries to run, stop him." Micah lowered his wrist as his jaw tightened with the effort to hold back the rage building inside him.

"We're going to have to go in, take him out quiet, and transport him to another location for interrogation," Jordan stated as the team watched him with clear, determined eyes. "We have a warehouse here." He pointed to the location on the city map he'd spread across the table. "This will give us the privacy we need for interrogation as well as confinement." He looked up at Macey March, the technical whiz kid of the Durango team. "Head out there with Tehya and get it ready."

Macey nodded before brushing past Micah and leaving the room. In the living room he motioned Tehya to follow before they both left the apartment.

"John, Micah, Travis, and myself will slip into the house and take Heinrick. The Durango team will cover. Nik, you'll cover here and keep Ms. Clay stationary until Micah returns."

Micah turned to Jordan. "Send Risa along with Nik to the secondary location until we have Heinrick there. I don't want her here without me."

Jordan's blue eyes looked like ice. "We can't risk that." He shook his head. "Nik will stay here with her and in constant contact with us. I need you on the team, Micah; you know that."

Micah turned and stared back at Risa, willing her to look up at him.

She was curled in the corner of the couch, her ball gown swirling around her like golden to black flames as she clutched a lap blanket around her shoulders. Her hair shielded her face, but he could see enough to know she was stark white.

Morganna sat on one side of her, while Kira had pulled a chair close to try to talk to her. She wasn't talking to them.

"Micah!" Jordan's voice was a slash of command despite the softness of it.

Micah turned to Nik. The Russian's face was devoid of expression, his icy blue eyes flat and hard as he stared back at Micah and nodded slowly.

"I don't like it," Micah breathed out roughly. "We don't have Orion yet."

"Heinrick is our key to Orion," Jordan reminded him. "This is what we've been working toward." He turned back to the other men. "We'll weapon up in the vans; we have everything we need there. Heinrick's estate is thirty minutes from here and secluded. He has no security or staff on-site. All we have to contend with is electronic security. Are we ready to roll?"

Micah turned back to Risa. She hadn't moved, hadn't changed position. He needed to talk to her before he left. He needed to take that look of dazed terror from her eyes before it destroyed him.

"Micah, are we ready to roll?" Jordan asked behind him.

He grimaced at the demand. *It wouldn't be much longer,* he promised himself. Once Heinrick was taken care of, then he would be back. He could ease her pain then. It would be a matter of hours.

He nodded slowly. "I'm ready to roll."

As the team shifted in the kitchen, Micah moved to the living room. Morganna and Kira were rising to their feet, their expressions worried as he neared them.

"Risa?" He knelt in front of her, taking her cold hands from her lap and staring into her dry eyes.

She looked shell-shocked. How the hell was he supposed to leave her like this?

"Nik will be here with you," he said softly.

She shook her head quickly. "Go. I'm fine. Nik is fine."

Her voice sounded hollow, distracted. Micah felt the fine tension that filled her body and he saw the pain in her eyes.

"A few hours, that's all," he promised.

She nodded sharply. "A few hours. I'll be here."

"Micah, we have to go," Jordan spoke from the door. "Black Jack is waiting. It's time to clear out."

Micah breathed in roughly before cupping her cheek and staring into her ravaged gaze. "I'll be back soon."

Her lips twisted in a facsimile of a smile. "I'm not a child," she informed him, her voice cool. "I'll be fine. Do what you have to do."

He was going to leave anyway, Risa thought as she watched him grimace. She accepted the brief kiss he brushed across her lips and stored it in her mental stack of memories. It was a lousy good-bye kiss, though.

She watched him leave. He was dressed in black. Black pants, black long-sleeved shirt and gloves. With his black hair and black eyes he looked like a dark avenger.

Finally, the apartment cleared out. She was left with the quiet, icy-eyed Viking-like member of the team, Nik.

She lifted her gaze to his. "Will he really be back?" she wondered aloud. "Does he return or just disappear into the sunset?"

Nik's expression never changed. "If he's smart," he finally said, "he won't come back. It would be better for both of you."

Her chest tightened at the statement. Forcing herself from the couch, she got to her feet and moved for her bedroom. Nik wasn't the talkative type, and that was okay, because she didn't have anything to say. She'd asked her question and he'd answered her. The fact that the answer still didn't tell her one way or the other if Micah would be back didn't matter.

She locked her bedroom door behind her and moved to the dresser. She pulled a pair of lounging pants from a drawer and a matching long T-shirt. Socks. Her feet were cold. It was too bad she had nothing in her room that would warm the cold, empty places within her soul.

As she removed the beautiful dress she had worn for such a short time and dressed in the warmer cotton pants and shirt, she rubbed at her arms, hoping to chase away the chill taking hold of her.

She washed the makeup off her face, smoothed lotion into her cold skin, and tried to tell herself everything was going to work out as Micah had promised.

They would take Oswald Heinrick and question him. He'd tell them who Orion was, and they would capture the killer. She would be safe then. And Micah would be gone. He would never return.

She pulled the clip from her hair after smoothing the lotion into her skin and stared at her reflection in the bathroom mirror.

She wasn't ugly. She wasn't a beauty queen. She would never stop traffic with her looks, or really even most men. But she wasn't ugly. She was a little plain. She might have flashes of prettiness if she was lucky.

Micah liked her. He was attracted to her. He got hard for her more often than just for a pity fuck.

She touched her cheek. Her skin was clear. Her eyes were a little pale, but her nose was straight. Her fingers trailed to her neck where a faint red spot marred her skin. Micah's mark.

Her knees went weak, a sob caught in her throat, and she had to brace her hands against the sink to keep from sinking to the floor.

He'd marked her flesh and her soul. And now he would make certain that demons from her past were eradicated.

He cared for her.

He might not love her, she thought, but perhaps he cared for her. She was certain he cared for her. It had been in his eyes before he left.

Caring wasn't love, though.

She shook her head and forced herself out of the bedroom and back into the living room.

Nik was sitting in a large easy chair, but he seemed to dwarf it. The man was seriously large. His shoulders were heavy and broad, his legs long and powerful. The hint of a beard and mustache darkened his strong jaw and emphasized the slightest bit of fullness in his lower lip.

He wasn't a handsome man, she thought. He was unique. Savage in his looks perhaps, with the prominent cheekbones and the dark tint of his skin.

He looked dangerous, with the same hard-eyed glint that Micah often carried.

Risa moved back to the couch, curled up in the corner, and dragged the blanket back over her. She was cold, though she knew the apartment wasn't really chilly. It was an inner cold that she wondered if she would ever be free of.

The cold that came from shock and disbelief.

How was her grandmother dealing with this? she wondered.

Abigail had been through a lot. She had faced the truth of what her only child had become, and now she had learned that the man she had been in a relationship with for nearly a decade was a rapist and the sort who would hire a killer.

"Will the world ever be sane again?" Risa whispered.

"Was it ever?" Nik asked with cool curiosity. "Most people live in whatever dreamworld they build for themselves, Risa. The key to survival is to see the world as it is. It was never sane."

No, it wasn't. At least not during her lifetime.

She sighed wearily and watched the clock across the room. She watched each second tick by and held on to the thought that Micah wasn't alone. He had a whole team as backup. He would survive.

He might not return, but he would survive.

MICAH WAS SILENT as the van pulled into place outside the brick wall that surrounded the estate on the back end. The van doors were thrown open, and like shadows he, Travis, Jordan, and Noah spilled from the vehicle. Behind the van Micah rode in, another eased to a stop and the four men of the Durango team joined them as they rushed the wall.

The six-foot perimeter stone wall was scaled in seconds as each man hoisted himself over it and dropped to a crouch before moving steadily for the three-story white brick mansion set in the middle of the five-acre property.

The house was silent. Oswald Heinrick's sporty personal vehicle sat in the drive at an odd angle. He'd rushed home from the ball at the same time that Risa had left. He'd known she remembered him. Standing there in the lobby surrounded by all his medical buddies in their pristine suits with their noses in the air, he'd known he was finished.

"Maverick taking main entrance." Micah spoke into the mic that curved along his jaw from the receiver at his ear as he eased up to the wide front doors.

"Black Jack back. Security disengaged," Travis responded.

Travis was at the back door where the main security terminal was located and disabled.

Micah pulled the electronic lock pick from the belt at his side, slid the metal spike into the lock, and engaged it.

The sound of the tumblers disengaging had a smile pulling at his lips. Within seconds both locks were disengaged. He eased the door open, weapon in hand, eyes narrowed against the pitch-black recess of the entryway.

"We have no lights," he announced quietly. "No sound."

"Maverick, proceed with night vision," Jordan ordered. "Let's not spook him yet."

Maverick adjusted the night-vision device over his eyes and scanned the entryway through the green haze that picked up each detail.

"Maverick moving in."

"Heat Seeker moving in," John announced through the receiver from the side entrance.

"Black Jack in," Travis announced from the back door. "Silent as a tomb."

"Team one, clear the way for teams two and three," Jordan announced.

Micah moved into place, the lightweight P-90 held comfortably in his hands as he covered the main staircase.

"Main case covered," he stated.

Two shadowed figures moved from the door and quickly up the stairs.

"Maverick scanning." He moved from the staircase to begin a search of each room in his designated area of the house.

It was huge. There were more sitting rooms in the damned place than there was anything else. Heavy, dark wood furniture graced each room. The green aura cast over it by the night-vision device gave it an unearthly appearance as Micah felt the hairs at the back of his neck rise.

"Scanning floor." Reno's voice slid over the communications link as his team reached the second floor.

"Scanning three," Clint announced as his team reached the third floor.

It was too damned quiet. The silence was heavy and filled with premonition as Micah moved through the rooms and headed for the kitchen.

"Maverick clear and moving to the kitchen," he informed the other agents.

"Black Jack moving in to your left," Travis informed him.

"Heat Seeker to your right," John stated.

They met at each doorway that led into the huge dining room and came to a stop. Weapons raised, the clicks of the safeties disengaging echoed in the silence.

"Son of a bitch," Heat Seeker breathed out roughly. "Live Wire, we have a small problem here."

"Report," Jordan demanded.

"Looks like Orion beat us to the bait. We have a hit, and it's messy."

Heinrick was spread out on his mahogany dining room table. His legs were chained to a heavy metal rod chained to a heavy hook in the ceiling above.

He was naked, his lower body lifted, his wrists chained to hooks at the floor, his head lying over the end of the table.

His throat and wrists were sliced. His eyes were opened wide, his expression one of horror as he stared back at them.

The scent of blood and death lay heavy in the room as the skylight painted a wash of moonglow over the macabre scene.

"Maverick?" Jordan snapped into the receiver. "What do you see?"

"Death," he stated before looking around the room.

There was a painting propped on the floor; where it should have hung was an open safe that had been recessed into the wall.

Micah caught Travis's attention and pointed to the safe.

"We have an open safe, digital code; it's empty," Travis reported.

"Teams two and three moving in," Reno reported.

"Team one, secure the scene; I'm coming in," Jordan ordered. "Pin lights only and watch where you step. Let's not leave anything for the authorities to find when the body's discovered."

Micah stared at Heinrick, then back at the safe. The contact Jordan had used for intel on this assignment had said Orion's employer had something on him, something that kept Orion from making his retirement plans. Evidently, Orion had found that information.

Was it the information that Orion was CIA? Or something more?

"Tehya, check in with Nik," Micah ordered as Jordan moved into the room.

"Checking, Maverick," Tehya stated.

Jordan eased in beside him and stared at the scene as Micah's narrow beam lit the area.

"Hell," he breathed out roughly. "Black Jack, you missed something. How did the bastard get in and out on us?"

"The same way we got in?" Travis asked. "Or he could have been waiting for him."

"What the hell is going on here?" Reno growled. "Orion was supposed to be at the party. He can't be in two places at once."

"And now he's gone," Jordan stated.

"Live Wire, Maverick, I can't raise Hell Raiser," Tehya announced into the link. "I repeat, Hell Raiser is not responding."

Micah froze. For the longest second, horror raced through him.

"Risa," he breathed her name out in a sense of dread. "Son of a bitch, he's gotten to Risa."

He turned and was moving before Jordan could stop him. He heard Jordan bark a command for his return, and it was ignored. He rushed from the mansion, aware of others following him.

He couldn't seem to run fast enough. Adrenaline poured through him, rage locked into every muscle and tendon of his body, and only one thought raced through his mind.

Risa.

RISA'S HEAD LIFTED at the firm knock on the door, her gaze turning to Nik as he moved from the chair, his weapon in his hands and ready as he moved for the door.

Risa drew the blanket from her shoulders as he motioned to her and moved to look into the peephole.

She sighed wearily at the sight of one of her clients.

"It's just Mr. Banyon," she told N.K. "I was expecting him. He's dropping off his quarterly receipts."

Banyon was quiet, professorish. A very distinguished gentleman who had always put her at ease.

Nik narrowed his eyes as he moved behind her. "Open the door easy. Don't let him in."

She disengaged the locks and opened the door a few inches.

"Mr. Banyon, I'm not really dressed—"

An explosion of light blinded her as she felt the door jerk out of her grasp, and she was thrown backward. There was no time to cry out. She felt the carpet burn across the side of her face as she was thrown into it, and then heard a thump behind.

Nik. She shook her head. He was huge. Banyon was shorter, softer. He'd never get past Nik.

She shook her head, her eyes tightly closed, as she fought the pain searing her head and tried to drag herself from the carpet.

"Easy, Miss Clay." Banyon's voice was cool, menacing, as she felt hard hands lifting her and placing her back on the couch. "The pain will only last for a few more seconds. Let me secure our friend here and then you and I will visit for a while."

A whimper fell from her lips as she shook her head and fought not to throw up.

"I was really hoping your boyfriend had stayed to protect you instead," he said as she tried to listen for his movements. "It took me a while, but I was finally able to figure it all out. Of course, Bailey Serborne helped. When this young man captured her in the back parking lot, I knew there was a bit more going on here than met the eye."

Bailey Serborne? Who the hell was Bailey Serborne?

"I'm still amazed at the ability of your security force. I've only been able to spot two of them, though there must be more. This young man and your lover." He seemed to grunt and then a thud sounded around her as the pain in her head finally began to ease.

"There we go," he breathed out in satisfaction as she tried to blink.

Her sight was blurry and with each attempt to clear it, a spike of pain drove through the sockets.

"There now, he's nice and trussed," Banyon chuckled. "He's an interesting fellow. Unlike your lover, I was unable to place his identity, but I guess the plastic surgeon took more care with his features than he did with Mr. Abijah's.

Now *there* is a worthy opponent. This is twice he's nearly had me. We're going to make certain there isn't a third time. Aren't we?"

She shook her head as she was finally able to open her eyes and focus on the man who had been hired to kill her.

He was unassuming, almost handsome with his beard and goatee and shaven head. His smile was comfortable, his gray eyes amused, as he glanced down at Nik's fallen form. Banyon had a quiet, confident look to his face that had always drawn her.

God, she'd been doing accounting for six months for a man who had just been awaiting the order to kill her?

Nik was tied securely and unconscious. At least he wasn't dead. Yet. She looked from him to the man who squatted beside him.

He was dressed to perfection, as always. A gray pinstriped suit, well pressed. Wing-tipped shoes. And he had a limp. That was why he was late bringing his accounts to her.

She glanced at his foot, then back to his face.

"Yeah, the foot is still kind of stiff," he chuckled. "I have to give your boyfriend credit, Risa. Even half-unconscious he was still a damned good shot. Then again, Mossad agents can almost shoot straight from the grave. Damned hard bastards to kill, you know."

She shook her head. No, she didn't know that.

"His mother was the one death I regret." Orion straightened and stared down at Nik with a thoughtful expression before looking back up at her. "Her name was Ariela Abijah. She was married to a CIA agent and her son was one of the best Mossad agents I've ever known. For a while, I guess they were friends." He shrugged his shoulders heavily as he sat down in the easy chair and watched her. He held Nik's gun comfortably and acted as though they were simply visiting.

The man had to be insane.

"You killed your friends?" she whispered. She wouldn't have a chance, then.

He nodded slowly. "Ariela was beautiful. I hated taking that job, but I had no choice. One of my employers knew a bit too much information about me." He smiled, a wide, satisfied curve to his lips. "He doesn't any longer, though, so that rather changes the state of my employment." He leaned forward confidently. "I've wanted to retire for several years and he kept calling me back."

"Heinrick," she guessed. "He's your employer."

"One of them." He shrugged. "He's the scientist Ariela was searching for, and the man Jansen allowed to rape you." He shook his head at that. "In all the years I've killed, I've never raped. Masturbated to death, maybe." He grinned at her shudder. "But I never raped."

He was crazy. Risa could feel the icy chill of his insanity reaching across the distance between them, threatening to freeze her with its cold.

"Heinrick's dead." He tilted his head to the side when she said nothing more. "Does that please you?"

She licked her lips nervously. "You killed him?"

He nodded like a little boy desperate for approval. "I found the evidence he had against me. I knew if I looked hard enough, I would. He was stupid. He kept it in his home safe." He shook his head then. "I should have thought of that, but I assumed he was more intelligent than to keep it there."

"Why are you here?" Her voice shook. She could feel the fear, and a burning fury churning inside her. "If you killed him, why didn't you just leave? Just retire like you wanted to do?"

His smile was amused and much too friendly. That was how he tricked her. He was able to fake a warmth and sincerity in his eyes, in his whole expression, that most people couldn't fake.

"Because you are a liability," he sighed. "Not that I'm worried about you seeing my face. Cosmetic enhancements are so reliable nowadays, but your boyfriend isn't going to let this go, is he?"

"You killed his mother. You were the reason his father died, and you tried to kill him. I somehow doubt he's going to let it go."

"But I left his cousin living," he sighed. "I could have killed her as well. I should have, she was CIA, another liability, but I allowed her to live."

"You believed he was dead," she argued.

"Well, that's true," he admitted with a light laugh. "But still, I let her live to atone for the death of the family of Abijah. And now, he's alive, and he still hunts me. What do you think it would take to make him stop?"

Risa shook her head. "He'll never stop hunting you."

He grimaced at that. "Ah well. I had hoped that by my allowing you to live, he would see the benefits in allowing me to finish my days as a retired assassin rather than prey. Oh well." He shrugged. "If nothing will stop him, then I can complete my assignment here and retire with a clean record." His eyes narrowed. "I've never failed to complete an assignment, you know."

CHAPTER 25

MICAH DIDN'T bother with the elevator when they reached the apartment building. He slammed through the door to the stairs, took them two and three at a time as the others followed behind him.

He could feel his heart pounding in his throat, fear clawing at his mind. He'd left her. He'd walked away from her when she had begged him with her eyes not to leave her. And still, he had gone.

How had Orion gotten past Nik? How could Micah have allowed this to happen?

He could feel a curious sense of disbelief and unreality filling him. He remembered racing in a similar manner for the location where his mother's body had been. Running around pedestrians and cars, his heart in his throat, adrenaline coursing through his body alongside his fear.

He had found her dead.

He had watched his father break. Kneeling in her blood, Garren Abijah had screamed out in horror, calling out his wife's name. Begging her to come back. Not to leave him.

Micah could feel a prayer burning in his head.

Be safe. Be safe. Ah God, keep her safe.

He pushed through the door to her floor and raced up the hall. He didn't pause. He threw himself into the door, crashing into the room and taking in the scene in one horrified glance.

Nik was conscious and bound with chains in one of the easy chairs, facing the kitchen. He was fighting the chains, throttled yells sounding behind the gag.

His horrified gaze was locked on the kitchen entrance.

Micah could feel the blood congealing in his veins as he moved to the doorway. Behind him, the others were pouring into the room.

Micah stepped into the kitchen and felt his knees weaken.

Risa was tied to her table. Her arms were tied by the wrists and held pointing to the floor by two large hooks that had been driven into the floor.

Her ankles were tied to a mop handle, the handle secured by a chain to another hook in the ceiling.

She was dressed. She was crying. Behind the gag, muffled sobs sounded as he moved to her, slowly, barely daring to believe what he saw. Tears easing from her eyes as she watched him, her chest rising and falling with her breaths. There wasn't so much as a smear of blood on her body.

"Risa." He touched her face, then eased the gag from her mouth. "Baby."

"Oh God." She strained toward him. "Oh God, Micah. I thought you were dead. I thought he'd killed you," she sobbed. "He said there was only one way to stop you and he'd do it if he had to. I thought he'd gone after you."

He shook his head, cupped her cheek, and laid his lips to hers. She was alive. She was struggling against the ropes; she was breathing. She was alive.

He pulled back and had to draw in a long, slow breath to fill his lungs with air. "Let me get you loose."

Jerking a knife from the sheath at his side, he cut her legs loose first and gently lowered them before bending and freeing her right arm. He moved to the left and stilled.

There, wrapped around her wrist by the leather choker that had always held it, was the pendant his father had given his mother at their engagement party.

The silver star was tarnished with age, but the golden teardrops in each point of the star still gleamed back with rich luster.

He released the ropes holding Risa's hand and lifted her wrist.

"He gave this to you?" he asked.

Her eyes, wide and still filled with fear, flickered to the pendant as he helped her sit up, only to pull her against him with one arm.

"He said it was a warning." She stared at the pendant before lifting her gaze to his face.

He lifted the pendant and turned it over. *Ad olam ani ehye lach. I'll be yours forever.* The Hebrew inscription had been engraved in the silver by his father.

It was a warning. A message that Orion knew who Micah was, knew who his parents were, Somehow Orion had managed to figure out Micah's former identity, and he had left the pendant as a warning that he knew who he was and knew how to hurt him.

Micah tucked the necklace into his pocket, then picked Risa up into his arms and strode through the apartment until he reached her bedroom and the bed they had shared.

"Did he hurt you?" He laid her on the bed, his hands moving over her arms before he lifted her wrists and rubbed at the reddened marks the ropes had left.

She shook her head quickly, her gaze locked on his face.

"Don't leave me," she whispered.

Micah froze. He stared down at her and saw the plea in her eyes.

He inhaled sharply before swallowing past the thickness in his throat and shaking his head.

"We'll talk about that later," he promised her.

He had no intentions of discussing it. There was only one answer, only one conclusion to this.

"I know what you'll do." Her breath hitched as her tears filled her eyes again. "You'll catch me asleep. Or in another room, and you'll just walk away, won't you?"

Micah could feel pieces of his soul breaking away, like a glacier cracking apart, piece by slow, agonizing piece.

He touched a tear that fell from her eye.

"I can't say good-bye to you." His hand cupped her cheek.

"I can't walk away while those beautiful eyes are begging me to stay. And I have no choice but to leave. We've always known, since that first night, that an end would come."

She flinched at the softly spoken words and Micah felt the pain of them resounding through his entire being. If anything in his life had ever been worth fighting for, then it was Risa. But there was no way to fight the agreement he had made. He risked her life by risking his own if he attempted to defy it. And he risked everything that she loved about him if he tried to break the one bond that was his alone. His word.

She trembled beneath his hand, her lips quivering as she tried to control the cries he could feel welling inside her. Could he walk away if she cried? Could he deny her anything when faced with her tears?

But she didn't cry. She drew in a ragged breath and nodded.

"Go," she whispered.

"Risa." He frowned, desperate to touch her one last time. To get the team out of her apartment, to hold her, to listen to her voice one last time as she cried out his name in passion before he was forced to walk away.

"Just go now," she cried out roughly. "Leave me my pride, Micah. Get the hell out of my life now if you're going to go. Don't sit here and make me beg you to stay."

He could hear the Durango team and the Elite Ops teams in the other room. Jordan's voice bled into the room. Micah knew he was needed. They were going after Orion's handler before dawn to learn his location.

Jordan was already pulling in information, tracking the assassin. Mac Knight was waiting in the other apartment, going over the pictures that had come through from the security camera on the elevator. They would have another identity on Orion soon.

And Risa needed to be debriefed. Micah couldn't do that. Jordan and the federal attorney would handle that. Micah could be in the room, but he couldn't touch her, couldn't hold her to comfort her as she was forced to answer the questions that would come.

"I could stay till morning." His jaw clenched as emotion swamped him and he saw the answer in her face.

"If you stay till morning you'll destroy me," she answered, her voice thick with the sobs she was fighting. "Please, Micah. If you're leaving me in the morning, then leave now. Don't wait until I'm asleep in your arms, or feeling the hope that you'll stay. I couldn't handle it."

She'd already been forced to handle so much. And she had endured it. She had held her courage and her strength, and she had fought to survive.

He tucked the loose strand of her hair back behind her ear to reveal the gentle slope of her brow, her cheek. He feathered the backs of his fingers down the side of her face and once again marveled at the smooth, silken feel of her flesh.

"Please don't . . ."

His head lowered. He couldn't stay, though he knew his heart would always linger with her. His lips touched hers and desperation slammed into his head.

He'd meant to kiss her with gentleness. He'd meant to only brush her lips with his. But her lips parted and a muted sob tore at her chest. He'd already lost his heart and soul to her; he may as well lose his mind.

His lips parted over hers, his tongue slid inside, and the taste of sweet heated passion and a woman's tears exploded against his taste buds.

A heavy groan tore from his throat. One hand gripped the back of her head, the other pressed into her back, pulling her against his chest as her head bent back beneath the force of his kiss.

He wanted to devour her. He wanted the taste of her seeped so deep inside him that he was never a moment without her.

The feel of her arms tightening around his neck, the sound of her sobbing moan of hunger, tore through him. Her lips opened to him like the petals of a flower to the sun as he slanted his lips over hers and tried to kiss her deeper, tried to draw her taste further into his senses.

He couldn't let her go. He couldn't walk away from her.

He couldn't live his life without the feel of this, her hunger and her need flowing into his until he couldn't breathe without the taste of her.

He stroked his hands beneath her shirt, felt the silky texture of her back. He couldn't touch her enough. He couldn't get enough of her.

Groaning, desperate for the feel of her, he bore her back on the bed, his lips taking hard, quick kisses before they settled against her again for another of the deep, drugging caresses that fueled his desire for her to a blazing level.

He pushed her thighs apart, settled his legs between them, and pressed the swollen length of his erection, covered by the black pants he wore, against the center of her thighs.

Grinding his cock against her, his hips shifting, rocking the thick flesh against her cotton-covered pussy, he groaned into her kiss.

Her knees lifted, bracketed his hips, moved with him as a strangled cry sounded in her chest.

He couldn't get enough of her. This was the last touch he would have, the last taste. He wanted every second of it, every flavor of lust, desire and hunger, and love, that he could draw from the experience.

He could feel her beneath his flesh. He tried to press himself into her.

"No!" she cried out as he tore his lips from hers and let them travel down the arched column of her neck. "Don't leave me, Micah. Don't . . ."

She shook her head as he pressed his forehead into her shoulder. Micah could feel her body trembling, shuddering as she fought to hold back her pleas.

"*Ani ohev otach.*" *I love you.* "*Me'achshav ve'ad hanetzach.*" *From now to eternity.*

He tore himself away from her.

His breathing rough, heavy, he watched as she rolled to her side, her back to him, her face buried against a pillow as her shoulders tightened, tensing against her tears, he knew.

"Risa . . ."

"Go!" she cried out desperately. "Just go. Please God, Micah. Just go."

He slid the pendant from the pocket of his pants and laid it on the bedside table after running his thumb over it. Regret slammed inside him with a brutality that nearly stole his breath.

"Dream big, love," he whispered as he gazed down at her. "Dream enough for both of us."

Turning, he moved to the door, jerking it open, and strode into the living room. A heavy silence filled the room as too many eyes watched him. He stalked past the broken door and moved down the hall.

"Micah, we're meeting here in five minutes," Jordan's voice carried to him as he neared the elevator.

Micah paused. He didn't turn back.

"Find someplace else to meet," he ordered his commander. "I'm out of here."

He didn't take the elevator. He pushed through the stairwell exit and took the stairs. Within seconds he was pushing through the back exit and entering the parking lot where the vans were parked. The vans and his replacement car.

He moved to the sedan, unlocked it, and settled into the seat as the overhead clouds opened up and rain poured around him.

He stared at the sheets of moisture washing over the windshield, unblinking. It reminded him of Risa's tears.

It reminded him of dreams he hadn't known he had, and ones he hadn't imagined he would ever want.

He closed his eyes, and just for a second he let himself imagine. Imagine the house of her dreams, her laughter in the yard as he watched her, her body heavy with his child. She would glow like the brightest star. Her eyes would fill with love and laughter; her expression would be serene with the dreams that surrounded them. She would soothe him after a mission, be waiting for him, arms wide open.

He wouldn't be a Maverick in her eyes; he would simply be Micah. Her husband. Her lover.

The image dissipated at the sound of a heavy knock on

the passenger window. He opened his eyes, breathed out a heavy sigh, and disengaged the lock.

Tehya slid in.

She tossed the wet jacket that covered her head to the backseat and stared out the windshield as he had.

"We need a drink," she stated.

"Why do we need a drink?"

She turned and stared at him.

"She locked her bedroom door and she's refusing to speak to anyone until her grandmother arrives. Jordan is sending Noah and Clint after Abigail Clay."

He nodded. She wouldn't be alone. He didn't want her to be alone. "That doesn't explain why we need a drink."

"It doesn't explain why both of us are escaping Jordan, either," she snorted. "For God's sake, Micah, just drive around and find a fucking bar. Buy me a whisky and we'll toast to a mission accomplished. How's that?" Anger filled her tone.

Micah looked at her askance. He'd not seen her angry. Not that she had been with the group long, a year or so perhaps.

She was pale now, though, her deep green eyes distressed, her expression tormented.

"Did something happen after I left? Is Risa okay?"

She turned to him, and in her eyes he saw the same torment he felt in his soul.

"Let's say, I may have seen my future," she whispered. "And if I don't get a drink fast, I just might lose what sanity I've managed to retain." She shook her head wearily. "I think I want to get drunk."

He started the car and slid it in reverse. "I think I'll join you."

And neither of them saw the shadow that watched from the exit.

Jordan leaned his shoulder against the narrow door frame and considered the couple as they left, the car easing through the pouring rain as he shoved his hands in the pockets of his slacks and lowered his head.

He stared at the cracked tile of the stairwell and breathed out roughly.

He hadn't expected this. He shook his head and ground his teeth together. He'd expected many things from Micah, but Jordan had to admit he hadn't expected him to walk away from Risa Clay.

"Are you going to tell him any differently?"

His head jerked up as his nephew's ruined voice sounded from behind him.

Glancing over his shoulder, Jordan considered the younger man. Noah Blake. At one time Noah Blake had been Nathan Malone, a husband, a SEAL. Until an assignment went to hell and he had become the prisoner of a fanatical drug lord.

Diego Fuentes was still alive, currently working in deep cover with Homeland Security. Nathan Malone had been listed as Killed in Action. And Noah Blake had been born.

It had taken Noah six years before he returned to the wife he had left. But once he'd returned, there had been no going back. The papers he'd signed, turning his life over to the Elite Ops, hadn't mattered. All that mattered to Noah was his wife, Nathan's wife, Sabella, and the child they were now expecting.

"No, I'm not going to tell him," Jordan finally answered, very well aware that Noah was talking about Jordan's refusal to impose the strict guidelines set down for the Elite Ops agents.

No weaknesses. No wives. No lovers. No relationships. They were dead men, and at no time could they ever risk being more than that.

Noah had broken every rule in the book earlier in the year when he had taken back his life in Alpine, Texas. He was now Noah Blake, garage owner, husband, and upstanding citizen.

"You'd let him just walk away from her?" Noah leaned against the wall facing Jordan and pushed his hands into the pockets of his jeans. "He's crazy about her, Jordan."

Jordan considered the question for long moments before asking, "Did you ask for permission to have your life back, Noah? Did you file papers, protest the guidelines, or ask for any quarter?"

Noah frowned. "I almost walked away from my wife the

second time. I almost lost a chance to know my child. Those papers I signed, the decision I made when I pledged my life to the Elite Ops, wasn't a joke, Jordan. Not to any of us. Especially Micah. We're the men we are because of the code of honor we've always adhered to. That's why you picked us up for this team. We took that decision seriously."

Jordan tipped his head to the side. "You didn't answer my question," he reminded his nephew softly. "Did you ask permission?"

"Fuck no. Without Bella, you'd have a shell that didn't care if he lived or died. That's what you'll have with Micah."

Jordan shrugged. "Then that's his choice. Not mine. Not yours. In this life, or death, Noah, every man has to make this choice himself. This won't be an easy life for you, for Bella, Micah, or Risa. The twelve years you pledged to the Ops is non-negotiable. The rest is a solitary decision that each man has to make on his own."

Noah's eyes narrowed on him. "It's a test."

Jordan shook his head. "It's not a fucking test. It's a choice. If he's strong enough to claim her, knowing what he's facing, then he's strong enough to keep her no matter the obstacles they face. That simple. It's a decision each one of you makes, on your own, without help."

Noah's lips pursed thoughtfully. "He left with Tehya," he said softly.

Jordan looked back to the parking lot and the rain pouring down. "Yes, he did."

"Some men can find comfort in another woman's arms." It sounded like a warning.

"Then some men aren't as smart as I originally thought." Jordan shrugged and let the door slam closed, cutting out the rain, cutting out thoughts he was better off not thinking. "Let's start cleaning out. I want Miss Clay transferred to her grandmother's home after Abigail arrives here. Clint and Kell can return with them and debrief her; let the two of them know what can be discussed and what can't. We're still on a job. Orion's still alive."

"He won't be for long," Noah stated.

Jordan glanced at him questioningly.

"I saw the pendant Micah took off Risa's arm. Orion left him a message. He knows who he is and he knows how to control Micah. Micah won't accept it. It's a threat to Risa. He'll make damned sure Orion is eliminated."

That was a problem. No one should know who any of Jordan's operatives were in their former lives. Those men had to stay dead; the complications of their ever coming back to life were too extreme.

Jordan blew out a hard breath. "Let's just hope Micah remembers the word 'teamwork.' "

"Do any of us?" Noah asked then with a grin. "Really, Jordan, you act like a damned father. You should have gotten married years ago and had a passel of kids. It would have kept you out of other people's problems."

He snorted at that. He didn't regret it. If he had lived that dream, he knew now, he would have lived it with the wrong woman.

But he couldn't have the right woman, either.

Damned if he did, damned if he didn't. It was the story of his damned life some days.

And it was raining to boot.

Chapter 26

Six Weeks Later
Atlanta, Georgia

THE SUN ROSE every morning; it set every evening. Risa stared into the darkness each night; most mornings she greeted the dawn. She stared out the window of her bedroom in her grandmother's home. Some nights Risa sat on the balcony and watched the shadows, imagining that she saw Micah in them. That he was watching her, that he lingered just out of sight and touched her with his eyes, caressed her with his thoughts.

How silly was she?

She touched her stomach beneath the cotton of her T-shirt and felt that surge of elation that she felt each time she thought of the child she carried there.

She was pregnant. She hadn't believed it at first. The doctor had warned her that the birth control she was on might not be effective during sexual relations because of the weaknesses of it. She wasn't using it at the time for birth control so much as regulation of her cycles. Evidently this was one of those pieces of information that she hadn't exactly listened to.

She thanked God she hadn't heard it, because she was carrying Micah's child now.

She rubbed her fingertips against her stomach and gazed into the darkness. No one knew yet. She hadn't told her friends yet, but she would soon. She would have to swear them to secrecy for a while. If their husbands knew, she knew Micah would soon find out. She didn't want him to regret leaving her. She didn't want his heart burdened more.

He loved her.

With her other hand, she touched the pendant she wore. She had finally found the nerve to do a search on the Hebrew phrases he had used.

How many times had he told her he loved her and she had never known? How many times had he whispered his regret that he couldn't stay?

For whatever reason, he was unable to be there with her. She accepted that. If he could be there, he would have been. He wouldn't have left her crying; he wouldn't have left her bleeding inside.

And she still cried. She still bled. She still stared into the shadows of the night and imagined he was there.

"Micah," she whispered his name, and felt the loss of breath, the weakness that assailed her as the pain washed over her. "I miss you, Micah. I miss you so much."

She missed him until she was certain she couldn't draw another breath without him. And then she thought of the child she carried and she found the strength.

Would it grow easier? she wondered. That lonely sense of bleak acceptance. The knowledge that a part of her was forever torn away from her. That the man who held her heart was out there, alone, fighting, in danger. Always in danger.

A tear slipped down her cheek.

"I love you, Micah," she whispered into the night. "I hope you know, I will always love you."

Two Weeks Later
Off the Coast of Africa

The island was several miles off the coast of Africa. A rising volcanic mountain thick with trees and undergrowth that surrounded and protected the mansion that sat in the middle of it.

The moonless night was perfect for a landing by water, but it was damned tricky getting through the heavy forest that ringed the mansion.

The team was alone on this mission. Five men made their way through the junglelike growth while Jordan manned the beaten, rusted freighter they had hijacked for the trip to the island.

It was a four hour hike. The jungle was thick with crawling, biting, sometimes lethal vermin. Snakes were in abundance here.

Micah ignored the conditions, the snakes and the mosquitos that Noah swore were bigger than his grandfather's cats.

Six weeks. They had tracked Orion for six long, unending weeks. He had slipped off the roster and gone cold a year before the rumored hit against Risa. The list of his aliases was two pages long; his ability to change his appearance was almost legendary. But after they'd found his handler, things had gone a little more smoothly.

The mousey little Cuban, Josef, had been their informant. He'd turned on Orion out of fear that with his retirement Orion would want to get rid of the last link to his former life. Josef had been right. Orion had blown the little Cuban's villa to hell and back, thinking Josef was still in it.

No messy bloodletting here. Just a lot of explosives. Josef had been with the Elite Ops teams. His butler hadn't been. Orion thought he'd killed Josef, while Josef was spilling his guts and every little secret he knew about Orion to the team. Those secrets had led them here, to an unnamed island, a whole lot of nasty privateers, and Orion.

Micah slipped up on yet another of the jungle soldiers Orion employed. His arm went around the thick neck, his hand braced against the other side, and with one sure movement, he broke another privateer's neck.

Nothing messy. No blood, no guts. Just silence.

Another little pop to Micah's side assured him that Noah had another of the bastards out of commission.

Hell, how many were there, anyway?

With the aid of the night-vision devices Micah wore, he

picked out two more. He was on them like their shadows. Silent as death. He twisted the first neck, popped it, and before the other man could turn around, he was dropping to the ground as well.

They were close. The lights set around the mansion could be seen through the thick growth of greenery now. There were a few dogs barking; a soldier snapped a command to shush them.

Cheap dogs equaled nervous dogs, Micah thought with a grin. The guards were so used to the animals' barking at shadows that they weren't even aware of the danger approaching them.

Moving into position, Micah shimmied up the nearest tree and braced himself in the thick branches as he pulled the tranquilizer gun from the pack on his back.

It was quieter than a gun and at times more effective.

He tapped the mic to his communication device twice to signal he was in place.

Three more taps came through the receiver at his ear. Noah, Travis, and John were in place as well.

The fifth tap signaled Nik's readiness to break the security on the gate once the guards were out of the way.

Micah took aim and began firing.

Pop. Pop. Pop. A series of muted shots seemed overloud in the silence surrounding him as he watched the first three guards drop. Three more shots and the dogs were down. If everything had gone according to plan, then the others were down as well.

"Heat Seeker clear."

"Wild Card clear."

"Black Jack clear."

"Hell Raiser clear."

Each obstacle was taken care of.

Micah climbed quickly down the tree, shoved the gun back into the pack, and sprinted for the front gate that barred the entrance to the estate.

They slipped quickly for the gate and ran for the guards' barracks. There would be a few more sleeping in there. They were taken care of quickly. Wild Card and Hell Raiser stepped inside, back-to-back, and used the remaining tranquilizer darts on the six men sleeping there. They'd be sleeping for a while longer.

The guns were shoved into a single pack along with the night-vision devices. P-90s were pulled from another pack and distributed along with extra clips. Micah strapped on a Kevlar vest and utility belt loaded with other goodies. Once he was weaponed up he lifted his fist to his shoulder in a signal he was ready to roll. Within seconds the others gave the same signal.

There was no radio contact, nothing spoken. Black masks covered their faces, and thin gloves protected their hands.

As one of the five of them sprinted across the grounds to the back door, Hell Raiser split off to the garage to secure a vehicle.

Black Jack pushed in the security code they had acquired, and within seconds the door was clicking open. Micah slid the knife from its sheath at his thigh. No gunfire unless there was no recourse.

The light of the back hallway glinted off five blades as they moved silently into the house.

The cook was sitting at the kitchen table, his heavy body perched on a chair that looked too small for his girth as he flipped through a magazine.

He was sleeping permanently after Micah twisted his neck, then laid his head carefully on the table. Micah worked his way to the far entrance to the kitchen, checked the next hallway, and lifted his fist in an all clear as Black Jack did the same on the other end.

They split off then. Maverick and Wild Card took the back hall and rooms while Black Jack and Heat Seeker took the other side of the house.

Minutes later they met at the central staircase.

Wild Card was now sporting a slash on his arm from the soldier who had very nearly surprised them in one of the bathrooms. Micah was minus a blade after burying it into the bastard's throat and leaving it there.

He jerked another from inside the Kevlar vest and started up the stairs, the others moving in behind him.

He had lived for this moment for six years. For the last six weeks he hadn't even lived; he had merely breathed. Orion's death was imperative. The message he had left with Ariela's pendant around Risa's arm had been unmistakable. He knew how to hurt Micah, and he would, if the team didn't back off.

There was no backing off.

Stepping along the hall, each man split off and begin entering bedrooms. They were empty. Orion didn't like guests, it appeared. At least not this early in his retirement.

Moving up the next flight of stairs, Micah turned and headed for the master bedroom.

He knew where Orion slept. He knew who he slept with. He knew that tonight one of them would die, and Micah had no intentions of being the one defeated.

He stepped to the door, then pulled free an electronic key from his belt. He inserted the key into the lock, pressed the activity button, and waited until the little red light turned green. A second later the tumbler snicked quietly, signaling the door was open.

He opened the door slowly, his eyes narrowed against the dim shadows of the room as he restrained his smile.

Orion.

He slept in the middle of the large bed. On each side a young girl slept. They couldn't be more than fifteen. One looked as though she had cried herself to sleep. Both had been kidnapped several weeks before from their parents' homes and brought here to Orion.

Micah stepped into the room.

It was definitely Orion. His features were the same as the ones that had been caught on the camera outside the elevator the night Risa was attacked.

He had an appointment to leave the island in the morning to travel to a Swedish plastic surgeon. It was a meeting he wouldn't make.

Micah stepped to the bottom of the bed.

Only a thin sheet covered the assassin and his little beauties.

"Orion, wakey wakey." Micah lifted the P-90 and waited.

Orion's eyes jerked open, his gaze caught immediately by the gun aimed on him as the two girls cried out and rolled from the bed in terror.

"They are well trained," Micah said quietly as he smiled back at Orion. "They know to run now when they see death coming."

Orion glanced at the gun, then into Micah's eyes. He sighed wearily. "David Abijah," he said mirthlessly. "I did you a favor, and this is how you repay me."

"David Abijah is dead, Orion," he stated softly. "Don't you remember? You put a bullet in his head and tossed him into the ocean."

Orion frowned. "He lived."

"He died."

Micah fired.

He watched the hole that bloomed with blood in the center of Orion's forehead, heard the whack of the bullet exiting and burying itself in the wall.

As Micah stared at the death mask that came over Orion's face, Black Jack and Wild Card grabbed the girls, wrapped them in robes, and hustled them out of the room.

Micah stood there, and he stared. Orion was dead. What was there left now? His heart was no longer his. His soul searched constantly for something he could no longer touch.

I love you, Micah. Her words stroked over his senses, caressed his empty heart.

He heard that much too often, as though her voice drifted on the breeze around him.

"Maverick." Heat Seeker tugged at his arm. "We need to roll."

He nodded slowly, took one last look at the corpse of the man who had destroyed the life of David Abijah, then turned and followed the rest of the team out of the house.

A jeep squealed to a stop at the front door as they threw the door open and raced out. The two girls were being carried by Wild Card and Black Jack. Nik was barking the extraction code through the link to Jordan as they piled into the vehicle.

No one tried to stop their exit. The few soldiers left raced into the house instead.

Micah stared into the night as the jeep sped along the rough path back to the jeep where Jordan waited with the inflatable speedboats to return them to the freighter. Once they were back in international waters, a Navy warship was waiting, a helicopter prepped and ready to fly them to American soil, all without anyone knowing who they were or where they came from.

It was over. Micah had signed his life away for vengeance, and now that vengeance had been exacted, he knew exactly how empty his life had been before Risa.

The jeep braked to a hard stop next to the boat. They piled out and rushed for the black inflatable. Within seconds they were tearing through the water toward the freighter.

Within twenty minutes the freighter was slicing through the waves, bearing them to the warship.

Micah watched the sun come up, saw the light blue perfection of the morning sky, and felt Risa's touch in his memories.

He had intended to stay as far away from her as possible, but he hadn't kept that vow to himself. He'd returned several times, stood in the shadows of her grandmother's property, and watched Risa as she sat alone on the balcony of her bedroom.

Some nights, he swore their eyes met. He wouldn't have been surprised in the least if she had left the house and come to him. The bond they had created during such a short time felt that deep, that enduring.

But she had continued to sit on her balcony during those few, brief visits, and Micah had forced himself to stay hidden. There were things that had to be done, choices that had to be made. He couldn't return to her as long as those obstacles still hung over their heads.

"It never goes away," Noah said as he leaned against the

railing and stared out to sea as Micah watched the sky. "You'll always see her. In the sky, in the night, in a breath or a sigh. She'll always be there."

And Noah should know. He had gone six years without his wife. He had lived as the walking dead, eating, breathing, sleeping death. Until the day fate threw them together again.

Noah had taken what was his. He hadn't demanded or asked. He had declared her his. He could have her and fight the battle he'd signed on to, or he could walk into true death from sheer grief.

The Elite Ops had a ton of money in their agents. They couldn't afford to lose them to broken hearts.

But could Micah afford to take what he needed so desperately? Would Risa even want the man he was now?

He shook his head, unable to answer his own questions.

"Think about it, Micah," Noah said softly. "Just think about it."

Hours later he was still thinking about it. That evening as the helicopter flew them back into base in Big Bend National Park, it was still weighing on him.

His flesh felt too tight over his bones. The need for Risa's taste, for her touch, was a fever burning inside him. Orion was over. He was gone. The nightmares of her past were finished; all that was left was any lingering nightmares she had.

And Micah wanted to be there. If she cried in the night, he wanted to be the one to hold her, to soothe her.

In the showers he washed the grime and blood from his body. He remembered her touch, her scent, and felt his cock thickening in torturous need. He spent too many nights like this, aching for her, needing her.

He laid his head against the cement wall of the shower and grimaced. He'd spent too many days and nights trapped inside this fucking mountain. He wanted to feel the sun on his face. He wanted to hold Risa in his arms, love her as the warmth of the coming spring days began to warm the land.

He wanted her. He was fucking dying without her.

He rinsed the soap from his hair and dried it quickly. He

jerked his clothes on, his boots. In his locker he dragged out his jacket, wallet, cash, and credit cards.

"Going somewhere, Maverick?"

He turned his head and almost growled like a damned animal as Jordan leaned against the end of the lockers and arched his brow curiously.

"Jacket, wallet, cash, and cards. Looks like a long unauthorized trip to me."

Micah shoved his wallet in his back pocket with the cards; the cash he shoved into the front pocket. The keys he kept in his hand as he pulled on the jacket.

"I'm due leave," he informed the other man. "Six weeks' worth. I'm taking it."

"We have another mission going out in a matter of days," Jordan stated. "We need you there."

"Too bad. I remember the contract," he snarled. "Six fucking weeks."

Jordan pursed his lips thoughtfully. "You have to sign out and list your destination as well as your intended activities while you're gone."

"Guess," Micah growled.

"It's against the rules, Micah," Jordan reminded him. "No weakness, remember? What is a woman if she's not a weakness?"

Micah walked slowly along the corridor created by the lockers until he stood only feet from his commander.

"She's mine."

Jordan's brows lifted. "Really? And the papers you signed state that you belong to the Elite Ops. Not a woman."

"Don't fuck with me," Micah leaned closer and hissed the demand. "I signed the agreement. Twelve years or until death. You want your twelve years? Don't stand in my way."

"You'll go rogue then?" Jordan asked dangerously.

Micah almost laughed. "No, Jordan, I won't go rogue. I'll catch a bullet and I won't give a damn if I come back from it. I can't fight without her. There's your destination and your intent. See you in six weeks."

"Say hello to Abigail for me," Jordan called back. "Ask

nicely and Reno might give you a ride in the helicopter waiting to take him home as well."

Micah lengthened his steps, heading for the stairs that led to the ground level of the base. The helicopter was waiting to fly Reno back to Georgia, and back to his wife and son. That same helicopter would take Micah back to the dream that he had thought he could live without.

What fools men could be, he thought. To think he could live without his heart, without the part of his spirit that he gave to his woman. How insane had he been to believe he could ever live without Risa when in truth, he hadn't known what living was until he learned what loving her meant?

AS HE ENTERED the ground floor of the base he saw Reno and Noah talking. Neither man looked happy. Micah moved down the stairs, aware of both of them watching him, glaring at him.

"I'm sharing your copter," he informed Reno. "Are you ready to fly?"

Reno's brows lifted. "I'm heading to Georgia, Micah, not the closest bar."

Micah grunted at that. "Let's fly, Reno, try not to piss me off."

He strode past the two men and headed for the exit. It wasn't as though he had become a drunkard. A bar was just more conductive to certain thoughts. When Micah felt as though his life had reached rock bottom, then sitting in the seediest, darkest bar he could find seemed the best option for those thoughts.

Not that he had done it often. But often enough, it seemed, that it had been noticed.

He pulled himself into the helicopter and watched as Reno followed in behind him. Reno gave the pilot the order to lift off and within seconds they were in the air and heading for home.

Once, Israel had been home. It was there that Micah's heart had leaned during the empty dark moments of his life since he had joined the Ops. Now, Risa was home. It was her where his heart had stayed. It was her that every part of his being longed for.

"She might tell you to fuck off," Reno stated as he leaned back in his seat and crossed his arms over his chest. He was still glaring at Micah.

"She might," Micah agreed absently, more involved with his memories of Risa than he was with Reno's advice.

But she would be there. If she told him to fuck off, he'd fuck her until she changed her mind. He hadn't spent six hellish weeks tracking down Orion and dying for her, only to be turned away like a flea-bitten stray.

"She's staying with her grandmother now," Reno told him.

"I know where the hell she's at." Micah jerked his head around and scowled back at Reno. "Worry about your life, Reno; stop worrying about mine."

Reno grunted at that and frowned. "She's too good for you," he snapped, obviously pissed over something.

Micah pushed his fingers through his hair and grimaced at that. "We agree there." There was nothing that could be done for it, though. He ached for her. He fucking hurt for her. The pain was like a wound that went to the bone and refused to heal. There would be no healing, no ease, until he saw Risa again.

She wouldn't turn him away, he thought. She couldn't turn him away. He had been a dead man in name only, but without Risa he would become a dead man in truth. Everything inside him belonged to her. Being without her was killing him.

"Hurt her again and I'll break your neck," Reno informed him harshly.

Micah turned his head and stared at Reno again. His gaze was flat and cold, hard. "Get off my back, Reno, or I'll toss you out of this helicopter," he snapped. "I don't need your threats or your advice."

Reno's lips tightened. "She's a friend, Micah."

"She's my soul."

Conversation ceased. Reno stared back at him for long

moments before he finally gave a quick, abrupt nod. Micah turned his gaze back outside. He stared into the clear blue sky and saw Risa's eyes. He heard the tears in her voice when he left; he felt the pain that had nearly ripped him in two when he had left.

He was going home. Now, he only prayed that she would give him another chance to love her. To touch her. To live within the warmth of her smile.

Chapter 27

RISA WAS SPENDING too much time at Raven's and Morganna's. She knew she was, and though that knowledge had her cringing a bit at the reasons, still she was helpless against it.

That evening after Raven had put Morgan to bed, Risa sat in the living room staring sightlessly at the wall, her hands twisting nervously in her lap.

She should leave.

She rose to her feet to do just that and the pain that bloomed in her chest nearly spilled the tears that seemed ever present from her eyes.

It was like tearing a piece of her body away.

Hugging her arms against her breasts, she paced to the large window that looked out over the driveway and told herself she had to leave. She'd been here for hours. Raven no doubt had things to do. Reno was due home today. She would want to get ready to greet her husband. He'd been gone for weeks this time.

Was Micah returning with him? Risa wondered.

She drew in a hard breath and shook her head. Turning quickly, she pulled her purse from the table by the couch and started for the door.

She wasn't going to do this to either one of them. If Micah had returned with Reno, then it was because of his job, because of an assignment. Because he no doubt had things to do and one of those things was not seeing the woman he had walked away from.

"Risa, are you leaving already?"

She turned at the sound of Raven's soft voice. Raven had piled her long dark hair atop her head. Her blue eyes were faintly alarmed, her expression anxious.

"I need to get back." Risa shook her head. "I'm sorry, Raven. I've been taking up too much of your time like this."

She had to stop talking. The pain rose inside her, searing her chest, her throat, as she fought to hold back the tears. It had to be the hormonal changes in her body, she thought. The doctor had warned her about the mood swings. With the absence of the small amount of Whore's Dust that had once been present in her brain, and her current pregnancy, he'd told her that it would be as though she didn't know which emotion she needed to feel. She would be learning herself all over again.

And maybe she was. She was definitely learning what it meant to hurt inside until she thought she was going to die from the pain. She was learning what it meant to miss someone, to watch for him everywhere she went. To cry for him each night.

She pressed her hand to her stomach and reminded herself that she wasn't alone anymore. She had a part of that love inside her. It eased her, but nothing could erase the living ache that beat at her chest.

"I enjoy your company, Risa," Raven said gently. "We're friends; no apologies are needed."

Risa shook her head and looked back to the window.

"I keep thinking he'll be here," she admitted, her voice hoarse. "That he'll return with Reno. That all I need is to see him one more time, to know he's safe, and I'll be okay."

"And you know better," Raven finished for her. "You know if you see him you're only going to hurt worse, and ache more."

Risa nodded jerkily. "It's not fair of me to put either of us in that position," she told her friend. "He had to leave. Didn't he?"

Of course he did. He wouldn't have gone otherwise, she told herself. But the absence tormented her. If he loved her, how could he stay away from her? Risa spent more time at Raven's, Morganna's, and Emily's than she spent at her own home now. Hoping to hear something. Hoping one of her friends would volunteer the smallest shred of information. And they never did.

"Did he?" Raven asked instead. "Only Micah knows that answer, Risa. Would he have left you if he could have stayed?"

Risa's lips trembled. "He would have stayed."

She had to believe in that. It was the only thing that got her through each night, the only thought she had to hold on to.

She almost laughed at the thought. "I've lost my mind," she told Raven then. "I managed to survive six years of nightmares, and even then, the nights didn't seem so long."

She slept, but rather than having nightmares, she dreamed of Micah. His touch. His kiss. His arms wrapped around her. Only to awaken alone. Awake was her nightmare now, because she hadn't yet learned how to survive without him.

"You haven't lost your mind," Raven sighed. "You lost your heart; there's a difference."

Risa shook her head. "No, Raven, I lost Micah."

And that said it all. Shaking her head, she turned from her friend and moved once again for the door.

"Risa," Raven stopped her again. "I wish you'd stay for a while."

Risa shook her head. "I can't stay," she whispered. "I shouldn't even be here for the reasons I'm here. I can't do this to him, or to myself, Raven. Not anymore."

She left the house, her head down, hoping her hair hid her tears, and moved quickly for her car. She had spent too much time in the past two weeks waiting for him, watching for him. She had worried, and she had paced the floors locked in a certainty that she was never going to see Micah again.

"Leaving so soon?"

She froze. Her head jerked up.

He was standing in front of her. His black eyes were as tormented as she felt; his face was lined with tiredness.

Her lips parted, her heart began to race in her chest.

Then he smiled. A crooked little grin that stilled the breath in her chest.

"You're a hard woman to catch up with," he told her as he straightened away from the side of her car and moved closer. "Reno called ahead. First you were at Emily's. I got there five minutes after you left for Morganna's. I went to Morganna's, but you weren't there."

She shook her head. "We went shopping."

"So then, Reno called home. You were going to leave before I arrived, Risa."

She tried to swallow past her tears. She tried to tell herself she could get through this. That she'd wait, see why he was here, why he was searching for her.

Six weeks of loss locked inside her. Her hand moved to her stomach as she sought the connection with their child that had eased her for the past few weeks. Nothing could ease the pain of losing Micah, of seeing him, certain he'd walk away again.

"I shouldn't have been here." She shook her head again. "I'm sure you're busy. Or something. I'll leave."

She moved for her car.

Micah stepped in front of her, his hands curved over her shoulders, and Risa felt her knees turn to jelly at the touch. Warmth flowed over her, inside her. It rocked her to her core; it stole her ability to breathe, to speak, to think.

"Come with me," he whispered as her head lifted. "Just for a while."

And she was supposed to refuse him? He made the request as though he expected just that.

She nodded and handed him the car keys. There wasn't a chance in hell that she could drive in the shape she was in.

She moved around the car and slid into the passenger seat as Micah moved in beside her on the other side. The car started and he was pulling away from the house.

Risa told herself it was just another dream. As he drove through town and pulled the car into the underground parking lot of one of the nicer hotels, she continued to tell herself it didn't mean anything. He just wanted to talk. Nothing more.

Six weeks. She had lived without his touch for six long weeks. Her hands fisted in her lap as she fought to keep her hands off him, to maintain her dignity, her pride.

He parked the car. When he got out, Risa drew in a hard breath, but she could sense the heady, rich warmth that flowed from his hard body.

"Risa?" He had opened her door and was waiting for her, his hand extended to her.

She lifted her hand. His fingers gripped hers, and when she was out of the car, he didn't release them.

Suddenly Risa felt sensations she was certain she had never known in her life. The feel of the hem of her dress sliding against her legs. The cool air of the garage against her bare arms. She had left her sweater at Raven's. She could feel her thighs, and the flesh between them. Her clit was swelling, aching. Her vagina was clenched tight in need and dampening with arousal.

Dampening nothing, she was wet. Slick, hot, and wet, and shaking with the need for his kiss.

The ride up the elevator seemed to take forever. When it stopped, the doors swishing open, Micah led her into a wide, elegant hallway and to the door of his room.

She stepped inside.

The door slammed closed and before she could speak, she found her back against it, his lips on hers, his hands touching her, and everything inside her exploded in pleasure.

Her hands slid up his chest, moved around his neck until she was holding him against her, straining to be closer as his head slanted and the already greedy, dominant kiss turned fiercer.

She couldn't get enough of him. She needed too much. She ached too much.

"I'm dying." He jerked back long enough to make the declaration in a hoarse, ragged tone. "Dying without you, Risa."

She tried to speak, but his kiss stole the words. His hands stroked under the hem of her dress. Her panties were pushed down her legs, and she didn't give a damn. She stepped out of them, her head falling back against the door as his lips moved along her jaw, then back to her lips.

His fingers slid through the slick folds of her pussy and he groaned into her kiss as she felt him struggling with the closure of his jeans.

He was here, in her arms. Warm and hard. She was lost in the sensations, the hunger. She was coming apart and she didn't give a damn.

"Micah," she breathed his name as she felt the buttons holding the dress together over her breasts pop.

The sensitive flesh was swollen, her nipples peaked against her bra. The dress and bra straps were pushed over her shoulder and a second later she was trying to scream from the pleasure as his lips covered one engorged peak.

At the same time, he lifted her, drew her leg to his hip, and tucked the fiercely swollen head of his cock into the wet folds between her thighs.

"I can't wait." He was panting; the muscles beneath his shirt were straining as Risa tore at the buttons. "I can't wait, Risa. I'm dying for you."

"Don't wait. Oh God, take me, Micah. Take me. . . ."

His cock pushed inside her snug entrance. Their cries mingled as he worked inside her. His hands were tight at her hips as her knees pressed into his. Her nails were dug into his shoulders, and pleasure consumed her with rapacious hunger.

"I have to have you." He was taking her, thrusting inside her, his hips shifting, rolling, pressing his erection deeper inside her. "Sweet love. Lovely Risa. I can't breathe for wanting you."

Another fierce thrust and he was buried deep inside her, a groan tearing from his lips as her muscles enclosed him, flexed against him.

Risa was locked in unbearable pleasure. She could feel the perspiration beginning to build on her skin, felt the heat radiating from his cock, heating her from the inside out as she tried to arch in his arms.

She was so close. Just that fast. Just his kiss, and in a matter of seconds she was so hot and ready for him that he'd had no problem burying himself inside her.

"Oh yes," he groaned against her neck. "Yes, baby. Take me. I've dreamed of this. Hungered for this."

He was moving and she was dissolving inside. Deep, hard thrusts began to pound his cock inside her, stroking it over nerve endings that blazed to life as he stretched her pussy, stroked inside it, and excited normally hidden nerve endings to violent life.

Risa heard herself crying his name; she felt her nails digging into the cotton of his shirt and trying to get to skin.

A second later he'd ripped his shirt off. The front of her dress was ripped. His lips moved back to her nipples and he thrust, hard and thick, deeper and stronger inside her.

She was a mass of pleasure. She was blazing out of control. She tightened around the heavy length of iron-hard flesh, each stroke pushing her higher, harder.

She was going to come. She could feel it. It was tightening inside her. It was going to destroy her.

"Micah," she cried his name weakly. "I can't stand . . ." She arched again. "Oh yes. Yes. Like that." He was pumping harder inside her. The slap of flesh against flesh echoed around her. Sensations, heated and too intense to survive, began whipping through her.

"Yes!" Her hands locked in his hair as he sucked her nipple, lashed at it with his tongue. "There. Like that. Like that," she was crying out her need as he stroked inside her harder, faster.

Desperate, powerful. The pleasure became overwhelming. Spirals of sensations were whipping through her, swirling around her, burning her, pushing her, driving her closer to a brink so intense she was losing her breath in anticipation.

It was there. Building. Tightening. She clawed at his shoulders, strangled cries falling from her lips as his hands gripped her rear, held her in place, and pounded inside her.

When it exploded through her, the darkness she had once feared washed over her, studded with starlight, filled with heat. Her gaze dimmed. She heard the muted wail of her cry, felt her pussy tightening on his shuttling cock and then the wash of an explosion so intense, she wondered if she would lose consciousness.

She heard his broken cry, her name on his lips, then the heavy, fierce jets of his release spurting inside her.

She lost herself in the pleasure, but it was okay, because Micah was holding her. He knew where she was. He was holding her against his body, sheltering her inside the storm, and allowing her to lose herself in a pleasure that had at one time frightened her.

"I love you." She heard the words at her ear. "Sweet Risa. I love you until I'm dying without you."

She shook her head. He couldn't die. He couldn't leave her. She locked her arms tighter around his neck; she felt him moving her, felt the soft give of the mattress under her back as he rose over her.

Her eyes opened, she watched as he propped his elbows beside her, holding his weight from her as he stared down at her. He stroked her hair back from her face, tucked a strand of hair behind her ear.

Was she dreaming? Was it only a dream that held her beneath him, that felt the fierce throb of his erection still buried inside her?

Her hand lifted, her fingers touched his face.

"You're really here," she whispered. "Please be here."

His eyes closed for a brief, suspended second before they opened and she began to believe.

"No dream," he promised her. "I'm here, baby."

He drew back, causing her to gasp as he pulled himself from her.

"You have too many clothes." His voice was whisper-soft as she watched him.

He pulled the tattered remains of her dress from her, then rose to the side of the bed and undressed himself. His shirt was ruined. Boots thumped to the floor; his jeans were disposed of quickly; then he was back, in the bed beside her.

He reached out, pulling her against him, sheltering her against his own body.

"You're not leaving?"

"I'm not leaving." He kissed her forehead, her cheek. His lips brushed over hers, as soft as a summer breeze, before he stared into her eyes. "I'm dying without you, Risa. I can't do this any longer." He swallowed tightly. "I wanted to protect you, love. From myself. From my past." He gave his head a hard shake. "Walking away destroyed me, Risa. I was more a dead man then than I ever have been."

Her lips parted on a gasp as emotion surged inside her.

"You love me? You're not leaving?" She couldn't believe he was back, that she was in his arms, that he loved her.

She touched his lips, her fingers trembling, heart racing.

"My heart was with you." A broken sob left her lips as she took his hand and slid it to her stomach. "Both our hearts were with you."

Micah felt a fist slam into his chest.

His eyes went from where his hand lay against her stomach and back to her gaze. Emotion swelled in his throat until he was certain he would choke from it.

"Risa?"

"Both of us, Micah," she whispered. "I didn't know. The birth control wasn't very strong."

He saw the uncertainty that filled her expression. The tinge of fear. He was shaking. He could feel himself shaking from the inside out.

"A baby?" He had to swallow past the need, the hunger rising inside him now. "You're pregnant?"

Her lips trembled and the sight of it tore through him.

He shook his head. He was swamped with feeling. Overwhelmed by it.

"Risa." His voice sounded broken even to him. "Sweet Risa."

He couldn't speak. He moved lower, his hand caressing her stomach before his head lowered and his lips brushed across the satiny skin.

His hand tightened on her hip as he fought to contain the emotions rising inside him like a wild wind across the desert. Blistering hot, surging through him with a force he couldn't contain.

"I am yours," he whispered. "I live to hold you, Risa. I breathe to touch you."

He was shaking, almost shuddering as his head lifted and he stared back into her tear-drenched eyes. "I love you."

"I love you, Micah." Tears fell from her eyes. "Oh God, Micah. I love you."

She was in his arms. He held her too tightly and he knew it. He couldn't help it. He rocked her. He let her sob against his chest and had to battle the tears in his eyes.

He was a Maverick. An unknown force, a man who adjusted the rules of his world as he moved through it. Until Risa.

She re-created his world. She re-created him.

No longer was he a dead man. He was a living, breathing extension of every emotion that one small woman could instill within a man.

He was her lover. The father of her child. He would be her husband.

"*Me'achshav ve'ad hanetzach*," he whispered. "From now until eternity, Risa. I will love you forever."

"Leigh's pages explode with a hot mixture of erotic pleasures."

—RT BOOKreviews

Wild Card

Navy SEAL Nathan Malone's wife, Bella, was told he was never coming home. But if he can get back to his wife, can he keep the secret of who he really is . . . even as desire threatens to consume them? And as danger threatens to tear Bella from Nathan's arms once more?

Maverick

The only way for the Elite Ops agent to uncover an assassin—and banish the ghosts of his own dark past—is to use Risa as bait. But nothing has prepared him for her disarming blend of innocence and sensuality, or for his overwhelming need to protect her.

Heat Seeker

John Vincent has every reason to want to remain as dead as the obituary had proclaimed him to be. He'd left nothing behind except for one woman, and one night of unforgettable passion. Now, both will return to haunt him.

Black Jack

The Secret Service can't control him. The British government can't silence him. But renegade agent Travis Caine is one loose cannon you don't want to mess with, and his new assignment is to die for.

Renegade

Elite Ops agent Nikolai Steele, code name Renegade, is asked to pay an old comrade a favor. This friend swears he's no killer even though he's been mistaken as one by Mikayla. Nik goes to set her straight, but the moment he lays eyes on her, he knows he's in too deep.

Live Wire

Captain Jordan Malone has been a silent warrior and guardian for years, leading his loyal team of Elite Ops agents to fight terror at all costs. But Tehya Talamosi, a woman with killer secrets and a body to die for, will bring Jordan to his knees as they both take on the most deadly mission.

ST. MARTIN'S PRESS

"LORA LEIGH *is a talented author with the ability to create magnificent characters and captivating plots."*

—Romance Junkies

Midnight Sins

Cami lost her sister in the brutal murders that rocked her hometown so many years ago. Some still believe that Rafe Callahan, along with his friends Logan and Crowe, were involved. But how could Rafe—who haunted her girlish dreams, then her adult fantasies—be a killer?

Deadly Sins

A newcomer in town, Sky O'Brien is a mystery to Logan Callahan. Like him, she is a night owl. Like him, she is fighting her own demons. Like him, she hides a secret in her eyes—a fire that consumes him with every glance. Could she be the one to heal him?

Secret Sins

Sheriff Archer Tobias has watched the Callahan family struggle to find peace and acceptance in the community—despite the murders that continue to haunt them. But he is torn between duty and desire when Anna Corbin becomes the next target.

Ultimate Sins

Mia, left an orphan after her father's death, was raised amid the lies and suspicions against Crowe Callahan. But nothing could halt the fascination she feels for him, or the hunger that has risen inside her.

St. Martin's Paperbacks St. Martin's Griffin